COFFIN ROAD

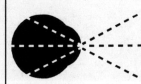

This Large Print Book carries the
Seal of Approval of N.A.V.H.

COFFIN ROAD

PETER MAY

THORNDIKE PRESS
A part of Gale, Cengage Learning

GALE
CENGAGE Learning·

Farmington Hills, Mich • San Francisco • New York • Waterville, Maine
Meriden, Conn • Mason, Ohio • Chicago

LIBRARY OF CONGRESS CATALOGING-IN-PUBLICATION DATA

Names: May, Peter, 1951– author.
Title: Coffin road / by Peter May.
Description: Large print edition. | Waterville, Maine : Thorndike Press, 2017. | Series: Thorndike Press large print reviewers' choice
Identifiers: LCCN 2016044030| ISBN 9781410496713 (hardcover) | ISBN 1410496716 (hardcover)
Subjects: LCSH: Amnesiacs—Fiction. | Murder—Investigation—Fiction. | Large type books. | GSAFD: Mystery fiction.
Classification: LCC PR6063.A884 C64 2017 | DDC 823/.914—dc23
LC record available at https://lccn.loc.gov/2016044030

Published in 2017 by arrangement with Quercus Publishing

Printed in Mexico
1 2 3 4 5 6 7 21 20 19 18 17

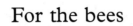

For the bees

"Scientists . . . submitting works on neonicotinoids or the long-term effects of GMO crops, trigger corporate complaints . . . and find that their careers are in jeopardy."

Jeff Ruch, Executive Director of PEER (Public Employees for Environmental Responsibility)

CHAPTER ONE

The first thing I am aware of is the taste of salt. It fills my mouth. Invasive. Pervasive. It dominates my being, smothering all other senses. Until the cold takes me. Sweeps me up and cradles me in its arms. Holding me so tightly I can't seem to move. Except for the shivering. A raging, uncontrollable shivering. And somewhere in my mind I know this is a good thing. My body trying to generate heat. If I wasn't shivering I would be dead.

It seems an eternity before I am able to open my eyes, and then I am blinded by the light. A searing pain in my head, pupils contracting rapidly to bring a strange world into focus. I am lying face-down, wet sand on my lips, in my nostrils. Blinking furiously, making tears to wash the stuff from my eyes. And then it is all I can see. Sand, stretching away to a blurred horizon. Tightly ribbed. Platinum pale. Almost bleached.

And now I am aware of the wind. Tugging at my clothes, sending myriad grains of sand in a veil of whisper-thin gauze across the beach in currents and eddies, like water.

There is, it seems, almost no feeling in my body as I force myself to my knees, muscles moved by memory more than will. And almost immediately my stomach empties its contents on to the sand. The sea that has filled it, bitter and burning in my mouth and throat as it leaves me. My head hanging down between shoulders supported on shaking arms, and I see the bright orange of the life jacket that must have saved me.

Which is when I hear the sea for the first time, above the wind, distinguishing it from the rushing sound in my head, the God-awful tinnitus that drowns out almost everything else.

Heaven knows how, but I am up and standing now on jelly legs, my jeans and trainers, and my sweater beneath the life jacket, heavy with the sea, weighing me down. My lungs are trembling as I try to control my breathing, and I see the distant hills that surround me, beyond the beach and the dunes, purple and brown, gray rock bursting through the skin of thin, peaty soil that clings to their slopes.

Behind me the sea retreats, shallow, a deep

greenish-blue, across yet more acres of sand toward the distant, dark shapes of mountains that rise into a bruised and brooding sky. A sky broken by splinters of sunlight that dazzle on the ocean and dapple the hills. Glimpses of sailor-suit blue seem startling and unreal.

I have no idea where this is. And for the first time since consciousness has returned, I am aware, with a sudden, sharp and painful stab of trepidation, that I have not the least notion of who I am.

That breathless realization banishes all else. The cold, the taste of salt, the acid still burning all the way up from my stomach. How can I not know who I am? A temporary confusion, surely? But the longer I stand here, with the wind whistling around my ears, shivering almost beyond control, feeling the pain and the cold and the consternation, I realize that the only sense that has not returned to me is my sense of self. As if I inhabit the body of a stranger, in whose uncharted waters I have been washed up in blind ignorance.

And with that comes something dark. Neither memory nor recollection, but a consciousness of something so awful that I have no desire to remember it, even if I could. Something obscured by . . . what?

11

Fear? Guilt? I force myself to refocus.

Away to my left I see a cottage, almost at the water's edge. A stream, brown with peat, washes down from hills that lift beyond it, cutting a curving path through smooth sand. Headstones rise up from a manicured green slope, higgledy-piggledy behind barbed-wire fencing and a high stone wall. The ghosts of centuries watching from the silence of eternity as I stagger across the sand, feet sinking nearly ankle-deep in its softness. A long way off to my right, on the far shore, beside a caravan just above the beach, I see a figure standing in silhouette, sunlight spilling down from the hills beyond. Too far away to discern sex or size or form. Hands move up to a pale face, elbows raised on either side, and I realize that he or she has lifted binoculars to curious eyes and is watching me. For a moment I am tempted to shout for help, but know that, even had I the strength, my voice would be carried off by the wind.

So I focus instead on the path I see winding off through the dunes to the dark ribbon of metaled, single-track road that clings to the contour of the near shore as it snakes away beyond the headland.

It takes an enormous effort of will to wade through the sand and the spiky beach grass that binds the dunes, staggering up the narrow path that leads between them to the road. Momentarily sheltered from the constant, battering wind, I lift my head to see a woman coming along the road toward me.

She is elderly. Steel-gray hair blown back in waves from a bony face, skin stretched tight and shiny over bold features. She is wearing a parka, hood down, and black trousers that gather over pink trainers. A tiny yapping dog dances around her feet, little legs working hard to keep up, to match her longer strides.

When she sees me she stops suddenly, and I can see the shock on her face. And I panic, almost immediately overwhelmed by the fear of whatever it is that lies beyond the black veil of unremembered history. As she approaches, hurrying now, concerned, I wonder what I can possibly say to her when I have no sense of who or where I am, or how I got here. But she rescues me from the need to find words.

"Oh my God, Mr. Maclean, what on earth has happened to you?"

So that's who I am. Maclean. She knows me. I am suffused by a momentary sense of relief. But nothing comes back. And I hear my own voice for the first time, thin and hoarse and almost inaudible, even to myself. "I had an accident with the boat." The words are no sooner out of my mouth than I find myself wondering if I even have a boat. But she shows no surprise.

She takes my arm to steer me along the road. "For heaven's sake, man, you'll catch your death. I'll walk you to the cottage." Her yappy little dog nearly trips me up, running around between my feet, jumping at my legs. She shouts at it and it pays her not the least attention. I can hear her talking, words tumbling from her mouth, but I have lost concentration, and she might be speaking Russian for all that I understand.

We pass the gate to the cemetery, and from this slightly elevated position I have a view of the beach where the incoming tide dumped me. It is truly enormous, curling, shallow fingers of turquoise lying between silver banks that curve away to hills that undulate in cutout silhouette to the south. The sky is more broken now, the light sharp and clear, clouds painted against blue in breathless brushstrokes of white and gray and pewter. Moving fast in the wind to cast racing shadows on the sand below.

Beyond the cemetery we stop at a strip of tarmac that descends between crooked fence posts, across a cattle grid, to a single-story cottage that stands proud among the dunes, looking out across the sands. A shaped and polished panel of wood, fixed between fence posts, has *Dune Cottage* scorched into it in black letters.

"Do you want me to come in with you?" I hear her say.

"No, I'm fine, thank you so much." But I know that I am far from fine. The cold is so deep inside me that I understand if I stop shivering I could fall into a sleep from which I might never wake. And I stagger off down the path, aware of her watching me as I go. I don't look back. Beyond a tubular farm gate, a path leads away to an agricultural shed of some kind, and at the foot of the drive, a garden shed on a concrete base stands opposite the door of the cottage, which is set into its gable end.

A white Highland pony feeding on thin grass beyond the fence lifts its head and also watches, curious, as I fumble in wet pockets for my keys. If this is my cottage surely I must have keys for it? But I can't find any, and try the handle. The door is not locked, and as it opens I am almost knocked from my feet by a chocolate Labrador, barking and snorting excitedly, eyes wide and smiling, paws up on my chest, tongue slashing at my face.

And then he is gone. Through the gate and haring away across the dunes. I call after him. "Bran! Bran!" I hear my own voice, as if it belongs to someone else, and realize with a sudden stab of hope that I know my dog's name. Perhaps the memory of everything else is just a whisper away.

Bran ignores my calls, and in moments is lost from sight. I wonder how many hours I have been away, and how long he has been shut up in the house. I glance back up the drive, to the tarmac turning area behind the house, and it occurs to me that there is no car, which seems odd in this remotest of places.

A wave of nausea sweeps over me and I am reminded again that I need to raise my core temperature fast, to get out of these clothes as quickly as possible.

I stumble into what seems to be a utility and boot room. There is a washing machine and tumble dryer beneath a window and worktop, a central-heating boiler humming softly beyond its casing. A wooden bench is pushed up against the wall on my left below a row of coats and jackets. There are walking boots and wellies underneath the bench, and dried mud on the floor. I kick off my shoes and rip away the life jacket before struggling unsteadily into the kitchen, supporting myself on the door jamb as I push through the open door.

It is the strangest feeling to enter a house that you know is your own, and yet find not one thing about it that is familiar. The row of worktops and kitchen cabinets on my left. The sink and hob. The microwave and electric oven. Opposite, below a window that gives on to a panoramic view of the beach, is the kitchen table. It is littered with newspapers and old mail. A laptop is open but asleep. Among these things, surely, I will find clues as to who I am. But there are more pressing matters.

I fill the kettle and turn it on, then pass through an archway into the sitting room. French windows open on to a wooden deck, with table and chairs. The view is breathtaking. A porthole window on the far wall looks out on to the cemetery. In the corner, a wood-burning stove. Two two-seater leather settees gather themselves around a glass coffee table. A door leads into a hall that runs the length of the cottage, along its spine. To the right, another door opens into a large bedroom. The bed is unmade and, as I stumble into the room, I see clothes piled up on a chair. Mine, I presume. Yet another door leads off to an en suite shower room, and I know what I must do.

17

With fumbling fingers I manage to divest myself of my wet clothes, leaving them lying on the floor where they fall. And, with buckling legs, I haul myself into the shower room.

The water runs hot very quickly, and as I step under it I almost collapse from the warmth it sends cascading over my body. Arms stretched, palms flat against the tiles, I support myself and close my eyes, feeling weak, and just stand there with the water breaking over my head until I feel the heat of it very slowly start to seep into my soul.

I have no idea how long I remain there, but with warmth and an end to shivering comes the return of that same black cloud of apprehension which almost overcame me on the beach. A sense of something unspeakable beyond the reach of recollection. And with that the full, depressing realization that I still have no grasp of who I am. Or, disconcertingly, even what I look like.

I step from the shower to rub myself briskly with a big, soft bath towel. The mirror above the sink is misted, and so I am just a pink blur when I stoop to peer into it. I slip on a toweling bathrobe that hangs on the door and pad back through to the bedroom. The house feels hot, airless. The floor, warm beneath my feet. And as that same warmth infuses my body, so I feel all its aches and pains. Muscles in arms, legs and torso that are stiff and sore. In the kitchen I search for coffee and find a jar of instant. I spoon it into a mug and pour in boiled water from the kettle. I see a jar of sugar, but have no idea if I take it in my coffee. I sip at the steaming black liquid, almost scalding my lips, and think not. It tastes just fine as it is.

With almost a sense of trepidation, I carry it back through to the bedroom and lay it on the dresser, to slip from my bathrobe and stand before the full-length mirror on the wardrobe door to look at the silvered reflection of the stranger staring back at me.

I cannot even begin to describe how dissociating it is to look at yourself without recognition. As if you belong somewhere outside of this alien body you inhabit. As if you have simply borrowed it, or it has borrowed you, and neither belongs to the other.

Nothing about my body is familiar. My hair is dark, and though not long, quite curly, falling wet in loops over my forehead. This man appraising me with his ice-blue eyes seems quite handsome, if it is possible for me to be at all objective. Slightly high cheekbones and a dimpled chin. My lips are pale but fairly full. I try to smile, but the grimace I make lacks any humor. It reveals good, strong, white teeth, and I wonder if I have been bleaching them. Would that make me vain? From somewhere, completely unexpectedly, comes the memory of someone I know drinking his coffee through a straw so as not to discolor brilliantly white teeth made porous by bleach. Or perhaps it is not someone I know, just something I have read somewhere, or seen in a movie.

I seem lean and fit, with only the hint of a paunch forming around my middle. My penis is flaccid and very small — shrunken, I hope, only by the cold. And I find myself smiling, this time for real. So I am vain. Or perhaps just insecure in my masculinity. How bizarre not to know yourself, to find yourself guessing at who you are. Not your name, or the way you look, but the essential you. Am I clever or stupid? Do I have a quick temper? Am I made easily jealous? Am I charitable or selfish? How can I not know these things?

And as for age . . . For God's sake, what age am I? How hard it is to tell. I see the beginnings of gray at my temples, fine crow's feet around my eyes. Midthirties? Forty?

I notice a scar on my left forearm. Not recent, but quite pronounced. Some old injury. An accident of some kind. There is a graze in my hairline, blood seeping slowly through black hair. And I see also, on my hands and forearms, several small, red, raised lumps with tiny scabs at their center. Bites of some sort? But they don't seem to hurt or itch.

I am awakened from my self-appraisal by the sound of barking at the door. Bran back from his gallivant among the dunes. I pull on my bathrobe and go to let him in. He jumps around me with excitement, pushing himself against my legs and thrusting his snout into my hands, seeking their comfort and reassurance. And I realize he must be hungry. There is a tin bowl in the boot room that I fill with water, and as he laps at it thirstily, I search for dog food, finding it finally in the cupboard beneath the sink. A bagful of small ochre nuggets and another bowl. The familiar sound of the food rattling into the bowl brings Bran snuffling hungrily into the kitchen, and I stand back and watch as he devours it.

My dog, at least, knows me. My scent, the sound of my voice, the expressions on my face. But for how long? He seems like a young dog. Two years or less. So he hasn't been with me for long. Even were he able to talk, how much could he tell me about myself, my history, my life before the time he entered it?

I look around me again. This is where I live. On the end wall of the kitchen there is a map of what I recognize to be the Outer Hebrides of Scotland. How I know that, I have no idea. Is that where I am? Somewhere on that storm-tossed archipelago on the extreme northwestern fringe of Europe?

Among the mess of papers on the table, I pick up an envelope that has been torn open. I pull out a folded sheet. A utility bill. Electricity. I unfold it and see that it is addressed to Neal Maclean, Dune Cottage, Luskentyre, Isle of Harris. And at a stroke I know my whole name and where I live.

I sit down at the laptop and brush fingers over the trackpad to waken it from its slumber. The home screen is empty except for the hard-disk icon. From the dock, I open up the mailer. It is empty. Nothing even in its trash. The documents folder, too, reveals nothing but blinking emptiness, as does the trash can in the dock. If this really is my computer, it seems I have left no trace of me in it. And something about the hard, white light it shines in my eyes is almost painful. I close the lid and determine to look again later.

My attention is drawn by the books that

line the shelves in the bookcase below the map. I stand stiffly and go to take a look. There are reference books. An Oxford English dictionary, a thesaurus, a large encyclopedia. A dictionary of quotations. Then rows of cheap paperbacks, crime and romance, vegetarian cooking, recipes from northern China. Well-thumbed, yellowing pages. But some instinct tells me they are not mine. On top of the bookcase, a pile of hardback books seem newer. A history of the Hebrides. A photo book titled simply *Hebrides.* There are some tourist maps and leaflets, and a well-thumbed booklet with the intriguing title *The Flannan Isles Mystery.* I lift my eyes to the map on the wall and run them around the ragged coastline of the Outer Hebrides. It takes a moment to find them, but there they are. The Flannan Isles. Eighteen, maybe twenty miles to the west of Lewis and Harris, well north of St. Kilda. A tiny group of islands in a vast ocean.

I drop my eyes again to the booklet in my hands and open it to find the introduction.

The Flannan Isles, sometimes known as The Seven Hunters, are a small group of islands approximately thirty-two kilometers west of the Isle of Lewis. Taking their

23

name from the 7th-century Irish preacher St. Flannan, they have been uninhabited since the automation of the lighthouse on Eilean Mòr, the largest of the islands, in 1971 — and are the setting for an enduring mystery that occurred in December 1900, when all three lighthouse keepers vanished without trace.

I look at the map once more. The islands seem tiny, so lost and lonely in that vast ocean, and I cannot begin to imagine what it must have been like to live out there, spending weeks or months on end with only your fellow lighthouse keepers for company. I reach out to touch them with trembling fingertips, as if paper might communicate with skin. But there are no revelations. I let my hand drop again, and my eyes wander down the southwest coast of Harris to find Luskentyre, and the yellow of the beach they call Tràigh Losgaintir. Beyond it the Sound of Taransay, and the island of Taransay itself, whose mountains I had seen rising out of the ocean behind me when I first staggered to my feet on the beach.

How had I come to be washed up there? That I had been wearing a life jacket suggested I had been on a boat. Where had I been? What happened to the boat? Had I been alone? So many questions crowd my confusion that I turn away, pain filling my head.

Bran sits in the arch, watching me, and when I catch his eye he lifts a hopeful head. But I am distracted by the bottle of whisky that I see on the worktop, several inches of gold trapping light from the window to give it an inner glow. In the cabinet above, I find a glass and pour in three good fingers. Without thought or hesitation I splash in a little water from the tap. So this is how I like my *uisge beatha.* Quite unconsciously I am discovering little things about myself. Even that I know the Gaelic for whisky.

It tastes marvelous, warm and smoky with an underlying sweetness. I look at the label. Caol Ila. An island whisky. Pale and peaty. I carry my glass and the bottle through to the sitting room, set the bottle on the coffee table and cross to stand at the French window, staring out at the sands and the light that sweeps across them between the shadows of fast-moving clouds. A flash on the opposite shore catches my attention. A fleeting reflection of light on glass. I look around the room behind me. Somehow, earlier, I had registered the binoculars sitting on the mantel. I fetch them, set my glass beside the bottle, and raise the twin lenses to my eyes. It takes me a moment, but then there he is. The watcher on the far shore, whom I had seen from the beach. A man, my own binoculars reveal to me now. I can see him quite clearly. He has long hair blowing back in the wind, and a patchy, straggling beard on a thin, mean face. And he is watching me watching him.

I am still shaking a little, and so it is difficult to keep the glasses steady and the man in focus. But I see him lower his binoculars and turn to climb up into the caravan behind him. I can see a satellite dish fixed to the end of the vehicle and what looks like a small radio mast. And, panning left, I find a battered-looking Land Rover with a canvas roof. Both sit elevated and exposed on what I know is called the machair, that area of fertile grassland around the coastal fringes of the islands, where wild flowers bloom in spring abundance and the lambs feed to bring almost sweet, ready-salted meat to the plate.

I return my binoculars to their place above the stove, lift my glass and sink into the settee that faces the view to the beach. I wonder what time it is. Hard to tell whether it is morning or afternoon, and I realize for the first time that I am not wearing a watch. And yet from the band of pale skin around my left wrist, on an arm that has been tanned by sun or wind, it is clear that it is my habit to do so.

Sun streams now through the window and I feel the heat of it on my feet and my legs. I sip slowly on my glass as Bran clambers on to the settee beside me, settling himself to lay his head in my lap. I run absent fingers across his head, idly stroking his neck to bring comfort to us both, and I have no recollection of even finishing my whisky.

CHAPTER TWO

I have no idea how long I have slept. Consciousness returns from a dark, dreamless sleep, bringing with it the physical pain of a still traumatized body, and the recollection that I recall nothing. Of myself, or what happened to me in the hours before I was washed ashore on Tràigh Losgaintir.

But I am startled, too. Heart pounding, aware that the sun has slipped beyond the hills and sunk somewhere in the west, sprinkling pink dusk, like dust, on the dying day. Something has wakened me. A sound. Bran has raised his head from his slumbers, sniffing the air, but doesn't seem alarmed.

A voice from the boot room calls out my name. "Neal?" A woman's voice. And she is not alone. I hear a man, too, as they shut the outside door behind them. I am on my feet in an instant, my empty whisky glass rolling away across the floor. Bran pulls himself up and looks at me quizzically.

Even before my visitors can open the door into the kitchen, I am out into the hall and turning toward the bedroom. "Neal, are you home?" They are in the kitchen now, and I search through the clothes on the bedroom chair to find a pair of jeans, hopping from one leg to the other as I pull them on, falling back on the bed to drag the waistband over my thighs and button them shut.

"Be right with you." I drag a T-shirt over my head. No time to find socks or shoes. I catch a glimpse of myself in the mirror as I hurry from the bedroom, face pale beneath my tan, hair a mess of curls.

They are standing in the sitting room when I come through. People, clearly, who know me. And yet I detect in myself not a flicker of familiarity in either of them.

They are both younger than me. Late twenties, perhaps early thirties. His blond hair is cut short at the sides, left longer on top and gelled back from a narrow forehead. He is good-looking, a man conscious of his image, a tightly trimmed beard that is longer than designer stubble dressing a lean face with almond-shaped green eyes. He wears what I am certain is a designer-labeled hoodie, and immaculate jeans above pristine white Adidas trainers that look as if they are just out of the box. With his hands pushed into the pockets of his jacket, he has a certain slouch, but you can tell from his shoulders and narrow hips that he is well built. He grins at me, a wide, open, infectious grin, and nods through the hall toward the bedroom. "Christ, have you got a woman through there? Hope we didn't disturb anything." His accent is very different from mine. North of England, but refined. Middle class. My guess would be public rather than grammar school.

"Sorry." I run a hand self-consciously back through my hair. "I fell asleep." My own voice sounds quite coarse by comparison. Scottish, but not island. Central belt perhaps.

She laughs. "Well, that's nice. Invites us for drinks then buggers off for an early night." Her accent is similar to his, but broader. A soft voice, with a slight catch in it. Almost hoarse. Seductive. She is six inches shorter than him, but still quite tall. Five six, perhaps, or seven. Short, boyish, auburn hair frames an almost elfin face. Deep brown eyes enhanced by a reddish brown eye shadow. Wide lips a slash of red. She is slim, a well-worn leather bomber jacket hanging on square shoulders over a white T-shirt and fashionably baggy jeans. "When we didn't see the car out front, we thought maybe you weren't here."

So I have a car, but no idea where it is. And I am suddenly overcome by an urge to tell them everything. Which is almost nothing. Just that I was washed up on the beach and haven't a clue who I am. These people know me. They could tell me so much. But I am scared to give shape or form to that black cloud of anxiety that hangs over me. Of events beyond memory. Things simply wiped from my mind that I fear I might never even wish to acknowledge. And all I say is, "I forgot."

"That's just what Sally said. 'Bet he's forgotten.' " And he does a very good imitation of her accent.

"So where is the car?" Sally says.

And I find myself panicking. "Pranged it."

"Aw, shit." She bends down to ruffle Bran's head, and he pushes his face up into her hand. "What happened? Is that how you cut your head?"

My hand goes instinctively to my hairline, where the blood I had seen earlier has dried now to a scab. But I don't want to go any further down this road. "Oh, it wasn't anything very much. I'll get the car back tomorrow."

He says, "How did you get home?"

My mind is racing. You can't just tell one

31

lie, and I'm very quickly learning that I am not a good liar. "The garage gave me a lift back."

Sally says, "All the way from Tarbert? Christ, that was good of them. You should have called. Jon would have come and got you."

Jon unzips his hoodie and allows himself to fall back into the other settee, legs spread, an arm extended along the top of the cushions. "More to the point, where's that drink you promised us?" And I am seriously grateful for the change of subject.

Sally slips out of her jacket and throws it over the back of the settee, before dropping down beside Jon, who lets his arm slide around her shoulder. It is clear to me that not only are they regular visitors, at ease in my house, but they are a couple comfortable with each other. "Yeah, come on, Neal, we're dying of thirst here."

"Sure," I say, happy to escape into the kitchen. "What would you like?"

"Just the usual," she calls through.

I feel panic rising again. I should know what they drink. How can I explain that I don't? I search the cupboards once more, this time looking for drink, but I can't find so much as a can of beer. Then I open the fridge, and there is a bottle of vodka, two-thirds full, in the door. Somehow I just know that vodka is not my tipple. I scan the shelves for tonic. Nothing. "I think I'm out of tonic," I call back, hoping I've got this right.

I hear her sigh. "Men! Do I have to do everything myself?"

And she slips through the archway into the kitchen, eyes alight and full of mischief. She puts a conspiratorial finger to her lips and, before I can even react, she reaches arms up around my neck to pull me toward her, mouth open, finding mine and forcing her tongue past my lips and teeth. Something in the scent and touch of her is arousingly familiar, and beyond that first moment of shock I find myself reacting. Hands sliding down her back and pulling her toward me, pressing myself against her. And then we break apart and I am both breathless and startled. She says loudly, "Did you check the larder?"

I look around. I have not the least idea where the larder is. "No."

She tuts, taking my hand and pulling me through to the boot room. "Let's see." I glance guiltily over my shoulder to make sure that Jon can't see us. Somehow I have been drawn into a conspiracy of deceit that must have been familiar to me only yesterday, and no doubt long before that. But now, in my ignorance of it, I find its sudden intimacy exciting, almost intoxicating.

To the left of the washing machine, she opens a floor-to-ceiling cupboard to reveal shelves stacked with tins and packet food, bottles and condiments. She stoops to the bottom shelf and lifts a six-pack of tonic in its plastic wrap. "Honestly, Neal, you'd forget your head if it wasn't screwed on." She grins and reaches up to kiss me lightly on the lips, then hurries back through to the kitchen. "I'll fix these. You go through and pour yourself a whisky and keep Jon company."

I go through to pick up my glass from where it has rolled under the coffee table and set it beside the bottle. I don't really want another drink. I need to keep my head clear.

Jon smirks. "Been at it before we got here, I see. That why you were sleeping?"

I force a smile. "No. I just had the one. And it was a while ago." I stand up and walk to the French windows and nod toward the far shore. "The man in that caravan over there was watching me through binoculars."

Jon breathes scorn through pursed lips. "Buford? He's a weird one, that. Apparently residents at Seilebost have been at the council to try and get him evicted. But it's common grazing or something, and he's claiming travelers' rights." Sally comes in and hands him a glass, and sits down beside him. "He must be mad parking his caravan there. He has it guyed and pegged all the way round to stop it blowing away. Must be like living in a bloody wind tunnel." He raises his glass. "Cheers."

Sally chinks glasses with him and cocks an eyebrow at me. "Not joining us?"

Jon grins now. "Think he's had enough already." Then, "I guess you didn't make it out to the Flannans yesterday. It was a real stinker. Start of the equinoctials, the locals say."

I cannot imagine why I might have wanted to go out to the Flannan Isles, but it seems safer to agree that I didn't. "No, I never made it."

"Thought not."

Sally takes a sip of her vodka tonic and I hear ice clinking in her glass and notice there is a slice of lemon in it. She really does know her way around my kitchen.

Jon says, "So how's the book going?"

Every sentence uttered feels like a trap set to catch me out. "Book?" I frown innocently, or at least hope I do.

Sally chides him. "You should know better than ask a writer a question like that."

Jon laughs and says, "What, has inspiration vanished like those lighthouse keepers you're writing about? Last time we spoke, you said you were almost finished."

I try to avoid further traps. "I expect to wrap it up sometime this month." And suddenly I realize that I don't even know what month it is. I glance around the room and see a Jolomo calendar hanging on the wall. A vividly colored painting of cottages standing above an outcrop of rocks, and boats at anchor in a stormy bay. Below it, the month of September is laid out in thirty squares.

Sally won't meet my eye. "I suppose that means you'll be leaving soon."

I nod, half-feigning regret. "I suppose it does."

It feels like an eternity before they go. We sit and talk. Or, at least, Jon talks and I listen, trying hard not to get involved in a conversation that I can't find my way out of. Concentration is difficult. In spite of sleeping earlier I am exhausted. My body feels battered. And I am aware of Sally watching me. Silent, appraising, as if she can read my mind, or the lack of it.

While he seems oblivious, Sally must sense my impatience to be rid of them, for it is she who stands, finally, and says they should go. "Neal's tired," she tells him. "We can do this another time."

Jon drains his glass and rises to his feet. "Maybe that bump in your car was a bit more than you're letting on, eh?"

I just smile and follow them through the house to the door. "Sorry to be such bad company," I say, and from the doorstep I look around for their car. But there is no vehicle in sight.

Sally kisses me lightly on the cheek and Jon shakes my hand. "Get yourself a decent night's sleep," he says. "You'll feel better tomorrow." Evidently it has not gone unnoticed that I am not myself. I almost smile inwardly. How could I be, when I have no idea who I am?

I stand on the step, the wind tugging my hair, and watch as they walk up to the road and turn left. Above them on the far side of the single-track, a house stands overlooking mine, and the beach beyond. For the first time, I cast eyes over the exterior of my own place. A traditional design, but it can be no more than a year or two old. Well insulated, double glazed, warm and comfortable inside, offering the protection of modern engineering from the elements of this harsh environment. How did I end up here? Have

I always lived on my own?

For a moment I am distracted by Bran racing among the dunes, barking and chasing rabbits, and when I look back I see Jon and Sally going up the drive of a house near the top of the hill. I realize they are neighbors. Sally turns and waves before they go inside. The house has a two-story glass porch in the design of a gable end, built out from the front of it. I can only imagine how spectacular the views must be from the inside, though given that Jon and Sally are neighbors, and friends, I must have seen them often enough.

There is only a handful of houses strung out along the road as it curves up over the hill beneath a brooding sky and failing light. A rising horizon unbroken by a single tree, and delineated by dry stone walls. Away to the west, beyond the beach and a sea that seems to glow with some inner light, the mountains of Taransay rise against the setting sun, the sky clearing beyond them in a freshening wind from the southwest.

I shout on Bran and he comes racing back.

Once inside, I hear him lapping water from his bowl in the boot room as I go into the kitchen and turn on the lights.

So I am writing a book.

I cross to the bookshelf and lift the booklet

on the mystery of the Flannan Isles and sit down to flip it open. In it I read that the largest of the seven islands, Eilean Mòr, which is Gaelic for Big Island, rises 288 feet above sea level and was chosen at the end of the nineteenth century as the site for a lighthouse that would guide passing vessels safely around Cape Wrath and onward to the Pentland Firth. The island is less than 39 acres in size, and the lighthouse they built there is 74 feet high. Lit for the first time on December 7, 1899, it flashed twice in rapid succession every thirty seconds, and sent a 140,000-candlepower beam 24 nautical miles out to sea.

It was almost exactly a year later, on December 15, 1900, that the captain of the steamer *Archtor,* headed for Leith on the east coast of Scotland, reported by wireless that the light was out. But whoever took that message at the headquarters of Cosmopolitan Line Steamers failed to report it to the Northern Lighthouse Board, and it wasn't until the 26th of the month that relief keepers, delayed by bad weather, were finally landed on the island to discover that keepers James Ducat, Thomas Marshall and Donald McArthur had vanished without trace.

As I read, I find myself being drawn into

the mystery. Printed in full is a colorful poem written about the event twenty years after it, by Wilfrid Wilson Gibson. In it he imagines that the relief keepers, on landing, were watched by three huge birds that flew from the rock, startled by their arrival, to plunge into the sea. And when the men entered the lighthouse, the smell of lime-wash and tar that greeted them was as "familiar as our daily breath," but reeked now of death. They found an untouched meal of meat and cheese and bread on the table, and an overturned chair on the floor. The men's bunks had not been slept in, and there was no trace of them anywhere on the island.

This fanciful version of events is contradicted in the booklet I am reading by extracts from the actual account given by assistant keeper Joseph Moore, who was the first man to enter the lighthouse after the arrival of the relief vessel *Hesperus*. Making no mention of a meal on the table or an overturned chair, he wrote:

> I went up, and on coming to the entrance gate I found it closed. I made for the entrance door leading to the kitchen and store room, found it also closed and the door inside that, but the kitchen door itself

was open. On entering the kitchen I looked at the fireplace and saw that the fire was not lighted for some days. I then entered the rooms in succession, found the beds empty just as they left them in the early morning. I did not take time to search further, for I only too well knew something serious had occurred. I darted out and made for the landing. When I reached there I informed Mr. McCormack that the place was deserted. He with some of the men came up a second time, so as to make sure, but unfortunately the first impression was only too true. Mr. McCormack and myself proceeded to the light-room where everything was in proper order. The lamp was cleaned. The fountain full. Blinds on the windows.

There are, it seems, two landing stages on the island. One on the east side and one on the west. While everything was normal on the east side, at the west landing a box holding ropes and tackle had gone, the railings were buckled, a 20-hundredweight block of stone dislodged, and a lifebuoy ripped from its fastenings — all 110 feet above sea level. Below, ropes lay strewn over the rocks, and the only conclusion that investigators could come to was that a freak wave had broken over the cliffs and carried the men away.

The one inconsistency in this theory, according to my booklet, was the fact that regulations stated that one of the keepers should remain always within the lighthouse. And while the boots and oilskins of two of the keepers were gone, the waterproof coat worn by the third, Donald McArthur, still hung from its peg in the hall. So if he had broken regulations and gone out at all, he had done so in his shirtsleeves. No one could explain why.

I close the booklet and run my hand over my face, aware for the first time of the bristles that cover my cheeks and chin. How long, I wonder, since I last shaved? But I am more focused on the mystery of the vanishing keepers, and wonder what I have written about them. Quite a lot, I imagine, since apparently I am close to finishing.

I shift seats to sit in front of my laptop and waken it from sleep, to be greeted, as before, by an almost empty screen. This time I search it more thoroughly. I open my browser to comb through its history. But there is none. It has been set to private browsing. Both the *cookie* and *download* folders are empty. A glance at the top of the screen tells me I am connected to the internet. And even as I look, I become aware of just how familiar I am with this laptop and its software. Computers are not some technology foreign to me. I know my way around. I check *Recent Items,* and find it, too, empty, apart from the mailer and browser that I have opened only in these last hours. And I realize that I must have been covering my tracks. Whatever use to which I was putting my computer, I did not want someone else knowing. All of which is very frustrating, when I am trying to learn what I clearly went to great lengths to prevent anyone else from finding out.

I breathe frustration through my teeth and am just about to shut down when I notice a folder sitting innocently between *Downloads* and *Music.* It is labeled, simply, *Flannans.* I double-click and it opens to reveal a long list of files. *Chapter One, Chapter Two . . .* all the way through to *Chapter Twenty.* Again I double-click, this time on *Chapter One,* which triggers the opening of my Pages word-processing software. The document opens. There are headers and footers and a chapter heading, but not a single word of text. I look at it, startled by its emptiness, before opening *Chapter Two.* Exactly the same. With an increasing sense of disorientation, I open every single document, and find every one of them empty.

Now I sit back and gaze at my blank screen, feeling more and more bewildered. Whatever I might have told Jon and Sally, or anyone else, I am not writing a book about the Flannan Isles mystery. I am a fraud.

I can feel the sense of frustration building inside me, bubbling up like molten lava to erupt as an explosion of anger. My chair falls to the floor as I stand up suddenly, just as in Wilfrid Wilson Gibson's poem. There must be, in this house, something that will reveal to me more about who I am. There has to be! I live here, after all. I'm not a ghost. I must leave traces.

And I spend the next half hour going through every drawer and every cupboard, pulling stuff out of them in a frenzy, searching for something, anything, I don't know what. I pull every book from the shelves of the bookcase, shaking each in turn by the spine, in case there should be something concealed among their pages. By the time I head for the bedroom, the floor is littered with debris, the detritus of my desperation.

But I stop in the doorway, my attention caught by a map lying on the coffee table, next to the bottle of whisky. An Ordnance Survey map, all neatly folded up within its shiny, cracked covers. I step over to the table and lift it up. A South Harris Explorer Map. It is well thumbed and torn along some of its folds. It is large and unwieldy as I open it up to reveal the myriad contour lines that delineate the shape and form of this lower half of the Isle of Harris. A landscape pitted by countless lochs, ragged scraps of water reflecting stormy skies. Red denotes the A859 main road, such as it is, with minor roads in broken black lines and yellow. Tràigh Losgaintir, where I washed up only hours ago, is a vast triangle of yellow. I find the cemetery, and my house next to it. Then my eye is drawn to a thick line of luminous orange, tracking part of a broken line from the south end of the beach, that heads almost straight up and over the hills toward a cluster of lochs on the east coast. It is a line I must have drawn on the map myself, with a marker pen. But not recently. It is quite faded, and I wonder how long I must have been here for the ink to lose its color.

Holding it under the light, and squinting to read tiny print, I see that the track my marker pen follows is called *Bealach Eòra-bhat.* Gaelic. But I have no idea what it means. I cannot imagine why I might have marked this track in orange, but if nothing else it gives me somewhere else to look. A starting point tomorrow. For there is nothing I can do about it now, in the dark.

I drop the map, still open, on the table and go through to the bedroom to continue my search. Here there is nothing but clean clothes and laundry. The spare bedroom at the other end of the hall is in use, it seems, as a dressing room. There are more clothes. A suitcase on top of the wardrobe, but it is empty. Only when I turn to go back out do I see the shoulder bag hanging from a hook on the back of the door. A canvas satchel. I grab it and sit on the bed to open it. Finally, something personal. My fingers are shaking as I undo the clasps and delve inside to find a blank notebook and a wallet. To my intense disappointment, verging almost on anger, I find only money in the wallet. Notes and some coins. No credit or business cards, no family photographs. Nothing. I throw the damn thing at the wall and drop my face into my hands, fingers curling into brittle claws to drag at my skin. And my voice rips through the silence of the house as I raise my head to the heavens. "For God's sake! Who the hell am I?"

Of course, no one replies, and I am left sitting here in the desperate silence, bereft. Perhaps I am a ghost after all. Perhaps I died somewhere out there at sea. Yesterday was a *stinker,* according to Jon. And I had canceled my trip out to the Flannan Isles. Or so I said. But what if I *had* gone? How did I get there, and what was the purpose of my visit? Certainly not to research a book. But something happened. I know it, I feel it. Something dreadful. Maybe I drowned. Maybe it was just my body that washed ashore on the beach. And it was only my spirit that rose from the sand to haunt this place. Perhaps that's why I can find no trace of myself.

I clench my fists and dig fingernails into my palms and know from the pain I feel that I am no ghost. I look up as Bran lopes along the hall to stand in the doorway and look at me. "Tell me, Bran," I say to him. "Tell me who I am. What am I doing here?" And he cocks his head to one side, ears lifted. He knows that it is him I am speaking to, and maybe he detects the question in my voice. But he has no answers for me.

Emotionally and physically spent, I rise stiffly and he follows me along to the bedroom. I do not even have the energy to go through and turn out the lights in the kitchen. Instead, I slip out of my jeans and T-shirt and flop on to the bed. If I could, I would weep. But there are no tears in my eyes, just a dry, burning sensation. My

47

mouth is parched. I should drink water. I should eat. But I am too tired. I lie on my back, reflected light spilling from the hall into the darkness of the bedroom, and close my eyes, only vaguely aware of Bran jumping up on to the bed and curling up at my feet.

CHAPTER THREE

I am awakened for the second time by a noise I don't hear, but which is somehow transmitted from my subconscious to send me spiraling up from the deepest of sleeps to break the surface of consciousness, blood pulsing in my head. I blink in the dark, pupils shrinking to bring focus to the light that falls in a skewed rectangle across the floor and far wall of the hall. And I see a shadow step through it.

"Who's there?" I know it is my voice, but it seems disconnected. I feel I should be scared, and yet I am not. I hear Bran issue a strange throaty sound and turn to see him lift his head into the darkness, sniffing furiously. But he has not been moved to rouse himself from the bed.

A silhouette steps into the hall from the sitting room, and I know immediately that it is Sally.

"Jesus!" I am not sure why I am whispering. "You scared the hell out of me."

"Why? Did you think I wouldn't come?"

"I didn't know I was expecting you."

"Idiot!" I can hear the smile in her voice, and roll on to my side as she starts to undress, clothes falling to the floor, until I can see the smooth curve of her hips and the darker circles of her areolae around hard nipples.

"What about Jon?"

"What about him? You weren't expecting him to join us, were you?" And she slips, grinning, into the bed beside me.

"Won't he wonder where you are?"

"He's still on that medication. Knocks him out. He won't surface for another eight hours." I realize I am supposed to know what the medication is for, so I don't ask.

I don't know whether to be alarmed or excited. The proximity of her naked body to my own is immediately arousing. The scent of her perfume, the warmth that emanates from smooth skin that suddenly slides over mine. Thigh on thigh as she moves between my legs, insinuating her body on top of mine. Hard breasts pressing into my chest, her breath in my face. I feel cool palms on each cheek as she holds my head and brings her lips to mine. I can only imagine we have done this many times before, but for me it is like the first time, and it feels as if she has lit a fire inside me. It rages and burns and fuels an unquenchable desire simply to consume her.

I grab her arms and flip her suddenly over on to her back and hear her tiny gasp of surprise. Almost subconsciously, I am aware of Bran jumping down from the bed and sloping huffily away along the hall. My mouth finds hers again and our hunger for each other is limitless. She writhes below me as I move my mouth across every part of her. Breasts, nipples, belly and the soft fuzz of her pubis. To breathe her in is intoxicating. I feel myself losing control, driven, possessed and wanting to possess her.

But she fights back, an equal battle for possession, and we go to war with our mouths and our hands, all intelligent thought sacrificed on the altar of physical desire, bringing us ultimately to a frantic, breathless conclusion that leaves us gasping and shiny with sweat, staring up at the shadows on the ceiling with wide eyes, awaiting the return of some semblance of sanity.

Finally she says, as if only now catching her breath, "That was amazing."

I nod, at a loss really for words. Then I realize she can't see me and say, "It was."

She hoists herself up to lean on one elbow and stare into my face in the semidarkness, lightly tracing fingers across my chest. "Better than the first time. Better than the last. What's got into you, Neal? You seem . . . I don't know, different."

A dozen responses flit through my head, each one flippant or evasive, and all failing to address the truth. I feel nerves like butterflies fluttering in my belly. It is the moment to share, because I am certain I cannot keep this in much longer. And yet still I am afraid to address what it is I can't even remember. In the end, all I say is, "I am."

I turn my head to see her half-frowning, half-smiling. "Are you? In what way?"

I draw a deep, tremulous breath. "They say that all any of us are is the sum total of our memories. They are what make us who we are. Take them away and all you are left with is a blank. Like a computer without software."

She seems to think about that for a moment. "I'm trying to imagine what that might be like," she says. "Weird. I suppose memories are just experience. We learn from our experiences. So without them . . ." She laughs. "We'd be just like children again."

"Not if all you took away were the memories of yourself. Who you are, what you are. Everything you have learned in life remains. It's only you who's been taken out of the equation." I suppose I am trying to find a way of explaining it to myself. But it's not easy, and I am not sure I am anywhere close, but now her half-smile has gone and only the frown remains.

"What are you saying, Neal?"

I sigh. There is no turning back. "Sally, the only reason I know that I am Neal Maclean is because I saw the name on a utility bill. The only reason I know your name is Sally is because that's what Jon called you."

She laughs. "Is that supposed to be funny?" Then, "I don't know why I'm laughing, because it's not." And that thought banishes her laughter, and the smile. "Neal, you're scaring me."

"I'm only telling you how it is, Sally. Eight hours ago, ten, maybe, I don't know how long it was, I found myself washed up on the beach out there. I was soaked through, freezing cold, and only still alive because I was wearing a life jacket. I don't know where I'd been, or how I got there." I sit up, knees drawn to my chest, cupping my face in my hands and breathing into them. Then I turn to look at her with an intensity that I see reflected in her alarm. "I had no memory of who I was, or what happened. And I still don't."

Her frown of consternation cuts deep shadows in her face. "How's that possible?"

"I don't know, but it is. I'm the blank that's left when you take away the memories. It's not just my life that I can't remember, my whole history, it's who I am. What I'm like. What I'm capable of." I hesitate, almost too frightened to shape the thought with words. "I feel as if I have done something . . ." I search for the right word. "Awful. I don't know. Shocking. Every time I try to force memories from my subconscious, I find myself lost in some black fog of dread. Beyond it, I know, there's clarity. But I just can't reach it. And I'm not sure now that I want to."

There is a long silence. "You were acting really strange this afternoon."

I nod.

"You didn't prang your car, did you?"

"No."

"So where is it?"

"I don't know."

She takes some moments to digest this. "You must have gone out to the Flannans after all."

I shrug. "I don't know why I would."

"You go out there all the time, Neal.

54

Research for your book."

"I'm not writing a bloody book!" My raised voice startles her.

"What do you mean?"

"It was you and Jon who told me that. That I was writing a book. About the Flannan Isles mystery."

"Only because that's what you told us."

I shake my head. "After you'd gone I checked my computer. I found twenty chapter templates and not a single word in any of them. If that's really what I told you, Sally, then I was lying. I'm not writing any book."

"Then what have you been doing here all this time?"

"You tell me, because I haven't the first idea." My frustration is bubbling out of me, and I hear my voice rising in pitch and volume. I force myself to calm down. "I'm sorry. It's not your fault. It's just . . . well, you must know so much more about me than I do."

Her voice is quiet, and I can sense that she has retreated into herself. "What do you want to know?" There is a lack of warmth now in her tone. "After all, I can only tell you what you told us."

"Well, let's start with that."

She rolls away to slip out of bed and start

dressing. The intimacy between us is long gone. When she finishes, she sits on the edge of the bed, her back toward me, and I cannot see her face as she speaks. "You've been on the island for about eighteen months. Taken this place on an open-ended long-term let. A sort of sabbatical, you said, from an academic career in Edinburgh. Time you were using to write your book on the disappearance of the lighthouse men." She half-turns her head toward me. "At least, that's what you said." Then, "You were always a little bit mysterious about yourself. What exactly it was you did for a living. Whether or not you were married. You don't wear a ring, but I could see from the paler band of skin on your ring finger that you had until recently."

"You didn't think it was strange that I never told you more about myself?"

I see her shrug her shoulders. "In the circumstances, I suppose I didn't really want to know. I sensed your reluctance and I never pushed you. Sometimes people can know too much about each other. Remove the mystery and you take away the excitement."

"What about you and Jon?"

"Jon and I have been married eight years. We came to Harris a little less than a year ago, from Manchester. A sabbatical of sorts, too. Only ours was to try and patch up a failing marriage." There is no amusement in the tiny laugh that breaks from her lips.

I break the silence that follows. "Should I feel guilty, then?"

"About what?"

"Us."

"No." Her voice is flat, without emotion. "It became apparent to Jon and I, very quickly, that the marriage was beyond repair. In the beginning it had all been so intense. But they say the light that burns twice as bright burns half as long." She pauses. "And we were all burned out." Then a sigh. "But we'd taken on the let for a year, so decided to stick it out." She half-turns again. "Then I met you." She swivels fully around so that she can meet my eye. "And that's what saved my sanity."

I search her face and find intensity there. In the line of her mouth, the darkness of her eyes. "And Jon has no idea?"

Her shrug this time is philosophical. "I don't think so. But, who knows? If he does, he's not letting on. And, anyway, he goes back to Manchester a lot, to take care of business, he says. Maybe he's seeing someone there." Her smile is wan. "At least it makes it easier for us." Pause. "Or did."

The look she gives me is so piercing and invasive that I almost cannot hold her gaze.

She says, "I can't even imagine what it must be like not to know who you are. You must have something in the house. Personal stuff. Things that would at least let you start filling in the gaps."

I shake my head. "That's what's so bizarre. There's nothing. No photographs, no passport, no checkbooks. Not even any credit cards."

"Well, then, how do you live?"

My gasp is born of utter exasperation. "I don't know. I have money in my wallet. But beyond that . . ."

Her frown deepens. "This is surreal, Neal, you know that? You couldn't make this up."

"I know. I know." Then I remember the map. "The only thing I've found . . ." And I slide past her and off the bed to go through to the sitting room. I hear her right behind me, and I lift the Ordnance Survey Explorer Map from the coffee table. "Is this."

She peers at it over my shoulder. "It's just a map."

I trace the line of the orange marker pen with my finger. "But I've drawn this on it. Following some kind of track that goes up into the hills."

She looks more closely. "Oh, yeah. *Bealach*

Eòrabhat." And somehow I know she gets the pronunciation of the Gaelic all wrong. "The coffin road. Jon and I walked the whole circuit last spring."

I look at her, filled with incomprehension. "Coffin road?"

"Apparently, right up till not that long ago, people on the east coast of Harris used to carry their dead across the hills to bury them here on the west side."

"Why?"

"The soil on the east side is so thin you can't dig down deep enough to make a grave. So they used to carry the coffins across what they called the *Bealach Eòrabhat* to bury the bodies in the west-coast machair." She smiles. "Though I'm not sure they actually used coffins. You could count the trees on this island on one hand, so there wouldn't have been much wood around. Maybe they only had one that they used again and again for carrying the bodies, and just buried them in a shroud or something."

"Why would I have marked out the coffin road in orange?"

Her smile is pale, and not exactly sympathetic. "You tell me, Neal." She turns back to the map. "But it stops about a third of the way up, so maybe there's something there."

"Like what?"

"How would I know? Jon and I didn't see anything in the spring. Well, I mean, apart from boulders and lochs and a bunch of cairns. I read somewhere that sometimes, when the weather was really bad, the coffin bearers would stop on the road and dump the bodies in a loch, or bury them anywhere they could find, and just mark the spot with a cairn."

I drop the map back on the table and sit heavily on the settee. "Only one way to find out. I'll walk the coffin road tomorrow."

She looks down at me, and for the first time since I have confessed my memory loss, I see her expression soften. "It's quite a trek just to get to the point where the coffin road begins, Neal. Right around the head of the bay and across the Seilebost causeway. How will you get there without a car?"

"I'll walk."

She purses her lips. "I could give you a lift. And walk with you over the coffin road."

"What would Jon say?"

"I'll tell him I'm going into Tarbert, and I'll pick you up at the far side of the cemetery. You can't see that far along from our house."

60

And I am suffused with a sense of gratitude.

Chapter Four

It is raining when I waken. A driving rain, blown in on the leading edge of a strong southwesterly. I can see it slashing across the beach, almost horizontally. The cloud is low, nearly black at its most dense. As I stand at the French windows, looking out across the Sound toward Taransay, I can see the rain falling from it in dark streaks that shift between smudges of gray-blue light and occasional flashes of watery sunshine that burn in brief patches of polished silver on the surface of the sea.

I have slept the sleep of the dead, untroubled by dreams, good or bad. The greatest nightmare was waking to face the dawn of a new day with memories that stretch back no further than yesterday. I feel hollowed out, empty, devoid of optimism and consumed by depression. The only light in my darkness is Sally.

I remember how it had been making love

to her the night before. All the mystery and excitement of sex with a stranger. How driven we had been, both of us, by some uncontrollable inner urge. And then my revelation of memory loss bringing distance between us, and a cooling of our warmth. I had felt her slipping away, the only thing of substance that I'd had to hold on to. And then her offer to walk the coffin road with me, like a lifeline. I was no longer alone.

While Bran polishes off the food in his bowl, I slip waterproof leggings over my jeans and push my feet into well-worn walking boots. My green waterproof jacket is fleece-lined and warm. I zip it up and select a hiking stick from the rack, before opening the door to face the rain.

Bran dashes out ahead of me, running for the beach until he sees that I have turned the other way, then comes scampering after me. In the window of the house that sits up on the other side of the road, I catch sight of the woman I met yesterday on the road. The one with the yappy little dog. She waves, and I wave back before turning east and tilting a little into the rain that drives in from the beach side, stinging my cheek.

The single-track winds between leaning fence posts, past the cemetery and a collection of houses on the other side of the road, a barn with its sloping expanse of rust-red roof. Ahead, along the rise, a handful of solitary trees that might be Scotch pines stand in silhouette against the luminous gray of the sky. Trees whose branches have been stripped and sculpted by the wind into strange, horizontal skeletons that reach to the east, like old television aerials seeking a signal.

Beyond the cemetery, the road bends and dips down to where a cattle grid sits between two red-topped white gateposts. Beyond it, a metaled path descends to the cottage on the beach that I saw yesterday. I turn in there to stand and wait, my back to the rain, out of sight of Jon and Sally's house, and Bran looks at me as if I am mad.

It is almost five minutes before Sally's car appears. A Volvo estate. She pulls up beside me and, as I climb in, she jumps out and runs around to lift the tailgate. Bran leaps in, unbidden. Evidently we have done this before.

The car steams up quickly and she puts the blower on full as she accelerates up the hill, past gnarled, stunted shrubs clinging stubbornly to sandy soil. More skeleton trees punctuate the bleak September land-scape, late-season heather bringing the only color to otherwise stone-gray hills. I am aware of Sally glancing at me.

"I guess you didn't wake up suddenly remembering everything?"

My laugh is without humor. "I wish." And it occurs to me that I am being shaped now only by the memories I am making, and have made since yesterday. Who I am, or rather who I was, is lost. A new me is being forged out of the moment, and I wonder how different that new me is from the old one.

We drive in silence on a road that twists and turns and undulates around and over the contours of the land, glimpses of the beach opening up at almost every turn, vast and dominating. Even on this greyest of mornings the water is the most extraordinary blue, somehow generating its own light. Then, as we follow the line of the shore, the hills rise up around us, the summer green of the grass already fading toward winter brown.

It is a long way to the head of the bay, and I am glad not to have been walking it on my own in this rain. We encounter no other vehicles, and at the road end we hit the main A859, which turns north toward Tarbert and south to Leverburgh. On our left, a rain-streaked perspex bus-shelter harbors a single miserable soul waiting for a bus into town, a phone box next to it placed there, perhaps, so that passengers might call someone to pick them up when the bus drops them off. On the hill to the north, we see lines of lorries and road-rollers laying a ribbon of thick black tar on a new, wider stretch of road. We turn south, and the road here is still single-track, with passing places. Half a mile on, we pass, coming in the opposite direction, the bus that will lift the spirits of the solitary passenger waiting at the Luskentyre turnoff. Then the long, straight stretch of causeway that arrows through choppy sea until it curves to the right, and on our left a huge expanse of salt marsh stretches away to the north, a startling green, shot through with snaking ribbons of still water reflecting gray sky.

At the end of the causeway, at the Seilebost sign, we turn left on to a metaled track, past a tiny pitched roof over a circle of stones, an ersatz well with a crudely carved wooden plaque depicting a hiker and the legend *Frith Rathad,* the Harris Walkway. Opposite is a sign for a rural sewer project funded by the European Union, and I wonder how people would survive in a place like this without the European money that would never have come from Westminster.

The track curls up past a clutch of cottages, lifting gradually into the foothills, the salt marsh stretching away in the plain below, the sheer scale of Tràigh Losgaintir behind us becoming apparent as we rise above it. We abandon the car where the tarmac gives way to stone and grass and rivers of water running in the tracks left by farm vehicles. And we walk, then, up to a wooden gate where we have the choice to continue north, or turn east. We take the latter, following Bran, who makes the turn without thought. A familiar route. He bounds over a stile, and we follow him along the track, heading off into a sodden wilderness of grass and heather that cuts between barren, rocky hills pushing up all around.

There has been no let-up in the rain. We are more exposed here in the hills, wind rushing between the peaks, hurrying east, the same wind that must have blown rain into the faces of all those carriers of coffins across the centuries.

I notice for the first time that, although Sally's parka is keeping her core dry, she is not wearing leggings and her jeans are already soaked through. A fair-weather hiker. I had dressed instinctively, donning those waterproofs I found in the boot room. Experienced in protecting myself from the elements. And Bran's confidence in where we are going tells me we have been this way many times before.

It is disheartening to look ahead, because the track climbs endlessly into the distance, and so we both focus on our feet, avoiding potholes and boulders on which ankles might get turned. And when, from time to time, we look up, our hearts sink, for we appear to have traveled no distance at all. Until we look back, and are rewarded with the most spectacular view of the beach, far, far below, a luminous silver and turquoise.

"Look!" Sally's voice makes me turn my head and I see where she is pointing, toward a small group of cairns gathered on the hillside. I see more of them ahead of us. Each one marking the place where someone has been laid to rest with the world at their feet. A view to die for.

Below us, on our right, a scrap of loch gathers in a hollow, reflecting the sky, its surface rippled by wind, and I check my map, folded into a clear plastic Ziploc. Not too much further before my orange line comes to its end. We circumvent three large boulders strung across the track to prevent vehicles from trying to go any further, and the path starts to climb even more steeply.

The hills lift almost sheer now on either side, to peaks lost in cloud, the track winding away into obscurity, still rising to what might or might not be its summit. There have been many faux summits before now.

"We must be nearly there," Sally says. She is breathless, her face pink from exertion and the sting of the rain. She glances away to our right. "Looks like they were quarrying here at some time." A cliff face is broken, seamed and jagged, with boulders lying in chaos below it, some of them as big as houses and canted at odd angles.

But I shake my head. "Explosions from a past ice age, Sally. Water freezing and expanding in the crevices until the rock shatters from the pressure." I find myself grinning. "Nature's dynamite." And I wonder how I know this.

Sally grins back at me. "What, are you a geologist now?"

I shrug. "Who the hell knows? Maybe I am."

I turn back to the track and stop. Two boulders, about the size of shoe boxes, but almost oval, sit balanced, one on top of the other. They are unusually shaped, and I can't see how nature could possibly have arrived at this precarious arrangement.

"What is it?" Sally follows my gaze but sees nothing out of the ordinary.

"Someone placed those stones like that."

She frowns. "How do you know?"

I shake my head. It's hard to explain. "It just doesn't look natural. But I guess most folk would have walked right past without noticing."

"I wouldn't have given them a second glance." Sally casts me a curious look. "So somebody put them there?"

"Yes, I think so."

A pause. "You?"

"It's possible." I pull out the map again, wiping away the rain from the plastic with icy fingers. "This would be about the right place."

"Where's Bran?" There is a hint of alarm in Sally's voice. I look up and cannot see him anywhere.

"Bran!" I shout at the top of my voice. And I hear him barking before I see him. Then he appears on the slope off to our right, emerging from behind one of those huge boulders deposited on the hill, part of the spoil from that ice explosion thousands of years ago. A great slab of rock, split along one of its seams. "Here, boy!" But he stands his ground, barking at me as if I am an idiot, and it occurs to me that he expects me to follow, as if that's the path we always take. I turn to Sally. "Come on."

I help her over ground that rises and falls

beneath our feet, peat bog sucking at our shoes, soaking them in a brown slurry. I use my stick for balance, climbing slightly as we reach the first of the boulders, and watch as Bran turns and runs down into a hollow ringed by rock spoil, like giant headstones randomly arranged around a level area of beaten grass beneath the cliff, completely protected from the wind. And as we reach the top of the rise to look down into it, we are stopped in our tracks.

"Jesus Christ," I hear Sally say, the words whipped from her mouth as she speaks them. Below us, completely hidden from view, and as protected from the elements as might ever be possible in this brutal environment, stands a large collection of bee hives. Square, boxlike hives, two and three levels high, some painted orange, others simply weathered, silver wood. They appear to have been positioned arbitrarily, raised off the ground on wooden pallets, roped down and weighted with small boulders on top. I do a quick count. There are eighteen, and I'm not sure that I have ever seen anything quite so unexpectedly incongruous in my life.

It takes us just a few minutes to scramble down into the hollow, and we wander among the hives like warriors walking among the dead of some battle fought long before our arrival.

"I don't understand," Sally says. "Who put them here? Was it you?"

I feel a strange calm descend on me, and I stop by one of the hives. "They call this a National," I say. "Well, a Modified National, because it was modified from the original Langstroth hive, combs set on hanging frames. Pretty much universal in Britain." And with an expertise that seems to come from race memory rather than conscious recollection, I lift the stones from its roof and untie the hive, taking away the roof itself to reveal what I know to be called the crown board. But it is no normal crown board. Clear plastic allows us to peer into the hive.

I am aware of Sally at my side as we look in on a burst-open pack of white sugar sitting on top of the eleven honeycomb frames that hang from rebates along either side. Bees are gathered together here on the right, between two or three of the frames, crawling over each other. Small, brownish, faintly striped. "What are they doing?" she asks.

"Clustering for warmth. *Apis mellifera.* Honey bees. This is their brood chamber. There will be anything up to sixty thousand bees in here." I have no idea where any of this is coming from. "To collect honey, you would have another chamber on top, a super, with a queen excluder, to prevent her from laying eggs in it. But it's the end of the season. The honey will have been harvested."

"What's the sugar for?"

"To feed the bees across the winter, since we've stolen most of the honey they would normally feed on." I replace the roof, carefully tying it down, then adding the weight of the stones. "There's still pollen around in the heather, but they'll not venture out on a day like this. The only real forage up here is the heather itself. But in the spring the machair will be covered with wild flowers. Not too far for the bees to fly, and a veritable feast of pollen and nectar."

I stand back to find her staring at me. Curiosity and confusion, and more than a hint of distrust in her eyes. "You remember all this stuff," she says. "And yet you don't remember who you are. Or me."

I shrug. I can't explain it.

"These are yours, aren't they? These hives."

"I'm guessing they must be."

"But you never told me about them. In all the time we've spent together, all those intimate moments, and you never once thought to say that you kept bees. You didn't *want* me to know, did you?" There is more than a hint of accusation in this.

I allow my eyes to wander over the hives, and then lift them to the boulders that stand around this tiny clearing, like so many silent witnesses. "It seems to me I didn't want *anyone* to know. They are completely hidden here. God knows how many walkers trek across the coffin road during the summer months, but not one of them would have had the least idea that there were hives beyond these rocks."

"But why?" I see doubt in her eyes. Suspicion. Though there is nothing I can say to allay that.

I very nearly shout at her, "I don't know!" And she takes a half-step back. Bran barks, wondering why I have raised my voice.

The rain has stopped as we walk back down the hill, but the wind has stiffened and blows directly in our faces. I suppose I must have seen it many times, but the view from here is quite magnificent. It feels like we are up among the clouds, looking down on the world. The cloud formations coming in off the Atlantic are torn and shredded by the wind, sunlight breaking through them in beams of pure gold against black, crisscrossing the incoming wash and the silver of the sand like spotlights on a stage. Nature's own theatrical production, dazzling and majestic.

Sally and I have not spoken for nearly fifteen minutes. Whatever is going through her mind, she is keeping her own counsel, while I am nursing an unreasonable guilt. In the end I cannot bear it any longer. "I'm sorry," I say, without looking at her.

"What for?" Her voice is cold.

"Everything. Shouting at you. Not telling you about the bees." And my frustration fizzes once more to the surface. "Jesus! Why the hell would I be so secretive about keeping bees?"

"You tell me."

"I wish I could."

It is easier going down than it was coming up, but the silence between us is still difficult.

I glance at her. "You said I went out to the Flannan Isles on a regular basis."

She flicks me a look. "Yes."

"Did someone take me, or do I have a boat?"

"You have a boat."

"Where?"

"You berth it in the harbor at Rodel."

"And where's that?"

She looks at me again to see if I am serious, then she very nearly laughs. But the laughter dies quickly, and the smile with it. "It's right at the southern tip of Harris. Beyond Leverburgh. It looks out across the Sound to North Uist."

"Would you take me there?"

"When?"

"Now."

It is a long time before she responds. "To be honest, Neal, I'm not sure why I should trust you anymore. You've lied to me, concealed things from me."

None of which I can deny. "But I must have had my reasons."

"Clearly."

I suck in a deep breath. "In all those hours we spent together, you must have got some sense of the man I am. Trusted me, had feelings for me."

"Yes, I did. And still do." She stops, forcing me to stop too, and I turn to face her. "But I never really knew you, Neal. Like I told you last night. I just didn't ask. And you weren't telling."

"Then give me the benefit of the doubt, Sally. Please. I'm not sure I can deal with this on my own."

She looks at me for a long time, before sighing in deep resignation. "Come here." And she opens her arms to wrap them around my waist and pull me to her. Holding me tightly, her head turned and pressed into my shoulder. I close my eyes and feel the wind whistling around us, yanking at our clothes and our hair. "Of course I'll take you to Rodel."

I'm not sure how long we have been standing like this, just holding each other, when I hear Bran barking somewhere on the track below us. We break apart and I see him a hundred or more yards away, barking at a man leaning against the gate at the foot of the hill. He has binoculars raised to his eyes, watching us. And, when he lowers them, I see, even from this distance, that it is the man who was watching me from the far shore yesterday. Buford, Jon had said his name was. A solitary traveler, with his caravan pegged down on the machair.

"What the hell does he want?" Sally says. "Do you think he was following us?"

"I don't know. Not up to the hives, anyway. Why don't we ask him?"

But even as we look, he pushes his binoculars into the deep pockets of his waterproofs and turns to hurry away toward the road, long ropes of hair blowing out in the wind behind him.

"Come on." I take Sally's hand, and we increase the speed of our descent. But the surface is difficult, slippery with mud and awash with rainwater running off the hills, and by the time we get to the gate, Buford has reached the semicircle of tarmac, where his Land Rover is parked next to Sally's Volvo. He backs up his vehicle and accelerates away down the track. When finally we get to the car, Buford has turned north on to the A859, and is picking up speed around the curve of the causeway.

CHAPTER FIVE

The single-track road from Leverburgh cuts through the hills above the southern coastline, before winding down into the tiny settlement at Rodel, where the sixteenth-century St. Clement's Church stands on a pinnacle above the harbor, facing out across the Sound. The church is clad in scaffolding, platforms erected on different levels to facilitate restoration work. We drive past its high stone wall, and gate, to turn down the narrow loop of road that drops steeply to the harbor below.

The harbor itself is tiny, built within encircling headlands that almost meet. Through the gap between them, the mountains of North Uist can be seen simmering darkly beyond clearing skies. The wind has dropped a little, and flashes of blue break the monotonous undulations of gray and silver that lie low across the sea.

There are eight or ten boats berthed here

within the protective arms of stone and concrete that mirror the larger, encompassing arms that nature has provided. A couple of fishing boats and half a dozen powerboats of varying sizes. And three small sailing dinghies. At the innermost end, reflecting on still, deep water, stand the huddled gray buildings of the Rodel Hotel. And parked out front, a blue Ford Mondeo.

"That's your car," Sally says. She pulls the Volvo over on to the grass and we walk around to it. The door is unlocked, key in the ignition, two other keys hanging from the fob that I imagine must be my house keys. I reach in to take them, and the small disc of polished wood through which the keyring is looped feels oddly, comfortingly familiar. Otherwise the car is empty, apart from the stale smell of wet dog. I lean over to open the glove compartment, but find only a couple of road maps, one of the Hebrides, another of Scotland. I straighten up and walk around to open the boot. There is a set of oilskins and a pair of mud-caked wellington boots. I slam it shut and gaze out over the boats that bob and shift on the gentle swell.

"Which is mine?"

Sally follows my eyes. She shrugs, puzzled. "It's not here."

And somehow I am not surprised. But still I ask, "Are you sure?"

"I should be. I've been out in it with you often enough. You may have hidden your penchant for bees from me, but your passion for boats was no secret."

A voice carried on the breeze and calling my name startles us, and we turn to see a man in jeans and wellies and a knitted Eriskay jumper climbing from one of the powerboats up on to the far quay. He pushes his hands into his pockets and walks around to greet us, a wide grin on a weathered face. Hair loss makes him seem older than he is, for as he reaches us I see that he has a young face. He thrusts out a large, calloused hand and we shake. "I was getting worried when you never brought *Dry White* back and your car was still sitting there." He glances at Sally and nods acknowledgment. "Mrs. Harrison."

She nods back, and the "Coinneach" she responds with is clearly for my benefit. I recognize it immediately as the Gaelic for Kenneth, but beyond that there is nothing else familiar about him.

"When did I take her out, Coinneach?" And as soon as I ask I realize what a foolish question it is.

He frowns. "What do you mean?"

81

Sally says quickly, "He means what time. We were trying to work out how long it took him to get out to the Flannans."

Coinneach sucks in air through thoughtful lips. "Couldn't say exactly. Early afternoon. But it must have taken you a good while to get out there. The weather was already deteriorating. You must have made it before the storm, though."

I nod quickly. "Yes."

"What did you do, spend the night out there?"

"That's right." I am almost grateful for his prompting my responses.

"So where is she now?"

I am aware of returning a blank look and feel panic rising.

"*Dry White,*" he clarifies for me.

And Sally steps in again. "He took her up to Uig. We're going to explore some of the caves up along the coastline there if the weather improves. I just brought him down to pick up his car."

I glance at her, marveling at how easily she can lie, while I become tongue-tied and completely unconvincing. Somehow, though, Coinneach seems less impressed, and he gives us an odd look, blue Celtic eyes flickering from one to the other.

■ ■ ■ ■

We drive both cars back up to the road and park one behind the other outside the church gate, where a sign reads *Fàilte Gu, Tùr Chiliamainn.* Welcome to St. Clement's Church. Earlier, as we drove into Rodel, Sally told me we had made love once in the tower, while a party of tourists was being given a lecture on the history of the church in the nave below. "It was insane," she said, laughing. "But the risk of being caught made it . . . I don't know, exciting." And I wonder now if perhaps revisiting the scene of our folly will stir memories.

Sun reflects on the wet stone path as we follow it up through the graveyard to the door. Inside, it is completely empty, ancient Lewisian gneiss green in places with the damp. Cruciform in design, there are tiny chapels in each of the transepts, and three walled tombs. We climb narrow stone steps leading to the chamber at the top of the tower, which stands at the west end of the nave, and squeeze into a tiny room lit only by a narrow slit from which archers might once have fired arrows to repel attackers.

I stoop and peer from its leaded window out across the Sound toward the Uists. The wind has dropped almost entirely now, and there seems no dividing line between sea and sky. "How could we possibly have made love in here?" I say. "Apart from the lack of space, any noise we made would have echoed through the whole building."

She laughs, and as I turn and straighten up, her face is very close to mine and I am aware of the heat of her body. "Actually, we were quite noisy. But they were noisier down there." I feel her breath on my lips before she kisses me. A soft kiss, full of tenderness. She draws back just a matter of inches, and I can barely keep her in focus. Her voice whispers around this stone chamber. "Anything coming back to you?"

I purse my lips thoughtfully. "Not yet. Maybe we should try a little harder."

This time the tenderness in the kiss is replaced by something more feral, and I feel my whole body infused with desire. When we break again, her breathing is rapid. "This is so weird," she whispers. "Everything about you is familiar, and yet it's like being with a stranger." She kisses me again, and I feel her hand move down to close around my arousal. I take a half-step back and she pushes me against the wall. The surface is hard and cold and rough. "Still nothing?"

"No. Keep going."

And we make love for the second time in my recollection. A strange, animal act, somehow beyond our control. Awkward and bruising in this confined space, each of us undressed only enough to make union possible. But extraordinarily intense, leaving us once more breathless and perspiring. I pepper her face and neck with tiny kisses, and she holds on to me as if she might never let go.

When finally she catches her breath she says, "And now?"

I shake my head again. "Nothing. But if at first . . ."

Her laughter reverberates around this tiny room, and something about the wanton quality of it provokes powerful feelings inside me. Until it dies away and her smile fades, and by the light of the window I see the intensity in her eyes. She runs her hand over my face, tracing all its contours, and I close my eyes. "Was I in love with you?" I ask her.

When she doesn't respond, I open my eyes to see her gazing at me, a quizzical look now in hers. "That's a strange, past-tense way of asking me. As if you no longer are."

"I know how I feel now, Sally. But I'm not the me I was two days ago. I want to know how *he* felt."

There is just the hint of sadness in her smile. "He told me he loved me, Neal. But, then, he told me lots of things, it seems, that aren't true."

Guilt washes over me. How could I have lied to her? About writing the book. About the bees, even if only by omission. "And what about you? Did you love me?"

I see her swallow back her emotion. "I did."

"And now?"

She smiles. "It seems that's a process of discovery."

CHAPTER SIX

For the third time in two days, something external wakens me. I am disorientated. It is dark, but not late. An old-fashioned clock with luminous hands on the bedside table tells me that it is ten past midnight. Then I remember lying down on the bed after Sally dropped me at the cottage sometime after lunch, and realize I must have slept all afternoon and through the evening.

We had eaten at The Anchorage restaurant on the pier at Leverburgh. Soup, then quiche and salad and a couple of glasses of white wine. Sally told me we had eaten there often, and we were greeted by hellos and friendly smiles from the staff. But I didn't remember the place at all.

Now I am on full alert. Because Bran has jumped down off the bed, a dangerous, low growling in his throat. I am wide awake in seconds and wishing I had left lights on in the house. But it had been daylight when I drifted off to sleep. I reach for the bedside lamp and knock it over, cursing under my breath as I hear the bulb break.

Bran barks. He is still in the room, but standing in the open doorway now. Not that I can see him. The darkness is so dense it is almost physical. No moon or starlight, no streetlights, or any light from nearby houses seeping in through windows.

"Sally?" I call out, more in hope than expectation. Bran would not react like this if it were her. I am rewarded by silence, broken only by Bran's continued growling, and I swing my legs out of the bed to stand and feel my way to the wall. To my dismay we remain in darkness, even after I have flicked the light switch down.

Now my alarm turns to fear. There is someone in the house that Bran does not recognize, and there is no power. I feel for the door frame and swing myself into the hall. I know that the door to the sitting room is open. I shoosh Bran and stand very still, straining to pick up any sound. But Bran can't contain himself for long and barks again. I take advantage of the noise to slip into the sitting room. Outside, a break in the cloud lets unexpected moonlight wash silver across the beach, and in the reflected light I see a shadow detach itself suddenly from darkness, filling my vision, a flash momentarily illuminating the length of a blade that signals deadly intent. I instinctively turn side-on to make myself a smaller target, reaching for the knife arm to stop its downward arc, and I put my full weight behind my shoulder as I push it into the chest of my attacker.

He is smaller, lighter than me, and I feel his breath exploding in my face, sour from stale cigarette smoke, as he staggers backward. I fumble desperately to hold on to his wrist as he struggles to free it, and then I push again, sending us both sprawling over the settee that backs on to the kitchen. I land on top, expelling all the air from his lungs, and we topple then on to the floor, his knife skidding away across the floorboards.

But as we roll over, my head strikes what must be the corner of the coffee table, and light and pain explode inside it. For several long moments I am quite disabled, all my strength dissipated, my limbs feeble and useless. I can hear Bran barking furiously in the dark, and am aware of my assailant scrambling across the floor to retrieve his knife. And there is not a thing I can do about it.

As I turn my head, I see his silhouette rising to its knees. The moon continues to sprinkle intermittent illumination across the beach beyond the French windows, and his face is mired in darkness. Not, it occurs to me in a moment of absurd lucidity, that I would recognize it even if I could see it. And along with this clarity comes the realization that I am not going to be able to prevent him from plunging his knife into me as many times as he likes. It is one of those moments when your own mortality becomes, perhaps for the first time in your life, more than something to be locked away and dealt with in a distant future. It is here and now, and death is just a breath away.

I make one last attempt to roll over and get to my knees, and find myself knocked back down by a shape that seems comprised only of darkness. But it is a darkness both solid and human, and it flies at the man with the knife. Bran is barking incessantly and my confusion is crowded with the noise of his bark and the crashing of two men locked in physical struggle. Merged into a single entity as I try to make sense of what is happening.

My attacker, and his, fall together on to the coffee table, which shatters beneath them. I feel flying glass cut my cheek, and one of them is up on his feet and running.

Through the kitchen and out into the boot room. The second man is slower to rise, winded, and I can hear him gasping for breath before he sets off in pursuit. Bran follows them, barking all the way to the door, and I lie for a moment, breathing heavily, letting my head clear before I try to stand up. I stagger into the kitchen, supporting myself on whatever I can reach, before stumbling into the boot room and out through the open door on to the steps.

The cold air is a physical assault, but it revives me sufficiently to enable me to step down on to the drive, from where I can see the shadow of a man sprinting away along the road in the direction of the cemetery. Just one, and I don't know whether it is the first man or the second. I spin around, scanning the horizon, and then the beach, for any sign of the other. But as the clouds overhead blow across the moon in the stiffening breeze, the night settles again in a blanket of darkness that smothers the land.

A light comes on in the cottage opposite. The old lady with the yappy dog awakened from her sleep. I turn and shout at Bran to shut up, and he stops his barking. And beyond the wind, I can hear the distant yapping of the old lady's dog, muffled by doors and windows.

I usher Bran back into the house and slam the door shut, turning the lock to secure it from the inside, and feel my way along the wall of the boot room to where I know the fuse box is set into a cavity above the boiler. Its plastic cover is down, and I fumble for the master switch. There is no light as I flick it up, but I hear the hum of the boiler as it springs back to life. Two steps to the door and I find the light switch, then stand blinking in the sudden painful glare of electric light.

I takes me some time, to come to terms with the fact that I am still alive, and that, apart from the mess in the other room and a gash in my head, nothing has changed. Except that it has. For someone has just tried to kill me. Some person, unknown, has come into my house in the dead of night and tried to put a knife between my ribs. Only by the grace of God, and the intervention of a second intruder, has my life been spared.

Nothing, absolutely nothing since I found myself washed up, semiconscious, on the Tràigh Losgaintir, has made sense. My memory loss. My failure to find a single clue to my identity, beyond my name, even in my own home. My affair with Sally. The book on the Flannan Isles mystery that I am not writing. Beehives on the coffin road. My missing boat. Now someone trying to kill me. And someone else stepping in to save me. The weight of it all is very nearly crushing.

Bran is still excited and excitable, dancing around me, snuffling and snorting, still on the brink of barking. But I hold him in the boot room with my foot while I shut the door on him. He doesn't understand, but there is shattered glass all over the floor of the sitting room and I know that I have to clear it up before I can let him back in. He barks his hurt through the door at me as I take a broom and shovel from the kitchen cupboard and start to sweep up. It takes me nearly fifteen minutes, searching out every reflecting speck of glass, and then vacuuming the floor just to be sure.

I right a small table that has been up-ended, replacing the lamp that stood on it, thankful that the bulb remains intact. Then move into the bedroom to pick up the pieces of broken bulb from the bedside lamp and run the vacuum cleaner over the carpet to suck up any shards I might have missed.

The very act of cleaning up after the attack has allowed me to calm down. My heart is beating almost normally again, and the focus on finding every skelf of glass has stopped me thinking too much about it. I don't *want* to think about it. I don't want to think about *anything.* I want to go back to the day before yesterday and be who I was then. With whatever secrets I might have had. At least I would have known what they were.

Finally I let Bran back through, and he runs around the house, sniffing in every corner. Strange, threatening scents. He is still on full alert, even if I have put it behind me. Well, not behind me, exactly. It's more like I have slipped into denial.

Which is when I notice the blade of my attacker's knife catching the light where it lies, almost obscured beneath the television cabinet. I drop to my knees and bend down to fish it out and hold it in my hand with a sense of awe. This is a hunting knife with a nine-inch blade, razor-sharp along its curved edge, serrated along the other. Its black haft has finger grips. My insides turn to water as I imagine how it would have felt to have this cold, deadly blade slice through my flesh and veins and organs. And I carry it with me through to the bedroom to slip below my pillow before climbing back into bed, Bran jumping up to stretch himself along my length for comfort. If anyone comes for me again, this time I will be ready.

Day two, AML. After memory loss. Morning greets me with dried blood on the pillow and a scab that has formed over my right temple where it struck the coffee table during last night's struggle. I have a thumping headache, which might owe as much to oversleeping as to my injury. Of the last twenty-four hours, I count up that I have slept away as many as fifteen. I suppose I must have needed to, but it hasn't improved either my physical or mental well-being.

It is just after six and Bran is already up, sitting patiently in the boot room, waiting for me to open the door and let him out. I oblige, and he scampers away across the dunes, watched by the Highland pony that grazes habitually among the beach grasses. I put out food and water for him and leave the door open for his return, then set the kettle to boil and spoon coffee into a mug.

As I wait, I go through to the sitting room. The only evidence of the life-or-death struggle that took place here at midnight last night is the buckled remains of the coffee table. I lift it up and carry it through to the spare room, and when I come back the sitting room seems bigger, empty somehow. I cross to the French windows and gaze out across the beach, watching sunlight chase shadows across turquoise and silver before they race each other over the purple-gray hills beyond. Buford's caravan draws my attention, and I realize it is because his Land Rover is gone. And I wonder where he might be at this time of the morning. What does he do all day, every day? And what is his interest in me?

The kettle boils and I make my coffee, pouring in milk to cool it enough to drink, then sit at the table with the view of the beach spread out before me. I close my eyes as I let the warmth of the coffee slip back over my throat, and try to focus on what it is I need to do now. Where do I go from here? I can't continue to live in this vacuum of ignorance. I have no purpose, no reason to get up in the morning without a past, or any future. Somehow I have to make sense of all this, figure out who I am and what I am doing here.

I incline my head to look at the map on the wall. If what I told Jon and Sally about an academic career in Edinburgh is true, why have I spent the last year and a half on the Isle of Harris pretending to write a book? My eyes come to rest on the cluster of dots on the map that are the Flannan Isles. I make regular visits to the islands,

Sally says. But if I am not writing that book, then why? I must have had a reason. I cannot for the life of me think of anything that would connect the Seven Hunters with eighteen beehives hidden off the coffin road. But those islands seem like as good a place to start looking for answers as any.

I hear Bran returning, claws scraping on laminate floor, and his thirsty lapping of water before the rattle of food as he sticks his face in his bowl. I move around the table to sit in front of the laptop and open up my browser, searching for images of the Flannan Isles. There are plenty, it seems, on the internet, mostly amateur photographs taken by tourists, and not particularly useful. I spend nearly ten minutes searching through them before I stumble on the site of the Royal Commission on the Ancient and Historical Monuments of Scotland, and a detailed map of the lighthouse island, Eilean Mòr.

Shaped a little like a turtle on its back, it reveals a ragged coastline, with cliffs rising all around it. Both landing stages are marked, east and west, on the south side of the island, along with the siting of the cranes which must have been used to lift heavy tackle and supplies ashore. Paths lead up from each to converge almost in the center of the island, before heading on up to the lighthouse itself. A helicopter landing pad is marked to the right of the path, which leads me to assume that service engineers must be brought to and from the island by helicopter. I am surprised to see a "Chapel" marked on the map, just below the lighthouse, and I wonder who must have lived here once, long enough to have built a place of worship.

Bran pads through to sit beside my chair and look up at me, then pushes my elbow with his snout, in search of my hand. I ruffle his head absently, and stroke behind his ears. My boat has gone, God knows where. And I wonder how I will get out there.

CHAPTER SEVEN

The harbor at Rodel is deserted as I drive down from the church and park in front of the hotel. There are a couple of other vehicles there, but not a soul in sight. I have no idea where Coinneach lives, and wander along the quay to the boat I saw him climb out of yesterday. It is a Sea Ray 250 Sundancer powerboat with a 454 Magnum Alpha One engine. I seem to know every little detail about it, although I am not sure how. It is a sleek beast, white with purple trim, and a plastic cowling that can be mounted to shelter the driver in bad weather. Though it would not, I know, last long in the winds it would encounter around these coasts. This is a fair-weather boat.

I am turning away when I hear my name called, and I swing back to see Coinneach emerging from below, climbing the couple of steps to the left of the driver's seat, and straightening himself with palms pressed into his lower back. "On your own today?" he says.

"Aye."

"So what brings you back to Rodel when your boat's up at Uig?" And something about the way he says this makes me think that he didn't believe a word of Sally's story yesterday.

"I was wondering if I could borrow yours."

He laughs, and his amusement seems genuine enough. "I'm not in business for the good of your health, Neal. But I'll rent you one. Where are you going?"

"The Flannan Isles."

He frowns and looks up at the sky. "Well . . . it's fair enough now, alright, but the forecast's for squalls moving up from the southwest. You'll maybe not get landed."

"I'll take my chances."

"You'll not be taking any chances with my boat, man. If the swell's too big, don't even try it. You'd best take the inflatable with you."

I nod.

He gives me a strange look. "What the hell is it you find to do out there on these trips, anyway?"

I wonder if he has asked me this before, and what I might have said if he has. All I say is, "I like the solitude."

"And what about your book?"

So I have told him that lie, too. "What about it?"

"Well, you must have gathered enough material for it by now, surely?"

"It's almost finished, Coinneach. I just need a few more photographs."

He cocks an eyebrow. "Not the best day for it today." Then shrugs. "But that's your business, not mine. Come up to the hotel and we'll get the paperwork sorted, and you can be on your way before the bad stuff comes in."

I see the islands, and the lighthouse, from some way off, and glancing back I can see the dark silhouette of the Outer Hebrides stretched out along the eastern horizon. The sea has been kind to me thus far, with a medium swell and light winds. I have studied Coinneach's charts, and although I have no recollection of having ever set eyes on them, they seem comfortingly familiar.

There is a sense, in all this water around me, of homecoming. I am fully at ease with it. And it instils in me a sense of confidence.

Approaching from the southwest, I throttle back and cruise slowly between Gealtaire Beag and the larger Eilean Tighe. Once round the headland, I bear west and see the extraordinary twin arches that rise out of the sea between the two Làmh a' Sgeires, Bheag and Mhor. Natural black rock stacks sculpted by nature and capped white with gannets, the air above them thick with wheeling seabirds, guillemots and shags, whose plaintive cries fill the air.

For the last mile or so, dolphins have followed me, breaking the surface of the water in playful arcs, circling the boat again and again. But they have gone now, and stretched out ahead is Eilean Mòr itself, lying deceptively low in the water. From a high point at its west side it dips toward a flat central area, before rising once more to a small summit in the east. The lighthouse sits on a central peak, which is the highest point on the island, rising it seems out of nowhere. But even as I approach it, the illusion of the island lying low is dispelled. Cliffs lift sheer out of the swell, rock laid in layers, one upon the other, and shot through with seams of pink gneiss.

Since the swell is coming from the southwest, I head for the more sheltered eastern landing, anchoring as close to shore as I dare. I lower the inflatable I have strapped to the stern of the boat, clamber carefully into it and pull the starter cord to kick the outboard into life.

I ride the swell into the jetty and see immediately that it has not been maintained in years, eroded and broken by time and the constant assault of the ocean. Concrete steps, encrusted with shells, vanish into dark green water, white breaking all around them on the rising tide. I nudge the inflatable slowly toward them, before turning side-on and cutting the motor, then leaping, rope in hand, on to the lower steps, hoping that my feet will find a grip. With difficulty I drag the tender the ten feet up to the broken concrete pier and secure it to a rusted iron ring set into the rock.

A hundred and fifty feet or more above me is the platform where the crane once stood, lifting loads from countless supply boats through wind and spray, to swing them on to an upper platform where a cable-drawn tram would haul them the rest of the way to the lighthouse itself.

The steps on which I have landed climb steeply up the side of the cliff before doubling back, still rising, to the concrete landing block where the crane would deposit the incoming supplies. On the sea side are the rusted stumps of what must once have been safety rails, long since torn away by the destructive power and fury of the Atlantic. It is a hell of a climb, puffins huddled in cracks and crevices, gannets and guillemots circling close to my head as if warning me to stay away, and as I near the top I feel the wind stiffening. Looking back across the water I have just covered, foaming in rings around the six other pinnacles of land that make up the Seven Hunters, I see the ocean rising and realize that I cannot stay too long.

I turn to find myself watched by a group of seabirds perched on a rock, huddled in hooded wariness. Large birds. Three of them, like the ghosts of the lost lighthouse men imagined in Wilfrid Wilson Gibson's poem.

We saw three queer, black, ugly birds —
Too big, by far, in my belief,
For guillemot or shag —
Like seamen sitting bold upright
Upon a half-tide reef:
But, as we near'd, they plunged from sight,
Without a sound, or spurt of white.

Spooked, I crouch to pick up a rock and hurl it at them. With huge wings outspread, flapping in slow motion against the wind, they rise, startled, into the air, wheeling away beyond the cliff and out of sight. I cannot explain why, but their presence creates in my mind a sense of foreboding, and I turn quickly to make the final ascent to the lighthouse.

The tram tracks are still visible in the concrete path, but the rails are long gone, and weeds and grass poke through the cracks. The climb leaves me breathless. Off to my right I see the helipad that was marked on the Historical Monuments map, and the chapel, such as it is. In fact little more than a crude stone bothy. A scaffolding erected along the south side of the complex supports thirty-six solar panels, answering the question I had in my mind of how the lighthouse was powered, if unmanned. The buildings are a freshly painted white, with doors and windows trimmed in ochre. The light room at the top of the tower is an impressive structure of steel, with glass prisms and a conical black roof. The whole is surrounded by a tall stone wall, cemented and topped with concrete copings.

The path leads through gateposts where some kind of gates must once have hung but are long gone. A weathered, cream-painted grille is closed over a green door. Both are locked. To either side of the path, within the walls, the ground is covered with thin, peaty soil and rubble. I have no idea what memory prompts me, but without hesitation I stoop to lift a large flat stone set in the peat, revealing two keys on a ring inside a clear plastic bag. I stare at them for several long seconds, wondering how I knew they were there, or even if it was me who had placed them beneath the stone. Carefully, I remove the keys and drop the stone back in place, then compare the keys in my hand with the locks on the grille and door. I get it right first time, unlocking both, and with an odd sense of excitement push the door open into darkness.

I am following now in the footsteps of Joseph Moore, who was the first man off the *Hesperus* to find the lighthouse empty and the keepers gone. I must have done it before, perhaps many times, but this time feels like the first, and I am burdened, somehow, by a sense of history.

I turn on the light switch on the wall to my right. The door to the kitchen lies open, just as it did when Moore came in. What were once bedrooms are mostly empty now, daylight flooding in through unshuttered windows. At the end of the hall, there is still a table and chairs in the room where a succession of keepers must once have shared their time, and where Gibson had conjured the image of an unfinished meal and an overturned seat. It is not limewash and tar that I smell in here, just cold and damp,

106

and something faintly unpleasant, like the distant reek of death.

Back in the hall, I see the row of coat hooks where oilskins and waterproofs must once have hung, including those of the unfortunate Donald McArthur who, for some inexplicable reason, had left the shelter of the lighthouse without them. And I can recall, almost word for word, the superintendent's account of conditions inside the lighthouse when the relief crew arrived, nearly eleven days after the light had been reported out by the captain of the *Archtor* on December 15, 1900.

The lamp was crimmed, the oil fountains and canteens were filled up and the lens and machinery cleaned, which proved that the work of the 15th had been completed. The pots and pans had been cleaned and the kitchen tidied up, which showed that the man who had been acting as cook had completed his work, which goes to prove that the men disappeared on the afternoon that Captain Holman had passed the Flannan Islands in the steamer ARCH-TOR at midnight on the 15th, and could not observe the light.

There were echoes of the *Marie Celeste*

about it all. What, really, had happened to those men? Could they truly have been carried off by some freak wave during a storm? A wave that must have crashed nearly 150 feet high against the cliffs, reaching almost to where the crane emplacement itself was set into the rock.

I climb the stairs that spiral up the inside of the tower, leading to a circular wood-paneled room. Above my head is the grille into which the lamp is set, providing a floor for maintenance and cleaning. I negotiate the last few rungs of an iron ladder that takes me up to the light room itself. And what an extraordinary space it is. Glass prisms acting as lenses, providing an unrestricted view of the Flannan Isles and the ocean beyond, through 360 degrees. The glass is misted, caked by salt carried on the wind and sparkling like frost. I hear the roar of the elements outside, and see white tops breaking all the way to the horizon. I can see, through the grille beneath my feet, down into the room below. The lamp itself is twice my height, spherical, comprising glass fins on its exterior to reflect the light, and set to revolve on a complex electrical mechanism set into the floor. To stand here, in the dark, with the lamp turning, would be blinding.

I stay there for some time gazing out at the world, feeling unsettled, insecure. Why had I come out here all those times? Where did I get the keys? And I realize that not only do I have no memories that predate the day before yesterday, I still have no idea what kind of man I was. Sally had said she loved me, but she also said that I had changed. Had I really? I had hidden so much from her, that the me she thought she knew had not been the real me at all, just a figment of my own invention. A liar. A deceiver.

It is with a great sense of dissatisfaction that I leave the lighthouse, finally, locking it up behind me and replacing the keys below the stone. I have learned nothing, least of all about myself. The first spots of rain whip into my face on the edge of a sudden squall, and as I hurry from the gate I see rain sweeping in from the southwest, a long trailing arm of it, darker even than the cloud from which it falls. I start down the steep concrete path, but realize I will never reach the boat before the rain hits. And it is too late to go back. Instead, I make a dash for the ruined chapel, which is just a short sprint away across the grass. Its roof of stone and turf has collapsed in places, but still affords a degree of shelter. I stoop beneath the lintel of the open doorway, and turn to look out and see the island vanish in the rain that sweeps across it like mist.

I move back, then, into the chapel and stumble on something beneath my feet, having to steady myself with outstretched hand on the cold, damp wall. There is very little light, and it takes some moments for my eyes to adjust.

At first I find it hard to believe what I am seeing. A man is lying spread-eagled on the floor, legs outstretched and twisted at an impossible angle. His head is half turned, and I can see where it has been split open, pale gray brain matter congealed in the dried blood that has pooled around it.

I feel acid rising in my throat, from shock and revulsion. I swallow it back, and find myself gasping for breath. My legs have turned to jelly beneath me and will hardly support my weight. After several long seconds, I crouch down, fingertips on the floor to steady me, and force myself to look at his face. He is an older man, gray hair thinning. Mid, perhaps late, fifties. Corpulent. He wears an anorak and jeans, and what look like relatively new hiking boots. If he is known to me, I have no memory of him. But it is clear that he has not been freshly killed. Certainly not today, and probably not yesterday. And since there is no decay that I can see, or smell, he cannot surely have been dead for more than a few days.

A crack in my mind's defenses opens up to allow in the unthinkable. Three days ago I was here. On this island. The next day I was washed ashore on the beach at Luskentyre, all memory lost in a cloud of black dread, knowing that something terrible had occurred.

I look at this man lying on the floor in front of me, his head smashed in, and I ask myself the question that has been clotting in my stream of consciousness. Was it me who killed him?

I close my eyes, fists clenching, sick to my stomach at the thought of it. But it is a thought that won't go away, growing inside me like a cancer. Is this why I have blocked all memory of the past? I stand up too quickly, blood rushing to my head, and stagger to the door, supporting myself on the stone as I lean out into the wind and rain to throw up acid and coffee.

I am shaking, tears springing to my eyes with the burning of the acid. It feels as if the earth has opened up beneath my feet and I am falling helplessly into eternity, or hell, or both. A short way off, to the east, I hear the growl of the sea as it rushes into a deep cleft in the cliffs nearly 200 feet below. And I am startled to see a group of people in brightly colored waterproofs, fighting their way up the concrete path toward the lighthouse, leaning into the wind and the rain. Tourists, I realize. A group almost certainly brought out on Seatrek's inflatable RIB from Uig, and landed below just before the squall struck.

Now shock at the thought that I might have killed this man combines with fear of being caught. Blinded by panic, and robbed of all reason, I dash out on to the slope just as the rain passes and a momentary break in the cloud sprinkles sunshine across the island like fairy dust. The tourists have almost reached the lighthouse above me, and I don't look back to register if I have been seen. Locked instead in my cocoon of denial, I slither down the wet concrete and run down the steps with an almost reckless disregard for my own safety.

Below me, Seatrek's red and black Delta Super X RIB rises and falls on the swell, anchored a few feet away from the jetty. I see a man waiting aboard her for the tourists to return. He calls to me as I reach the foot of the steps as if he knows me, voice raised above the wind and the sea. But I ignore him, dragging my tender back down the steps and leaping recklessly into her, almost capsizing her in the process. I don't even look in his direction as he calls again, pulling instead on the starter cord, almost frantic in my desire to be gone from this place. It coughs into life on the third pull, and I gun the throttle, banking away against the incoming waves to race out across the bay to where Coinneach's Sundancer awaits me.

I nearly fall overboard as I transfer from one to the other, but scramble safely on to the stern, before hauling the inflatable aboard and tethering her. I fire up the motor and accelerate hard away to the southeast. I look back only once as I round the eastern tip of Eilean Tighe, and see the distant figure of the man who called to me still standing in his boat, watching me go.

CHAPTER EIGHT

I am seized now by a sense of urgency. I desperately need to know who I am and what it is I have done. And since I got back to the cottage I have been tearing it apart, without a thought for what the owner might say. I am beyond caring.

I have tipped the mattresses off all the beds. Stripped them of sheets and blankets. I have emptied every cupboard. Pots and pans are strewn across the floor, the kitchen table piled with crockery.

I have already been through the car, checking under seats, searching for hidden pockets. I have torn up the carpet and removed the spare wheel from its well in the boot. And I am alarmed to realize that I have no logbook for this vehicle, nor apparently a license to drive it.

The cushions from the settee are piled in the middle of the sitting room floor. I have unzipped their leather covers in search of anything I might have hidden inside them.

And I am slumped now at the kitchen table, almost in tears. To describe my mood as despairing would be the antithesis of hyperbole. I feel hopeless and helpless and scared, frustration welling up inside me, ready to explode in anger or violence, or both. I find myself wishing now that I had drowned in the aftermath of whatever happened out on Eilean Mòr the night I lost my boat. I grip my hair in both hands, tipping my head back and shouting at the ceiling.

Bran, who has been following me around, excited and bewildered, barks now. He must wonder why this lunatic who has been rampaging about the house has the same scent as his master. And the tears of vexation that have been gathering in my eyes finally spill over to burn my cheeks as they run down my face.

I wipe them away with my palms and force myself to stop hyperventilating, and try to think clearly. It is not easy. There is simply nothing in the house to tell me who I am, beyond a name. When the money in my wallet runs out, I have no idea how I will buy food, or petrol for the car. If I am stopped by the police while driving, I will be unable to show them a license or papers of ownership, and will then have only five days in which to confess my loss of memory, or run.

I daren't even contemplate the man in the ruined chapel on Eilean Mòr. Because, the more I think about him, the more convinced I become that it was me who killed him. The urge simply to run is almost irresistible. But where would I run to, and how would I finance it?

I don't know how long it is I have been sitting at the table before I get up and wander through to the hall, thinking vaguely that perhaps I should start to clear up. The day has passed in a blur, and the light is fading outside. Bad weather has set in again, and rain is battering against the windows, running like tears down the glass.

Bran pushes my hand with his head and I realize I have just been standing here in the hall, inert, my brain and all my thinking processes on hold, unable to recall exactly why it was I had come through. Which is when I notice for the first time the hatch in the ceiling outside the spare room. I don't know why I didn't see it before, because it now feels as if I always knew it was there.

I wonder how I will reach it, for I can't recall seeing stepladders anywhere in the house. Then I remember the garden shed, which would be an obvious place to keep them. I hurry out into horizontal rain that catches the last light of the day and streaks the coming darkness. I am soaked within seconds. But the shed is securely padlocked, and I know that there was no key for it among the ones I recovered from the car.

Back in the house, I check the kitchen cupboard again, in case somehow I had missed a pair of stepladders. But, of course, there are none. Only brooms and shovels, and cleaning fluids on a shelf above them. I have almost shut the door when I see it. A pole about two meters long, with a shallow S-shaped hook on the end of it, hanging on the back of the door, and I realize immediately what it is for.

Outside the spare room, I look up and see the cream-painted metal loop set into the hatch. I raise the pole, slot the hook into it and pull it down. Initially it resists the pull of the spring that holds it, until finally it locks in place and reveals the bottom rungs of a folding ladder. I hook the pole now into the ladder and extend it down to the floor.

Bran leaps out of the way of the pole as I let it fall, and I climb rapidly up into the roof space. It is dark, and I reach into it, fumbling about until I find a switch that fills the attic with light from a solitary naked bulb. Apart from the layers of insulation between the rafters, it is quite empty. With the exception of a single black briefcase that stands up, just within reach.

My fingers are trembling as they close around the handle, and I pull it toward me before climbing quickly back down to the hall. I want to throw the briefcase on the floor and open it right there and then. But I force myself to stay calm and carry it through to the kitchen, where I sit down and set it on the table in front of me. And now I am almost afraid to open it. Perhaps it is better to live in ignorance than be confronted with an unpalatable truth.

Finally I lay it flat, release the clasps and lift the lid. I am not sure what I might have been expecting, but I could hardly have been more startled. The briefcase is filled with bundles of £50 notes. Twelve bundles altogether, with space left by others that have clearly been taken. Spent, no doubt. With the silence of the house ringing in my ears, and a sensation of blood pulsing in my head, I lift one of the bundles and count twenty notes. £1,000 per bundle. £12,000 in total, and there might easily have been another eight bundles in the case to begin with.

At least I know now how I financed my life here. With cash. But whose cash, and why? Is it stolen money, or payment of some kind? One answer simply raises more questions. I sit staring at the notes in disbelief for a very long time, at the end of which I hear my own voice. "Jesus!" It is a whispered oath, as if I am almost scared to speak out loud.

Then I notice the fold-out compartment in the lid. If it were empty, it would be sitting flush. But it isn't. I pull it open and draw out a blue folder. I push the briefcase aside and lay the folder in front of me to open it. My mouth is very dry, my tongue almost sticking to the roof of my mouth, but it doesn't even occur to me to get a drink.

Inside the folder, held together by a paperclip, is a bundle of badly photocopied sheets of A4 paper. I say badly photocopied because these are duplicates of newspaper cuttings that are almost unreadable. Too much ink has made the letters and words of the text thick and furry, and the accompanying photographs so dark as to be very nearly black.

I remove the paperclip and start to sift through them, aware that my breathing is so rapid and shallow that I am starting to become light-headed. I stop and take a deep breath and examine the sheets that I hold in my hands. They are all clippings of articles taken from newspapers and magazines dating back to 2009. And they are all about me.

"Thirty-five-year-old champion yachtsman, Neal Maclean." "Thirty-six-year-old team trainer, Neal Maclean." "Neal Maclean (37), successful Scottish youth coach . . ."

A champion in my own right as a young man, it seems I am now training youth groups and individuals participating in single-handed racing events organized by the Royal Yachting Association of Scotland. One on the Clyde coast. Another in the Firth of Forth. A weekend of racing on Loch Lomond. Coach of the winning team at the 2012 West Highland Yachting Week. Head coach of the Scotland team sent to Weymouth to compete in the Youth Nationals in 2013. Heading up the RYA Scotland Junior Class Academy summer program that same year.

The photographs are mostly of young men and women who have won competitions, but there is one taken of the entire Scotland youth team. Black-smudged smiling faces with me at their center. My features, along with everyone else's, are virtually indistinguishable, but my curly black hair, longer then, is unmistakable.

I scan each article, hungry for personal details. But there are none. Just my age. And I read about myself getting older with almost every piece. By my reckoning, I must now be either thirty-eight or thirty-nine. No mention of family, or occupation, or home city. None of these posts is professional. Sailing is my hobby. While I know more, now, about how I spend my spare time, I know nothing further about myself.

I turn over the final sheet and stop dead. This is no newspaper article. It is an extract of birth that bears the embossed seal of the General Register Office, Scotland, issued almost exactly two years ago. Neal David Maclean, son of Mary and Leslie, born 1978 at Edinburgh Royal Infirmary. Not just any birth certificate. My birth certificate. I sit looking at it, held in shaking hands. A strange affirmation, somehow, that I actually exist. And there, written on the other side, in a hand I recognize as mine, is the address of a house in Hainburn Park, Edinburgh.

Reconnecting with who I am seems just a touch away. I pull the laptop toward me and load up my browser to type *BT phone book* into Google. A link takes me to the home page of British Telecom's phone directory. I type in my surname and the address on the back of the extract of birth, then hit return. Up comes my full name, with phone number and address, including post code. I am very nearly afraid to breathe, in case it all vanishes like smoke in the wind. But as I sit staring at the screen it remains there, burning itself on to my retinas.

I know now exactly who I am and where I live.

I have found an empty overnight bag in the bottom of the wardrobe, and it sits on the bed beside the clothes I am laying out for my trip. Underwear, socks, a spare pair of jeans, a couple of shirts. I have no idea how much to pack, or how long I will be away. For this is a journey into the unknown, with no predetermined destination and no return ticket. At least, not yet.

I hear the door open into the kitchen and freeze, listening intently. But I can barely hear anything above the pulsing of blood in my head. Bran, who has spread himself on the bed, unsettled and depressed at my packing, lifts his head for a moment, then drops it again to sink back into his huff. But I am not taking any chances. I reach below the pillow to feel for the hunting knife left by my attacker last night and move carefully into the hall.

"Neal?" Sally's voice is shrill and carries more than a hint of alarm in it.

I step into the sitting room and see her framed in the archway to the kitchen. She looks pale, shocked, and her eyes drop to the knife I hold in my hand.

"For God's sake, Neal, what's going on?"

The relief that courses through me is almost disabling. I lay the knife on the table beside the lamp and take three quick steps toward her, to pull her into my arms and hold her. I feel her surprise and initial resistance, before her hands slip around me to spread themselves on my shoulders. Her head tips back to look at me. I see confusion and fear in her eyes.

"What on earth's happened?"

I kiss her softly and close my own eyes to rest my forehead on hers. "I missed you today," I say. "I really missed you."

"I had to go up to Stornoway with Jon." She kisses me. "I'm sorry." Then she steps back, holding both my hands, and stares at me earnestly. "Who did all this?" And a flick of her head indicates the mess that surrounds us.

"I did."

Her astonishment is patent. "Why?"

"I was looking for me."

Confusion clouds her eyes before they flicker toward the table. "And the knife?"

I lead her to one of the settees, replacing the cushions, and sit us both down. We are turned, half-facing each other, still holding hands, and I tell her everything. About my attacker the night before, and the intervention of a third party that almost certainly saved my life. I see her eyes widen in horror and disbelief.

I tell her about my fruitless trip out to Eilean Mòr, but omit the discovery of the body in the chapel. I am afraid to even put that into words. Then my frantic search of the house to find something, anything, that would provide a clue to the real me.

I stand up and lead her through to the kitchen and open up the briefcase to reveal the bundles of cash. Her eyes are like saucers. She lifts one, as if only by touching it will she believe it really exists. "Neal, this is scary."

I nod. "And it's not all." I show her the cuttings and the birth certificate, and the confirmation of my address in the BT phone book. Neal David Maclean, from Hainburn Park, Edinburgh. "I'm going there tomorrow."

Her eyes crinkle with concern. "Is that a good idea? You might find you have a wife and family."

"I've got to know, Sally."

She seems resigned to it. "Will you fly?"

"I have no credit card or photo ID. But I checked the internet. I can pay cash for a ferry crossing from Tarbert to Skye tomorrow and drive down."

"Without a license or logbook?"

"The chances of me being stopped are negligible, Sally, unless I'm in an accident."

She slips her arms around me, and I hear her voice, very small, as she presses her head against my chest. "I'm scared I'm going to lose you."

"Don't be silly," I say, but there is little conviction in my words.

She looks at me. "Whoever you are — whoever you really are — you might not want to be with me once you know. Once you remember."

"Of course I will."

But she just smiles, a sad, wistful little smile. "You should go to the police, Neal."

I step back, surprised. "Why?"

"Why? Because someone tried to kill you, that's why. And, because they didn't succeed, there's a good chance they'll try again."

"I can't."

"Why not?"

"Because I'd have to tell them that I've lost my memory. That I've been lying about why I'm here. That I've got twelve grand in cash stashed in a briefcase in the attic and I don't know where it came from. There's so much more I still need to know, Sally. I can't go to the police." I hesitate, and realize that there is something else I need to confront. But, still, I can only address it obliquely. "Besides, chances are they're going to come looking for me soon enough."

She is startled, eyes wide with surprise. "Why?"

"Because, when I was out at the lighthouse today, I found a man's body in the old ruined chapel. Someone killed him, Sally. Smashed his head in." I swallow, my throat dry and swollen. "And I think it might have been me."

CHAPTER NINE

Karen lay on the bed with her earbuds in and the volume up high on her iPhone. Still, somehow, she could hear them. Or perhaps feel, rather than hear them. Modern houses with stud walls and composite wooden flooring left little to the imagination. And she had known plenty of them, moving as they had from house to house when she was young, always in the wake of her father's career. London, Leicester, Edinburgh. So many houses in such a short life.

She closed her eyes and tried to quell the sick feeling that had lain like a stone in her belly ever since her mother had broken the news.

Karen had changed in the two years since her father's death. From a hormonal, but almost painfully conventional teenager to a hormonal, rebellious little bitch. A change of which she had been the conscious architect. Short hair, shaved at the sides and dyed green in a lick across the top, but still black at the back. The nose and eyebrow studs, the rings in her lip that they made her take out for school. The pictures of One Direction on the wall had been torn down to be replaced by Marilyn Manson posters she had found in the goth shop.

The first tattoo had caused a monumental row with aftershocks that went on for days. But there was nothing her mother could do about it. *Fait accompli.* Tattoos were for life, and this one had been such a small thing. A delicate little butterfly just above her left ankle. The others that followed had reduced it to insignificance. A winged skull on her chest, just below the neck. An elaborate and colorful snake that coiled its way around her left arm, from shoulder to wrist. An eagle with wings spread across her back and shoulders. And a couple she hadn't even told her mother about.

Dressed discreetly, it was possible for all of them to be hidden. But pointing that out had done nothing to allay her mother's fury with each addition. And after every grounding she had simply gone out and got another. They couldn't lock her up in her room forever.

Her mother had demanded to know where she had got the money. But Karen only ever shrugged, infuriating her further. How could she tell her that the tattoo artist was a friend returning favors? An older friend, with a penchant for teenage girls.

She had gone from being Daddy's little girl to Mother's nightmare in twenty-four short months. A deliberate decision. To leave behind the fragile, broken child, so filled with regret, and become . . . she didn't know what. Anyone but who she really was.

Finally, she couldn't stand it anymore and jumped off the bed, ripping out her earbuds and crossing to the laptop on the dresser. She scrolled down a list of recently downloaded albums. Anathema, Motionless in White, Dark Princess, and a host of others whose music she really didn't care for. A culture mostly from before her time. Loud, frenetic, violent music that her mother detested even more than Karen. She selected an album by We Are The Fallen called *Tear The World Down,* clicked *play,* and cranked up the volume on her sound system. Classic metal, screaming lyrics about sorrow, pain and tears in a song called "Bury Me Alive." The perfect accompaniment to the unwanted sounds of sex.

It was less than five minutes before her mother stormed into the room, pulling a black silk dressing gown around her to cover her nakedness. She was flushed from more than anger, pupils dilated, her blond-streaked hair a tangled mess. "Will you turn that bloody noise down!"

Karen stood her ground defiantly. "Funny. I was just going to ask you to do the same thing."

Her mother frowned and shook her head. "What are you talking about?" And she stalked across the room to the computer and grabbed the mouse to click *pause.* The sudden silence seemed even louder than the music.

"You and baldy boy, fucking on the other side of my bedroom wall. You think I want to listen to that all night?"

"Don't you use that kind of language with me!"

"Oh. Oh. So you're not fucking then? You're making love, is that it? Well, it doesn't sound much like love to me. More like war. All that banging and screaming." She drew a deep breath, sucking up all her anger from deep inside. "I don't need that shit all night, every night."

Perhaps it was guilt that stopped her mother from coming straight back at her. But it was the ruthless streak Karen had been cultivating that led her to press home her advantage.

"Cos that's what it's going to be, isn't it? Now that he's moving in. Sleeping in my dad's bed, sitting in his chair, screwing his wife. Telling *me* what to do." Her mouth curled in anger as she almost spat the accusation at her mother. "You didn't wait very long, did you?"

"Christ, Karen, it's been two bloody years! What did you think I was going to do? Spend the rest of my life in mourning? Dress in black and live like a nun? I'm not even forty, for God's sake."

"And what about me?"

"What about you?" The words exploded from her mother's lips in anger. "You're only seventeen! You've got your whole life ahead of you, and all you want to do is romanticize some imaginary past that never even existed. You did nothing but fight with your father."

"I loved my dad!" The words, shouted in defiance, were out of her mouth before she could stop them, and she was immediately embarrassed.

But her mother just shook her head. "Well, you'd a funny way of showing it. He's dead, Karen. Gone. Get over it!"

She slammed the door shut behind her, and Karen heard her angry footsteps all the way along the hall. Then the low murmur

131

of voices next door. But there was no resumption of hostilities.

Her desk was at the window side, about halfway up the row, and she looked out on trees, and pale gray buildings and acres of glass. Suburban hell. The greens and bunkers of the golf course simmered silently beyond a high hedge. She could hear Mrs. Forrest speaking, but she wasn't listening. Everything that made Karen different was hidden from view. Except for her hair and a few face studs. White blouse, school blazer and tie reduced her to conformity. Almost. The green lick always singled her out for attention.

It was the third or fourth time of her name being called that finally drew her eyes toward the front of the class.

Mrs. Forrest was a formidable woman. She taught English and math and was very much of the old school. She belonged to a generation whose own teachers would have wielded the taws. And Karen had no doubt that, were it acceptable today, Mrs. Forrest would have taken pleasure in dishing out its singular punishment herself.

"Are you listening, Karen?"

"Yes, Mrs. Forrest."

"Then what did I say?"

"I haven't the faintest idea."

"So you weren't listening."

"I was. You just weren't being interesting enough to register in my consciousness." Karen's IQ was probably twenty points or more higher than most of her teachers'. It never endeared her to them and almost invariably created a sense of their inferiority, which made them dangerous.

The teacher sighed. "You do realize that you are the only girl in the class who has failed to hand in her assignment."

Karen was aware of classmates turning heads in her direction. None of them would dare to cross Mrs. Forrest, with or without the taws. She was a big personality. "What assignment would that be?"

Mrs. Forrest's silence would have intimidated nearly any other girl in the room, but Karen was past caring. She didn't even know why she had bothered coming back for a sixth year. Except that she had no idea what else to do. She could have applied for university at the end of the last school year, and would have been accepted by any one of them that she had cared to ask. But another three or four years in education was an unappetizing prospect. With depression leading to apathy, leading to more depression, her downward spiral into lassitude had

133

led her more recently to speculate upon whether suicide was genetically heritable. "The assignment that every other girl in this class has completed. Apparently they had no problem in understanding what was being asked of them."

"You must have spelt it out in words of one syllable, then."

Mrs. Forrest pursed thin lips. "I think, young lady, it's time we made an appointment for you to speak to the school counselor. You can stay behind after school this afternoon and we'll arrange a session."

"I'm busy after school."

"Oh, are you? Doing what, exactly?"

"Frankly, Mrs. Forrest, it's none of your fucking business."

There was a collective intake of breath, and Mrs. Forrest paled visibly. "Get out of my class," was all she said.

Karen scooped up her books and jotter and slid them into her satchel. "My pleasure." And she stood up and walked out in silence, letting the door bang behind her.

Gilly found her sitting smoking behind the gym after class. She was the only girl that Karen had ever met in all her years at school with whom she felt she could talk as an equal. But their relationship was fractious and competitive, and for all their closeness there was always a certain distrust between them. Gilly was a plain girl, with straight, mousy-brown hair and over-large hips that Karen would say, when she was being mean, made her perfectly suited for childbearing. Karen swore she would never have children. What a waste of intelligence, she would say, to spend your life raising children for some shit of a husband who regarded you as little better than a glorified nursemaid and house-keeper.

Gilly sat down beside her and lit a cigarette of her own. It was her sole concession to rebellion. She had not gone down Karen's road of facial piercings and tattoos. She was certain to go to university, where she would probably get a master's degree or a doctorate, then spend the rest of her life raising children. She said, "You're in deep shit, girl."

"Yeah? Whose?"

"Mrs. Forrest's, for a start."

"Aye, well, she's pretty full of it."

"She went straight to the headmaster's office after you'd gone. Left us a good fifteen minutes on our own." She grinned. "The place was in uproar. If you stood in the election for student rep you'd be a shoo-in."

"That might be a little difficult after

they've expelled me."

"They won't expel you!"

Karen shrugged. "That's a pity. Guess I'll have to quit, then."

Gilly gave her a skeptical look. "And do what?"

Karen inclined her head very slightly but said nothing.

"What's got into you, anyway? You're being a right pain today."

Karen took a pull on her cigarette and stared at the ground. It was a long time before she said, "That bald-headed bam's moving in with my mum."

"What, that guy she's been going out with?"

"Yeah, her boss at work."

Gilly shrugged. "So?"

"So he thinks he's just going to walk in and take over where my dad left off. Well, he's got another think coming."

"Could be worse, she might have married him."

"She can't. It'll be another five years before she can apply for a legal declaration of presumed death. As if it's not pretty fucking conclusive as it is. An empty boat and a suicide note. At least it means she'll not be changing her name and trying to change mine, too." She flicked her cigarette away across the tarmac and watched the sparks kick up from it as it hit the ground. "Think it's probably time I moved out."

Gilly was taken aback. "Moved out? Where would you go? How would you live?"

"I'll figure something out. But I'm not staying there to let him boss me around, and spy on me in the shower."

"Is that what he does?"

"Not that I know of. Not yet, anyway. But he probably will." She grinned and stood up. "I'm out of here."

She took a bus into town, then rode out to the airport and back again on the tram. The airport was somehow symbolic of escape. But it was only ever a dream. An impractical fantasy.

The tram was fun, and she was still newfangled with it. The outward and return journeys took her through western suburbs she didn't know, and then slap bang through the city center. Priority for the tram, and unrivaled views of the gardens and the castle through panoramic windows. And no matter how busy it was, no one would speak to you. People traveled in their own little bubbles, listening to music or reading books, or simply staring into space, like Karen.

She had removed her tie, opening the top of her blouse to reveal a little of her tattoo, lipsticked her mouth deep purple and reinstated her lip rings. She was determined to be as defiantly ugly as possible, staring down anyone who had the temerity to look at her.

But today she wasn't catching anyone's eye. And, contrary to all outward appearance, she was bleeding inside, where Daddy's little girl hid from the world, succumbing to guilt and grief.

It was still a mystery to her why she had given him such a hard time. Driven by some internal devil that made her say and do things that she really didn't mean. Just to be difficult, or obstinate, to hurt with malice aforethought. She had felt almost possessed, driven to truculence, and always filled, in the aftermath, with regret that she could never admit to.

Her mother had doted on her when she was wee, an only child, an only daughter. But it was always her father's approval she had sought, him she had wanted to spend time with. And in those early years he'd had endless patience, and limitless time, or so it seemed. He'd played games with her for hours on end — hide the sweetie, snakes and ladders, checkers — and read to her every night. Silly, childish stories, but they had given her an appetite for reading. Only now did she realize how desperately boring it must all have been for him. But he had never stinted on his time. He had taught her to swim on holiday in France, to ride a bike in the back garden, running along beside her, holding the saddle. "Don't let go, Daddy, don't let go," she had shouted, unaware that he had let go long ago.

She glanced from the window of the tram, out across the roofs of Waverley Station, and, jumping focus, saw her reflection in the window. An involuntary smile on her face with the memory of it. And tears sprang suddenly to her eyes.

From the age of twelve or thirteen she had become unaccountably angry with him. Not entirely her fault, because his work had taken up more and more of his time, leaving less and less of it for her. And she had punished him for it, mercilessly, with her moods, and sullen sulks, and sudden outbursts of anger. Even when he had gone out of his way to make time for her, to take her out sailing, or walking in the Pentland Hills, she had found excuses not to go. Hurting herself just to hurt him.

And then the very last time she'd seen him. He had been going to come and watch her in the school debate. The proposition was that GMOs were the future of food and the only way to feed the world. She knew that it was one of her dad's hobby horses. He had always been implacably opposed to the idea of genetically modified crops, and so she had boned up on the subject and was the principal speaker against the proposition. He had called off at the last moment. A problem at work and he had to deal with it. He said that he would drive her to the school but couldn't stay.

That he hadn't even been going to hear her speak, after all the work she had put into it just to please him, had seemed like the last, unforgivable straw. She blew up at him, accusing him of being hopelessly selfish, of not caring about anyone or anything in the world but himself. And least of all her. As usual, he had stayed calm and patient and tried to explain. But that only infuriated her further, and she had screamed in his face, "I hate you, I hate you, I hate you!" And fled from the room in tears.

She never saw him again. They found his boat that weekend, out in the Firth of Forth. Empty. All the life jackets still on board. And then the note her mother had discovered that night, left on the pillow, beneath the duvet, so that she hadn't seen it until going to bed.

For the longest time, Karen had been utterly overcome by guilt. It was her fault. Somehow he'd been driven to take his own life because of her. The way she behaved, the things she'd said. And she had wished with all her heart that she could just go back and undo it all. Tell him that she'd never meant any of the things she had said, that she loved him really. But there was no way to do that, no way to unsay the things she'd said. And in the end her only means of dealing with it was by growing a hard outer shell that would never let anything in to hurt her ever again.

She became aware of a middle-aged woman sitting opposite, staring at her, and caught a reflection of herself again in the window, her face streaked now with black mascara, and shiny with tears.

It was midafternoon when she got back to the house. Her mother would not be home for nearly three hours yet, returning no doubt with Derek, since it seemed he had already moved in.

Karen could not for the life of her see what it was that her mother found attractive about him. His head was completely bald on top, smooth and unnaturally shiny. But he had a ring of dark hair around the sides and back, greying a little at the ears. And he wore it far too long, as if that could make up for the lack of it elsewhere. It might not have been so bad had he just shaved off the lot. That's what men did these days when they went bald. And it looked so much better.

She supposed he was quite well built, but old fashioned in the dark suits he habitually wore — estate agents, it seemed, were always on call — or the neatly pressed jog pants and sweatshirt that he wore to go running at the weekends. He was invariably nice to Karen, smiling and obsequious, believing apparently that it might endear him to her. She detested him.

She dumped her bag in her bedroom and changed into a T-shirt and black jeans, then wandered through to her mother's bedroom. In the months after her father's death, she had come in here often. Her father's clothes had been left hanging in the wardrobe, and they smelled of him. His smell. She would bury her face in one of his jackets and simply breathe him in. And it choked her every time. Because somehow it was as if he was still there. How could he be gone when she could smell him? That comforting, familiar smell that she had grown up with. Whether it was aftershave, or some other scent, or just the natural oils that the body exudes, it was a smell that always took her back to childhood, conjured those happy days when she had loved him unconditionally.

His clothes had long gone. Her mother had removed them all one day when she was at school, and taken them to the charity shop. Karen had been distraught when she returned home to find his half of the wardrobe empty. Those suits and jackets and trousers on their hangers, the folded piles of jumpers and T-shirts, the drawer full of socks were her last connection to him. Somehow deep down she might even have believed that one day he would come back to wear them all again. But even that had been taken from her with their removal.

Now, when she opened the wardrobe, they were Derek's clothes hanging there, like the intruder he was in their lives. And all she could smell was the powerful, pungent odor of the aftershave he applied far too liberally to his shiny, shaven face.

She banged the door shut and went through to the dressing room off the bedroom. Her mother's little den. Karen knew that her mother kept an old photo album in here in one of the dresser drawers. An anachronism, really, in this digital age. Color prints from film negative. Her paternal grandfather had been a portrait and wedding photographer, and her father had inherited all his cameras, and continued to use them almost until his death, though it had become more and more difficult to get film processed. Only very late did he succumb to digital, seduced by the gift of a Sony Cybershot from Karen's mother, who was fed up being asked to take photographs she couldn't immediately see and post on Facebook like everyone else.

Shooting on film had meant that there were fewer photographs taken, which had made them more precious, and it was nice to have an album to sit and flick through. Pictures you could touch, almost as if touching the people themselves, a direct connection with a happier past.

Karen sat on the floor, her back against an old armchair, pulled her legs up and opened the album on her knees. She smiled at the tottering two-year-old, arms raised, hands held by her daddy as he encouraged her to walk on her own. A picture taken by someone of the three of them, with Karen in the middle. She would have been about five then, and already her mother and father seemed dated. His hair had been longer at that time, falling in dark curls over his forehead. And her mother was slim, before she put on the weight, hair drawn back in a ponytail from a small, pretty face.

There was one taken of Karen and her dad when she was about eleven. She had been quite tall then, following a period of rapid growth that had left her awkward and leggy. She was grinning shyly at the camera. Her dad had his arm around her shoulder and was smiling down at her adoringly.

She felt the tears welling up again and bit her lip to stop them from spilling. Blinking furiously, she closed the album and slipped it back in the drawer. The last photographs would all have been digital and kept, she knew, in files on her mother's laptop.

The laptop sat open on the little dresser, where her mother would spend time posting and commenting on the videos and pics posted by her boring friends on Facebook. An endless succession of pointless quizzes, of babies and gardens, smileys and saccharine aphorisms. *Share if animals are worth fighting for.*

Karen sat in front of it and tapped the trackpad to waken it from sleep. The desktop was a shambles of icons and folders, files and photographs, jpegs and PDFs. She clicked the *Photos* icon on the dock and the software that stored all her mother's photographs opened up to fill the screen. The sidebar listed photo events going back several years. Karen went through them at random, but couldn't find any of her father, and wondered if her mother had trashed them. The most recent were of her and Derek. A barbecue in the back garden, a picnic in the Pentlands. Drunken faces at a party leering for a selfie taken on her mother's smartphone.

Karen breathed her exasperation and shut down the software. She was about to put the computer back to sleep when a folder among all the items on the desktop caught her eye. It was labeled simply, *Derek*. She hesitated to open it. It would be like spying, and she knew how pissed off she would be if she thought her mother was trawling through files on *her* laptop. But curiosity overcame reticence, and she double-clicked. The folder opened up in a separate window to reveal a long list of files, tracing email communications between Derek and her mother, going back nearly five years.

Karen wasn't quite sure why she was disappointed. Dozens of what would inevitably be boring work emails. Houses for sale. Schedules. Adverts. Appointments with clients. Photo attachments. She pushed the cursor arrow toward the red *Close* dot, then on a sudden impulse double-clicked to open a file at random. It was dated a little less than three years ago, and, as Karen read it with growing disbelief, her blood turned cold.

She felt as if she were fevered. Her face was hot and red and her throat burned. She could hear Derek retreating from conflict out in the hall and tiptoeing downstairs. Her mother was flushed and defensive.

"You had no right to go poking through my private correspondence!"

"No, I didn't. But I did. And that's not even the point. You and that baldy bastard were cheating on my dad long before he died."

"We weren't *cheating!*"

"Okay, fucking behind his back, then."

"Stop it!"

"No." Karen was fired up by hurt and righteous indignation. "What did you do, bump him off so you could be together?"

Exasperation exploded through her mother's teeth. But she held her voice in check. "Don't be ridiculous."

"What's ridiculous about it? I never believed he committed suicide anyway. Why would he?"

"Look . . ." Her mother was fighting to stay calm. "Yes, Derek and I were having an affair."

"Fucking, you mean. Over the desk in that back office at the estate agency, probably."

For a moment, her mother didn't know what to say, and blushed to the roots of her hair. And Karen realized that's exactly what they'd been doing. But her mother recovered quickly, speaking in calm, measured tones. "My marriage to your father had been over in everything but name for a long time. Work had always been his mistress, the one he ran to when he needed to escape from me." She looked pointedly at Karen. "From us. And then it became more than a mistress, more than an escape. Like he was married to the damn job. It took over his life. He was never here. Well, you know that." She paused, breathing rapidly, and Karen couldn't think of a single thing to say to fill the silence. "So, yes, Derek and I became lovers. But there was no cheating involved. I told your father. I'm no saint, but I'm no sinner either. I asked him for a divorce. One day, when you stop being a child and grow up, maybe you'll understand what it feels like to be neglected by a partner."

Stinging from the *child* jibe, Karen fired

148

back. "What, you mean like the way I feel right now?" Which didn't miss its mark, and she pressed home on it. "What if it was your affair, asking him for a divorce, that made him kill himself?"

Her mother stood with her hands on her hips, eyes upturned toward the heavens. "A moment ago you were accusing us of murdering him."

"Well, maybe you did." Her eyes were burning now, too. "Dad would never have *fallen* overboard. And even if he had, he'd have been wearing his life jacket. So how come it was still in the boat?"

"Because he took his own life, you stupid girl! Have you forgotten that he left a note?"

"Oh, yes. The famous note. The one you've always refused to let me see. How do I even know it exists?"

Karen's mother stabbed an angry finger at her. "Don't you fucking move." And Karen was shocked to hear her swear. She stormed away down the hall, and Karen could hear her banging about in her den, slamming drawers and doors. When she returned, she was very nearly hyperventilating, and she thrust a folded sheet of paper at her daughter. "It's not the original. The police still have that. But this is the copy they made for me."

Karen stood looking at it, her heart in her throat, and she didn't even want to touch it.

"Go on, take it. You're a big girl now. Or so you keep telling me. Time to face the truth. After sixteen years of marriage, this is all he could think to leave. Nothing about me. Not a word of apology. Or regret. Nothing." She pushed it at Karen again. "Go on, take it. It was only ever about you."

Karen was shaking as she took the folded sheet from her mother's outstretched hand. She opened it up very slowly, and saw her father's familiar scrawl. Somehow she had expected there would be more. But all it said was, *Tell Karen I love her, even if I never could be the dad she wanted me to be.*

Chapter Ten

Broken clouds are painted roughly across the sky, like a sketch in preparation for a painting. They reflect crudely in the still autumn waters of the Firth of Forth, off to the west. To the east, beyond the suspension cables of the road bridge, the triple humps of the rail bridge are painted rust-red. A paint that lasts much longer now, doing men out of work.

I can see the sails of occasional yachts tacking out toward the North Sea, and somewhere beyond the low-lying smudge of the south shore, the city of Edinburgh nestled tightly beneath Arthur's Seat.

I am tired. It has been a long drive down from the Isle of Skye after an early ferry crossing from Tarbert. With stops, I have been nearly eight hours on the road.

Traffic is gathering already for rush hour, and I am glad to be heading into Edinburgh rather than out of it. Until I hit the town itself, and it all grinds to a halt. At Haymarket I smell the malt bins of the breweries. The all-pervasive stench of them, like stale beer in a pub at midnight, hangs in the air and suffuses the senses with strangely elusive memories that remain infuriatingly just beyond reach. Oddly, the streets of the city are familiar to me. I need no maps or GPS to guide me to the King James Hotel at the top of Leith Walk, where Sally booked me a room for two nights using her credit card. But I will pay with cash.

I am glad now that I thought to reserve a parking place in the tiny car park below the hotel. Driving in the city, I would be at much greater risk of being stopped by the police than I have been on the open road. Although that did not reduce my paranoia to any significant degree on the drive down.

The girl at the reception desk is tall and willowy. And difficult. "I'm sorry, sir," she says, "I need your credit card."

"I don't have one."

"The room was booked using a card."

"A friend's card. I am not authorized to use it. I'll pay cash."

She glances at her computer screen. "Well, the lady has authorized its use to pay for the room. We'll add any other charges to that."

"No." I shake my head in frustration. "I want to pay cash."

"I'm sorry, we need a credit card to cover payment of any additional costs you might run up. Meals, room service, bar . . ."

"I'll give you a deposit. In cash."

She sighs, as if I am the one who is being difficult. And I wonder how it can possibly be this hard to pay for something with real money. "I'll get the manager." My turn to sigh.

The manager, who looks no older than fifteen, insists on deducting the room and parking charges from the credit card, since those amounts had been preauthorized by the card holder, and in the end accepts a cash deposit of £1,000 to cover additional room charges, although he refuses to allow me to charge meals or drinks to the room. I am going to have to reimburse Sally when I get back.

When I dump my bag in my room, I am tempted to jump into a taxi and go straight to the address on the back of the birth certificate. But it is too late in the day, and I am tired, and even if I do not sleep well, I know it would be better to start fresh in the morning.

So I drink a couple of whiskies at the cocktail bar, trying not to think about why I am here, and have a salad in the restaurant, before retiring to my room to lie on the bed watching television until finally, sometime in the small hours, I drift off to sleep.

The taxi driver looks at me as if I am mad. It is a black hackney cab, and I have already slipped into the back seat and fastened the seat belt when I tell him that I want to keep him for the day. He shakes his head. "I don't do that. Wouldn't be worth my while."

"Well, what would make it worth your while?" It's strange how having all that cash makes me reckless.

He laughs. "Forget it, pal, you couldn't afford me. I'll take you and drop you wherever you want to go."

I take out my wallet and count out a sheaf of notes, which I push through the gap below the glass separator. "Five hundred quid. And it might not even be the whole day."

The driver looks at the notes, and I see him run his tongue thoughtfully between his lips. He takes the bundle without comment. "Where are we going?"

"Hainburn Park. It's just north of the —"

He cuts me off. "I know where it is." And he pulls away from the front of the hotel into the early morning traffic.

It is a dull morning that camouflages the beauty of this gray-stoned city. It seems flat and lifeless. The only color is on the pavements, where multicolored umbrellas are lifted in protection from fine rain that falls like mist. The green of Princes Street Gardens seems end-of-season weary, and a pall of gloom hangs over the capital, as if in anticipation of winter, just around the corner.

I watch the city slide past rain-streaked windows as we head south over the Bridges into Nicolson Street, and I suppose that this is my town. The place where I live. It all seems familiar enough to me, but I have no idea whether I grew up here, or moved back here later. What is my work, my job, my profession? I told Sally and Jon that I was an academic. If that is true, what is my subject, my area of expertise? Am I a teacher, a lecturer, a researcher? I close my eyes and stop trying to remember. If any of it is going to come back to me, I need to let it happen naturally. Trying to force it is only giving me a headache.

I start to get lost as we turn west at Newington. The streets have become unfamiliar. The leafy suburban streets of upmarket Morningside, where grand detached houses lurk discreetly in mature gardens behind screens of trees and hedges made impenetrable by leaves starting to turn toward autumn.

It takes little under half an hour to get there, passing finally through the blue-collar suburb of Oxgangs before turning into the warren of detached villas and bungalows that is Hainburn Park, with its view out beyond the bypass to the green rise of the Pentland Hills. Today they are almost lost in mist.

I have been watching the numbers, and spot the house on our right as we pass it. "What number, mate?" the driver asks.

"This is it," I tell him. "Go to the end of the road and turn, then pull in about three houses down." I see his eyes flicker toward me in the mirror, but he does as I ask.

When we have pulled in at the side of the road and he cuts his motor, he says, "What now?"

"We wait."

I sense the driver's unease, but ignore him and sit gazing out of the window at my house. It is a modern, detached villa with its own drive and what looks like a double garage. Tall wooden gates lead through to the back garden beyond, and I can see trees behind that.

A white Nissan X-Trail is parked in the

drive next to a short flight of steps that leads up to a front porch. There are net curtains on the windows of the front room, so it is impossible to see inside. All I want to do is walk up and knock on the front door, but something makes me hesitate. A need, perhaps, for some hint of familiarity, some memory, no matter how distant, as confirmation that this really is where I live. That I really am Neal Maclean.

The driver has opened his window and is smoking, and reading a copy of the *Scottish Sun.* The windows in the back are starting to steam up, and I lower the one on the pavement side to get a clearer view of the house. Still nothing comes back to me. It all feels like nowhere I have ever been. And yet, why else would I have an extract of birth for Neal David Maclean, with this address written on the back of it?

Even as I am watching, the front door opens, and I tense as a woman steps out. I strain to look at her through the fine drizzle as she skips down the steps and climbs up into the Nissan. I am almost disappointed by her ordinariness. Brown hair streaked blond, not excessively tall. A woman in early middle age. Forty, perhaps, and inclining to plumpness. She wears jeans and a sweater beneath a light summer raincoat which flaps open, and block-heeled sandals. A black bag on a short strap hangs from her left shoulder. She throws it into the car ahead of her as she gets in, then starts to back out into the street.

I rap on the driver's window. "We need to follow her."

He looks up, taking in the X-Trail, then glances back at me. "I hope this is kosher, mate, and you're not some bloody perv. Cos I don't want any part of stalking a woman that you've got a fancy for."

"She's my wife," I tell him emphatically, and an unpleasant smile spreads itself across his face.

"Oh, I get it. Been a bad girl, has she?"

"Just follow the car, please."

His lip curls in annoyance, and for a moment I think he is going to tell me to get out of his cab. But if he was, he reconsiders, and turns to start the motor and accelerate away in pursuit of the white Nissan. It is clear that he does not like me, or this hire, but he's taken the money, and I am happy that at least he does not try to engage me in meaningless small talk.

She drives to a large shopping center at Cameron Toll and takes a shopping trolley into Sainsbury's. We park two rows behind her in the car park and wait.

It is hot and stuffy in the back of the cab and I roll down the window part of the way and lean my head back against the rest, closing my eyes. I am not sure if it is a memory or a dream, or perhaps a mix of both, but I see a woman in blue who looks very familiar to me. If I breathe deeply I can smell her scent, and it takes me tumbling back through time to childhood. Patchouli. I know, without being told, that she is my mother. She has many rings on her fingers, long dark hair held in place by braided lengths from the front of it tied back. Her jeans flare over brown leather boots, and she wears a loose, tie-dyed top. A child of her age, caught in a time-warp from the era of her youth, when the world was still full of hope. She is leaning over me, kissing my forehead, smiling. And just beyond her a man is speaking her name. But somehow I can't quite catch it.

"What do you want me to do now?"

I am startled by the driver's voice, annoyed that the interruption has prevented me from hearing my mother's name. It had been so close, so tantalizingly just out of reach. I blink and see the woman we have been following, loading bags of shopping into the back of her Nissan. "Just keep on her tail."

We follow her through a maze of streets before finally she pulls up in a parking space outside a row of single-story suburban shops. My driver draws in on the opposite side of the street and the taxi's diesel engine sits idling noisily as the woman goes into a hairdressing salon called *Coif'n'Cut.* Through the window we can see her being greeted by what looks like the owner. There is a kiss on each cheek, laughter, and then the coat and bag are dispensed with before she is led away, beyond our field of vision.

"Knowing women, she could be in there for a while," the driver says. "And I canny sit parked here."

We end up parked in a fifteen-minute meter bay a hundred yards up the road, and I am in and out of the cab feeding it for the next hour and a half. My frustration is growing by the minute, and I can feel my driver's impatience keeping pace with it.

When eventually she emerges from the hairdresser's, I can see no difference at all in her hair.

"Hah," the driver grunts, looking in the mirror. "Either she snuck out the back to keep some secret rendezvous, or she's paid a bloody fortune for fuck all."

Her next stop is at a Costa Coffee, but mercifully she emerges again after a few minutes, sipping a large takeaway cup and slipping back into her Nissan. We follow her to the house, then, and park further down the street to watch her carry her shopping into the house and shut the door.

By now I have had enough. It's time to confront her. I am about to step out of the cab, when I see a group of schoolgirls approaching from the direction of Oxgangs Road. Three of them. And some instinct makes me stop to watch. They are in school uniform. Teenagers from fifth or sixth year, swinging bags and taking their time as they make their way toward us in animated conversation beneath two umbrellas. At the drive to my house they stop briefly, then one of them detaches herself from the others and runs up the path to open the front door with her own key. She is too far away to see clearly in the rain, and is obscured by her umbrella. Sixteen or seventeen years old, I would have said. Quite a tall girl, but it's impossible to make out her features.

"Your kid?" the driver says.

I nod. "Yes." And it gives me the strangest feeling to realize that I have a daughter. I check the time and see that it is nearly one o'clock. She must have come home from school for lunch, and will probably leave again in half an hour or so. I decide to wait, to get a better look at her.

"So we wait again?"

"Yes."

The driver sighs extravagantly, then reaches down to his left to retrieve a bag from which he takes a flask and a bag of sandwiches. And I realize how hungry I am myself. I ate very little yesterday, and had no breakfast this morning. So I lay my head back once more against the rest and close my eyes.

Almost immediately, I see myself running alongside a child's bicycle. A little girl is clutching the grips on the handlebars with whitened knuckles, wobbling as her short legs stretch fully to turn the pedals. "Don't let go, Daddy, don't let go," she shouts, and I realize that I am not holding the bike at all. I open my eyes again, blinking furiously. Karen. I don't know where it comes from, but that is the name on my lips. I say it out loud. "Karen." And see the driver looking at me again in his mirror.

"That your kid's name?"

I nod.

"Quick eater, then. That's her finished already."

And I realize that the driver, too, has finished his packed lunch, and that I must have dropped off to sleep. I am awake in an instant and, peering through a windscreen made almost opaque by fine droplets of rain, I see my daughter running down the drive to meet her friends, the three of them again sharing two umbrellas and huddled together beneath them.

"What now?"

"Follow them."

The driver turns to glare at me through the glass. "No fucking way am I following a bunch of teenage girls in my cab."

"It's my daughter, for Christ's sake."

"I only have your word for that." He pauses. "And anyway, they'd see us. A big black fucking cab crawling along behind them." I don't know what to say, and he looks at me appraisingly. "Tell you what. I'll take you to the school ahead of them. Got to be Firrhill High, in this catchment area. And you can watch her go in."

We get there a full ten minutes ahead of them, and I assume they must have waited to take a bus up Oxgangs Road. Pupils straggle through the gates in groups of two and three and four. The rain has got heavier, and no one is lingering in the street or the playground. When I see them, they are instantly recognizable. Three lassies huddled under two umbrellas, hurrying down from the main road, and I am disappointed again not to see her face.

We sit along from the house in Hainburn Park all afternoon with the rain drumming on the roof of the cab. I can feel the driver becoming increasingly restive. And the only reason I can contain my own impatience is because I have decided to wait until my daughter returns from school, when I will step down from the cab to greet her in the street. It is more passive than walking up the drive and knocking on the front door to confront my wife. And I wonder if I am, by nature, a coward, or a prevaricator, or simply someone who shies away instinctively from the possibility of confrontation. Does she even know where I have been for the last year and a half, or why? What was the state of our relationship when I left? Are we still married? As the clock ticks away, I am becoming increasingly nervous.

By the time I see the three girls hurrying down the street toward us, what had begun the day as light drizzle has become a torrential downpour. Raining like stair rods, my mother used to say. And I catch my breath. Another memory. But it arrives like a lone horseman from the clouded depths of my mind, and slips away into insignificance.

I refocus. The gutters are in spate and I can see almost nothing out of the windows. I am wearing a waterproof jacket, but have no hat or umbrella. As soon as I step from the cab I will be drenched. They are almost upon us, and I swing the door open and step out on to the pavement, almost bumping into them. One of the girls releases a tiny, startled yelp, and all three faces turn up toward me from under the umbrellas. Fleetingly, I catch Karen's eye, and see a face full of indifference, without a trace of recognition.

The girls hurry on, leaving me standing in the rain, my hair streaked in wet ropes down my forehead, and I am filled by the awful, hollow pain that comes with the realization that the girl I had thought to be my daughter didn't know me. Looked me straight in the eye and away again. Dismissive. Some stupid guy that bumped into them on the pavement. Certainly not her father.

I watch them carry on up the road, one of them detaching from the others and running up to the door of the house I have been watching all day, before vanishing inside. I open the door of the taxi, cast adrift again on a sea of utter confusion, and see the driver leaning toward me.

"That lassie didnae know you fae Adam.

You're taking the piss, pal. You can find your own way back to the hotel. Shut the fucking door!"

In a state of semishock, I do as he says and hear him start the motor and rev fiercely. I watch as he pulls away up the street, leaving me standing at the side of the road. Perhaps it is only my imagination, but it seems to me as if the rain has intensified. I feel it beating a tattoo on my head, soaking into my jeans, washing around my shoes. I run a hand back across my scalp, sweeping my hair out of my eyes. With the rain running down my face, it would be hard to tell if I was crying. And if I were to cry, they would be tears of pure frustration. Along with the return, perhaps, of fear. For the rock of certainty on which I have built my hopes turns out to have been the sand of self-deception. If I had been Neal Maclean, resident of this Edinburgh suburb, father of Karen, then surely that girl would have known me? But if not her father, who else could I be? I feel as confused and disorientated now as I did those first moments on the beach at Luskentyre when I opened my eyes and realized I had no earthly idea who I was.

A strange, unaccountable anger takes hold of me. Why would I have all those newspaper cuttings about Neal Maclean? His birth certificate, with this address written on the back. It is incomprehensible. At the very least, somehow, I have to make some kind of sense of it.

I turn and walk briskly through the rain and turn into the drive of the house where the white Nissan is parked. Neal Maclean's house. Where Neal Maclean's wife and daughter live. At the front door, I knock three times in rapid succession, and such is my impatience that I barely wait a handful of seconds before knocking again. Then I spot the doorbell and ring it.

When the door opens, the woman with the blond-streaked hair looks startled, and it is immediately clear to me from her eyes that she doesn't know me. Her daughter is hovering in the gloom of the hall beyond her, a towel in her hands. She, too, looks blankly toward me.

"Can I help you?" the woman says.

I have no idea what to say, and I blurt, "Don't you know me?"

"No, I don't. What do you want?"

Her daughter calls, "He was standing out on the street when I got back."

The mother says to me, "I think you'd better go."

I don't know what possesses me to say it,

because I know now it's not true. And I feel like a drowning man grasping at flotsam that I will simply drag under with me. "You must know me. I'm Neal Maclean. We're married."

Her eyes open wide with fear, all color draining from her face in an instant, and she slams the door shut on me. From the other side of it, I hear her shout, "If you don't leave immediately, I'll call the police!"

There is a bar in the hotel called The Boston Bean Company. I have no idea why, and it seems to me like an absurd name for a bar. But tonight it offers refuge and escape to a man with no name, no past, no future. I am reacquainting myself with my only friend, Caol Ila. A friend who offers warmth and escape. And ultimately oblivion. A friend who doesn't care who I am, good or bad, lost or found. A friend who will stay with me to the end, and ultimately hasten my departure.

It was quiet here when I first arrived, my hair still damp, a chill in my bones. But the in-crowd have arrived. Young people. Noisy. Drinking, talking, laughing. And above all, confident in who they are. They make an island of me. A solitary, silent island of confusion in their sea of certainty. I sit on a stool at the counter, watching my glasses come and go. A pale amber procession of them, evaporating before my eyes. And there is one refrain that plays again and again in my head like an earworm. If I am not Neal Maclean, who in God's name am I?

CHAPTER ELEVEN

I am tempted by the hair of the dog. Not only because I feel like death on this gray September Edinburgh morning, but because I would like to rediscover the level of oblivion I achieved last night. The real world, today, feels even harsher and less forgiving.

It is only a short walk from the hotel to the top of Leith Street, and the turn into Princes Street. The equestrian statue of Wellington stands mounted on a plinth at the foot of the steps to General Register House, looking out over North Bridge.

For some reason I am acquainted with the history of this building. Built in the eighteenth century with funds seized from defeated Jacobite estates, it lay empty for nearly a decade, becoming known as the most magnificent pigeon house in Europe. It also provided a refuge for thieves and pickpockets before work resumed on its

interior, turning it into what it is today —
one of the oldest custom-built archive buildings still in continuous use anywhere in the
world. Only nowadays they call it the Scot-
landsPeople Center.

At the reception desk in the main lobby, I
buy, for fifteen pounds, a day search pass,
and am escorted through the magnificent
circular, glass-crowned Adam Dome, where
the ancient records of sasines are stored on
shelves that follow the contours of the room
and rise in majestic procession to the golden
dome high above. Desks with computers
are set at intervals around the walls, but
this is not the place where I will conduct
my search.

The assistant takes me through a hall, past
the Reid stairs, which lead to the historical
and legal search rooms on the first floor,
and into the Reid room itself, where computers sit before blue chairs in serried rows,
on tables set along either side of the room.
A man and a woman sit at a table in the
center, and the woman looks up and smiles
as I approach, and asks to see my pass.

"Have you used a computer in the search
center before?" she asks.

If I have, I have no recollection of it and
shake my head. She leads me to a desk and
I sit down in front of a computer, feeling

like a child on his first day at school. She pulls up a chair beside me, to boot up the computer and log me in.

"Now, what exactly are you looking for?"

"Anything at all about a Neal David Maclean." I fumble in my shoulder bag and bring out the extract of birth.

"Ah, you must have accessed Scotlands People online to get that?"

"No." I am thinking as quickly as my hangover will allow. "It was given to me by a friend. I promised to do a search for him while I was here in Edinburgh."

She touches the extract. "And that's your friend? Neal Maclean?"

"No. It's a relative of his. He just wanted me to find out as much about Neal as I could."

"Well, you have his birth certificate, so that's a good start. Is he married?"

"I think so, yes."

"Let's have a look then." She leans across me to tap at the keyboard. I suppose this is something I should be doing myself, but she seems happy to help, bored perhaps from sitting for endless hours at her desk in the library silence of this room. "Yes, here we are, this looks like him. Married to Louise Alice Munro, February fifth, 1998. Married young. Just twenty years old."

I squint at the screen and see that Louise Alice Munro is two years older than Neal, which is unusual. And she must have fallen pregnant very quickly after their marriage. Or perhaps a premature pregnancy was their reason for marrying at such a young age in the first place. "Is there any way of establishing whether they have had any children?"

"That might take a while."

And I think there is no point. I know they have a daughter. "Let's skip that, then."

"Do you want to go back the way? Parents, grandparents."

I shake my head. "No."

And she frowns. "I don't really understand —" she glances at my pass — "Mr. Smith. What exactly is it you think you can find here?"

I am at a complete loss. I really have no idea.

"I take it he's still alive?"

"Who?"

"Neal David Maclean."

"I believe so, yes."

"Well, if you only believe so, maybe we should check that first."

And as she leans across me again, I smell her perfume — something floral sweet — and I feel the warmth of her body. She initiates another search and hits the return key to bring up the result. She straightens in her seat, pulling down her jacket where it has ridden up over her breasts.

"Well," she says, and gives me the strangest look. "Your friend might have briefed you a little better, Mr. Smith. Neal David Maclean has been dead for over two years."

And I gaze at the winking cursor on the screen. A fit man, a sailor, used to the outdoor life, Neal Maclean had died in his late thirties from a heart attack. Was it any wonder his wife had looked at me as though she had seen a ghost?

CHAPTER TWELVE

Karen's trip out toward the airport was not on a tram this time, but in a taxi. Which took a much more direct route, heading west on the A8, past Corstorphine and the old art deco Maybury Roadhouse at the roundabout, freshly painted and home now to the Maybury Casino. But the airport was not her destination.

She was unaccountably nervous. Not because she had skipped school, or stolen money from her mother to pay for the taxi, but because she was embarking on a voyage of discovery, to confront the demons she had tried so hard to keep in check these past two years.

Guilt had been the most prominent of them. A creeping, destructive sense of guilt that had eaten away, like so many termites, at the very foundations of her self. So much so that she had felt compelled to invent a new self, to gloss over the old, to pretend that she was someone else altogether, raising two fingers to the world as if she didn't give a damn.

Her father's final words had stripped away all that self-delusion.

Tell Karen I love her, even if I never could be the dad she wanted me to be.

Who had she wanted him to be? She had no idea, and looking back she realized that she was the one who had changed, not him. He had been *everything* she had wanted him to be when she was younger. She had adored him, would have done anything for him. Just, she knew, as he would have done anything for her.

How hurt and frustrated must he have been when the daughter who adored him turned into the sullen, resentful teenager she had become?

Of course, she'd had no idea, then, of the estrangement that existed between her parents. She had been far too self-absorbed for that. But again, in retrospect, she could see all the signs. Remembering the whispered arguments in the bedroom, the silences at the dinner table. How increasingly he was detained at work and came home late. And although her mother had claimed the other night that he had used his work as a means of escaping *her,* Karen now wondered. Perhaps it was disappointment in his daughter that had kept him away from home, and that was what had driven the wedge between him and Karen's mum.

Yet more guilt.

Tell Karen I love her.

The written words had gone through her like a knife. Cold, hard, sharp-edged. And they had met with little resistance. Her mother's spoken words had echoed in her mind for hours afterward. *It was only ever about you.* What had she meant? Had she been jealous of the relationship between Karen and her dad? Or was she blaming Karen for her father killing himself? Karen might have asked, had she not been afraid of the answer. Though, she hadn't spoken to her mother since. And, the way she felt now, never would again.

The hours after she read the note had been spent crying in her room until she physically ached. Then had followed a stripping away of all the layers of pretense she had built around herself since her father's death. In the bathroom, she had hacked away the longer, green hair on the top of her head, and then dyed it black like the rest. One by one, the piercings and lip rings were removed, leaving tiny holes in pale, naked skin. She scrubbed her face until it was devoid of the least trace of makeup, then stood staring at herself in the mirror, searching blue eyes for truth. Wondering not who it was she had become, but who she had been. And what she had done.

As she sat in the taxi now, she could see that same reflection staring back at her from the glass screen. She barely recognized herself. A pale, plain face beneath a head of close-cropped black hair with a few stray curls gelled back on top. There were penumbral shadows beneath her eyes from lack of sleep, and a puffiness still from all the crying. She was dressed, for her, very conservatively. Jeans, white tennis shoes, a plain white T-shirt beneath a long-sleeved dark jacket. There was not a tattoo in sight. Purple nail varnish had been removed from short nails that she had always had a tendency to bite, and she looked down at her hands and thought how small and ugly they were. Then remembered the tattoo artist laughing as he told her that men liked women with small hands, because it made their manhood seem bigger. She burned with shame at the recollection of things she had done in the name of rebellion.

Her taxi cruised through the underpass at the Gogar roundabout and, half a mile further on, took a left leading down to a smaller junction, before swinging left again and heading south. This was green, open country, transected by the Gogar Burn and punctuated by stands of dark trees. The road swooped over a rise in the land, and she saw the Gogarburn Golf Course off to their right, before the curve of the tarmac took them down in a wide sweep to a sprawling complex of steel and black glass that filled the hollow. It was built on two levels, and lay surrounded by mature trees that almost hid it from casual view. An enormous car park, very nearly filled to capacity, stood in grounds of manicured lawns. Her taxi swung into the turning circle at a concourse which led to revolving glass doors at the entrance to the main building, and Karen saw a long marble plinth set into the grass. It was engraved with the words *The Geddes Institute for Scientific Research.* This was where her father had worked for the two years before his death, and she had never once set foot in it.

A large, uniformed security guard standing at the door refused to let her in. "You need a pass, love." But he didn't look at her as if she were his "love."

"I'm here to see my godfather."

He cocked a skeptical eyebrow. "And who would that be?"

"Professor Chris Connor."

He hesitated.

"My dad used to work here, too."

"Used to? Where is he now?"

"He's dead."

Which tilted him slightly off balance, and she saw the first crack in his implacable veneer. "What's your name?"

"Karen Fleming."

"And your dad?"

"Tom."

He stabbed a finger at her. "You wait there." And he slipped inside and crossed the lobby to a reception desk. Beyond him, Karen could see through the glass, a long atrium rose up to a pitched glass roof that spilled light down on to what looked like the kind of shopping street you might find in a mall. There were coffee shops, restaurants, a bakery, a clothes store, a supermarket, even a bookshop. And the concourse was crisscrossed by people drifting from shop to shop, or riding the escalators up and down to a gallery running along either side of the first floor. Others stood in groups talking, and sipping skinny lattes from Starbucks cups.

The security guard returned to wave her through the revolving door and lead her across to the desk. A young woman wearing a headset with a microphone smiled at her. "Professor Connor will be down in a moment. I'll need to make out a pass for you." She slipped a form across the counter for Karen to fill in with her name, address, telephone number, date, time and reason for visit. When it was done, she peeled away a second copy sheet for filing, and folded the top sheet to slip into a plastic visitor holder that she gave to Karen to clip on to her jacket. "Just sit over there."

Karen crossed to sit uncomfortably in one of several leather armchairs grouped around a handful of coffee tables whose tops were marked by stains and rings.

Voices raised in idle chatter and laughter echoed all around the atrium and Karen wondered where it was that people worked here. And what it was they did. She had only ever had the vaguest notion of what it was her father worked at for a living. A research scientist employed by the university was all she had ever known. His field had been neuroscience, though she had no real idea exactly what that was.

In the center of the lobby, the black bust of an impressive-looking young man with a thick head of hair and a full beard was raised to head height on a marble plinth. She saw the name *Sir Patrick Geddes,* and beneath it his birth and death dates. *1854–1932.*

"Hello, K-Karen." His voice broke into her reverie. She looked up and was as shocked by her godfather's appearance as he seemed to be by hers. He was, perhaps, a little older than her father and had always been inclined to plumpness. But since she last saw him he had shed more weight than was good for him and looked gaunt and wan, his once luxuriant thatch of sandy hair now thin and scraped back to disguise advancing baldness.

She stood up and kissed him awkwardly on each cheek. His brown eyes, watery and bloodshot, darted here and there and seemed reluctant to meet hers directly. He nodded toward the bust of Patrick Geddes, a way of distracting them both from their unease.

"Amazing chap," he said. "Botanist, sociologist. And probably one of the world's first environmentalists. Taught zoology right here in Edinburgh for a while. Then founded the university of Bombay." He forced a smile. "Or Mumbai, as they call it now. Planned the Hebrew University in Jerusalem, too, and founded the Collège des Écossais at Montpellier in France. As if that wasn't enough, he was pretty much known

the world over as the father of urban planning. Not bad for a laddie from Aberdeen-
shire. And all of it achieved in seventy-eight
short years."

Seventy-eight seemed very old to Karen.
"That would be two of my dad's lifetimes,
then."

Connor became self-conscious again, and
he glanced around as if looking to see who
might be watching them. Though, as far as
Karen could tell, no one was paying them
the slightest attention. "Wh-what are you
doing here, Karen?"

"I came to see my godfather."

Connor looked instantly guilty, and Karen
noticed that he was turning his wedding
ring constantly around the third finger of
his left hand, without any apparent awareness of it. "I'm sorry, Karen. I should have
kept in touch. I . . . I know your dad would
have wanted me to. It's just . . ." He
searched around for some excuse. "Things
have been, you know, not so great at home."
But he didn't elucidate. "Y-you shouldn't
really have come here. It would have been
better if you'd called." He took her by the
arm, gripping her too hard, and she was
sure that his fingers would leave bruises.
"You'd better come up to the office."

As they glided up to the first-floor gallery

on the escalator, Karen looked down on to the concourse. "What is this place? It looks like a shopping mall."

Connor smiled. "We're a research institute attached to the university."

"What do you research? The shopping habits of employees?"

He shook his head, and for the first time his smile came quite naturally. "You sound like your dad." And for some reason that thought made tears well in her eyes. She blinked and looked away to avoid embarrassment. "There are five thousand employees and students based here, Karen, and we're a long way out of town. I think Ergo took a leaf out of The Royal Bank of Scotland's book. Their headquarters is just over the hill there, and they have a very similar arrangement. The place is like a small town. People do everything but actually live here. Shop, eat, work, socialize. It narrows our focus and keeps it concentrated on work."

Karen noticed that his stutter seemed to have disappeared. "What's Ergo?"

They had reached the gallery now, and he led her along it, past offices and meeting rooms with glass walls and open doors. "It's a Swiss agrochemical company. Probably bigger than Monsanto and Syngenta combined. They derived the name from the shortened form of the Greek word *ergosta-sio,* meaning *plant.* But, of course, Ergo itself also means *therefore.*" He turned to smile at her. "I think, therefore I am. I think." When she didn't return the smile, his faded. "Anyway, Ergo is the institute's primary benefactor. They fund ninety percent of our research."

"Which they then exploit commercially?"

Connor flicked her a look, surprised perhaps by her perception. "Well, yes. But it provides a wonderful resource for the university, professors and students alike." He glanced around the gallery that lined the atrium. "These are all just offices and conference rooms for staff and administration. Lab facilities and lecture theaters are located in the outlying buildings."

At the end of the gallery, they turned right into a long corridor, then left into a small office with two desks pushed together beneath a window looking out across trees, toward the airport. Karen could see planes landing and taking off, but triple-glazing and engineered insulation cocooned them in silence. Connor closed the door carefully behind them, and closed blinds on the glass wall to shut them off from the corridor beyond. "Wh-what is it you want, Karen?" The uncertainty crept back into his voice with the return of the conversation to personal matters.

"I want to know about my dad."

His agitation increased. "W-well, why? Your mum could tell you much more about him than me."

"I'm not talking to my mum right now. And, anyway, I'm not sure she really knew that much about him. You've known him since you were students together. You were his best man. And my godfather, for Christ's sake."

He looked at the floor, his arms hanging awkwardly at his sides. "I'm sorry. I . . . I've been pretty lousy at that."

"Well, maybe you can make up for it now." She saw him wince, as if she had stabbed him. "I want to know what he was like. Really like. What he was working on." She paused. "Why he killed himself."

Her godfather turned away to shuffle papers on his desk. She saw him shaking his head. "I wish you'd called me at home."

"Why?"

"B-because this isn't the place to talk about stuff like that."

She sighed her frustration. "I couldn't find a number or an address for you anywhere. This is the only way I figured I could contact you. It's like, you know, you haven't made it very easy."

"I'm sorry," he said again.

She finally lost patience. "Stop apologizing, Chris! Just talk to me." And she thought how strange it seemed to be calling him Chris. When she was a child, he'd encouraged her to call him "Toffee," which had been her father's nickname for him. Not remotely appropriate now.

But if "Chris" seemed inappropriate to him, he didn't show it. He leaned across his desk and, with slightly trembling fingers, lifted a business card from a clear plastic holder. He took a pen and wrote a number on the back of it, then turned and handed it to her, still avoiding her eye. "Call me at home tonight. W-we'll arrange a time and place to meet."

CHAPTER THIRTEEN

Detective Sergeant George Gunn lodged himself firmly in the pale blue airplane-style seat on the starboard side of the 42-foot MV *Lochlann* as she plowed her way through the medium-gray swell of this mid-September afternoon. He had hoped that by bracing himself with outstretched arms on the seat in front, keeping his eyes away from the window and the tipping horizon, he would survive the trip without being afflicted, as he normally was, by the curse of seasickness. But just fifteen minutes out, he had already begun to feel like death.

Murray sat up front, guiding the boat toward the dark profile of the Seven Hunters, strung along the distant horizon like so many oddly shaped beads. It was a trip he had made countless times, and Gunn envied him his easy way on the water. He was as much at home on it as on the land.

To his annoyance, Professor Angus Wilson

seemed actually to be enjoying himself. Gunn glanced across the cabin at the pathologist, and resented the way the man almost invariably made him feel like a rank novice. Who knew how many postmortems the physician had carried out, how many murder victims he had dissected. How many mangled bodies he had vandalized with his knife, probing for cause of death, uncovering hidden trauma. While Gunn, serving most of his career at the police station in Church Street in Stornoway, had only rarely been exposed to violent death in all its bloody technicolor and ugly stench. And had never got used to it. He liked to think of himself as a student more of human nature than of human physiology.

It was pure chance that the professor had even been on the island. A messy, suspicious death that had turned out, as Gunn expected, to be a suicide. A man who, for some unaccountable reason, had thrown himself from the cliffs in Ness. The pathologist was due to catch the late afternoon flight back to Edinburgh. And after getting the call from Murray, Gunn had only just caught him as he was checking out of his hotel.

Neither of the two uniformed officers they had brought with them from Stornoway seemed afflicted by Gunn's inability to keep the contents of his stomach in place, and they looked at him in surprise as he dashed suddenly out of the cabin to double up over the back of the boat and heave into its wake.

There was no color at all in his face as he ventured slowly back to resume his seat. He had grown more inclined to portliness in recent years, and the life jacket fastened tightly around his woolen jumper meant that he had to squeeze himself into it. He ran a hand back through dark hair that grew thickly from a widow's peak on his forehead, greying now at the temples, and became aware of Professor Wilson looking at him across the aisle.

"I'm not surprised you're feeling nauseous, Detective Sergeant, given the pungency of the aftershave you seem to sprinkle so liberally on that shiny face of yours. I'm amazed you need to shave at all. I've seen more hair on a whore's fanny."

Gunn heard the stifled laughter of the uniforms somewhere behind him.

"Honestly, man. You get sick in the autopsy room, queasy in the car, bilious on the boat . . . You'd think, by your time in life, you might have mastered the vagaries of your stomach."

Gunn refrained from comment as he felt

a second wave of nausea rising. He glared instead at the professor, diverting his thoughts from his stomach by focusing his hatred on this vulgar, bullying pathologist who never seemed to tire of baiting him. Everything about him was irritating to Gunn. From his smug smile to his tangle of ginger whiskers, as coarse as fuse wire, and the wispy, greying fuzz that ringed a bald, shiny head spattered by large brown freckles. Thin as a whip, and tall, with long, bony fingers, he towered over Gunn, making him feel small in every sense.

"About forty minutes from here," Murray called back to them, and Gunn groaned inwardly.

When finally they arrived at Eilean Mòr, there was a spit of rain in the air and the wind had risen out of the southwest. The eastside landing stage was relatively sheltered from the incoming swell by Làmh a' Sgeire Mhor, and Murray anchored the *Lochlann* in the bay and moved aft to lower the inflatable tender into the rise and fall of deep green water. Gunn's focus on not falling into the sea as he transferred from one to the other took his mind off the nausea. When they were all aboard, and Murray had fired up the fifteen-horsepower outboard,

Gunn clung on to the sides with knuckles that glowed white with tension.

The inflatable skimmed fast across the surface of the bay, sending spray up into their faces, then Murray throttled back to turn the boat side-on and nudge it gently in toward the steps. One of the constables jumped out with a rope to tether it to the rusted rung set in the wall, and one by one they made the jump from boat to landing stage, timing each leap with the highest point of the swell. Professor Wilson made it look easy, and it seemed to Gunn that the older man had the agility of a mountain goat. In stark contrast to Gunn himself, who almost fell, and was only saved from doing so by the steadying hand of the professor, who grabbed his arm. Gunn shrugged it free. "I'm fine," he said curtly.

To the accompaniment of screaming seabirds circling overhead, the five men made the long, windswept climb up the steps, doubling back to the crane emplacement, then following the tracks of the old tramway up to the intersection, from where a single concrete path led up to the lighthouse itself.

By the time they were on a level with the old ruined chapel, Gunn had to stop, leaning forward with his palms on his thighs, just to catch his breath. He felt the wind tugging at his clothes and filling his mouth as he sucked in oxygen.

Wilson shook his head. What was left of his hair was standing almost on end in the wind. "Are you not required to maintain a certain level of fitness in the force these days, Detective Sergeant? Man, you wouldn't be fit to chase a sloth up a tree!"

Gunn straightened up in an attempt to recover a little of his dignity, but was certain that his face would be puce, and he avoided the eye of the uniforms, who he knew would be enjoying this ritual humiliation of their senior officer.

Before setting out from Uig in the boat, Gunn had interviewed the tourists who found the corpse. And he turned now to Murray. "You weren't with the group that discovered the body when they went to look inside the chapel?"

Murray shook his head solemnly. "No, I usually stay with the tender. It wasn't until they came and told me what they'd found that I went to take a look for myself. I wasn't going to call you folks out on some wild goose chase."

"So it was just you and one other who actually went in?"

"Aye, that's right. The first fella in backed

out before the others could follow, and threw up all over the grass." Murray nodded toward a discolored area of ground near the entrance to the chapel. Most of the vomit had soaked away, but the evidence of the man's breakfast was still visible.

Gunn felt his stomach heave. He waved the uniforms toward the old stone ruin. "You'd better do your stuff, boys."

And as the two constables hammered in the metal stakes they had brought on the boat, linking them with fluttering crime-scene tape to cordon off an area in front of the entrance, Gunn and the professor pulled on latex gloves and plastic shoe covers in preparation for taking a look at the body for themselves.

Gunn knew he was not going to enjoy this, and took a deep breath. He steeled himself, glancing out across the ocean, where sunlight played in burnished silver patches that fell through broken cloud, and wondered what on earth anyone would be doing out here to get himself murdered in the first place.

He followed Professor Wilson under the tape and into the narrow entrance to the chapel. There was a smell of damp in the gloom, and something else. Something unpleasant, a little like rotten eggs. Light

194

fell in daubs through the broken roof, and the dead man lay twisted at an unnatural angle, his head turned to one side in a pool of long-dried blood and pale gray matter.

Professor Wilson dropped down to sit back on his heels and Gunn crouched beside him. There was very little room in here, and they were in very close proximity not only to each other, but to the body itself. Gunn gritted his teeth, determined to stay in control of his stomach, and watched as the pathologist began going carefully through the dead man's pockets. First his dark blue anorak, which was unzipped. The outside pockets were empty, apart from a sweetie wrapper, and all he recovered from the inside pocket was a pen and a small spiral notebook whose virgin pages were quite blank. His trouser pockets yielded a car key on a tab. Very carefully, the pathologist half-rolled the body on to its side, and, with fingers like forceps, recovered a wallet from the back pocket.

Supporting the corpse with his free hand, he let it fall gently back to its resting place, then opened the wallet. He raised his eyebrows in surprise and turned his face toward Gunn. "Just cash. No credit cards, no driver's license —" he slid two fingers into an opening just behind the empty card slots and drew them out empty — "or anything else, apparently, that might identify him." He handed Gunn the wallet, then turned his attention to the body itself, drawing a torch from his jacket pocket to play over the waxen features of the dead man. A slack face, lined by the years, fat accumulated in the jowls and folds of flesh beneath the jaw. Hair, thin and greying. Impossible now to say what color it might once have been. The pathologist made a moue. "Very unscientific, but at a guess I'd say he was in his fifties. There will be better indicators once I get him on the table."

In spite of himself, Gunn said, "Can you tell how long he's been dead?"

The professor turned a withering look in his direction, then turned back to the body, lifting an arm and bending it at the elbow, before raising and lowering it at the shoulder joint. He spread fingers across the man's jaw, which was quite slack, allowing him to open and close the mouth without resistance. The lips seemed vaguely swollen. Gunn watched as he unbuckled the trouser belt, unzipping the fly and pulling up the jumper, and the T-shirt beneath it, to expose the belly.

"Greenish tinge to the abdomen," the pathologist said. "And slightly bloated, probably with gas. Though there's fat there anyway, and the liver may well be distended. Help me roll him over."

Gunn lent him both hands to roll the man on to his side and hold him there as Wilson pulled the trousers down over the buttocks, revealing red-purple discoloration where they had been resting on the ground. He pressed a thumb deep into the discoloration, then removed it. There was no change of color. "Hmmm," he said. "Livor mortis is well defined. And fixed. Can't blanch it with my thumb."

Gunn knew better than to ask.

The pathologist then spread his palm on the man's back and moved it gently back and forth. "A little skin slippage, too. Okay, let's lay him back where he was." And when the body was lying once more as they had found it, Professor Wilson leaned over the head to examine the wound with the beam of his torch. "He'd been struck several times, I'd say, before the skull was breached. Abraded lacerations, and contusions. Something rough, like a rock or a stone." And almost involuntarily, they both looked around the confined space of the old ruin for what might have been the murder weapon, the beam of the professor's torch playing over several possible candidates.

"We'll need to go through this place with a fine-toothed comb." Then he returned the torch to the face of the victim and pulled back the eyelids in turn to shine its beam directly into the eyes. "Corneas are quite opaque." He snapped off his torch. "Let's get out of here."

Gunn was only too pleased to be able to scramble out and straighten himself up to breathe cold, fresh air. Professor Wilson followed him out. Murray and the two constables stood some twenty feet or more away on the path, watching them. There was more rain in the wind now, although oddly it was brighter than before, great swathes of ocean around the foam-ringed islands of the Flannans reflecting dazzling sunlight from huge rents in low, bubbling raincloud.

The professor lowered his voice as he turned his back on the onlookers and spoke directly to Gunn. "So Murray said it was two days ago that this fella Maclean was seen running from the chapel?"

"That's right."

"And nobody thought to take a look inside it then?"

"They were driven back to the boat by the rain, apparently."

"Well, I can tell you this, DS Gunn, if it was Maclean that killed him, he didn't do it two days ago." Something like a smile flitted across his lips. "In answer to your earlier question, I can't tell you exactly how long this man has been dead, but it's more than two days, that's certain. And, at a guess, I'd say at least four. But that's all it would be at this stage. A guess." He lifted his head, as if sniffing the air. "Tell me," he said, "there was no boat found, was there?"

"No, there wasn't, sir."

"So how did he get out here?"

Gunn shrugged. This was more familiar territory for him. "Who knows? Perhaps brought out by the killer himself."

"Perhaps." The pathologist scratched his chin thoughtfully. "Funny thing to do, though, don't you think? Bring a man away out here just to kill him, then leave him in the chapel where he's bound to be found, sooner or later. I mean, if you were a man of murderous disposition, Detective Sergeant, though I'm not suggesting for a minute that you are, wouldn't you push the body over the cliff? Let the sea take him? Chances are he would never be found."

Gunn nodded, and gazed up at the rows of dark solar panels along the front of the white-painted lighthouse. He knew the story of the vanishing lighthouse keepers, of course. The sea had claimed them. Or, at least, that was the theory. And it occurred to him that this man's killer had either wanted his victim to be found, or what had taken place here had been unplanned, and that the killer had simply fled in a blind panic.

He became aware of the pathologist speaking again. "We'd better call the coastguard and get the body helicoptered back to Stornoway. I'd like to get this fella on the table as soon as possible."

Gunn put on his greens and face mask before entering the autopsy room, but nothing ever prepared him for the smell. The perfume of putrefaction, and the gut-wrenching stink released by the bowels during dissection. In his limited experience, pathologists never seemed to notice it.

Outside, the light was fading fast and Gunn was hungry and anxious to get home for his tea. It had taken a considerable effort of will to force himself to attend this postmortem, which he knew would rob him of his appetite, and he had been putting it off as long as he could. Unlike the professor, who had already expressed his delight at spending another night in the Royal at the Scottish government's expense, and dining again at the Indian in Church Street, with its luridly colored curries. He must, Gunn reflected, be a man blessed with a cast-iron constitution.

Much of the postmortem had been completed. The cadaver lay opened up on the table, the liquids released by the pathologist's knife draining into a bucket beneath it. The organs had been weighed and bread-loafed. And the damaged brain, removed from its fractured skull, was suspended now in fixative.

The victim's clothing was laid out on a separate table, along with the rock they had recovered from just outside the chapel. A jagged piece of gneiss, about twice the size of a fist, that a man could spread his fingers around. It had blood, hair and tissue still clinging to it, but they had been unable to secure any fingerprints.

"Seems he put up quite a struggle," Professor Wilson said. "Forearms are covered in bruises and abrasions where he raised them to protect himself from the attack. Then his killer got through with the first blow to the head, and that, or maybe the second, might have dropped him to his knees, if he was on his feet. Considerable bruising there." He tapped both knees. "He was struck four times on the left side of the skull, any one of which might have been enough to incapacitate him. But his killer kept going anyway. The final blow was what killed him and did the worst of the damage. You'll get all the measurements and gory details in my report."

"Can't wait," Gunn said dryly, drawing a look from the pathologist. "You're confirming for me, then, that he was murdered?"

"That, Detective Sergeant, was never in doubt." The professor paused. "Have you found his car yet?"

"No, we haven't."

"Identification?"

Gunn shook his head. "The picture taken by the police photographer will be released to the press tonight. We'll see what that brings."

The professor grunted and lifted the dead man's right hand. "Bruises and grazing on his hands as well. The chances are the poor sod got in a few strikes himself. His fingers are ingrained with dirt, and maybe oil, and his fingernails are short and filthy, so it's impossible to tell if there's blood or skin from his attacker under any of them. I've taken scrapings from them all, and the lab will reveal in time if they captured any DNA from his killer." He ran his latexed palm lightly over the back of the hand he was holding. "Strange thing, though, and I only know about this because my wife used to keep bees. He has several bee stings on the back of his hands."

Gunn moved closer to take a look.

"You see? These little red lumps with tiny scabs at their center. Looks like he was stung quite recently, too."

CHAPTER FOURTEEN

Gunn enjoyed the drive down to Harris. Southwesterlies had blown great ragged clumps of black raincloud across the islands overnight, and everything looked shiny and new in the early morning sunlight, as if freshly painted.

As he passed from Lewis into Harris, even the Clisham, whose peak was normally mired in cloud, stood sharp and clear against the deep blue of the autumn sky, casting its shadow west over the Abhainn Langadail, which ran north into Loch Langabhat itself, a continuation of the extended valley rift that transected the center of the island from north to south.

On the long descent toward Tarbert, the southern half of the Isle of Harris, he knew, stretched off in obscurity beyond the hills, but it wasn't until he crested the rise past the town itself, after the turnoff to the Episcopalian Church, that he saw it laid out before him, shimmering in this startlingly luminous morning.

The tide was out, and the sands of Luskentyre glowed silver, very nearly filling Gunn's field of vision. They never ceased to take his breath away. Ringed by hills to the south, the mountains of North Harris, and the peaks of Taransay to the west, beyond all that simmering turquoise, he wondered if there could be any more beautiful spot on earth.

But he very quickly became firmly re-grounded in reality when his car bumped and rumbled over the hardcore being laid for the new road, then sat for minutes on end at successive stop lights regulating the two-way flow of traffic during the road-works.

Finally, gliding down over a new smooth unpainted ribbon of black tarmac laid only the week before, he reached the turnoff to Luskentyre itself, and spent the next five minutes avoiding the ditch as his glance was drawn repeatedly beyond the single-track road to the glimpses of paradise beyond the dunes. He had often spoken to his wife of buying a wee cottage down here when finally he took his retirement. But there were a few years to go before then.

He spotted the sign for Dune Cottage at

the side of the road just beyond the cemetery, and then saw the police car parked
behind the house itself. He turned in over
the cattle grid, and parked beside it, stepping out into the fresh, blustery breeze that
blew in off the beach, and zipping up his
quilted black anorak. The uniformed sergeant from the police station at Tarbert
eased himself out of a car that was far too
small for his six foot, six inches, and unfolded himself to stand upright and shake
Gunn's hand. They knew one another well,
the sergeant being of a similar age and having served most of his time on the islands.
He nodded curtly, and "George" was all he
said.

Gunn retrieved his hand from the other
man's grip. "Donnie." He looked around.
There was not much here. A handful of
houses climbing the hill behind the cottage,
following the road over toward the far
beach. An agricultural building of some
sort. A garden shed. And the graves of
generations of *Hearachs*. He felt the wind
lift his carefully gelled hair into a quiff.
"Been here for long?"

"Arrived just ahead of you, George."

Gunn nodded toward the cottage. "Is he
at home?"

"Doesn't look like it."

They walked around to the gable end and knocked on the door. When, after a full minute, there was no response, Donnie followed Gunn down to the front of the property, which looked out over the dunes to the beach. A couple of Hebridean ponies, one white, one gray, stood, heads down, grazing on beach grass. The two policemen climbed the steps of a weathered deck, to where a circular wooden table and two chairs sat looking out at the view. Gunn shaded his eyes and peered through the glass of the French windows into Neal Maclean's sitting room. There was nothing much to see. Two sofas and a table with a lamp on it. A wood-burning stove in the corner. On the far side of the room, an archway led back through to the kitchen.

As he turned away to look out over the beach, he saw reflected light flashing several times from the far shore, and shielded his eyes from the sun to see a figure standing in front of a caravan, binoculars raised and pointed in their direction. "Who the hell's that?" he said.

Donnie followed his gaze. "Oh, that's Buford. An Englishman. Claims to be a traveler. The locals have asked us repeatedly to shift him, but there's nothing we can do." He lifted his cap to scratch his head. "We've had several complaints from folk that he's been spying on them with those binoculars of his, but when we ask him about it he just says he's birdwatching." He replaced his cap. "Seems to know his stuff, too. North Harris, apparently, has the highest concentration of nesting golden eagles in Europe. So he told me when I went to speak to him. I've lived here all my life and I didn't know that."

"Can I help you?" A sharp voice made them both turn to see a small, elderly lady standing at the end of the house. She wore knitted leggings and pink trainers, and a quilted body warmer over a green cardigan. Her silvered hair was drawn tightly back and gathered in a bun.

Gunn went to greet her, hand outstretched to shake hers. "Detective Sergeant George Gunn, from Stornoway, ma'am." He half-turned toward Donnie. "And Sergeant Donnie Morrison from Tarbert. We were looking for Mr. Maclean."

"He's not here," she said, still eyeing them suspiciously.

Gunn said, "And you are . . . ?"

"Flora Macdonald. I live across the road there, and Mr. Maclean rents this house from me. Are you a Gaelic speaker, Mr. Gunn?"

"I'm afraid I'm not."

He clearly went down in her estimation. "Pity. Though you've certainly got the *blas.*" She looked toward Donnie. "Mr. Morrison?"

To Gunn's consternation, Donnie responded in Gaelic, and the two of them had a brief exchange that was warmer than hers with Gunn. Then Donnie turned to him. "She'd be happy to make us a cup of tea up at the house and answer any questions we might care to ask."

Gunn smiled coolly. "Thank you, ma'am." And wondered why she couldn't have said that to him in English.

It was hard to tell whether Mrs. Macdonald's house was an old one remodeled, or a recent build. Gunn suspected the former. It was toasty warm, and double glazing protected them from both the wind and the sound of it. Although modern in its insulation and finish, it was like stepping back half a century when the policemen walked inside, Mrs. Macdonald's yappy little dog running about between their legs and snapping at their ankles. There was a clash between the floral wallpaper and the rose-patterned carpet. The furniture itself came, it seemed, from another era altogether. Soft, worn sofa and armchairs with embroidered antimacassars on the backs and arms, and cushions so giving it felt like they were trying to swallow you. Darkwood furniture polished to a shine. A dresser, a table, an old bookcase laden with china plates. A traditional tiled fireplace, with peat smoldering in the hearth, which filled the room with the timeless reek of the islands.

Gunn sank into the settee and wondered how he was ever going to get out of it. Donnie, having suspected there might be a problem, remained standing. "Milk, sugar?" the old lady said, as she went through to the kitchen.

"Both," Gunn called after her.

"Not for me," Donnie said.

She called back to them, "This house is built on the site of the original crofthouse, you know. Not the blackhouse. You'll see the remains of that out the back. The croft itself extends right down to the shore, and my son had Dune Cottage built on it for the rental. To keep me in my old age."

"And has it?" Gunn said.

Mrs. Macdonald appeared at the kitchen door, the sound of the kettle fizzing behind her. "Oh, son, it's been a marvelous investment. I get a thousand a week for it during the season."

"But Mr. Maclean has it on a long-term let?"

"Yes, he has. Been here . . . now, let me see . . ." Her eyes darted sightlessly around the room as she made the calculation. "About eighteen months. Arrived early spring, last year. We gave him a good rate, too, because in the winter months it would usually lie empty, and it made the administration of it a lot easier."

"But he's not here just now, you said."

"No, he's not." And when she didn't volunteer to tell them where he was, Gunn sighed and asked. "Och, he's away to the mainland, Mr. Gunn."

"You're expecting him back, though?"

"Well, he didn't say he wouldn't be. Though his let runs out in about four weeks." A whistling from the kitchen distracted her. "That's the kettle now." And she disappeared back into it.

Gunn raised his voice a little. "Do you have an address for him?"

"No, I don't." Her voice came back through the open door. "Funny thing, we never dealt with him directly. The booking was made through an agency and paid for up front with a bank transfer. He just turned up one day and moved in."

"And what's he like?" Gunn glanced at

Donnie, who had started wandering around the living room, examining ornaments on the shelves, occasionally picking one up to look at it. He was paying not the least attention to the conversation.

"Oh, a nice enough young man, Mr. Gunn. Keeps himself to himself, mind. Except, of course, for . . ." She broke off and Gunn waited patiently for her to finish. But she didn't. And she then appeared carrying a tray from the kitchen, laden with teapot, cups and saucers, milk jug and sugar bowl. All in chintzy china. She laid it down on the shiny surface of the coffee table.

"Except for what, Mrs. Macdonald?"

She started to pour. "I shouldn't really gossip, Mr. Gunn." Though Gunn could tell that's exactly what she was going to do. She dropped her voice to conspiratorial. "His relationship with her along the road."

Donnie paused, a china figurine held in his hand, interest finally piqued.

"Her along the road being . . . ?" Gunn prompted her.

"Mrs. Harrison." She stood up and drew in her chin. "Shameless, she is. In and out of his house —" she corrected herself — "*my* house — at all hours of the day and night. And right under the nose of her husband, too."

212

Gunn cocked an eyebrow. "So she and Mr. Maclean are having an affair?"

"I really couldn't say, Mr. Gunn. But anyone who's been watching the goings-on across the road would be entitled to draw their own conclusions." She handed a cup and saucer to Gunn. "Help yourself to milk and sugar." Then she turned to hand a cup to Donnie, who quickly replaced the figurine and grasped the saucer with both hands.

Gunn struggled to escape the clutches of the sofa to perch on the edge of it and milk and sugar his tea. "And her name is . . . ?"

"Sally. And her husband, Jon. They stay in the big house at the top of the hill. The one with the glass front. Incomers, too. But just renters like Mr. Maclean."

As he stirred his tea, Gunn said, "Have you noticed anything odd about Mr. Maclean's behavior recently, Mrs. Macdonald?"

She frowned. "Odd in what way?"

"Well, anything out of the ordinary."

"There's nothing very ordinary about Mr. Maclean, Detective Inspector." And Gunn noticed she had promoted him. "Says he's here to write a book, though I've never seen any evidence of it, and he doesn't seem to spend much time writing."

"A book about what?"

"The disappearance of those poor lighthouse men on the Flannan Isles." Though their disappearance was more than a century old, she spoke as if she knew them personally. "He was back and forth to the islands quite a lot, by all accounts."

Gunn and Donnie exchanged looks. "So he has a boat, then?" Gunn said.

"Well, he must have." She paused to think about it. "Yes, he does. Because I met him on the road the other day and he said he'd had an accident with it."

"What kind of accident?"

"He didn't say. But he was in some state, Mr. Gunn. Soaked to the skin, and wearing one of yon bright orange life-jackets. Came up from the beach, he did, shivering so much he could hardly speak. Bleeding from his head, too."

"When was this?"

"Oh, let me think . . . About five days ago, it would be. He hardly even seemed to know me."

"I don't suppose you'd know where he keeps this boat?"

"I really couldn't say, Mr. Gunn. Tea's not too strong for you, is it?"

"No, no, it's fine, thanks." Gunn sipped at it. "Is there anything else you can tell me about him? How he spends his days when he's not writing? I imagine there's not a lot to do around here."

"Well, he's never once been to the church, I can tell you that. Godless folk they are that come from the mainland." She raised her cup to her lips, then lowered it again without drinking. "He goes for long walks with that chocolate-colored Lab of his. Frequently on the beach, though he heads up quite often over the coffin road."

Gunn had heard of the coffin road, and knew that these days it was a trekking route for hill walkers. "What's up there?"

She shrugged. "Nothing. Rocks and heather and a few wee lochs and cairns. Though it's a long time since I walked the coffin road myself."

"I suppose he must have taken his dog with him to the mainland?"

"No, I've seen Mrs. Harrison out walking it, so he must have left it with them."

Which suggested to Gunn that his intention was to return. "Anything else you can tell me about him? Does he have visitors?"

"Not that I've seen." She blew on her tea then took a sip. "But he's back and forth all summer to the Post Office in Tarbert with wee packages."

"What sort of packages?"

"Well, they're not big, but, you know, quite bulky. He uses yon padded envelopes."

"How often?"

"Every week or so, I'd say. I don't always see him leaving, myself, but I have a friend at the Post Office, Mary Macleod, who tells me he's in there all the time. He has one of those PO boxes, you know? I can't imagine why; there's a perfectly good postal delivery to the house. Mary says he's in and out all the time, from May to September, but hardly ever in the winter." She sipped pensively on her tea. "Never goes up the coffin road in the winter months either, or very rarely, anyway. Not that I blame him. Very exposed to the weather up there, it is."

Gunn placed his cup and saucer carefully back on the tray and stood up with difficulty. He searched in his pockets to retrieve the photograph of the dead man, taken at the mortuary the previous night. He held it out for her to look at. "Do you know this man, Mrs. Macdonald? Has he ever been a visitor at Dune Cottage?"

She frowned. "He doesn't look very well." Then shook her head. "No, I've never seen him before. And I've a good memory for faces."

Gunn slipped it back in his pocket and handed her a dog-eared business card. "I'd be obliged, Mrs. Macdonald, if you could give me a call when Mr. Maclean gets back."

She took the card and examined it carefully. "I knew a Gunn once. From South Uist, she was." She hesitated, pursing her lips slightly. "A Catholic." Though she didn't ask, the question was in the eyes that she turned toward Gunn.

"Church of Scotland," he said. And she nodded, apparently satisfied.

"So what's all this about, then?" She glanced from one to the other. "Has he done something he shouldn't?"

Gunn scratched his cheek, and fleetingly recalled Professor Wilson's aspersions about his facial growth. "No, no, nothing like that, Mrs. Macdonald. Routine stuff." He hesitated. "I don't suppose that you would mind if we took a wee look around his house?"

She folded her arms, only too aware that he had just fobbed her off. "Well, you'd suppose wrong, Mr. Gunn. It may be my house, but since Mr. Maclean has it long-term it's effectively his. You'll have to get his permission if you want to go inside it."

They stood on the road outside, with the wind whistling about them. Donnie pulled his cap low over his brow to stop it from blowing off, but Gunn had given up the unequal struggle to keep his hair in place and spoke animatedly into his mobile phone with tendrils of black hair waving about his head like the tentacles of a sea anemone. When he finished his call, he hung up and slipped the phone thoughtfully into his pocket. "I've asked them to get a search warrant from the Sheriff, but it might be a while. You'd best head on back to Tarbert, Donnie, and I'll give you a call when we get the go-ahead."

He watched Donnie's blue and white wending its way past the cemetery along the single-track toward the main road, before turning and walking up the hill to the house with the glass front. There was a Volvo estate parked in the drive, and he walked up to the door of a porch that rose in a double pitch to the second floor like a two-story conservatory. He rang the bell and turned to take in the view. A handful of small clouds raced across acres of blue, chasing their shadows over the sands below. On the far machair, he could see the Seilebost primary school, and wondered how it must have been to grow up and go to school in such a place. Though he imagined that generations of kids had probably taken it quite for granted, and only with the experience born of life and age would they have come to understand how privileged they had been.

He turned as the door opened to find himself looking at an attractive young woman with short dark hair. She cocked her head, eyes wide and quizzical, and smiled. "Hello. Can I help you?"

"Detective Sergeant George Gunn," he said. "From Stornoway. I wonder if I might have a few words."

"Of course." She opened the door wide. "Come in, come in."

He followed her through a hall flooded with light from the conservatory, and into a sitting room with a large picture window looking out across the bay. A young man was sitting smoking in an armchair by the fire, and he stood up, stubbing out his cigarette as they entered. He cast an inquiring look toward his wife, who shrugged and said, "Detective Sergeant Gunn would like to talk to us."

The young man seemed startled. "Police? What could you possibly want to talk to us about?"

A chocolate Labrador, which had been stretched out in front of the fire, eased himself to his feet and came snuffling around Gunn's legs. Gunn absently ruffled his head. "It was actually Neal Maclean I was looking for, but I hear he's gone to the mainland."

"Yes," said the young woman. "We're looking after Bran while he's away."

"And you are Sally and Jon Harrison, is that correct?"

"Yes," Jon said. "Is there a problem? Is Neal okay?"

"As far as I know, sir. We're just making some routine inquiries."

"About what?" Sally, it seemed to Gunn, had paled a little.

"We found a body on Eilean Mòr, out on the Flannan Isles, Mrs. Harrison. And I understand Mr. Maclean was a frequent visitor out there."

Jon said, "Yes, he was. He's writing a book." Then, "A body? Whose body?"

Gunn retrieved the photograph of the dead man and showed them it. "Do you know him?" He watched carefully as they both took a good look but shook their heads, and he saw no sign of recognition in their eyes.

"Who is he?" Jon asked.

"We don't know yet, sir. But Mr. Maclean was seen near where the body was found a couple of days ago, and we'd just like to ask him about anything he might have seen. Did he give you any idea when he might be back?"

The couple exchanged glances and she

220

shrugged. "No," she said. "He didn't. We're not that close, really. Just neighbors who share the odd drink."

Gunn glanced down at Bran and ruffled the dog's neck. "Close enough for him to leave his dog in your care, though."

Jon said, "He knows how fond we are of Bran. And it's no trouble at all, really."

Gunn avoided direct eye contact with Sally. "So what do you know about Mr. Maclean?"

"Very little, really," Jon said. "We've only been here for a year. Neal arrived about six months before us." He smiled awkwardly. "We incomers tend to stick together."

"He's on a sabbatical of some kind," Sally said. "To write his book."

"Sabbatical from what?"

They both shrugged, and it was Jon who responded. "He didn't say. He's a pretty private sort of bloke, and you kind of know instinctively when not to ask."

"But you know he was going back and forth to the Flannan Isles?"

"Yes, of course."

"In his own boat?"

"Well, whether he owns it, or he's just chartered it, I really couldn't say. But, yes, he has one." Jon glanced again at Sally.

"And he kept it where?" Gunn asked.

"Rodel," Sally said.

Gunn hesitated, and knew that this would be embarrassing. "Would you mind, Mr. Harrison, if I had a word in private with your wife?"

Jon and Sally looked at each other in surprise. He said, "What on earth for?"

Gunn smiled awkwardly. "Well, if I were to say, then I wouldn't need to speak to her in private, would I?"

Jon became defensive. "There's nothing you can't say to my wife in front of me."

Gunn glanced at Sally, a wordless appeal for help, but there was none forthcoming. She said, "I'm perfectly happy to answer anything you might ask in the presence of my husband."

Gunn's mouth was dry as he turned toward Sally. "I've been led to believe, Mrs. Harrison, that you and Mr. Maclean have some kind of . . . relationship."

Jon frowned, preempting any response from his wife. "Bollocks! Who told you that?"

"You've been speaking to that nosy old cow down the road, haven't you?" Sally said, her face flushed, and Gunn couldn't tell whether it was from anger or embarrassment. "Curtains twitching every time we're in and out the house."

Gunn said, "I thought you weren't regular visitors."

"We're not," Jon said. "But I'm back and forward to the mainland on business, and I know that Sally sometimes pops in for a drink with Neal. Only natural. But folk round here like to put their own twisted construction on things."

Gunn wondered if that were true, or whether he might have got a different response had he been able to speak to Sally on her own. But there seemed no point in pursuing it any further now. "Well, I'm sorry to have troubled you," he said. And he fumbled through his pockets, the nylon of his anorak swishing loudly as he searched for another business card. When he finally found one, he handed it to Sally. "I'd be obliged if you'd let me know if you hear from him, or ask him to give me a call himself when he gets back."

She took it, avoiding his eye. "Of course."

At the door, he turned and said, "By the way, what is it, exactly, that you are doing here?"

"We're on a sabbatical of sorts ourselves," Jon said. "A year out."

"And what business are you in, back on the mainland?"

"Concrete." Jon forced a smile. "Up to

223

my neck in it. Have to go back to Manchester every so often to make sure the mixer's still turning."

Gunn nodded. "Well, thanks for your help."

Outside, he thrust his hands deep into the pockets of his anorak and hunched against the wind as he walked back down the road. That they were both lying about her relationship with Neal seemed entirely possible, although whether they were simply in denial about a fracture in their own relationship or there was some more sinister motive, he couldn't judge. Whatever the truth, he didn't much care for either of them.

He checked his watch. There was still plenty of time to get to the Post Office at Tarbert, but first he wanted a quick chat with the traveler who had installed himself on the far machair and liked to watch folk through binoculars.

Beyond the metaled road, the path that led down on to the horned peninsula at the far side of the bay was little more than two sand-filled tire tracks. Gunn bumped his car over the humps and dips and wondered if he would ever manage to get back again.

It was hopelessly exposed here to all the incoming weather. Not a place, he thought, that you would choose to site a caravan. Certainly not on a permanent basis. And when he arrived, he saw immediately how Buford had secured it by roping it all around to metal stakes driven deep into the sandy soil. There was a radio mast on the lee side of the mobile home, also pegged down with guys, and a small generator. A large satellite dish was securely bolted to the southeast corner. Gunn wondered what kind of "traveler" it was who watched satellite TV and required high-tech radio comms.

An old, battered Land Rover with a canvas roof sat parked a few yards away. Gunn opened his car door and stepped out into the wind that drove in off the Sound of Taransay, and wondered how much more exposed it might be here if the island itself weren't there. He crossed first to the Land Rover and rested his hand briefly on the engine cowling. It was stone cold. Then he turned to look at the caravan. It had seen better days, scarred and dented by who knew how many miles. The nearside tire looked almost flat. A washing line extended from the caravan to a securely fixed pole, and several items of gray-looking underwear strained in the wind at the clips that held them. A salt-bleached wooden box, pegged to the ground, stood below the door, acting as a step. Gunn leaned beyond it and knocked firmly on the door itself. He waited nearly half a minute before knocking again. Still there was no response. He tried lifting the handle, but the door was locked. Unusual for these parts. Still, the man was an incomer and wasn't to know that no one around here ever locked their doors. There was no reason to. All Gunn's instincts, however, were telling him that the man called Buford hadn't gone off somewhere and locked up behind him. With his Land Rover sitting there, and no sign of the man on the road, Gunn had the strongest suspicion that Buford was, in fact, at home, had locked the door from the inside and was simply ignoring Gunn's knock.

He pursed his lips and raised his voice above the wind. "Mr. Buford. This is the police; open up, please." But it was only the wind that responded, incessant in its eternally mournful cry. Gunn stood for some moments, nursing his frustration, before returning to his car, turning it in a wide circle, then bumping back along the path toward the road.

The Harris Post Office in Tarbert was housed in a harled bungalow with a gray-tiled roof that stood below the anonymously roughcast Free Presbyterian Church of Scotland. Almost opposite, a house with rusted yellow gates displayed incongruously ornamental lambs atop each gatepost. The Post Office was set halfway up the hill above the town, and, beyond the shambles of parked cars and red Post Office vans, Gunn could see the bright yellow railings of the car ferry terminal below.

He passed a row of black bins lined up along the outside wall and ducked into a dark interior, lit in patches by burned-out sunlight that fell through the windows of the cluttered little office.

Mary Macleod was younger than her friend from Luskentyre, but only by a few years. "I'm just part time now," she told Gunn quite happily when he showed her his warrant card. "But I've not much else to do with my time, so I spend most of it here. I've worked for the Post Office close on thirty years, since my husband died and the children went off to make their own lives." But her face clouded when Gunn asked her about Neal Maclean. "Oh, I don't know that I'm at liberty to divulge confidential details about customers, Mr. Gunn," she said.

Gunn cocked one eyebrow. "That doesn't seem to have stopped you from relaying them to Flora Macdonald at Luskentyre,

Mrs. Macleod."

She flushed to the roots of her silver hair. "I'm sure I didn't tell her anything I shouldn't have."

"Then you won't mind telling me, too."

She glanced about self-consciously, aware of the eyes of customers and staff upon them. "You'd better come through." And she led him into a small private office, its wall pinned with posters and leaflets. "What exactly is it you want to know?"

"Mrs. Macdonald tells me that Mr. Maclean is in the habit of sending regular packages from here."

The old lady nodded. "Yes. At least once a week. Sometimes twice."

"But only during the summer?"

"Well, I couldn't say exactly when he starts and stops. He's only been here two seasons. But I can tell you that we hardly saw him all last winter."

"And when was he last in?"

She thought about it. "About two weeks ago, I'd say."

"And how does he send these packages? Registered post, or . . . ?"

"Special Delivery."

"So you'll have a record of the address he sends them to?"

"Well, I suppose it'll be in the computer.

But I wouldn't be at liberty to divulge that information to you, unless you had some kind of official authorization."

"Well, I can get that if I think it's necessary, Mrs. Macleod. But perhaps you might just remember. Off the top of your head, that is. Since he's been in so often."

She glanced nervously toward the door. "We handle so much mail here, Mr. Gunn, I really couldn't say."

But he let it hang, and she became uncomfortable.

"It was somewhere in Edinburgh, I remember that. Some kind of laboratory. But where, exactly, I really don't remember."

Gunn nodded. "Mrs. Macdonald told me he had a PO box here."

"Oh, did she?" And something in Mrs. Macleod's tone told him that she would be having words with her old friend from Luskentyre.

"So he has all his mail delivered here?"

"No, no. Most of it goes to Dune Cottage with the postie. The mail that comes to his PO box is usually Special Delivery, too. From the laboratory he sends his packages to. Though he doesn't always pick it up straight away."

"Is there anything waiting for him to pick up right now?"

She gave him a look. "No, there is not, Mr. Gunn. And even if there were, I'd need permission to let you see it." Then she relented a little. "He's not had anything for about ten days or so."

Gunn reached into the inside pocket of his anorak and produced the photograph of the man whose body they had found on Eilean Mòr. "Have you ever seen this gentleman in here?"

She lifted the reading glasses that hung on a chain around her neck and put them on to squint at it closely. But she shook her head. "No, Mr. Gunn, he doesn't look at all familiar to me."

The bright early sunshine which had accompanied Gunn on his drive down from Stornoway was intermittent now as cumulus bubbled up from the southwest, blown in on a strengthening wind and casting more shadow than sunlight across the southern half of the island.

Occasional rain spots spattered on his windscreen as he headed down through Northton and past the Seallam genealogy center, to Leverburgh. But it didn't come to anything, and was brighter when he reached the southern coastline and headed through the hills on the long straight road to Rodel.

It was a long time since Gunn had been here. He had once brought his wife on a weekend drive from Stornoway, and they had eaten the most marvelous seafood in the Rodel Hotel. But he imagined it would only be a matter of weeks now before the hotel would shut down for the season, and the little harbor below it was quite deserted. Despite the absence of people, there were plenty of boats. Fishing boats and motor launches, a couple of sailing boats and a handful of rowing boats which had seen better days, all lined up side by side, nudging each other playfully on the incoming swell, pulling on ropes and creaking in the wind. Many more boats than Gunn remembered from his previous visit.

He was about to walk up to the hotel when a voice called from the far side of the harbor. "Can I help you?" Gunn turned to see a man walking round the quay toward him, and could only assume he had come from one of the boats, because there had been nobody there a moment ago. He wore heavy boots and yellow oilskin over-trousers, and an intricately patterned Eriskay jumper. His weathered face was young, but thinning hair aged him.

Gunn showed him his warrant card. "That all depends," he said. "You are . . . ?"

"Coinneach Macrae." He held out a hand to shake Gunn's and very nearly crushed it. "I run a boat-charter business out of the harbor here."

"Ahhh," Gunn said. "Didn't think there were this many boats last time I visited."

"It's my first year at Rodel," Macrae said. "Used to be based at Leverburgh, but Rodel's a bigger attraction for the tourists." He turned and ran his eye around the harbor. "Doesn't come much prettier than this."

Gunn nodded. "Gone well, then, has it? Your first season."

Macrae's shoulders rose and fell noncommittally. "Could have been worse. So what can I help you with, Detective Sergeant?"

"I'm wondering if you know a fella called Neal Maclean."

"I do indeed."

"He keeps his boat here, I believe."

"He does that."

Gunn turned toward the boats tethered in the harbor. "And which is his?"

"It's not here."

Gunn frowned. "So where is it?"

Macrae ran a hand back through what was left of sandy hair. "No idea. It's all very odd, really."

"What is?"

"Well . . . five, maybe six days ago, he went off to the Flannans, like he quite often does. But he never came back. His car sat parked over there in front of the hotel for a day or so. Then he shows up with a woman I've seen him with a few times. A Mrs. Harrison." He crinkled blue eyes and turned them skywards, thinking hard. "Sally," he said suddenly. "That's what he calls her. Anyway, they arrive in her car to get his, and he seems surprised that his boat's not here." Macrae took in Gunn's expression and laughed. "I know, I know. Sounds crazy. How would he not know his boat wasn't here? Anyway, she jumps in with this cock and bull story about them having berthed it up at Uig, and he shuts up. I didn't believe a word of it."

"So where do you think his boat is, then?"

"I wouldn't have the foggiest idea, Mr. Gunn. But he shows up here again the next day wanting to hire one of mine."

"And you hired him one?"

"Why wouldn't I? He's an experienced sailor, and he paid me in cash right there and then."

"So that would have been when? Two days ago?"

"No . . ." Macrae scratched his chin. "Must have been the day before that. I'll

233

have a record of it in the books."

"And did he say where he was going?"

"Aye, the Flannans. I was a wee bit worried, because the weather was on the turn."

"But he brought it back?"

"Oh, aye, he did. A few hours later. Looking like he'd seen a ghost, too. Face so white it was green. You know, like folk get when they're seasick."

Gunn knew only too well.

"Only, a man like him doesn't get seasick, Mr. Gunn. So I've no idea what his problem was. But he was in no mood for chitchat, and he was off like a bat out of hell."

Gunn dug out his photograph of the dead man. "Ever seen this fella at all?"

Macrae took it and examined it closely before handing it back. "Afraid not." He paused. "Is that the dead man, then?"

Gunn scowled. "How do you know about that?"

And Macrae grinned. "It's a small island, Mr. Gunn. You should know that better than anyone. It bothered me, you know, Mr. Maclean's story about taking his boat up to Uig. So I called Murray at Seatrek last night, just out of curiosity. Turns out Maclean's boat's not at Miavaig at all. And, of course, that's when he told me all about taking you folk out to Eilean Mòr yesterday, and what it is you found there."

Gunn slipped the photo back into his inside pocket and breathed his annoyance. "Tell me, Mr. Macrae, how would you get out to the Flannan Isles if you didn't have a boat yourself?"

Macrae pushed his hands deep into his pockets and sucked air in through his teeth. "There's a few excursion operators that run trips out to St. Kilda and the Flannans, Mr. Gunn. One at Leverburgh, another at Tarbert, and then of course there's Seatrek itself."

"Scotland The Brave" began playing in Gunn's pocket, and he fumbled to pull out his mobile. "Excuse me," he said, and turned to walk, swishing, away along the quay to take the call. It was the desk sergeant at Stornoway to say he had just dispatched a constable to Luskentyre with the search warrant from the Sheriff.

CHAPTER FIFTEEN

It is after three thirty when I drive off the ferry from Uig on to the ramp at Tarbert. Brightly colored yellow railings guide the disembarking traffic on to the road that leads out of the town, past the Harris tweed shop. It is spitting rain, and my windscreen wipers smear it across the fly-spattered glass.

It is hard to say that I am glad to be back, but this feels more like home to me than anywhere I went to in Edinburgh. Wherever I might truly belong, I have spent the last eighteen months of my life on this island, and so there is a sense, however illusory, of returning to the womb. Here, for better or worse, there are people who know me, or at least know me in the part I have been playing this last year and a half.

But, during all the long hours of the drive back from Edinburgh, I have been wrestling with the concept that I have no name I can answer to. The only name I am known by is that of a dead man. Since I have no past, I am without a present. And without a present I have no future. It is a thought that has driven a wedge of depression deep into my consciousness, and I am falling into a trough of sheer despondency.

I am tired now, my concentration shot, and I almost collide with another vehicle as I turn south on the main road. The blast of the other car's horn sets my heart racing and clears from my mind the cloud that has been obscuring my immediate future in all its uncertainty. I have no idea what I am going to do when I get back to the cottage. I desperately want the comfort of Sally's arms around me, soft and warm. I want to breathe in her scent, drift off in her embrace, like a child. And, who knows, maybe waken with tomorrow's dawn, memory fully restored, knowing exactly who I am and why I am here.

Everything on the drive to Luskentyre feels reassuringly familiar. The sign on the left for the Episcopalian Church, the road signs for Rodel and Geocrab and Manais. The Golden Road. Even the roadworks on the brae leading down to the fabulous expanse of silver and turquoise in the bay.

The bizarrely wind-sculpted Scots pines to the right of the single-track seem to be welcoming me home as I turn at the cottage before the cemetery and come up over the rise to see a phalanx of police and other vehicles crowded on to the tarmac behind my house.

It comes like a punch in the gut. Debilitating and painful, suffusing my entire being with a sense of utter hopelessness, and very nearly robbing me of the ability to turn the wheel and guide my car over the cattle grid. For the briefest of moments I consider driving past, as if just passing by. But the road goes nowhere, except to the beach at the end of it, and I would have to turn and come back. And then what? I have to face up to the reality of my situation some time.

As I draw in behind all the other vehicles parked in my drive, I cut the motor and close my eyes. There can only be one possible reason for this congregation of policemen at my house. And I see once again the face of the man I found dead in the ruined chapel on Eilean Mòr, the blood and brain tissue, and know that they, too, think that I killed him.

The afternoon is blustery, gray and depressing as I step out of my car. The clouds over the beach are low, almost purple on their underside. The wind is fierce and I feel it filling my mouth and bringing tears to my eyes. A uniformed policeman climbs out of one of the cars and approaches me. "Excuse me, sir, what's your business here?"

And I hear myself saying, "I live here."

I see his eyes open wide. "You're Mr. Maclean?" I nod, knowing that it is absolutely not who I am. "Better come with me, sir." I feel his fingers closing around my upper arm, and he is leading me down the drive toward the door of the cottage, which is standing wide open. We reach the foot of the steps and I can see several uniformed officers moving about inside my house. The constable who has my arm calls, "George!" And after a moment a stocky man in a black quilted anorak appears at the door. His face is pink and round and shiny, and a black widow's peak cuts a V into his forehead. He looks at the constable, then at me, and the constable says, "Detective Sergeant Gunn, this is Mr. Maclean."

I see Gunn's expression change in an instant. He looks at me again, but with different eyes this time. "Mr. Neal Maclean?" he says.

"What's going on?" I ask, although I know perfectly well.

Gunn comes down the steps and a wedge of his gelled hair lifts up in the wind. "Three days ago, Mr. Maclean, you were seen by several witnesses, running from the old ruined chapel at Eilean Mòr, out on the Flannan Isles. Yesterday, the body of a dead man was discovered in that building. A death we are treating as murder. I'm wondering how you could have entered that building without seeing the body and, if you did, why you didn't report it."

Thoughts tumble through my head, disordered and incoherent. I know that I have to come up with a convincing story, but I am finding it almost impossible to think clearly. And it occurs to me in that moment that I should just tell him the truth. The whole truth. What kind of relief might that be? But equally, I realize that the truth will sound even more unlikely than anything I might invent. And it seems to me now that the black cloud which has been masking my memory since I washed ashore on the beach must be obscuring something worse even than murder. Because it is still there. So I rush into a lie. "You probably know by now, Detective Sergeant, that I am writing a book on the disappearance of the Flannan Isles lighthouse men."

"So I've been told, Mr. Maclean." There is a strange little sardonic smile playing about his lips. "I'd be interested in seeing that manuscript, sir, if you wouldn't mind showing me it a little later." And I know he knows that I am not writing a book. Still, we both keep up the pretense.

"Of course," I say. "Anyway, I was out at the lighthouse for a bit of research and got caught in a squall. I was going to take shelter in the chapel, but the rain eased off a bit, and I decided to make a dash for the boat instead. So I never actually went into the building."

That little sardonic smile has gone. He seems quite impassive now, and it is impossible to read anything into his face. But I am sure he doesn't believe me. After a moment he nods his head beyond me, toward the garden shed. "Would you mind unlocking that shed for me, sir?"

I turn and glance at the shed, surprised. The large padlock hooked firmly through the clasps is locked. I remember that I couldn't get into it when I was looking for stepladders. "I don't have the key," I say, and fish my keys out my pocket. An ignition key for the car, and a couple of smaller keys for the house. "These are the only ones I have."

Gunn purses his lips. "The owner of the house tells us that a key to the padlock on the garden shed was among the keys that she gave you when you first moved in."

I shrug. This is probably true. But I have no idea where that key might be now. "Then I must have mislaid it," I say. "I've never had any cause to use the shed." And no sooner do I say it than I wonder if I have.

"You won't mind if we force the lock then, sir?"

"Not at all." There is a sick feeling evolving in my stomach. "Perhaps the owner won't be too pleased, though." I cannot imagine how my attempt at a smile comes across to the policemen standing watching me. Their expressions remain grave.

Gunn nods to one of the uniforms, and he goes to the boot of the nearest vehicle, returning with a wheel brace, a single length of iron with a socket wrench at one end. The constable steps past us and goes to the shed, inserting the other end through the loop of the padlock and levering it hard against the door. The sound of splintering wood is quite clearly audible above the howling of the wind, and the clasps held together by the padlock rip free of the door, screws and all. And I wonder why anyone ever bothered to padlock it.

The officer who is still holding my arm passes me over to Gunn, who leads me to the shed. With his free hand he forces it open against the wind, then uses his body to keep it there, before reaching inside to feel for a light switch. When he finds it, the late afternoon gloom is banished and the darkness of the interior is thrown into sudden, sharp, fluorescent relief.

For a moment, I could almost believe that the wind had stopped blowing. For, in that instant, I simply can't hear it. And I can feel the sense of shock and confusion all around me, as everyone crowds around to look inside.

The first thing that hits us all, I think, is the smell. The powerful, sweet, pungent odor of cedar wood and honey. And the reek of old smoke, like a cold chimney when you clean out the hearth. But we are distracted by what we see.

"Jesus," I hear someone say. "It's like a bloody laboratory."

And that's exactly what it is. A makeshift laboratory that must have cost a small fortune to equip. Worktops lining three sides, rows of shelves above them cluttered with bottles and jars and flasks. Pieces of equipment, large and small, on the worktops or on the floor. A scattering of microtweezers and scissors, micropipettes and rows of yellow tips in a bright red holder. Boxes of latex surgical gloves. To my amazement, much of it seems familiar to me. A handheld field microscope with an XY slide indexer. A white box, about the size of a laser printer, with a screen set into its beveled front. The make and model, Sure-Cycler 8800, is engraved into the plastic above the screen, and I know that this machine is used for amplifying DNA. A small freezer unit sits on the floor against the back wall, and, on the worktop above it, what looks like a fridge, with a black box set into the top of it. But I know that it is not a fridge. It is a digital image system used for DNA gel photography. I see the gel tank itself on the counter beside it, and its small black power pack.

There are piles of padded envelopes, kitchen scales, and larger, industrial hanging scales dangling from a hook on the wall. A MacBook Pro laptop computer sits next to an SLR digital camera set into a holding frame and bracket, and the wall above it is pinned with dozens of printout photographs of honeycomb frames. A laser printer/photocopier/scanner sits on a low table in one corner. Hive frames and foundations, and a shallow wooden drawer that I know to be a pollen trap, are propped all along the right-hand wall, from which hang a beekeeper's protective clothing. Hat and mask, gloves, jacket, wellington boots beneath them. There is a hive tool dangling from a hook, a smoker with its carrying cage and nozzle for directing smoke into the hive, and rolls of cardboard tied with string on a shelf next to a red plastic cigarette lighter engraved in white with the logo *Ergo*. The top shelf groans with jars of rich, amber honey. Makeshift wasp traps fashioned from old plastic Coke bottles hang from the ceiling. They are filled with clusters of drowned wasps, attracted into the shed by the honey in the jars, then drawn into the traps by a mix of jam and water. And black electric cables loop back and forth bringing power to sockets set at intervals along the worktops.

I can feel the skin of my face burning red as Gunn turns to look at me with the strangest sense of incomprehension in his eyes. "So you've never had cause to use the shed, sir?"

I cannot think of a single thing to say. The silence that hangs in the air is blown away in the wind, which I hear again, suddenly, as if someone has just pressed the un-mute button. I do not need to look around me to know that every eye is upon me. They have no idea that I am as lost for an explanation as they are. And I hear myself say, stupidly, "I can't explain it."

"May I see your hands, please?"

Confused, but compliant, I offer him my hands, and he takes them in his, turning them over, and I see the odd bee sting on my fingers. Small red lumps with tiny scabs at their center.

He lets go of my hands and takes me by the arm again. "Come with me please, sir." And he leads me through the silent, standing police officers, up the steps and into my house. Everything is in chaos as we pass through the boot room and into the kitchen. Beside the laptop on the kitchen table, the briefcase I found in the attic sits with its lid up, exposing the bundles of banknotes inside. The folder of newspaper cuttings on Neal Maclean is open, its contents spilled across the table. "Maybe you'll have more success in explaining this," he says. And hell simply opens up beneath my feet.

CHAPTER SIXTEEN

The skyline beyond the promenade that ran the length of the Portobello sands had probably not changed much since its heyday as a beach resort in the nineteenth century. Grand Victorian stone-built villas, and colorfully tarted terraces. Church spires and redbrick factory chimneys. For much of the twentieth century it had fallen out of fashion, only recently undergoing a renaissance that had seen the beach as crowded on a summer's day as in the old photographs taken in the late eighteen hundreds that Karen had found on the internet.

Now, on this gray, blustery September morning, she and her godfather were the only souls leaving tracks in the sand. It was where he had suggested they meet. An unlikely place, but Karen had taken the bus out from the center of town with butterflies colliding in her stomach. If Chris Connor had behaved oddly on her visit to the Geddes Institute, then his manner on the phone had been even stranger. Terse, almost monosyllabic. It was Karen's clear impression that he could barely contain his impatience to hang up. But they had, at least, arranged to meet, albeit in this most unexpected of places.

Beyond their initial greeting, they had walked together in silence. Karen had wanted simply to blunder into the conversation, but she sensed Connor's reticence, and forced herself to be patient. Bad weather out in the North Sea had driven seabirds back up the firth, and gulls wheeled overhead in the breeze, shrieking their anger at the sky. A little sunlight played through breaks in the cloud along the coastline of Fife on the far shore.

"M-my wife's left me," Connor said suddenly, and Karen was startled to a standstill. But he didn't seem to notice and kept walking, and she had to run to catch him up.

"Why?"

He shrugged. "She says I'm n-not who I used to be."

"But . . . why?" Karen struggled to make sense of this unexpected turn. "I mean, what's changed about you?"

He kept his eyes on some distant place that only he could see. "Everything, I suppose. Since your dad's death." He drew a deep breath. "We were compatible, I think, only because we were so different. M-me and your dad, that is. He was . . . cavalier. Adventurous. Strong. I . . . I admired him enormously. But he was also impetuous, Karen, sometimes to the point of just plain foolishness. Headstrong and, well, for want of a better word, arrogant. No one was going to push him around, tell him what to do."

Karen was wide-eyed and breathless. This was all new to her. A different picture of her dad. And she realized that the man she had known as her father was also someone else, someone she hadn't really known at all. "And you?"

For the first time, her godfather smiled. "Oh, I was the sensible one. Conservative. Safe. Maybe that's what he liked about me. I . . . I moderated his excesses. I was his anchor. Everywhere he went, he wanted me to go, too. Which is how, I suppose, we c-came to follow such a similar academic route, and both ended up working at the Geddes Institute." He turned to look at Karen for the first time. "Losing him was like losing the better, stronger half of me." And she was shocked to see his eyes fill with tears. He looked away quickly. "You see,

I . . . I knew what he knew. And if he didn't have the strength to deal with it . . . if a man like your father could take his own life . . . To be honest, I don't know how I've got through these past two years. But a part of me died with him, Karen, and what was left couldn't be the man my wife had married, the man she wanted me to be. It's been . . ." He searched for a word to express it, but could only come up with the mundane. "Difficult."

Karen could no longer contain herself. "What do you mean, you knew what he knew? What did he know? Why did he kill himself?"

But he just shook his head. "It's not that simple, Karen. There are no easy answers."

"Well, give me the difficult ones, then." Her frustration lent an edge to her voice that made him turn, forgetting himself for a moment and smiling fondly, his hesitancy disappearing like smoke in the wind.

"You really are just like him, you know. I couldn't get over that the other day when you came to the Geddes." Then his smile faded, and his gaze wandered off toward the far shore. "Your dad had been working on a study of bees, funded by Ergo."

"Bees? I didn't know he was interested in bees."

"He wasn't, particularly, before undertaking the study." Now he looked at her quite directly. "Wh-what do you know about bees, Karen?"

She shrugged. "They make honey. They sting you."

He raised a rueful eyebrow. "Not unless they absolutely have to. It kills a honey bee to sting you, did you know that?"

Karen shook her head.

"Unlike a wasp, or a bumble bee, which can sting you again and again, a honey bee's sting is barbed, so it hooks into your skin, and when they try to fly away it rips their insides out. Eviscerates them." He plunged his hands deep into the pockets of his coat, and his heels seemed to dig deeper into the wet sand with each step. The tide was well out now, and every so often they had to climb over the groynes that subdivided the beach. "There are more than twenty thousand different species of bee, most of which aren't even honey bees, but together they are the biggest single pollinators of plants on earth. You understand the process of pollination?"

Karen was indignant. "Of course I do. I got an A in biology. Transferring pollen from the male to the female reproductive organs of plants makes babies. It's all about sex, really."

He grinned and she knew she was making him think of her father again. "Exactly. And those babies are the fruits and nuts, or the vegetables and grain that feed us." The stutter had vanished as his passion kicked in. "Bees pollinate seventy of the roughly one hundred crop species that feed the world, Karen. Einstein was once quoted as saying that if the bee became extinct the human race would die out within four years. Apocryphal, of course, but not that far from the truth. Without the bee, there is no way we could sustain the current human and animal population of the planet. People would suffer from poor nutrition, increased disease. There would be mass starvation. Those of us left would have to survive on a radically reduced and very expensive diet. Workers would have to be employed on the grand scale to hand-pollinate plants. Can you imagine? But they've already started it in China. In the end, only the rich would be able to eat well."

"Wow." Karen tried to absorb all that her godfather was telling her. She had known, though she didn't know how, that bees were important, but just how important was news to her. "Wouldn't affect meat, though, I guess."

But Connor shook his head. "Oh, yes, it would." And she saw how there was fire again in his eyes, replacing the cataracts of uncertainty that had clouded them earlier. "The production of animal fodder is bee dependent, too. In the US alone, bees pollinate more than thirty million hectares of alfalfa that gets cut and bailed as hay for horses and cattle, and fermented as haylage for dairy cows. Without it, they would have to return to traditional grazing, winter feed would be poor, and meat production would plummet." He fixed her with staring eyes that seemed somehow to be seeking her approval.

Karen whistled softly. "Guess we can't do without the bee, then."

He drew a deep breath. "We might have to, Karen. The agrochem industry claims that bee populations have varied hugely over the centuries. Affected by disease, environmental change, any number of different factors. Which is true. But here's the thing: bees are dying off now faster than they've ever done in history." He stopped in his tracks and turned his face toward her. "Christ, Karen, between thirty and fifty percent of the bee population of the United

States alone is dying every year."

Karen found herself gripped by his intensity. "And we don't know why?"

"Well, yes. And no. A few of the causes we've identified and understand. Changes in farming practices, the destruction of natural habitat, disease, parasites. But other causes are a mystery. You know, in the US, they harness bees on an industrial scale to pollinate crops, truck them all over the country and sell their services to farmers. There's a phenomenon there that they call CCD. Colony Collapse Disorder. The bees simply vanish. Leave the hive and never return. No one knows why. But it's destroying that industry and threatening to ruin crops. There are barely enough of them left to pollinate the almond crop in California." He turned abruptly and started walking quickly toward the next groyne, and Karen almost had to run to keep up. "It is going to cost the US economy billions, Karen. Not millions. Billions! Replicate that on a worldwide scale and we're talking hundreds of billions." He gave a bitter little chuckle. "As with all things in this world, money's never far from the center of them."

Karen grabbed his arm to make him stop. "What's any of this got to do with my dad, Chris?"

He turned to face her and wild eyes searched hers. "You would think, wouldn't you," he said, "that, with so much at stake, everyone everywhere would be doing what they could to solve the problem, to protect the bees?"

"Well, why wouldn't they?"

"Money, Karen. Fucking money!" His voice rose almost to a shout, and Karen was startled, but more by his language than his tenor. She had never heard him swear before. Just as she had never heard her father use bad language. She supposed that adults did swear, just not in front of the children. But it still came as a shock to hear it. He relented, and uncertainty consumed him again. "I . . . I'm sorry."

Karen stood awkwardly, looking at him. And he wouldn't meet her eye. After a moment, she stepped in and put her arms around him. He tensed, then after a few seconds she felt him relax, and his arms slipped tentatively around her, and they stood in a long, silent embrace. Two solitary figures on an empty beach. Beyond them, somewhere out there in the firth, they had both lost someone they loved.

When, finally, they broke apart, she said, "Tell me."

He was pale now, and resigned somehow.

He nodded, and they resumed their walk toward the distant pavilion. But their pace was more leisurely now. He watched his feet as they walked, scliffing the wet, compacted sand left by the recently retreated tide, and she slipped her arm through his. She felt as close to her father in this moment as she had in years.

He said, "The project that Ergo had funded Tom to pursue was . . ." He forced a smile. "You'll laugh. It sounds so prosaic." And he put an emphasis on each of the words. "The impact of floral diversity on bee resilience and learning capacity." He looked at her and took in her expression. His laugh was spontaneous and genuine. "Yeah, exactly. In other words, they wanted to find out how poor diet affected the performance of bees." He hesitated. "But they wanted your dad to do something else, which I think was the real object of the exercise. You've heard of neonicotinoids?"

Karen shook her head. "Sounds like it might have something to do with tobacco."

"Close. It's actually a class of insecticides that are chemically similar to nicotine. They have unpronounceable names like *clothianidin* and *imidacloprid*. Anyway, a bunch of them got banned by the European Union about three years ago, because there was strong scientific evidence that treating crops with this stuff was harmful to bees. Some scientists were even claiming that it was the primary cause of the sudden decline in bee populations. Trouble is, there was no actual proof. No smoking gun. And the big agrochemical companies, Ergo among them, were furious. Loss of revenue from the banning of these products was running to billions a year."

Connor stopped suddenly and stooped to pick up a shell lodged in the sand. A classic small scallop shell. He turned it over in his fingers.

"Big corporations run the world, Karen. Biotech, agrochemical, oil. They are bigger than a lot of governments. And in certain cases they turn over more in profit than the GDP of many small countries. They wield enormous influence. Politicians and political parties, particularly in America, rely on them to fund election campaigns. They are powerful lobbyists. Which is why the US has not banned the use of neonicotinoids, and thousands of tons of the stuff are still being used on crops there every year. Biggest usage is on oilseed rape. They coat the seeds with insecticide, so that, when it germinates, the insecticide is diffused throughout the plant, including the nectar and pollen that's harvested by the bees."

"In spite of the danger to them?"

Connor laughed. "Well, of course, the agrochem companies say there *is* no danger. They produce all these studies showing that the level at which their insecticides are found in the environment has no effect on bees."

Karen raised a skeptical eyebrow. "Well, they would say that, wouldn't they?"

"Which is why Ergo was keen to have an independent researcher — your dad — show unequivocally that neonicotinoids do not kill bees, and are therefore not responsible for the decline in bee populations."

"And did he?"

Connor nodded. "He did. They got him to repeat an industry experiment that exposed bees to levels of insecticide one hundred and forty times higher than you would typically find in areas where the stuff had been used on crops. An absolutely toxic level of imidacloprid, which you might think would simply wipe out all the bees exposed to it. It didn't. Only about fifty percent died. A level they call LD50. And proof that, at normal levels, neonicotinoids were not at all toxic to bees."

"Wow. So what did my dad do?"

"Well, Ergo were keen to have him speak

out in support of his findings."

"And he did that?"

Connor sighed and nodded. "He published his research, Karen. Ergo put out press releases and made his findings available to every media outlet on the planet. He spoke at several industry conventions. Making him very unpopular with the environmental lobby." He shrugged. "I mean, your dad was a scientist, Karen. These were his findings."

Karen said, "Why do I have the feeling there's a *but* somewhere in our future?"

Connor's smile was rueful and sad. "Oh, yes. Remember the research project on the impact of floral diversity on bee resilience and learning capacity?"

"How could I forget?"

Now his smile widened with genuine amusement. "Well, Tom had handed that over to one of his students. A bright lad called Billy Carr. And since half of your dad's bees had survived his experiment, Billy borrowed them to use in his. He employed them as his control group. In other words, they were fed a normal diet, while another group of bees was given a restricted diet, so the effects of the poor diet could be compared with the normally fed control group." Connor spread his arms and his hands. "It was pure bloody chance, Karen. A complete accident. But, in the course of his experiment, Billy found that your dad's bees were the ones suffering from learning difficulties. They were unable to associate floral scent with the reward — the pollen and nectar they would find in the flower. Their memories were screwed. And, Karen, memory is everything to a bee. It's how they find their way to food and convey that information to other bees. It's how they find their way back to the hive. Without it they can't find tomorrow's food, and the colony in the hive breaks down."

Suddenly Karen saw the significance of it. "So the imidacloprid hadn't killed the bees directly, but it had left them brain-damaged."

"And unable to function properly. Exactly." Connor's face was shining as he took pleasure in Karen's intelligence. Her ability to see things clearly, and reason as her father had done. But, just as quickly, it clouded again, as if a shadow had passed directly over it. "But, for such an intelligent man, Tom could be so bloody naive."

"What do you mean?"

"Well, he and Billy took the results from that experiment and reran it, this time using bees that had only been exposed to environmental levels of the neonicotinoid. Same thing. The bees suffered neuronal brain damage and weren't able to forage properly for food. Tom went straight to Ergo to warn them that there was a major problem. Their neonic insecticides were fucking with bees' brains and leading ultimately to colony collapse." He threw back his head and hollered at the heavens. "So fucking stupid!"

Karen grabbed his arm. "What happened?"

"What happened, Karen, was that his whole damn world just fell apart. He barely even had time to draw breath before he found himself summoned by the director of the Geddes and told that he was being made redundant."

Karen was shocked. "And was he?"

Connor nodded vigorously. "Oh, yes. Totally unconnected with his research, they said. Cuts and natural wastage. And, of course, your dad being your dad, he accused them of trying to cover up his findings. Being scared of losing their research funding from Ergo. Which only hastened his departure. He was told to clear his desk and go. And when he threatened to publish the results of his research anyway, they had him escorted from the building. Security people came to his office and the labs and seized everything. Notes, results, computers, hard drives."

"You mean the results of his research were never published?"

"Never. And there was no way he could ever repeat the experiment. The cost of these things is prohibitive. Way beyond the means of any individual."

"I never knew he'd been sacked," Karen said. "I'm not even sure my mum did. Why wouldn't he have told us?"

Connor shrugged. He was still holding the shell in his hand. He looked at it briefly, then turned and hurled it into the water. The tide was turning. He resumed walking, and Karen slipped her arm through his again. They covered several hundred yards before Connor spoke again.

He said, "Billy Carr, the student who conducted the experiments with him, tried to smuggle stuff out to him in the weeks after he'd been kicked out."

"Weeks? How long after he'd been sacked did he kill himself?"

"Must have been a couple of months, Karen."

"Jesus . . ." She shook her head and wondered how he could have kept it from them for so long. And why.

"Anyway, Billy himself disappeared after about a month. No idea what happened to him. He just . . . vanished. Didn't turn up one day, and no one ever saw him again."

Karen was struck by a sudden, dreadful thought. "They didn't kill him, did they? My dad, I mean. Ergo. To stop him from publishing?" In her mind, it explained everything. The empty boat. The life jacket still aboard. And then she remembered the note. *Tell Karen I love her.*

Chris was shaking his head. "I don't think so, Karen. They're pretty damned ruthless, these big corporations, but murder? I doubt it. Your dad was depressed. Never saw him so low. He went to all the big environmental campaign organizations, like Friends of the Earth, Buglife, the Soil Association. Looking for funding to repeat the experiment. But none of them had the resources. In the end, I think he just gave up. They'd beaten him, and he had no way to fight back."

A huge wave of anger welled up inside Karen. Ergo might not have murdered her father, but they had killed him as surely as if they had. With their greed and their arrogance and their total disregard for the planet, and every man, woman and child on it. "Bastards!" she said. "Fucking bastards!" It was out before she could stop herself,

263

and she glanced, embarrassed, at her god-father. But he seemed not even to have heard her. His eyes were glazed and gazing off into some unseen distance.

Then he turned toward his god-daughter. "Come back to the car with me, Karen. There's something I want to give you."

Chris Connor's car was parked in Straiton Place, beyond a children's play area with swings and a chute. Almost as soon as they left the beach to follow the path one street back, he seemed to Karen to lose the confidence he had found talking to her on the sands. He appeared nervous again, and his eyes were everywhere, directed at every movement. Every pedestrian, every passing car. Until his gaze fell on some kids kicking a ball about on the grass. Tiny kids, the ball almost as big as themselves. And he seemed briefly absorbed by them. He stopped, watching, oblivious to Karen's impatience. Then, absently, he drew the remote from his pocket, and the lights flashed on his white Renault Scenic as the doors unlocked.

He looked at Karen, almost as if seeing her for the first time. "She took the kids."

Karen frowned. "What do you mean?"

"My wife. Took both the kids. My boys.

Seven and nine now. Said they deserved better."

And while her godfather was clearly feeling sorry for himself, it was his boys that Karen's heart went out to. She knew only too well what it was to lose a father. And after the revelations of the past half hour, her guilt and regret had been replaced by an anger that filled her up, very nearly consuming her. But she was used to containing her emotions, and there was no outward sign of the internal fury that was firing her impossible desire for revenge. Her father might have taken his own life, but he had been driven to it. Someone had to pay. "You said you had something for me."

"Oh, yes . . ." He rounded the car and lifted the tailgate, then reached inside and drew out a shoebox. Literally a shoebox — it had a Clarks logo on the side of it. Its lid was held shut by string wrapped length and widthwise and tied in a knot on top. It was rough, frayed string, and the knot looked impossibly tight. The green color of the box had faded, as if it might have been sitting somewhere in sunlight for a long time. He thrust it at her. "Here. It's for you and your mum."

Karen took it, holding it slightly away from her, as if it might be contaminated.

"What is it?"

"They never did give your dad time to clear out the things from the drawers in his office. Not that there was much in the way of personal stuff, anyway. So I did it for him. And then forgot to give it to him. It's been sitting in the house all this time."

And suddenly Karen wrapped her arms around it and pulled it close. It was as though she was holding a little piece of her father in them. There was enormous comfort in it, and she found herself both excited and scared by the prospect of opening it. Excited because she knew it would be a voyage of discovery, however brief, and that it would put her in direct contact with her dad again, in a way she hadn't felt since her mother had given his clothes away to charity. Scared, because maybe it wouldn't be enough, and she didn't want to be disappointed. She saw her godfather lift his eyes from the box and glance each way along the street.

"And something else." He reached into an inside pocket of his coat and pulled out a long white envelope. He held it in his left hand and ran the fingers of his right gently over it, and Karen could see her name written on it in the bold, clear handwriting of her father. But Chris didn't give it to her immediately, as if reluctant to part with it. "He gave me this just a couple of days before he went missing." He sighed deeply. "I should have seen it, I should have known. But at the time, and even now, I couldn't conceive of your dad as being a man who would take his own life."

She wanted to snatch it away from him. It had her name on it. It was hers. "What's in it?"

"I don't know. He gave it to me sealed, and made me promise to keep it safe, and only give it to you when you had turned eighteen." He expelled air in frustration with himself. "I can see now why he gave me it. But at the time, I really didn't understand."

"I'm not eighteen yet," Karen said.

"I know." He looked at the envelope again. "But, after you came to the Geddes the other day, I knew I had to give it to you. What was the point of waiting? Seventeen, eighteen. What difference does it make now? It's something he wanted you to have." Almost reluctantly he held it out to her, as if he were giving away the last piece of his friend, saying a final, belated farewell to the man he had loved, too.

Chapter Seventeen

Outside, the light was fading. September was evolving toward October. Summer to autumn. The shadow of winter already loomed large on the horizon.

Karen stood in the bathroom, staring at herself in the mirror. More than once, her godfather had told her that she was just like her dad. He hadn't meant her appearance, of course.

She had always thought that, in looks, she took after her mother. Her dyed-black hair was naturally brown. A mousy, insipid sort of brown, somewhere between chestnut and blond, but without the distinction of either. Just like her mum's. Although it was curly like her dad's. For years, her mother had dyed her hair blond, though now, Karen thought, there was perhaps as much platinum white in it as any color.

Her mother was a pretty woman. Not beautiful, but she had small, attractive features. Petite and perfectly formed. Cute. Somehow *cute* had bypassed Karen. Her features were not unlike her mother's, but their arrangement was not as pleasing to the eye. She regarded herself as plain. Not the sort of girl that would turn heads.

But now, as she stared in the mirror, she was looking for any sign of her father. It pleased her to think that she had inherited his intelligence, and perhaps some of that belligerent personality that Chris Connor had spoken of. But she was desperate to detect some physical manifestation of it. Something of him that she could see every time she caught her reflection in a mirror, or a window. If she had inherited any of his physical attributes, it was in the blue of her eyes. Her mother's were green. She had her mother's mouth, but the lips were pale, like her father's. And she gazed hard into her own eyes, as if perhaps her genetic inheritance might be staring back at her through the blue lenses of her dead father, critical, appraising.

For some reason, she still hadn't opened the box, or her letter. And the longer she left it, the harder it became to do. She couldn't really explain it to herself, but she felt sick every time she thought about opening either. She went back down the hall to her bedroom, pausing briefly on the landing at the top of the stairs. She could hear Derek and her mother talking in the lounge below, but the burble of the television masked their words and she couldn't make out what it was they were saying.

She hadn't been to school for days, and she knew that sooner or later they would contact her mother. But not yet, evidently. She slipped into her bedroom and shut the door carefully behind her. The Clarks shoebox and the white envelope sat on the bed, beckoning her to come sit beside them and open them up, to reveal the secrets she wasn't at all sure she wanted to know.

She had not said a word to her mother, about going to the Geddes, or meeting her godfather on the beach at Portobello, and she wasn't sure she had ever felt quite so alone in all of her short life. Even at the moment of learning about her father's death, her mother had been there with warm, protective arms. But that umbilical had been cut now forever. She was adrift on her own in a world vacillating between fear and uncertainty.

Tentatively she sat on the edge of the bed and lifted the shoebox on to her lap. The knot in the string was impossible to unpick and, in frustration, she reached for a pair of scissors on the dresser and slashed through it. The lid toppled to the floor. She peered into the box and, as she had feared, felt disappointment wash over her. There was really very little in it. Pens and pencils, a couple of erasers, a small stapler and a sprung implement with opposing claws for removing unwanted staples. There was a box of Gaviscon double-action antacid tablets, strawberry flavor, a fluorescent yellow marker pen, a small brown resin Buddha. She remembered something very similar to it sitting on his study desk here in the house, but bigger. And she wondered suddenly what had happened to all that stuff.

She lifted out two sheets of folded A4 paper and opened them up. The top sheet was the draft of a letter applying for a job at a university in England. She glanced at the date, and realized it could only have predated his redundancy by a matter of weeks. Or days. Had he seen the writing on the wall? If he'd got the job, would that have meant moving the whole family south? Or were he and her mother already bound for divorce? The second sheet was his résumé. All the jobs he had held over the years, and then a long list of his qualifications. She had not realized that he'd had so many degrees. An M.Sc. in Molecular Biology, a B.Sc.

Honors in Genetics, a Ph.D. in Cell Biology. He had also studied ecology, and conducted investigations into chronic neurological conditions in both humans and insects.

She had known none of this about him. The years he must have studied, the jobs he had taken, research projects he had worked on. He left in the morning, he came back in the evening. He was the man she knew at nights and weekends, and on holidays. He was her dad. The other person he'd been had simply never existed for her. What kind of pain and pressure had he kept to himself? The loss of his job, the destruction of his research, a wife who'd been having an affair. Karen had been oblivious, and when it seemed to her that he hadn't been there for her, she'd accused him of caring only about himself and screamed in his face, *I hate you, I hate you, I hate you.*

She did not even know she was crying until she saw her tears blister the paper she held in her hands. She laid it aside and quickly brushed away the tears with the back of her hand. At the bottom of the box was a picture frame lying face-down. On top of that, a grubby white business card. She lifted it out. It belonged to a Richard Deloit, Campaign Director of OneWorld.

Karen had heard of the organization. A high-profile, very vocal, international environmental group based in London. They were, it seemed to Karen, always in the news. Well known for gimmicks and stunts designed to attract media attention, if nothing else. She could even picture Deloit himself. A glamorous sort of man with curls of palladium white, full of righteous indignation and silky self-confidence, who seemed more impressed by himself than the causes he spoke for. She flipped the card over. There was a mobile phone number scrawled on the back of it, and the words, *Call me*.

She laid it aside and reached into the box again to retrieve the final item. As she turned it over, she saw that the frame was fashioned from hand-worked pewter and engraved with a Rennie Mackintosh design of interweaving tulips. She caught her breath when it revealed to her the picture it framed. She remembered it well. A photograph taken one year on holiday in France, when she was maybe five or six. She was wearing a pale blue print dress, and a wide-brimmed straw hat with blue ribbon over curling hair, much fairer than she remembered. It fell in soft loops to smooth, tanned, bare shoulders.

She gazed at that smiling, innocent face,

and ached inside for those happy days of childhood spent, lost to the turbulence that would come in later years and wreck her young life. Her dad must have had it on his desk. And maybe he, too, had longed for those forgotten days and years when the sun seemed always to shine, and love and happiness just existed, like the sea and the sky.

She refused to let more tears fall, and reached over to place the photograph in its frame on her bedside table, determined to let it remind her that life had once been worth living. That, if she had been happy once, then maybe one day she would be again.

Now the box was empty, and she had no excuse for further procrastination. She lifted the letter and weighed it in her hands. But there was no weight in it at all. At least, not in the paper. The words inside, she knew, would be considerably more laden, and she couldn't put off reading them any longer.

Suddenly, as if impelled by some outside force, she ripped open the envelope and pulled out the folded sheet from inside. Her fingers trembled as she opened it up and saw, in virgin ink, what may very well have been some of the final words her father ever wrote. Between his writing of them and now, no one else had ever read them.

My darling Karen,

I have no idea how to apologize for the pain I must have caused you. I know I never lived up to the father you wanted me to be, and I won't make excuses for that now. One can always find excuses for one's own failings, but when you reach the place that I have reached there is no room left for self-delusion. I know that suicide will have invalidated my life insurance, but I also know that your mother's relationship with Derek will have ensured financial security. One of the great regrets of my life is that I failed your mum. I hope you didn't blame her. I don't. And, who knows, maybe Derek has been the father to you that I couldn't. But however much you might hate me for what I have done to you, I want you to know that I love you, and that I always have, even if I couldn't be the dad you deserved. Maybe one day, when the dust has finally settled on all of this, we can find again the happiness we knew when we were both so much younger.

Dad.

Karen sat with the skin tingling all across her scalp. Every fine hair rose on the back of her neck and on both arms . . . *find again the happiness we knew* . . . How could they find happiness again when he was dead? She read the letter once more, quickly, hungrily, and every nuance of tense, every choice of word screamed only one thing. He wasn't dead. Her dad was alive. He had written this letter thinking that she would not read it for another year, by which time he was assuming she would know things she didn't know now. Primary among these being that he wasn't dead. That he hadn't committed suicide. It was a postrevelation apology, an appeal, however tentative, for some kind of rapprochement. Asking for her forgiveness and a second chance.

Karen's mother was less than pleased with her. "Derek lives here now, too," she'd said when Karen demanded to speak to her alone.

"Well, come upstairs, then."

But her mother had dug in her heels. "Anything you've got to say to me, you can say here and now. Derek and I have no secrets between us, and nor should you."

"Oh, well, forget it, then!" And Karen had started for the hall.

"No, it's okay." Derek had been the one to pour oil on troubled waters. He stood up. "I'm for an early night, anyway."

He half-smiled at Karen's mum as he left the room, but Karen refused to meet his eye. And now that he'd gone, she wasn't quite sure where to start.

Her mother stood, arms crossed defensively, a face like thunder. "Well?"

"Why didn't you ever tell me that dad had been sacked two months before he went missing?"

Whatever her mother might have been expecting, it wasn't this. She unfolded her arms and blinked, surprised, at her daughter. "Well, that's nonsense."

"It isn't. He was kicked out of the Geddes Institute weeks before his boat was found out on the firth."

"Who told you that?"

"Chris Connor."

A name that came out of the blue and struck her mother like a slap across the face. She shook her head, green eyes filled with confusion. "Chris . . . ? When were you talking to him?"

"I went to the Geddes a couple of days ago."

"Why?"

Karen pulled a face. "Why do you think?"

"Oh, for God's sake, Karen, why can't you just let it go? Your dad's dead. Get over it."

Karen almost bit her tongue in trying to hold back the truth. Instead, she said, "Are you telling me you didn't know he'd been sacked?"

"No, I didn't. Why wouldn't he tell me something like that?"

"You didn't know what he was working on, then?"

Her mother sighed in exasperation. "I don't know. Something to do with bees. He'd been coming home with stings all over his hands. What kind of nonsense has Chris been putting in your head?"

"It's not nonsense! Dad was doing experiments on the effects of insecticides on bees. When he came up with something the industry didn't like, they got rid of him. Forced him out of the institute by threatening to withhold its funding."

Her mother shook her head. "I don't know what Chris's game is, but this is pure fantasy."

"No, it's not!" Karen shouted so violently at her that her mother took a half-step back, almost as if she had been physically assaulted. In the silence that followed, Karen glared at her, breathing hard. "He gave me a letter that my dad wrote and asked him to give me when I was eighteen."

"Well, he was a bit premature then, wasn't he?"

"After I went to the institute, he decided to give it to me, anyway. I opened it tonight."

Her mother crossed her arms again. "And?"

Karen steeled herself. "He's not dead."

Her mother gasped her disbelief, turning her head away, shaking it and raising her eyes to the ceiling. "Oh, for God's sake!"

"He's not!"

"Oh, don't be so bloody stupid!" She drew a deep, tremulous breath. "Karen . . . I've been talking this over with Derek . . . and we both think it's about time you saw a psychiatrist." She blurted it out before she could stop herself. What might have been discussed as one of many possible approaches to dealing with her troublesome daughter was suddenly right out there, top of the agenda.

Karen felt the skin on her face redden, stinging as if she had been slapped on both cheeks. "Go to hell!"

She turned and stalked out of the room. Her mother's voice came after her, laden with regret at words spoken in haste and anger. "If there's a letter, show it to me."

Karen swiveled on her heel in the doorway. "Oh, yeah. So you can accuse me of making it all up. Writing it myself. Cos, of course, I'm off my fucking head!"

She took the stairs two at a time, and saw a startled-looking Derek standing at the far end of the hall as she stormed into her bedroom and slammed the door shut, locking it behind her. Two strides took her to the laptop, and she selected a Marilyn Manson album to blast out at full volume. Then she threw herself facedown on the bed, wrapping her pillow around her head to shut out the music and the banging on her bedroom door, her mother's voice shrill and hysterical somewhere far beyond it.

She supposed she must have cried herself to sleep, for she had no recollection of the album coming to an end, or the silence that followed it. Her mother must have given up trying to reason with her through the door long ago.

She rolled over on the bed and lay staring up at the ceiling. Her dad was alive, whether her mother wanted to believe it or not, and she had no idea which of the two conflicting emotions of joy and fury had gained ascendancy over the other. Initial euphoria had given way to a searing anger. How could he have done this to her? Faked his suicide and put her through two years of hell believing that he was dead, and that she was somehow responsible for it. Which, in turn, had subsided with the realization that, as usual, she was only seeing things from her own selfish perspective. For her dad to do what he had done, he must have had powerful cause. And that it was linked in some way to the research which had got him fired and physically ejected from the institute seemed beyond doubt.

The fog of mixed emotions was starting to dissipate, and she began to think more clearly, in spite of the throbbing headache that had come with the spilling of her tears. If her dad was alive, where was he, what was he doing? She needed to know. She needed to find him. And she knew that she was entirely on her own. Who was going to believe her? Certainly not Derek and her mother. Clearly they thought she was *disturbed,* in need of psychiatric treatment. And psychiatrists, she knew, liked to give you drugs to dull the senses and mute the emotions. Well, nobody was going to make her take any pills. She wanted all her senses about her. But where to begin?

She lay with her eyes closed for several long minutes before she remembered the business card in the shoebox. She sat upright and leaned over to lift the box from the floor. The card was lodged in amongst all the pens and pencils. When finally she retrieved it, she flipped it over to look again at the two words which implored, *Call me.* Okay, she thought, I will.

She grabbed her mobile from the bedside table, pausing only briefly to glance again at the photograph of herself with the blue dress and straw hat, before focusing on dialing the mobile phone number on the back of the card.

She listened to it ring several times, certain that it was about to go to voicemail, when suddenly it was answered by a sleepy, gruff, male voice that barked out across the ether. "Hello?"

She blinked, and glanced at her digital bedside clock, realizing with a start that it was almost one in the morning. She very nearly hung up, but forced herself to stay calm. "Is this Richard Deloit?"

There was a pause at the other end. "Who wants to know?"

"My name is Karen Fleming. I'm Tom Fleming's daughter." She had no idea what reaction to expect, if Deloit would even know or remember who Tom Fleming was. This time the pause was even longer. But when finally the man responded, his voice was low and threatening, and very much awake.

"Do not ever call me again, do you understand? Never." And he hung up.

The mornings were darker now, and there was only the faintest of gray light in the sky when Karen stepped silently from her bedroom, a small backpack dangling from one hand. She closed the door silently behind her and tiptoed down the stairs. Avoiding the third step from the bottom, which always creaked, like standing on wet snow.

In the downstairs hall, she waited for several long minutes, listening for any sign that either Derek or her mother were awake and might have heard her. But the silence in the house was thick, almost palpable. Yellow light from the street lamps outside fell in through glass in the front door and lay on the hall carpet in long, subdivided rectangles. She moved through it like a ghost, into the living room. Derek's jacket still hung over the back of the chair where she had seen it the previous evening.

In an inside pocket, she found his wallet. There were two credit cards and a bank card visible when she opened it up. Those he used most often, she suspected. She unclipped an internal flap and turned it over. There were three more cards. One was the membership of a gym. One was his driving license. And the third, another credit card. The one he was least likely to miss immediately. She slipped it out of its sleeve and checked the expiry date. It was valid until the end of the year. But there was still the problem of the PIN number. When people had several cards, she knew, they would write their PIN numbers down somewhere. Everyone lived in an age now where too much was expected to be committed to memory. PIN numbers, passwords, user names. Impossible to carry it all in your head.

She searched through the rest of the wallet, more in hope than expectation. It would be foolish to keep the numbers with the cards. But you'd want them with you. She thought for a moment. His phone!

She found his iPhone 6 in another pocket, and was relieved to discover that he hadn't PIN-protected it. Idiot! She went straight to his address book and tapped in his name. In the notes field, below phone numbers and address, were all his PINs, along with several passwords and user names. Nothing if not predictable. Karen found the PIN she wanted and closed her eyes for a moment, committing it to memory. Five was the key, then two. Five, plus two, minus two, plus two. 5735. She returned phone and wallet to his pockets, then opened up her mother's handbag, which lay on the table. She took £25 from her purse. Some cash to get her on the road. Then moved silently back out to the hall.

She laid her backpack on the floor, lifted her hoodie from the hall stand and pulled it on. Then she slipped her arms in turn through the straps of her bag and swung it on to her back.

The front door opened without a sound, and she immediately felt the damp of an autumn mist in her face. She paused to zip up her hoodie and flip the hood over her head. Then she double-checked her pockets, just to be sure. Phone and charger. Headset and change of underwear in her bag. No need for keys. She wasn't coming back.

Very gently, she pulled the door shut behind her, stood for a moment on the top step to draw a long breath, then hurried down the steps to the path and the front gate, before turning into the street. There were haloes of mist around all the street lamps, and she had gone no more than fifty yards when she looked back to see that her home was already lost from sight. Vanished like the past she had no intention of ever revisiting.

CHAPTER EIGHTEEN

I have no idea what time of day it is. Early afternoon, maybe? I am hungry and tired, and still far from convinced that I have done the right thing. Because now, I know, I am in more trouble than I ever thought possible.

It feels like hours since the interview concluded. A difficult interview that increased the intensity of my headache with every unanswered question. I suppose it must have begun somewhere around mid-morning.

I spent the night at Dune Cottage. Alone. In turmoil. Before he left, Gunn warned me that under no circumstances was I to drive my car, since I was unable to produce a valid license. And I was absolutely forbidden to leave the island. An unnecessary additional stricture, it seemed to me, since I could not achieve the latter without doing the former.

When it got dark, I could see lights on in the Harrison house up the road, but they didn't come visiting, or bring my dog back. The cottage seemed so very empty and lifeless without Bran. The only visitor I had was Mrs. Macdonald from across the road. She was so very pleasant and helpful to me that first day we met on the road, but last night her face might have been chiseled from ice as she told me that I was to quit the cottage by the end of the week, and I realized it was she who had been renting it to me. She would refund the last few weeks of my let, she said, but could not tolerate the idea of my staying there for another four weeks after the shame I had brought on her and her family. I am still not sure how anything I say or do reflects well or badly on her family in any way. But she was not to be argued with.

The police sealed up the shed again so that I would have no further access to it. What I find so extraordinary is how familiar its contents seemed to me. All that equipment. I knew and understood what almost every piece of it was for. But why it was there, and the use it was being put to, is still a mystery to me. That I must have equipped the shed myself seems undeniable. I must have had a reason for it, but what it might be I can't think.

I barely slept all through what felt like an interminably long night. At first I was tense, listening for Sally. I was sure she would come. But she didn't. By 2 a.m. I came to realize that she wasn't going to. It's hard to describe how lonely it seemed in that place where I had spent the last eighteen months of my life. Perhaps lonely is the wrong word. It doesn't really convey how utterly alone I felt. Abandoned. Hopeless. And still do.

I suppose I must have drifted off sometime shortly before dawn, because I was awakened by a knocking at the door. I had not undressed the night before, but simply lain on the bed, still with my shoes on. And it wasn't until I opened the door to the uniformed officer who stood on the step that I realized how I must look. Unshaven, hair a mess, clothes disheveled and creased. I recognized him as one of the policemen who had been searching my house the day before. He was young — ten years or more younger than me — and was trying to appear professionally impassive, but I could see the eager curiosity in his eyes. This was a story he would tell to gatherings of friends in pubs and at parties for years to come.

He said, "Detective Sergeant Gunn has asked me to invite you to help him with his inquiries."

"Has he? And if I decline?"

"I'll have to arrest you."

I tried a smile, but it probably didn't seem like one. "Then that's an offer I can't really refuse, is it?"

There was not a flicker in his face. "I'll be driving you to Stornoway, sir. It might be advisable to bring a toothbrush and pack some underwear. In case we don't get back tonight."

I thought, So this is what volunteering to help the police with their inquiries is like.

At least he didn't make me sit in the back of the car, like a prisoner. I sat up front in the passenger seat beside him, with my overnight bag on my knees, and saw Mrs. Macdonald watching from her window as we turned out on to the single-track road.

Toward the end of the road, where it meets the A859, we passed a man out walking. He moved on to the verge as he heard us coming, and turned as the car drove by. It was the man from the caravan across the bay. I recognized his distinctive stoop and long, tangled hair. He wore a shabby green parka, with a pair of binoculars on a strap dangling around his neck, and carried a walking stick. A worn and torn cloth cap was pulled down on his brow, but for the first time I saw his face quite clearly. It was a long, guarded face with a cultivation of several days' growth on it. His eyes were dark and, in the moment that they met mine, seemed almost black.

But it was a moment that passed in the blink of an eye, and then he was gone. I glanced in the wing mirror and saw him move out on to the road again, to resume his walk. We rounded a bend in the road and he vanished from view.

I am not sure how long my interview with Gunn lasted. When we arrived in Stornoway I was taken into the police station through a back entrance. We passed a charge bar from behind which a uniformed sergeant glowered at me, and in a corridor off to my right I saw doors opening into cells on either side of it. The interview room where I am sitting now is somewhere upstairs. There is a table, the chair I am sitting in and two chairs opposite. A window looks down into a courtyard, and I can see a yellow-painted rough-cast wall.

I know that Mr. Gunn found my answers to his questions irritating. I am sure that he thought I was just being difficult, or obstructive, covering up my role in the murder of the man they found on Eilean Mòr. My difficulty was that I could not say with any degree of certainty whether I had killed him or not.

He came into the room with another officer, whom he named when identifying those present for the benefit of a digital recording machine. But I don't remember the name. Just that he was tall and thin and never once opened his mouth. But his eyes, any time I looked at him, spoke volumes. I was guilty as sin.

We got off to a bad start, and Gunn's veneer of patience quickly wore thin. "You are Neal David Maclean, is that correct?"

"I'm sorry, Mr. Gunn, I really can't say."

He gave me a look. "Can't or won't?"

"Can't."

He frowned, and I could see the wheels turning behind his eyes as he decided how to proceed. "Neal David Maclean is the name under which you have been living at Dune Cottage, Luskentyre, for the last eighteen months, is *that* correct?"

"Yes."

"And yet there was nothing in the cottage or carried about your person to confirm your identity. No credit cards, no checkbooks, not even a driver's license."

I nodded. "That's right."

"So how do you explain that?"

"I can't."

By now, I am sure, his irritation was morphing into anger, but he hid it well. "And the newspaper cuttings on Neal Maclean, and the bundles of cash in the briefcase?"

I shrugged. "I found them in the attic, just as you did."

"Are you saying you didn't put them there?"

The more I tried to answer his questions honestly, without telling the truth, the more blind alleys I stumbled into. "I think it's very probable that I did."

He sat back and drew a long, slow breath before deciding on another tack. "You are writing a book about the disappearance of the lighthouse men on the Flannan Isles in the year nineteen hundred, yes?"

"Apparently."

"Well, are you or aren't you?" An edge to his voice now.

"Since neither you nor I can find any trace of a manuscript in the cottage, Mr. Gunn, I think we'd probably have to assume that I'm not."

"But you've been making trips back and forth to the Flannans ostensibly to research it."

"From all accounts, yes."

"I take it you're not denying that you went

out to the Flannan Isles five days ago in a boat hired from Coinneach Macrae at Rodel?"

"I'm not, no. And I did, yes."

"But you do deny finding a body in the old ruined chapel below the lighthouse?"

I had lied about this yesterday, though every fiber of my being was now screaming, *Tell him, tell him, tell him!* But I still wasn't ready to let go. "I'd rather not say."

Which clearly threw him. I could see his eyes narrow, not just with anger or frustration, but from consternation. "Yesterday, when we opened up the hut at Dune Cottage, we found all kinds of scientific equipment in it, including what would appear to be the accoutrements of a beekeeper. Do you keep bees, Mr. Maclean?"

I nodded. "It seems that I do."

"Where?"

"Hidden. Off the coffin road."

He seemed taken aback by this, and took some moments to frame his next question. "When you showed me your hands yesterday, you had what appeared to be several bee stings on them."

"Yes."

"During the postmortem on the man found murdered in the old chapel on Eilean Mòr, the pathologist discovered very similar

294

stings on the back of *his* hands."

This came as a devastating blow to me. Until now, there had been no link between myself and the dead man. There had been nothing about him that I recognized. But bee stings on our hands? That was an irrefutable connection, beyond the possibility of coincidence, that I couldn't explain. And it made me even more inclined to believe that perhaps it *was* me who had killed him. I felt my face redden.

"Can you explain that?" Gunn asked.

"No, officer, I can't."

I became aware for the first time, when he flipped it open, of the beige folder that he had brought in with him and laid on the table. He began shuffling through sheets of typed notes. He seemed to find what he was looking for and read for several moments before looking up.

"Do you know a lady called Sally Harrison?"

"I do."

"And do you deny having a relationship with her?"

"I don't."

He seemed surprised. "She claims not to be having one with you."

I felt my brows creasing. "You asked her?"

"How else would I know she'd denied it?"

I thought about that. "In the presence of her husband?"

I saw his mouth tighten. "Yes."

"Well, then, that would explain it."

Now he pursed his lips. "So how long have you had this . . . alleged relationship with Mrs. Harrison?"

I shrugged. "I'm not really sure."

Then, out of the blue, "You have a boat, I believe. The one you've been using to go back and forth to the Flannans."

"Yes, I believe I do."

"Where is it?"

I realized that I had no satisfactory answer to this. "I don't know."

"Yet you told the boatman at Rodel that you had taken it up to Uig. I know, because I have checked, that you did no such thing."

"Sally told him that. Rather than have me try to explain that I'd lost my boat."

"And why would she do that?"

"I told you, Mr. Gunn. We're having an affair. Why else do you think she was with me at Rodel?"

Gunn nodded thoughtfully. "Are you married yourself, sir?"

I sighed and went for honesty. "I don't know."

"Do you have any children?" This time there was discernible aggression in his voice.

And for me it was the tipping point. I simply couldn't keep it up any longer. For better or worse, I knew that I was about to relinquish what little control I had left over my own life. I dropped my face into my hands and closed my eyes, aware that my breathing had become quite erratic. When I let my hands fall away and lifted my head again, I saw both men looking at me with strangely concentrated stares. I said, "Mr. Gunn, I wasn't entirely straight with you yesterday. I did find that man in the chapel the day I visited the island. I have no idea who he is, but obviously the bee stings connect us somehow. If you were to ask me whether or not I'm the one who killed him, I'd have to tell you that I really don't know. But I guess I'm scared that maybe I did."

There was an extraordinary silence in the room. Thick enough to cut into slices. It seemed as if both police officers were holding their breath. But I had started down the road of truth, and I knew there was no way back. So I told them everything. About washing up on the beach at Luskentyre with no memory of who or where I was. Discovering that apparently my name was Neal David Maclean, and that I was in a relationship with a married woman. Learning that I was writing a book I could find no trace of.

I had gone out to the Flannan Isles in search of answers and found a body. Then searched my house from top to bottom looking for anything to confirm my identity, but finding nothing. Just the money and the cuttings.

Gunn glanced down at his notes, perhaps looking for inspiration among them, but finding none. When he looked at me again, I could see that, although he was skeptical, I had also cut away the ground of certainty from beneath his feet. Finally he said, "You say you learned that *apparently* you were Neal David Maclean. Does this mean you think you might not be?"

"I know I'm not."

"How?"

"I went to Edinburgh to find out."

"And?"

"Neal David Maclean has been dead for two years."

Now, as I sit here on my own, I regret telling them the truth. Because I can't prove a word of it, and I am no longer the master of my own destiny. I cannot imagine what will happen now, and perhaps they are as uncertain as I am about what to do next.

I can hear the sound of distant voices from somewhere deep inside the building, the clack of computer keyboards, the odd trill of a telephone. I can hear, too, the rumble of traffic out in Church Street, and the call of gulls drifting up from the harbor. There is rain running down the window, driven in on the edge of a blustery wind.

I turn, startled, as the door opens unexpectedly, and Gunn returns with the tall, thin officer whose name I can't remember, and the young man in uniform who drove me up from Harris.

Gunn says, "I'd like your permission, sir, to take your fingerprints and a swab of your DNA. If you are in either of those databases, then we'll be able to make a positive identification."

"And if I'm not?"

"One step at a time, sir." He looks awkward. "Would you be prepared to submit to a medical examination?"

I think about it. Perhaps, if there is some medical explanation for my loss of recollection, diagnosis might lead to treatment and a return of memory. I nod. "Okay."

"Then Constable Macritchie will escort you to the Western Isles hospital."

"Am I under arrest, Detective Sergeant?"

He presses his lips together in grim resignation and his upper lip whitens, as if he has drawn a chalk line along it. "Not yet, sir."

From the *yet,* I take it that my arrest is therefore imminent, and almost certainly on suspicion of murder.

CHAPTER NINETEEN

When the door to the interview room closed behind the suspect, Gunn stood for a moment, gazing from the window, his mind a firestorm of mixed emotions. He became aware of Detective Constable Smith watching him, and he turned to find himself fixed in the other man's hawklike stare.

"What?" he said, almost defensively, as if there were an accusation in Smith's eyes.

"You believe him?"

"It's the most unlikely story I've ever heard, Hector."

"Aye, but do you believe it?"

Gunn thought about it. "On balance, probably not." But there was still a part of him that found quite compelling the tale that Maclean, or whatever his name was, had told them. And something in the way he told it that had the ring of truth. "We need to check out his story about Neal David Maclean." He opened his folder on the desk and shuffled through its contents, finding and retrieving the birth certificate. He handed it to Smith. "Should be simple enough to check this out. There's an address written on the back. Let's see if the man whose birth certificate it is lived or lives there, and if he's dead, as our man says."

"And if he is?"

"Then we'll know that at least a part of his story is true." He glanced at Smith and saw in his face that his junior officer was dubious of the credence Gunn seemed to be giving the suspect's story. And as if to justify his thinking, Gunn said, "Mrs. Macdonald, the lady who owns Dune Cottage, told me that she met our man on the road about a week or so ago, around the time the pathologist thinks the bloke on Eilean Mòr might have been killed." He consulted his notes. "He was soaked to the skin, she said, and wearing a life jacket. He'd come up from the beach, head bleeding, and was shivering so much he could hardly speak. Her exact words? *He hardly seemed to know me.*" He looked up at Smith. "All of which would tie in with his claim to have been washed up on the beach, unable to remember what had happened."

"Very convenient, if he'd just killed that fella."

"Well, to be fair to him, he's admitting that's a possibility. Though we don't have a single piece of evidence, for the moment, to suggest that he did."

"Well, it'll all be out of our hands soon enough."

Gunn grunted. "When does the CIO arrive?"

"On a flight from Inverness sometime tomorrow."

Gunn closed his folder. With an average murder rate on the islands of just one a century, it was felt that investigating officers in Stornoway didn't have the requisite experience. And so any time anything interesting happened, Police Scotland liked to send a more senior officer from the mainland to take charge. Gunn breathed his frustration. "It would be nice if we could have this all wrapped up before he gets here."

"It would," Smith said, though it was clear from his expression he didn't think it likely. "Oh, by the way, our man's car . . . It's a long-term rental, paid for by some company down south. Might take a while to find out exactly who's behind it." He turned toward the door. "I'll check out this bloke Maclean."

"While you're at it, Hector, might as well

run a wee check on that couple who're staying up the road from Dune Cottage." He ran an eye over his notes again. "Jon and Sally Harrison. From Manchester, apparently. She clearly lied to me about her relationship with our man. And her husband says he's in concrete."

Smith chuckled. He knew there was a joke in there somewhere, but he couldn't think what it was and his smile faded. "Will do," he said.

CHAPTER TWENTY

It was Karen's first time in London. When she had boarded the train in Edinburgh, her hands had been shaking almost uncontrollably. She felt sick, and a part of her had just wanted to give it all up and go home. To pretend that none of this had happened. That her dad was still dead, and she could retreat to the comfort of self-recrimination and absolve herself from any further responsibility for her life.

But, as the hours wore on, her fear had slowly dissipated, and she saw all the negatives of her life, self-pity, blame, anger, exposed like dead fish washed up on a beach. And she realized that she had simply wasted the last two years.

Fear, gradually, had been replaced by quiet determination, so that by the time she stepped on to the platform at King's Cross she was focused and clear on exactly what it was she had to do.

Still, her sense of being alone, and in a strange and dangerous place, at first nearly overwhelmed her. London. It had only ever been a name. A place she had seen on TV and in movies. Edinburgh seemed tiny by comparison, and the sheer scale and volume of noise in this conurbation of eight million people was daunting. Her parents, she knew, had lived somewhere just outside of London when she was a baby, but she had no recollection of it, no affinity with it, and beyond an initial sense of awe, found herself disappointed. It was really just another big, dirty, ugly city. Same shops, same people, same cars, same ads on the billboards.

In the Underground, people squeezed into small, noisy, overlit capsules that rattled through the bowels of the city. There was no Underground in Edinburgh, and Glasgow's Clockwork Orange simply didn't compare. Passengers sat or stood in bubbles of isolation, lost in their private worlds, oblivious of the sweaty, overscented and indifferent hordes of humanity traveling with them in these dark, smelly tunnels. And when finally they reached their stations, they emerged blinking in the daylight on to blackened pavements shiny with discarded chewing gum, and streets choked with traffic belching poison into the air. For the first time in her life, Karen felt invisible. And in a strange way there was a comfort in that.

The offices of OneWorld were tucked away in a crumbling building in an alley off Dean Street in Soho. Karen had taken the Tube to Leicester Square, and used her phone to navigate her way through Chinatown to Shaftesbury Avenue. Rusted railings and bars on the windows characterized the dirty little backstreet where OneWorld had its headquarters. Scaffolding made the street almost impassable, stone cleaners at work, blasting away decades of grime and repairing the decaying stone and brickwork beneath it. Despite its decrepitude, Karen knew that this was a prestigious and expensive address, and she wondered how much of the money raised by OneWorld went on maintaining its image here, however illusory.

She pushed open a black-painted door with shining brass hardware, and found herself in a gloomy hallway with stairs climbing steeply to a first-floor landing mired in darkness. On her right, a sign on a darkwood door revealed this to be the *Office*. Opposite was the *Conference Room*. She knocked, and stepped tentatively into the office.

A girl who looked not much older than Karen sat behind a desk in front of a computer terminal. The wall behind her was pasted with OneWorld campaign posters on GMOs, oil pollution, clean water, CO_2 emissions, whale hunting. She had dyed-blond hair tied back in a ponytail and wore a black OneWorld T-shirt and skintight jeans tucked into calf-high leather boots. The window that looked out on to the alleyway was barred on the outside and opaque with grime. Ed Sheeran leaked almost subliminally from her computer speakers, and she was speaking animatedly on the phone. She glanced at Karen and raised a finger indicating that she should wait. There were three chairs lined up against the back wall, and a coffee table groaning with magazines. Karen sat down and inclined her head to read the cover of the magazine on top of the pile. It was a copy of the *New Internationalist,* and its headline screamed "TTIP — Now It Gets Political." Karen had no idea what TTIP was, and she suddenly felt very ignorant and insignificant. A country girl arriving in the big city for the first time, foolish and naive.

When the girl finished her call, Karen stood up. "I'd like to see Mr. Deloit."

But still the girl held up a finger, and scribbled something on a notepad before looking up. "Do you have an appointment?"

"No."

"Then, I'm sorry, you'll have to make one and come back another time. Mr. Deloit is a very busy man." She opened up a desk diary. "If you want to leave me your name and number, and preferably an email address, I can get back to you. What is it you want to see him about?"

Karen stood her ground. "Just tell him Karen Fleming is here. He'll see me."

The girl shook her head. "He won't. Now, either you can give me your details or you can leave."

Karen sat down. "I'm not leaving till I see him."

The girl sighed. "He's not here."

"I'll wait till he comes back, then."

Karen could see the workings of the girl's thought processes revolving behind dark brown eyes. "He won't be in today."

"I don't believe you."

"I don't care what you believe. He's not going to see you without an appointment."

Karen stood up again and crossed the room to the desk. She leaned over it, aware that with her cropped black hair and face full of holes she was probably quite intimidating. She knew, too, that the Scottish accent sounded aggressive to the English ear. "Just tell him I'm here, alright?"

If the girl was intimidated, she wasn't going to show it. She glared back at Karen and there was a momentary hiatus. Then she lifted the phone and pressed a button. After a moment she said, "There's a very hostile young lady here who refuses to leave without seeing you." A pause. Then, "Karen Fleming." Karen could hear a man's voice raised on the other end of the line. The girl flinched, and colored slightly. She hung up as she hoisted herself out of her chair, and said in a voice that could have turned salt water to ice, "Come with me."

Karen followed her up the stairs into darkness, and as they neared the top, a light came on, triggered by a sensor. There were unmarked doors at either end of the landing, and the stairs went up into yet more darkness. The girl knocked on the nearest door, then held it open for Karen, waiting until she had entered, and then closing it behind her.

It was an old-fashioned room with wood-paneled walls and a high ceiling. A thick, dark red carpet soaked up every sound and movement, and there was a sense of hush in the room. Daylight spilled in through layers of filth on a large window that looked down into the lane, and a green glass and brass lamp on Deloit's desk cast a pool of bright yellow light on the surface of it all around his laptop. It was a large, leather-tooled mahogany desk, and Deloit eased himself out of a matching captain's chair.

He was heavier, Karen saw, than he looked in his press photographs, a jawline deformed by jowls and a paunch that stretched the lettering on his OneWorld T-shirt. His platinum curls grew almost to his shoulders. Perhaps natural once, but dyed now. He had probably been a good-looking man in his youth, and in some ways still was. But the ravages of time and good living were starting to show, and his face was ugly with anger as he rounded his desk toward her.

"You stupid little bitch! Which part of *never call me again* did you not understand?"

"I'm not calling you, I'm calling on you. And don't you call me a fucking bitch!" Which took the wind out of his sails, at least for a moment. Karen used that moment to her advantage. "My father's still alive, isn't he? And you know where he is."

He regained his composure, and his anger, and took two steps toward her, grabbing her arm and pushing his face into hers. "You fool! You're risking everything. Were you followed here?"

Karen was startled. "Followed? Who by?

Who would want to follow me?"

He breathed his anger and frustration in her face. "You have no idea, do you? What even gives you the notion that your father's not dead?"

"He left a letter for me with my godfather. I wasn't supposed to get it for another year, but he gave it to me yesterday."

Deloit tipped his head back, eyes directed to the ceiling. "Goddamned stupid fucking idiot!" Then he seemed to collect himself and directed his ire back at Karen. She felt his fingers tightening around her upper arm, bruising her, she was sure. "You have to leave. You have to leave now! And you have to forget that any of this ever happened."

"Why?" Karen very nearly shouted in his face.

But he shook his head. "What you don't know, you can't tell. But what you do need to know is that your father gave up everything for you. Everything! And if you go on like this, you're going to fuck it all up." He pulled her across to the window and peered through the dirt, down into the lane. "We've got to get you out of here. But not the front way. Come with me." And he dragged her toward the door. As he opened it, she pulled her arm free.

"I'm not going anywhere till you tell me

what's going on."

His eyes were wide and wild, tiny drops of spittle gathering in the corners of his mouth. "If you care remotely about your dad, if you value his life, and his work, then you'll go, Karen. Just go. And take my word for it. You are putting his life in danger."

His words struck her like blows from a fist. Each and every one of them. *You are putting his life in danger.*

He took her arm again and hurried her downstairs. But instead of opening the front door, he led her back along the hall and into a small kitchen where she smelled stewed coffee and stale food from empty carryout containers on the worktop. He unlocked a reinforced metal door and pulled it open. Outside was the narrowest of lanes lined with bins that overflowed on to the cobbles. She caught the movement of some creature scuttling off into the late afternoon gloom.

He glanced either way along the lane then propelled her out into it. "Go home. And if you care at all about your dad you'll not breathe a word of this to anyone. Do you understand?"

Karen nodded, and stood mute and bereft in the shadow of the brick facades that towered above her, the tiniest sliver of sky dividing them a long way overhead. The slamming of the door echoed in the silence, and she heard him locking it again. Somewhere distantly she became aware of the rumble of traffic, and she rubbed her arm ruefully where fingers of steel had gripped them. She wanted to cry. And perhaps just twenty-four hours ago tears would have been spilled. But however aggressively Richard Deloit might have screamed in her face, ejecting her from the back door of One-World and telling her to go home and forget everything, she knew with certainty now that her dad was still alive. Which made her even more determined than ever to find him.

Karen sat in a tiny Starbucks in the Trocadero, just off Leicester Square, nursing a grande caramel macchiato. On one side stood a bureau de change, on the other, a homeless man wearing a baseball cap and wrapped in a torn and dirty coat squatted on the pavement, leaning back against the pillars. The two extremes of modern Britain sandwiching an American coffee shop. Her anger, by now, had been given time to ferment and was fizzing inside her. Why had she let Deloit treat her like that? Why had she not stood her ground and demanded the truth? How pathetic was she that she had allowed him simply to push her out of the back door and leave her standing like an idiot in that back alley?

Such was the level of her indignation that she was tempted to go back and hammer on his door, screaming for answers until she got them. But the one thing that stopped her was the recollection of the words he had almost spat in her face. *You are putting his life in danger.*

She had no idea how that was possible, or why. But it scared her. He had faked his own suicide. And you didn't do something like that without a pretty damn good reason. *Were you followed here?* Deloit had demanded of her. Who would have followed her, and how would she have known if someone had? She glanced around all the faces in the coffee shop. They were young people, mostly, heads buried in phones or tablets or laptops, as oblivious as people in the Underground of everyone else around them. No one was paying Karen the least attention.

For a long time she sat in a state of mental paralysis, letting her coffee grow cold. This had been a wasted trip. All those hours on the train from Edinburgh. The cost of it, charged to Derek's credit card, had seemed excessive, and she had her first and only pang of guilt about it. It didn't last long. Because words spoken on the beach at Portobello came tumbling back into her consciousness. *I knew what he knew.*

She had asked her godfather what it was he knew, and he had not really answered her. But if anyone could tell her what was going on, it had to be him. She took her phone out and dialed his mobile. It rang four times before going to messages, but she didn't leave one. She hung up, and almost immediately her own phone rang. The display told her it was her mother, and she muted the ringer until it stopped vibrating. She sipped on the lukewarm remains of the sweet chemical concoction that passed for coffee, and thirty seconds later the phone vibrated briefly and she knew her mother had left a message.

"Karen, for God's sake, where are you? We're worried sick. I should have called as soon as I woke up this morning and saw that you were gone. You've been acting so weird lately, but I never thought for a minute that you'd run off like this. Now the school have phoned to say you've been absent for days." A sigh of exasperation. "Oh, babygirl, don't do this to me. Call me, please." There was a long pause before she hung up, as if she believed that Karen was there, listening, and might respond.

Karen deleted the message and wondered why she didn't feel at least some tiny sense of remorse or regret. All she could think was that Derek hadn't discovered yet that one of his credit cards was missing, or her mother would have said something. But it surely wouldn't be long before he did, and the likelihood was that he would have it canceled.

She left Starbucks and searched for a cash dispenser. She needed money as a backup in case the card stopped working. And she had to make a decision quickly about what to do next. The light was fading faster here than it did back home, and she didn't relish a night spent on her own in London. There was no reason for her to stay. She had already decided that returning to hammer on the door of OneWorld would be a waste of time. A triumph of head over heart. She needed to talk to Chris Connor again. The night train to Edinburgh would get her there first thing tomorrow morning. But she would need to buy her ticket fast, while Derek's card was still active.

The sleeper left Euston at ten to midnight, the guard's shrill whistle echoing among the dark rafters of the long, gloomy platform as the train creaked and eased its way out of the station at the start of its seven-and-a-half-hour journey north. Karen found herself sharing a cabin with an overcoiffed middle-aged business woman. She was wearing a gray suit and black high-heeled shoes, and regarded Karen warily. Neither of them was comfortable undressing, and as the lights went out, each lay self-consciously on her back on the narrow bunks, listening to the rhythm of the wheels on the rails, frightened to go to sleep. The rolling stock groaned and complained as the train jerked and shuddered its way through suburban stations, gathering pace with the darkening of the night, and leaving the wealthy veneer of a decadent and decaying south behind them.

Karen was too tense to sleep, and certain that her traveling companion was equally awake. She lay for a long time staring at a ceiling that only occasionally took form as light leaked around the window blind from some street-lit conurbation. Finally, the relentless tempo of the train carried her off into a restless slumber.

She woke with a start in darkness some-time later. Her fellow traveler was on her feet, and for a moment Karen panicked. *Were you followed?* She sat bolt upright, heart pounding, before realizing that the woman was simply returning from a visit to the toilet. After several long moments, she lay back down again, forcing herself to be calm. This was crazy. She was starting to become paranoid, without the least idea why. She tried to make herself breathe normally, but they were long, deep breaths with the hint of a tremor in them, and she knew that she would not sleep again tonight.

But when the train eased its way gently into the gray, early morning Edinburgh light that fell through the glass of Waverley Station, Karen woke to the realization that she had in fact succumbed. The lady with the suit was up and dressed, teeth brushed, hair immaculate, and was closing the clasps on her small suitcase. Karen swung her legs out of her bunk and rubbed the sleep from her eyes. She felt grubby and gritty and had a filthy taste in her mouth. She glimpsed her reflection in the window and saw how pale she was.

The business woman forced a smile. "Goodbye," she said, although they had never said hello, nor exchanged any other words between them during the entire night.

Karen paid to go into the station's public toilets, where she washed in the sink and changed her underwear in a cubicle. In the buffet, she bought a coffee and a custard-filled croissant, and began to feel vaguely human again. Self-confidence had been restored by her return to Edinburgh. She was on home ground again. She took out her phone and saw that there had been another five calls from her mother. There were three messages, but she didn't listen to them. Instead she redialed Chris Connor. Again her call went to messages, but this time she left one. "Chris, it's Karen. We need to talk. I know you didn't like me coming to the Geddes, but that's what I'm going to do. I'll see you there in about an hour."

By the time her taxi swooped down toward the turning circle in front of the concourse at the Geddes Institute, the sky had broken up a little, letting sunlight through in peeps and patches to sprinkle itself across the rolling green woodland to the southwest of the city. Karen paid her driver and hurried across the concourse to the revolving glass doors. It was a different security guard who barred her way this time. "I'm here to see Professor Chris Connor," she said.

"Are you expected?"

"Yes." After all, he had almost certainly picked up her message by now.

"Wait here, please." He crossed the foyer to the reception desk, and the same girl who had made out the pass on her previous visit looked up to see Karen standing at the door. She exchanged a few words with the security man, then stood up and came out from behind the desk to accompany him back across the atrium. Beyond them, the coffee shops and bakery in the mall were doing brisk business as students and researchers fueled themselves up for the morning ahead.

The girl gazed very earnestly into Karen's eyes. "You're looking for Professor Connor?"

And something about her manner set alarm bells ringing in the back of Karen's head. "Yes."

"I'm so sorry, you obviously haven't heard. Chris was killed in a car accident on the bypass yesterday."

CHAPTER TWENTY-ONE

Karen sat at a table outside the Kilimanjaro Coffee shop in Nicolson Street, oblivious of the fact that she was smoking in full view of the British Heart Foundation next door. Buses and taxis rumbled past, filling the air with noise and fumes, and obliterating the view of the church opposite.

But she heard nothing, saw nothing. Felt nothing. Except for the fear that seeped in behind the numbness.

Poor Chris, she kept thinking, over and over again. And wondering whether he would still be alive if she hadn't gone to see him. If he hadn't given her the letter and told her the things he had. She had spilled tears for him in the taxi on the way back to the city, but her eyes were dry now, burning, and red like the paintwork on the facade of the coffee shop.

She stubbed out her cigarette and lit another with shaking fingers.

An accident on the bypass, the girl at the Geddes had said. And maybe, after all, that's just what it had been. An accident. But given how agitated Chris had been about speaking to her at all, and Richard Deloit's behavior in London yesterday, Karen found it hard to believe. *You are putting his life in danger,* Deloit had said of her father. Did that mean she had also put Chris's life in danger? Was she responsible for his death? She buried her face in her hands and couldn't bear to face the thought. Because if she was, then perhaps she really was putting her dad's life in danger, too. But if it was true, she still had no idea how that was possible.

She lifted her head from her hands and breathed deeply. There was no way, now, that she could go home, having stolen money and a credit card, and refused to answer a single one of her mother's calls. Never mind the fact that she had barely been at school in the last week. No, there was no way back.

But what was the way forward? Where would she stay? How would she survive once they canceled the credit card? Who could she turn to? There was no one else. Deloit wouldn't speak to her. Chris was dead. Again, she choked on the thought.

She closed her eyes and replayed her final moments with him, walking together on the beach at Portobello, occasional daubs of sunlight burnishing patches out on the firth. And suddenly she remembered that there *was* someone else. A loose thread that it had never even occurred to her to follow back to its source. Her father's student. The one who had conducted the experiment with him. Billy . . . What was it Chris had called him? Billy, Billy . . . Carr! It returned to her suddenly as she replayed Chris's voice in her head. Billy Carr. What had happened to him? He had just vanished, Chris said. There one day, gone the next. But people, Karen knew, didn't just vanish without trace. People leave tracks, most of them electronic, and Karen had a thought about how she might find and follow Billy Carr's trail, like the loose thread that he was, back to its source.

By late afternoon it was spitting rain, and Karen had her hood pulled up as she leaned back against the sitting rail in the bus shelter. But not because of the rain. A lot of the kids passing would probably recognize her, so she kept her head down, face obscured by the hood, and only revealed it on occasion when she glanced up the road in search of a familiar figure.

It had been an unbearably long day, treading water, counting off the minutes and the hours until school would be out. Walking the length of Princes Street, sitting in the park at lunchtime, eating sandwiches from a plastic wrapper and watching the trains rumble in and out of Waverley. Feeling small and very vulnerable in the shadow of the castle. Now she was starting to fear that she had wasted her time, and that Gilly was not at school today. Maybe she'd been off sick, and Karen could have gone straight to her house hours ago. The thought almost induced her to kick out at the perspex wall of the bus shelter.

But then she saw her. On her own, as usual. Sauntering down the road in no particular hurry, absently swinging her school bag from her free hand. Raising a cigarette to her lips with the other. The only time she wasn't on her own was when she was with Karen, though Karen was aware that Gilly was actually one hundred percent self-reliant. She only really tolerated Karen because they were cerebral equals. Or very nearly. Karen was certain that she topped her friend by a couple of IQ points, and that Gilly knew it, which is why she had never revealed to Karen the result of the

Mensa test she had taken last year. But what was a couple of points between friends? The truth was that no one else in the school came anywhere close to their level of intelligence. Which made them at the same time outcasts and misfits.

Gilly didn't even notice her as she wandered by. It was only Karen's "Hey!" that caught her attention. She turned, surprised, not immediately recognizing her, until Karen pushed back the hood. And then her eyes widened. "Jesus, girl! What have you done to your hair?" But she didn't wait for an answer. "And . . ." She peered at her. "Christ! I knew there was something different about you. All the ironmongery's gone." She wrinkled her nose. "Hated that stuff. But, bloody hell, you look naked without it now." Then she frowned. "You been crying? Fuck's sake, you look hellish."

Karen struggled to prevent tears welling up in her eyes again. "Thanks," she said. "Can always rely on you to make a bad day worse."

Gilly sighed. "You are in such trouble, I can't begin to tell you."

And in spite of everything she felt, Karen smiled. "See?"

Gilly grinned. "Jesus Christ, come here." And she put her arms around her friend and squeezed her so hard she almost stopped her breathing. By the time she let her go, the tears were coursing down Karen's cheeks and she had to use both palms to wipe them away. Gilly gazed at her with concern. "Your mum's been up at the school. And I think she's been to the police to report you missing. Officially."

"Stupid bitch," Karen said, and remembered Deloit calling her exactly that just yesterday. "I need help, Gilly. Can I come back to your place? I need to use your computer."

Gilly shrugged. "What am I going to tell my mum?"

"Does she know I'm . . . *missing*?"

"Well, *I* haven't said anything to her. Your mum spoke to me at school this morning. Wanted to know if I knew where you were. Of course, I didn't. So she'd have no reason to go asking my mum. I mean, they're hardly big pals anyway, are they?"

"Good. I might need her to let me stay over tonight."

"Shouldn't be a problem. We'll just tell her your mum's away at a wedding or something." She tugged on the strap of Karen's backpack and grinned again. "And look, you've even got an overnight bag. So who'd ever know different?"

■ ■ ■ ■

Gilly's mum wasn't at home when they got
to the house, and they went straight up to
Gilly's attic room. Karen took off her
hoodie and backpack, dropped into the two-
seater settee pushed against the far wall and
lit a cigarette. Four velux windows were set
into walls that sloped up to the ceiling, and
Gilly's desk, with its impressive array of
computer equipment bought by adoring
parents to indulge her, stood against the
wall below one of them. A top-of-the-range
iMac with two ancillary Thunderbolt
screens, a 12-terabyte external hard drive, a
state-of-the-art sound system. If Karen had
the edge on IQ points, Gilly's family were
wealthier than hers by a mile. The room,
however, was a tip, as it always was. Gilly's
pathological untidiness as counterpoint to
Karen's manic sense of order.

Gilly slumped into her computer chair
and lit a cigarette for herself. "You going to
tell me?"

Karen thought about it. *You are putting his
life in danger,* Deloit had said. And Chris
was dead. "Nope."

Gilly shrugged. "Fair enough. You don't
get to use my computer, then, and you can

find somewhere else to spend the night."

"Bitch," Karen said.

Gilly raised an indifferent eyebrow. "You always knew it, didn't you?"

Karen sighed and leaned forward. "Look. This is serious, okay? You don't tell a soul. Not your folks, not anyone. People have died."

"Yeah, right. Who?"

"My godfather, for a start."

Gilly didn't look impressed.

"And what I'm doing, right now, might be putting my own dad's life in danger."

Gilly very nearly laughed. "Karen, your dad's already dead."

Karen closed her eyes and pulled on her cigarette. When she opened them again, she looked at Gilly very directly. "That's just it: he's not."

Gilly's cigarette paused halfway to her lips. For the first time, Karen had caught her interest. "So tell me."

And Karen told her. Everything. About her meetings with Chris Connor, her father's experiment with bees that had so upset Ergo, the box of her father's belongings from the Geddes Institute, the letter from her dad. The phone call to Richard Deloit and her subsequent visit to London. And then the news, when she got back, of her godfather's "accident."

"I need to find this Billy Carr," she said. "My dad's student. He's the only remaining link to him."

"A guy who disappeared nearly two years ago?"

"He can only be a few years older than us, Gilly. Chances are he'll be on social media. Twitter, or Facebook, or Snapchat or something. That's why I need to use the computer." She stood up.

But Gilly didn't move from her chair. She stubbed out her cigarette in an overflowing ashtray. "What you need is help."

"Why do you think I came to you?"

"No, I mean adult help. We might be smart, K, but we're just a couple of teenage girls. And if you really are up against a giant agrochemical corporation like Ergo, we're no match for them. I mean, really! Get serious."

Gilly's words came like darts out of the dark, puncturing her fragile veneer of self-confidence and deflating all her hopes. "There *is* no one," she said.

"Come on, think, K. Think. There must be. What about your dad's family?"

Karen sighed. "His parents are dead. He has a brother somewhere in England, but they were never close and I haven't seen

330

him since Dad vanished. And that was the first time in years. I wouldn't even know where to start looking for him." But even as she said it, she knew that she did. "Wait a minute! He sent me a friend request on Facebook about a month after Dad died. Of course, I accepted, but we never shared or commented on anything. In fact, I can't even remember him making a single post. I'd forgotten all about him." She pushed Gilly out of her chair and swapped places with her in front of the computer.

"Help yourself, why don't you?" Gilly said dryly.

But Karen wasn't listening. She brought up Facebook on Gilly's browser and logged in. At the top of her profile page, she clicked on *Friends* and the short list of her twenty-seven friends appeared, most of whom she barely knew and almost never interacted with. All but one had postage-stamp profile pics alongside their names. The one blank was a white profile on a gray background of an anonymous male head beside the name Michael Fleming. "That's him." She clicked on his name and brought up his page.

It was blank. He had never posted a profile pic or cover photo. He had never entered any details about himself, where he lived or worked, or where he had been educated. There were no photos, no posts, and he had a single friend. Karen.

Gilly peered over her shoulder at the screen. "This is a dead account, girl. Maybe he thought it was a good idea at the time, and then never followed up on it. He obviously doesn't use it."

Karen sat staring at the screen. "That creeps me out, G. Like he's just been watching me. All my posts, all my pics."

"Or he set it up on an impulse then forgot about it. One way of finding out."

Karen turned to look up at her. "Send him a DM?"

Gilly shrugged. "Worth a try."

Karen opened up a new message box and tapped in her uncle's name. She thought briefly about what to say. Something that would grab his attention, elicit a response. If he ever checked it. And she typed, *Uncle Michael, I think Dad might still be alive. Please get in touch.* Short and to the point.

Gilly said, "Let's give him a little time to respond. Depends what app he's using. Some of them put alerts up on the screen."

They heard a door banging shut downstairs, then Gilly's mum's voice. "Gilly? Are you home?"

"Upstairs, Mum. Karen's here."

Karen whispered, "What if she's heard I'm

missing?"

Gilly grinned. "Let's find out." And she raised her voice. "Can she stay over tonight? Her mum's away at a wedding."

"No problem, love. You girls want something to eat? I can order pizza."

"Brilliant!" Gilly called back down the stairs, then turned to high-five her friend. "What topping do you want?"

"Chorizo?"

"Awesome!"

They sat eating the pizza, when it came, at the breakfast bar in the kitchen. Karen, Gilly, and Gilly's mum prattling inconsequentially as she made them mugs of tea. Karen had never much cared for her. She thought her vacuous, and really not very bright. Gilly got her brains from her dad, as Karen's had come down the genetic line from hers. She was equally sure that Gilly's mum seriously disapproved of her daughter's friendship with the goth punk. But she smiled at Karen and asked politely how her mother was doing these days. As if she was interested. Out of wickedness, Karen said, "She's doing fine since her lover moved in." Gilly's mum's mouth hung open, a slice of pizza on pause midway between it and her plate. "Her boss from the estate agency.

Turns out they'd been having sex for years."

When they got upstairs again, Gilly said, "Is that true? About your mum and her boss."

"Yep." Karen didn't want to talk about it anymore. Its shock value was all used up. She sat in Gilly's seat and banished the screensaver. The brief message to her uncle was enclosed in a speech bubble that issued from her profile pic. The cursor was winking in the text box. But there was no reply. She sat staring at it, motionless, for too long, and Gilly became aware that something was wrong.

"What is it?"

Karen's voice was small and hushed. "What if it wasn't my uncle I friended at all? What if it was Ergo pretending to be him so they could keep an eye on me?"

"Oh my God!" Gilly's hand flew to her mouth. "Then you've just tipped them off that you know about your dad."

Karen turned frightened blue eyes toward her friend. "How could we be so fucking stupid!" She raised her eyes to the heavens. "Christ!" Then, "We've got to find this Billy Carr guy. And fast."

"Okay, let me in." Gilly shoved her friend out of her seat and logged out of Karen's Facebook. "First thing we do is disguise my

IP address. Though that might just be shutting the barn door after the horse has bolted." She pulled up a piece of software called VPN Unlimited, and connected to an IP address registered somewhere in the south of England. "Okay." Now she logged into her own Facebook account and typed Billy Carr into the search window. A long list appeared of Carrs and Carvers and Carrolls and Carringtons, and other variations on Carr. But there were fewer Billy Carrs than either of them had expected, and it didn't take long to narrow the list down to three in Scotland. The second one that Gilly brought up to look at in detail elicited a yelp from Karen.

"There!" She pointed at the screen. "Studied genetics and neurobiology at Glasgow University, then won a research fellowship at the Geddes Institute of Environmental Sciences in Edinburgh. That's him."

Gilly scrolled through his personal details, but most of them were blank. Apart from his school. "He went to Springburn Academy in Glasgow," she said. "So the family home must be somewhere in that catchment area. Let's see how many Carrs there are in Glasgow." She switched screens and brought up the home page of the online BT Phone Book, tapping in *Carr* and *Glasgow.*

"Twelve," she said, then grinned from ear to ear. "And only one in Springburn. A certain W. Carr in Hillhouse Street. Balornock, actually." She swiped to another screen and initiated Google Maps. She typed in the Hillhouse Street address and watched as a map of Springburn and Balornock materialized. "And just about two streets away from Springburn Academy."

"That must be him." Karen's mouth was dry. "W for William; that'll be his father. Probably named after him."

But Gilly was back on Carr's Facebook page on another screen. "Wait," she said. "Look at this." She was scrolling through an album of photographs he had posted and stopped suddenly on a group of young men gathered outside a four-in-the-block house on a street corner. A tidy garden lay beyond a black, wrought-iron fence, and a shiny new red car sat at the curb. The young men, most of whom seemed to be in their late teens or early twenties, were gathered around it, grinning and laughing. Billy's post read, *My first car.* Billy, the proud owner, was at the center of the group, with several of his friends pointing fingers at him.

Karen leaned in to get a closer look at him. It was hard to judge his age, but the pic had been posted about eighteen months ago, and he looked around twenty-two or twenty-three. Judging by the car, he had done alright for himself after leaving the Geddes. His hair was longer than fashionable and drawn back in a short ponytail, and he sported a sparse-looking beard and mustache. But she could see that he was a good-looking boy, and with a car like that wouldn't have trouble pulling girls.

But Gilly was pointing at the street sign bolted to the railings behind the group. "Look," she said, and Karen refocused her gaze. The sign read, *Hillhouse Street*. Gilly turned a smile toward her friend. "I knew Facebook would come in useful for something one day." Her smile faded. "What will you do? Phone? He might not be living at home anymore."

Karen shook her head. "No. It's too easy for someone to hang up on you. I'll get the train to Glasgow first thing tomorrow and go knocking on the door."

CHAPTER TWENTY-TWO

The Carr family home was situated on the ground floor of the four-in-the-block house on the corner of Hillhouse Street. It stood opposite half a dozen semiderelict corner shops which had once served a community where most people did not have cars. Only three of them were still occupied. A launderette, a Chinese takeaway and a minimarket. The rest were shuttered up and covered in graffiti and old posters.

In front of the house, a neatly manicured square of lawn was surrounded by red chippings and framed by close-cropped hedges. The original windows had been replaced by brand-new hardwood and double glazing. Shiny red paint glistened on the stone sills and on a low wall leading to a door of polished mahogany with beveled glass and brass fittings. Scrupulously pruned roses were still in bloom, red and yellow and white, in finely turned flowerbeds.

Someone, Karen thought as she stepped from her taxi, cared about this place, and had lavished time and money on it. She opened the gate and walked up the path to the front door. Decorative blinds were half-drawn on the bedroom and living room windows. She rang the bell and waited with a sick feeling in the pit of her stomach. Behind this door lay what might very well be her last chance to connect with her father. And if that did not work out, she knew, there was nowhere else for her to go. No one else to turn to. She had cut the umbilical and cast herself adrift in a hostile world. And whatever happened, she would never go home again.

The door opened a crack and, from the darkness beyond, she was struck by a warm, antiseptic smell, like stepping into a hospital. The pale face of an elderly woman peered out at her. From buds that fitted into her nostrils, clear plastic tubing was hooked back over her ears, looping down to meet below her chin and then curling away behind her. Steel-gray hair was cut short around a thin face, prematurely lined, Karen saw now. The woman was not as old as she had at first appeared. Dark, sad eyes gazed up at her. "Can I help you, lassie?" Her voice was the texture of sandpaper.

"Mrs. Carr?"

"That's me."

"I'm looking for Billy, Mrs. Carr. We were research fellows at the Geddes Institute together." Karen knew she was taking a chance.

"He's not here. What did you want with him?"

"Billy said if I was ever in trouble I should look him up."

The woman chuckled. "That's oor Billy. Generous to a fault." Then her smile faded. "Are you in trouble, lass?"

"My father died a while back and my mother's in hospital. The bank's repossessed the house and I'm looking for somewhere to stay for a few nights." Karen had no idea where any of this was coming from. Spontaneous fiction. But she understood that she needed to win this woman's sympathy if she was going to get any information from her.

"Aw, jings, that's tough . . . What did you say your name was?"

"Karen."

"Karen. Your story's not that different from mine. My man died, too, and I have cancer of the lung. But at least I've got my Billy to look after me. No idea what I'd have done without him." She opened the door wide. "Come away in." And Karen saw, as she walked into the hall, that Mrs. Carr was dragging an oxygen tank behind her on a wheeled contraption not unlike a shopping trolley.

The woman closed the door and led Karen through to a small sitting room that gave on to a kitchen in the back. A gas fire sat in the original tiled fireplace, and although it seemed to be on low, the room was stiflingly hot.

"Sit yourself down, lassie."

Karen perched on the edge of an oxblood leather settee and looked around the room. Two leather recliners flanked the fireplace, and a sheepskin rug covered the carpet in front of the fire. A cat had stretched out on the rug and was fast asleep. In the corner by the window, a large flat screen TV stood on a table next to a sleek, low cabinet housing a high-end stereo system. Mrs. Carr parked her oxygen and eased herself into the recliner nearest the kitchen. Just that small effort left her breathless. An array of remote controls and an iPad cluttered a small table at her right hand, and Karen was shocked to see a packet of cigarettes and a lighter on it.

"Not sure there's much I can do for you, Karen. Billy's away the now and I don't know when he'll be back." She tilted her head and gave Karen a good looking over. "Were you and he . . . ?"

"Oh, nothing like that. Just friends."

His mother seemed relieved. "He's a good boy, my Billy. My only regret is he never finished his studies. He's got brains that lad. Not like me, or his faither. Not sure where he gets it from. But he's smart."

"Yes, I know."

"I don't suppose you would have some notion of why he quit?"

"The Geddes?"

"Aye."

"I've no idea, Mrs. Carr. He was there one day, and not the next." She recalled and repeated her godfather's words. "Never did find out what happened to him."

"Aye, well, he got himself a job, that's what happened to him. More interested in earning money than studying. But he's done well for himself, the laddie." She looked around the room. "Got me all this. And a man to do the garden. And minicabs to take me back and forward to the Royal. I canny complain, Karen. He's been good to his mammy."

Karen nodded her appreciation of Billy's sacrifices for his mother. "I don't suppose you could tell me where I can find him?"

A shadow flitted briefly across her face.

"I'm very sorry, Karen, but I canny. He made me promise."

Karen frowned. "Promise what?"

"Not to tell anyone where he was."

"Why?"

"Och, lassie, I've not the foggiest idea. He can be a funny one sometimes. He's working up north somewhere, and he told me if anyone came looking for him I wasn't to say a word about where he is." She stole a guilty glance at Karen. "I'm sure he didn't mean you, right enough. But I wouldn't like to give out his address or phone number without asking him first." She nodded toward the iPad on the table beside her. "He got me that so we could keep in touch by email." She said *email* as if it might be some foreign, and therefore highly suspicious, word. "I'm not very good at it. But I'll send him one tonight to ask if it's okay." She seemed embarrassed by having to put Karen off and eased herself out of her chair. "You'll take a wee cup of tea?" A distraction.

Karen said, "Oh, don't trouble yourself, Mrs. Carr. It's alright." She started to get up, but Billy's mother waved her back into her seat. "No trouble at all. I was just about to make one for myself anyway." And she dragged her oxygen off into the kitchen.

Karen sat awkwardly on the edge of the settee and wondered what she was going to do now. Billy would know immediately that Karen wasn't a fellow student from the Geddes. She stood up and glanced almost sightlessly around the room, a sense of panic rising inside her. This was her last hope.

Mrs. Carr was gabbling to her through the open door, and she could hear her banging about in the kitchen. There was no point in staying for tea and meaningless conversation. This was a dead end. In every possible way. She was about to turn and slip quietly out of the door when she spotted a postcard sitting prominently on the mantelpiece next to the clock. It was a Highland scene. A loch. Mountains rising up behind it. Pine forest. On an impulse, she lifted it down and turned it over. It was addressed to Mrs. Agnes Carr, and the message was written in biro by a spidery hand. *Hi Mum, here are my new home and email addresses. Keep them safe . . .*

When Mrs. Carr came to the kitchen door to ask if Karen took sugar or milk, the girl was gone. And so was the postcard.

CHAPTER TWENTY-THREE

I hate hospitals. I don't know why. Some bad experience in my past, I expect. But there it is, an odd mix of feelings. Fear and sadness. No. More than sadness. Depression. And that smell. Always that smell. Antiseptic. But something else, too. Something sharp and unpleasant. If death had a smell, then maybe that's how I would describe it.

They gave me a CT scan earlier. Looking for brain damage to explain my memory loss, I guess. They have poked and prodded and X-rayed and asked me endless questions, and now I have been sitting here in someone's office for the last half hour or more, staring at posters on piss-yellow walls. Looking at them, but not seeing them. I couldn't tell you what a single one of them was declaiming, or selling, or warning me to avoid.

There is a desk and a filing cabinet, and a

window looking out over a car park. Beyond that, I can see the road rising up to the great interior expanse of the Barvas Moor. When you drive that road, it seems as if there is no end to it. The moor stretches off as far as you can see in every direction. Flat, featureless, except for the scars of the peat-cutting near the roadside. In the very far south, the mountains of Harris are just visible on the distant horizon. And when you have driven for half an hour, you will see the Atlantic washing up along the west coast in a fury of white froth whipped up by a wind that has blown itself in anger across 3,000 miles of uninterrupted ocean.

It is strange how I am remembering these things now. Things I must have seen and done. And yet I am still without any sense of who it is that I am.

The door opens and a man in a white overall steps into the room. He is quite tall, and maybe around my age, or older. I can see that beneath his overall he wears a T-shirt and jeans. His hair is unconventionally long for a medical man. Reddish in color, and luxuriant once, perhaps, but thinning now a little across the top. He has a warm smile, and the freckled complexion of someone who spends time out of doors. I have not seen him before.

As I rise, he waves me back into my seat, shaking my hand and telling me not to disturb myself. I would have thought I was probably pretty disturbed already, without any further prompting, from myself or anyone else. He has an odd accent, almost imperceptible, and his English is just too perfect to be British. "Dr. Wulf Kimm," he says. "I am the resident psychiatrist. You'll excuse me if I don't use your name, since neither of us seems to know it." He smiles as if this is a joke, and I return the smile to humor him. Germans, and their sense of humor.

He sits down on the other side of the desk, opens up a folder that he has brought in with him and lays it before him, spreading the several sheets it contains across the desktop. He takes a pair of silver-rimmed reading glasses from the breast pocket of his overall and puts them on to skim-read the notes in front of him. Then he removes them, letting them dangle from his thumb and forefinger as he looks at me thoughtfully.

Quite unexpectedly he says, "I was a junior doctor at this hospital more than twenty years ago, you know. Best days of my life. I spent most of my time, when I wasn't working, riding around the island on my motorbike. Of course, it was a pretty rackety old thing in those days. Now I have a Honda CB1000R." As if this should mean something to me. "I went on to specialize in psychiatry back in Münster. You can imagine my joy when this job popped up on the online noticeboards. I jumped at the chance to come back."

"Sometimes," I say, "the past doesn't live up to your memory of it when you revisit."

He cocks his head and looks at me curiously. "And you know this how?"

I shrug. "Experience, I suppose."

"But you can't recall the experience that taught you it?"

"I wish I could."

He takes out a large spiral notebook from a desk drawer and opens it up. Selecting a pen from the same drawer and replacing his reading glasses on his nose, he scribbles some notes in it, then looks up again. "My colleagues can find no physical reason to explain your loss of memory. Neuroimaging reveals no brain damage."

"Which is why I have been handed over to you."

"Indeed." He pauses. "I am going to ask you a few questions, sir. I would appreciate it if you would answer me as honestly as you can."

"Of course."

"But first, let me establish . . . You remember nothing at all about yourself?"

I think about it. "I can remember feelings. Emotions. Over the past few days I have had some fleeting fragments of recollection. Mostly from my childhood. My mother. Another child. I'm not sure whether it's a brother or a sister. But nothing concrete or detailed. It's like dreaming. You wake up and the detail of it is gone, like a mist evaporating in sunshine." I scratch my head. "You know, it's weird. When I washed up on the beach, I had no idea at first where I was. And yet, now, the island seems very familiar to me. But I'm not sure if that's a familiarity I've learned or remembered." I turn toward the window. "Just a few minutes ago, I was looking out across the moor. I know it's the Barvas Moor, and I know that I have driven across it sometime in my past. But I don't actually remember doing it."

He nods and makes some notes.

"Later, we'll go over the experience of finding yourself on the beach, exactly as you remember it. But for the moment I'd like to focus on other parts of your memory. Have you ever, to your recollection, had black-outs? Blank spells? Memory lapses."

I shrug and smile at the irony of it. "I

don't really remember."

He doesn't smile. "What about time? Do you ever lose time? You know, have gaps in your experience of time?"

And suddenly I remember driving. It was night. I was going home. From work, perhaps. Things on my mind. And when I turned my car into the drive, I couldn't remember a single thing about the journey. Not one gear change, not one set of traffic lights. Nothing. Just as if it had never happened. So I tell Dr. Kimm and he makes some more notes.

"From what you remember about yourself, would you say you were someone preoccupied with details? You know, rules, lists, schedules, that sort of thing."

"I know that detail is important to me," I say. "Just from my experience of the last few days."

"To the point, perhaps, of losing sight of the reasons for having them in the first place?"

"I have one single preoccupation, Doctor. And that is to find out who I am, and why I am here. So, of course, every detail is important. But I'm not likely to lose sight of why."

"And the detail of what happened that led to your being washed up on a beach with no memory, that is just as important to you?"

"Of course."

"You *want* to know what happened."

And for the first time, I hesitate. Do I? Do I really want to know? What if I killed that man? Is that something I want to find out about myself? That I am a murderer. That I am capable of taking the life of another human being by smashing his head in. I look up and find the doctor watching me closely.

"What did you think when you found the body of that man on that island?"

I can't even bring myself to answer.

"Did you think you had killed him?"

I did. It was the first thought that went through my head, and I can barely make myself meet the doctor's eye as I nod my head.

CHAPTER TWENTY-FOUR

Gunn made a half-hearted attempt to clear away the mess on his desk to make a place for the good doctor's interim report. He shared his office with DC Smith, who was out on a job, and it was his chair that he offered to Dr. Kimm when he came in. He had heard the roar of the motorbike out in Church Street, but had not associated it with the imminent arrival of the psychiatrist from the Western Isles Hospital. Until the man entered wearing his leathers, a helmet under one arm, the other holding out his report.

"I knew you were in a hurry for this, Mr. Gunn, but it will take me some time to produce a detailed report. This is just a digest, a summary of my findings."

Gunn glanced over the printed sheets and his heart sank. This would not be light reading. "Maybe you'd like to give me a quick verbal," he said optimistically.

The doctor glanced at his watch. "I'm hoping to get down as far as Leverburgh today," he said. "Taking the Golden Road. The forecast's good, but I want to leave myself time to get back before dark."

"Doesn't have to take any longer than you want it to, Doctor. Just a thumbnail sketch of your conclusions." He knew he wouldn't have a chance to wade through the report, interim or not, before his meeting with the CIO, and he didn't want to face him without all the details at his fingertips.

Dr. Kimm laid his helmet on Smith's desk and unzipped his jacket. "Well, Mr. Gunn, it is a good job that this psychiatrist is also trained in basic psychology. You got two for the price of one." He grinned, but Gunn didn't see the joke. "Your man, for want of a better way to describe him, has no physical injury, no brain damage to explain his memory loss." He paused. "He is suffering, in my opinion, from dissociative amnesia."

"Dissociative . . ."

"It's one of a number of dissociative disorders, which also include multiple personality disorder. Which was interesting, given your account of the patient having spent eighteen months here pretending to be someone else. Dead or otherwise. I'm not so sure I would go so far as to say he

353

was suffering from MPD, but he does display some elements of OCPD."

Gunn frowned. "Which is?"

"Obsessive-compulsive personality disorder. Which you mustn't confuse with OCD, obsessive-compulsive disorder, which is anxiety-based. The patient in this case shows a certain preoccupation with orderliness and perfectionism. Excessive attention to detail. He would want to be the boss in any given situation, but would not make a good team member."

"What does any of this have to do with losing his memory?"

"Well, I explain all that in my report, Mr. Gunn. But it's all associated." He grinned. "Or, in his case, dissociated."

Gunn looked lost.

Doctor Kimm said, "A joke." He leaned forward. "We had a good long chat, Detective Sergeant, your suspect and I. I learned a lot. Not his name, or his job, or where he lives. But about him. His personality. Who he is, in that sense. He displays mild symptoms of OCPD and anankastic personality disorder. That doesn't make him mentally ill. Lots of us show those kind of symptoms to a greater or lesser degree. But it's his very personality that has forced him to shut out the events that led up to, and caused, his memory loss. A trauma of some kind, that he is simply unable to process in relation to himself. So he has just removed, or dissociated, himself from it. And the only way he has of doing that is by blocking his memory of it. And himself."

"You mean he's doing it on purpose?"

"No, no, no, no. It's quite involuntary."

Gunn scratched his chin. "No chance he's faking it?"

The doctor shook his head. "Impossible to rule it out, but I don't think so."

Gunn leaned back in his seat and sighed. None of this was going to be easy, and he found himself almost glad to be able to hand over accountability to the CIO. "Do you think he killed that man out on Eilean Mòr?"

"I have no idea, Mr. Gunn. You might have evidence to suggest that he did, but I suspect that you don't, since you are asking for my opinion." He smiled, and rubbed his hands together, as if washing them of all further responsibility. "But here's the interesting thing." He reached for his helmet and stood up. "The patient himself believes that he might have done it. In fact, he is scared that he did. Which might very well be what is blocking his memory of the whole thing."

Gunn stood up, too. "Will it ever come

back to him? His memory."

"It could come back in the blink of an eye, Mr. Gunn. Or it might never return. Or he might start remembering bits, fragments, like the pieces of a jigsaw puzzle, which will eventually enable him to put together a picture of what happened."

"Treatment?"

The doctor shrugged. "None, really. Hypnosis might help. It might not. But I can't give him a pill that will restore his memory, if that's what you're thinking. It's his subconscious that has turned the key in the lock. And it's only his subconscious that can unlock it again." He beamed. "Interesting case." And he glanced out of the window. "Sun's shining. It's going to be a lovely ride down to Harris."

The CIO was younger than Gunn. He had been a newly promoted Detective Constable at Inverness when Gunn first met him. A smug little bastard who was going places and knew it. Though Gunn, then his senior officer, had still been tasked with drying him behind the ears and preventing him from getting unwittingly tangled up in the ropes. But Gunn's ambitions had never extended beyond returning to his native Stornoway and providing a safe and stable environment for raising a family. And so, while Gunn remained a Detective Sergeant, Jimmy "The Hammer" Chisholm, as he became known, leapfrogged him up the ranks and was now *his* senior officer. Which Gunn found quite hard to swallow. Although Chisholm himself had no difficulty in hammering the point home.

He looked up from his desk as Gunn came in. There was no smile, no acknowledgment that they had not seen each other for nearly two years. His face was leaner than Gunn remembered, his nose more bladelike. And Gunn was pleased to see that he was losing his hair while Gunn's still grew in thick abundance.

"George." It was DCI Chisholm's only acknowledgment. And even that rankled. He had once been *Jimmy* to Gunn's *sir.* Now it was the other way around. The desk in front of him was strewn with reports. "Clear enough from the pathologist that it was murder," he said. No preamble. "We still don't know who he is?"

"Afraid not, sir."

"What are we doing to find out?" Meaning, what was Gunn doing.

"As you know, sir, his photograph has been in all the dailies, as well as on BBC and STV. It'll be in all the periodicals before the week's out."

"And down south?"

"*Crimewatch* is running an item this week."

"Nothing from fingerprints or DNA?"

"I think I might have told you if there were, sir." Gunn beamed as if he was making a joke, but Chisholm's glare made it clear he recognized insolence when he heard it.

Gunn said, "We're still awaiting a report back from the lab to learn if the victim had any skin from his attacker under his fingernails. If there is, then we'll know soon enough if there's a match with the suspect."

Chisholm leaned back in his seat, stroking his chin with pensive fingers, and looked at Gunn reflectively. "Why do I have the feeling you don't think there will be?"

Gunn lifted his eyebrows in surprise. "I have no idea, sir."

"DC Smith seemed to think you were quite sympathetic to our suspect's story."

"Oh, did he?" Gunn filed that one away for later retribution. "I just happen to think he's telling the truth, as far as he knows it. But that doesn't mean he's not our killer. Borne out by the report from the psychiatrist."

Chisholm looked up, interested. "You've

spoken to him?"

Gunn nodded and dropped Kimm's interim report on Chisholm's desk. "That's a holding report on his findings."

Chisholm opened the folder and ran his eye down the first page. Gunn saw his jaw clench and eyes widen almost imperceptibly before he looked up. "Tell me what's in it." And Gunn was glad he had persuaded the psychiatrist to delay his run down to Harris for the verbal briefing.

"According to Doctor Kimm, he's suffering from dissociative amnesia."

"And what's that when it's at home?"

Gunn said smugly, "It's one of a group of disorders, sir. Psychological. There's no physical reason for his memory loss. No injury. The psychiatrist believes that he is blocking a trauma of some kind."

"The murder of our man on Eilean Mòr."

"Very possibly. The suspect has no memory of committing the murder, but is afraid that he did. The memory loss is a way of dissociating himself from the act. Assuming that he did it."

Chisholm looked almost impressed. "And do we think that he did?"

"Well, that's the problem, sir. We have no physical evidence to tie him to the murder. We can't even prove that he was on the island at the time, although he himself admits it's a possibility." Gunn sucked in air before he continued. "As you'll see from my report, he was living down on Harris under an assumed identity for eighteen months prior to the murder. The identity of a dead man, as it turns out. So neither he, nor I, have the least idea of who he actually is."

"So we have a victim and a suspect, neither of whom we can identify, and no evidence whatsoever linking one to the other?"

Gunn shifted uncomfortably. "Well, there is one thing, sir. We found a bunch of scientific and beekeeping equipment in the suspect's shed down at Luskentyre. He claims not to know what any of it is doing there, but both he and the victim have bee stings on the back of their hands." And he could see from Chisholm's expression that the DCI was as nonplussed by this as he was himself.

Chisholm sighed and looked again at the psychiatrist's notes, but it was clear to Gunn he wasn't reading them, and he suspected that Chisholm was wishing they had sent someone else to take charge of this case. Finally he looked up. "So should we detain him or not?"

"Well, given that we only have one shot at

that, sir, it might be better if we didn't. Since we have no actual evidence to link him to the crime. Apart from charging him with driving without a license, we don't have a single reason to hold him."

"Then you'd better find one pretty damn fast, George." And Gunn noticed that the *we* had morphed to *you*. A case of dissociative responsibility, he thought wryly. "And I don't want him leaving the island until he's been either cleared or charged."

Chapter Twenty-Five

If anything, it feels even stranger to be chauffeur-driven home by a uniformed police officer than it did being taken away the other morning under suspicion of murder. But there is no more clarity now than there was then. The fact that they have let me go does not mean they think I didn't do it. They just can't prove it. That much is clear to me, at least. But I am none the wiser. About anything. About who I am, why I am here, or whether or not I am a murderer.

They have warned me not to leave the island, and since I am forbidden to drive my car, I am effectively under house arrest in a cottage whose owner wants rid of me as soon as possible.

Still, there is a comfort in seeing the beach laid out ahead of me beyond the dunes, beach grass blowing in the wind. That white Highland pony is still grazing there, silhouetted against the startling blue of the sea behind it, and a sky glowing red and gray beyond that. Long strips of dark cloud almost obscuring the sun as it dips toward the horizon.

I think Mrs. Macdonald has some kind of radar installed in her house, or a long-range listening device. Because there she is at the window as we turn down over the cattle grid on to the metaled parking area behind Dune Cottage. Watching. I see the net curtain fall to obscure her as I get out of the car and glance across the road in her direction.

My car sits where I left it, and the constable gets out of the driver's side of his own and says, "Detective Sergeant Gunn has asked me to take your car keys, sir."

I go into the house, which is not locked, and find my keys hanging on the hook just inside the door. I remove my car key from the ring and step out again to hand it to the policeman. He nods and gets into his car to drive off without another word.

I go back inside to close the door and lean my back against it, eyes closed. The nightmare goes on.

The house is a mess as I wander through it, the detritus of the police search lying about the place like so much debris washed ashore by the same sea that dumped me, semiconscious and without memory, on the beach.

I feel compelled to tidy up, to reintroduce at least some order to a life in chaos. And I wonder if perhaps the psychiatrist is right, and that I do suffer to a greater or lesser degree from some kind of obsessive-compulsive personality disorder. If I knew myself better, I might have been able to confirm that diagnosis.

In the back bedroom, I come across the wrecked remains of the coffee table whose glass was smashed the night I was attacked by an intruder. And I wonder why I didn't tell the police about what happened that night. It wasn't a conscious decision, but I suppose I knew that, since there was no way of proving it, my whole story might only have been made to sound even more ridiculous. How often it is that an awkward truth is easier to dismiss than a comforting lie.

It is dark by the time I go outside with a stout screwdriver to prise off the strip of wood the police have used to seal the garden shed shut. I don't want Mrs. Macdonald's radar to alert her to what I am doing, so I pull the door closed behind me before turning on the light.

Looking again, with fresh eyes, I see how ordered it all is. How I have arranged shelves and hooks to accommodate different, though associated, items. My first impression of seeing it the other day was of something quite random, almost chaotic, but I realize now that there is a logic at work. Even if I am not quite sure what it is. I look at the neat row of microtweezers and scissors lined up beside a standing microscope with twin eyepieces and a stage plate. Next to it, a cardboard box filled with tiny, tapering plastic tubes, sealable at one end with flip-over tops.

What was I looking at through this microscope, and why would I require such tiny tweezers? I bend over the microscope and put my eyes to the lenses, and suddenly I see it. A bee in sharp focus on the stage plate, brightly lit. With the scissors and tweezers, I am carefully opening up its head to tease out the brain and drop it into one of those tiny plastic tubes.

That fleeting flash of recollection is like an electric shock, and I step back, recoiling in surprise. I am both scared and energized. It is the first real fragment of returning memory. No matter how perplexing, it is a step toward discovering who I really am. But also a step into that dark cloud of obscurity that hides the truth of what happened to me, and what I might have done, that night out on Eilean Mòr.

I hear my name called from somewhere outside and I am startled out of the moment. I recognize Sally's voice and then the sound of the door opening into the cottage. I quickly turn out the light in the shed and step out into the dark, closing the door behind me and fixing it shut as best I can.

As I hurry up the steps and into the house, Bran barks excitedly and rushes to greet me, paws up on my chest, very nearly knocking me over. I am almost as glad to see him as he is to see me. The one living creature in my life who trusts me unreservedly. I make a great fuss of him, then look up to see Sally standing framed in the arch that leads to the sitting room.

She is watching us with a curiously neutral expression on her face. How often in these last days I have wanted to hold her. To feel the comfort and warmth of another human being. To feel loved and wanted, and not just by a dog. But something, even in the way she is standing, places a barrier between us, and I know instinctively that she will not be that source of warmth and comfort tonight.

I gaze at her in the half-light of the living room lamp that she has turned on, and feel pangs of both lust and regret, and I remember running my hands through her silken, cropped hair, her naked skin next to mine. In the bedroom along the hall. In the tiny, cold chamber at the top of the tower in St. Clement's Church.

"The police were asking about us," she says.

"You and Jon?"

"You and me."

I nod. "Gunn said you denied we were having a relationship."

"Did you tell him about us?"

"No. He already knew. Didn't seem any point in lying about it. He said he asked you in front of Jon."

"Yes." She gazes at the floor for a moment, then back at me. "He's been behaving pretty strangely ever since."

"You mean he didn't believe you?"

"I don't know. We never spoke about it after the cop went. But he's being cold and distant." She pauses. "I think we should stop seeing each other."

I am not sure why, but I am devastated by this. Sally is the one person I trust. The one person I have felt able to tell everything. Without her, I know I will be utterly, overwhelmingly alone. "Why, Sally? Why? You said it was as good as over between you and Jon."

"It is."

"Then why would we stop seeing each other?"

She takes a deep breath. "Because I have no idea who you are, Neal." She almost laughs. "Neal. I don't even know if that's your name."

"It's not."

A slight frown creases her eyes.

"Neal Maclean is dead."

And now they open wide. "Then who the hell are you?"

"I don't know." Hopelessly alone in my ignorance, as I knew I would be.

Her jaw seems to set, a hint of defiance in it. "And that man they found on the Flannan Isles . . . Did you kill him?"

I close my eyes and hold them shut for what seems like an inordinate length of time, before opening them again to see that she has not moved a muscle. "It is almost impossible for me to think that somehow I have it in me to take the life of another human being. But I think I probably did."

The dark of the night outside seems profound. Tangible, enveloping, as if it had simply wrapped itself around me. In my bedroom, the only light comes from the luminous hands of the bedside clock. I have left the side window on the latch, and I can hear the wind and the ocean. And, in the room, the sound of Bran's heavy breathing. He is happy to be back with me, oblivious of my misery, and has fallen easily into a deep sleep. I feel his legs kicking from time to time as he dreams, perhaps of chasing rabbits across the dunes.

It is hours since Sally left, and I can't sleep. For fear that I share this body I inhabit with a killer.

CHAPTER TWENTY-SIX

It was almost two hours since Karen had boarded the train at Inverness. She was travel-weary after nearly three and a half hours on the train from Glasgow, and then hanging around at Inverness Station, waiting for her connection. The time had been passed with coffee and sandwiches in the Pumpkin Café, and an almost incessant stream of banter from a young Polish guard who seemed to have nothing better to do while waiting for his train than regale Karen with tales of his lazy Scottish girlfriend.

Since then, the West Highlands had slipped past the window of her seat on the train to Kyle of Lochalsh in a gloomy blur of lochs and mountains. Places like the Valley of Drizzle, and Raven Rock, seemed somehow reminiscent of Tolkien in this land torn and shaped by the great glaciers of some past ice-age. Tree-covered islands in vast, still lochs cast dark reflections on darker water, great jagged mountains rising above the tree line to vanish in brooding low cloud.

It was Karen's first time in this part of the country. She felt dwarfed by it, lost and insignificant, and it cast a doubtful perspective on her foolish endeavor to track down Billy Carr in some distant, hidden valley. But his address, at least, had a postcode, so it couldn't be impossible to find.

At last the train rumbled into the tiny station at Strathcarron, the village of Lochcarron strung out along the far shore of the loch itself, the jagged peaks of the Torridon mountains rising into an ominous sky. She was the sole passenger to leave the train here, stepping down on to a deserted platform, a blue and cream-painted rusty metal bridge straddling the track. As the train pulled away, she felt dumped and deserted in the middle of nowhere. She zipped up her hoodie and went out into a small car park. There wasn't much here. A line of whitewashed cottages stretched away along a narrow lane. There was a Post Office in what might once have been the old station house, and beyond the car park, the Strathcarron Hotel.

Here, she asked a smiling young receptionist if she could call her a taxi. "Where are you going?" the girl asked, and Karen showed her Billy Carr's postcard. She frowned. "No idea where that is. The driver'll probably know, though."

The driver didn't. It took fifteen minutes for him to come and pick her up from the car park behind the station, and when he looked at the address he shook his head. "Strathdarroch? Never heard of it, and I've lived here all my life." Then he grinned. "Thank the good Lord for GPS, eh?"

Programmed with Billy Carr's postcode, the GPS took them off into the wilderness on a single-track road that rose up through wild, uncultivated country in the approximate direction of Loch Kishorn, or so the driver said. They passed through Forestry Commission plantation, and then what might have been the remains of ancient Caledonian forest, stands of ragged Scots pines and the deciduous oaks and birch and aspen of Scotland's long-vanished temperate rainforest.

It took almost twenty-five minutes before the driver turned into a metaled cul-de-sac, where a wooden gate blocked their further progress and the road became a rutted track that cut up the hill through thick forest.

"It's up that track somewhere, love. But I'm afraid this is as far as I can take you.

Rip the underside off my car if I try and drive her up there."

Karen was reluctant to get out of the taxi. If she couldn't find the Darroch Cottage of Billy Carr's address, she would be stranded out here with nowhere to go, and no way back. They hadn't seen a cottage, or a car, or any other sign of life for the last fifteen minutes. The light was already starting to fade from the east, and there could be no more than a couple of hours of daylight left. If she let the driver go, she was absolutely on her own. She checked her phone. There wasn't even a signal here to call for help. "How much do I owe you?" she said, in a voice that sounded a great deal more confident than she felt.

"Forty-five quid, love." He paused. "Sure you know where you're going?"

She nodded, almost afraid to speak in case the fear that was churning in her stomach would make her throw up.

After she had paid him, she stepped out into the dusk and watched as he turned the car and headed back the way they had come. She stood for a long time, listening to the sound of its motor fading into the early evening, until she could hear nothing except for the birdcall that filled the air all around her and, somewhere, the distant sound of running water.

Finally, with feet like lead, she unlatched the gate and slipped through it, fastening it again behind her, and started up through the trees, darkness closing in around her. She had never felt so entirely alone.

With her eyes turned down, watching each and every step on the ridges and ruts of the track so that she didn't turn her ankle, she failed to notice how the trees around her were beginning to thin. And when finally she looked up, she saw that the track was leading her out of the forest and into a beaten clearing that sat in the lee of the hills.

Off to the right, on the very edge of the forest, stood a dilapidated stone cottage with a lean-to extension. To the left, a tiny loch lay still and dark in the gathering gloom, its waters lapping gently against the edge of the clearing. On the far side of it, a small waterfall tumbled through trees and rocks to send ripples arcing out toward its center. A dusty, mud-spattered red Mitsubishi four-wheel-drive Outlander sat at an angle under the shade of a mountain ash growing among a cluster of rocks. Billy Carr, it seemed, liked red.

As she crossed the clearing, a couple of brown hens went skittering and clucking away into the trees, and she called out,

"Hello, anybody there?"

She was rewarded with a silence broken only by the birds. The door to the cottage stood ajar, and she could see that the place lay in darkness beyond it. She reached out a hand and pushed the door open into the dark. The hinges creaked like a sound effect from a bad horror movie.

"Hello?"

Still nothing. She stepped inside and allowed a few moments for her pupils to dilate. Most of the footprint was occupied by a single room, cluttered with old furniture standing at odd angles on an uneven stone floor. A sofa and a couple of armchairs, horsehair bursting through where the upholstery was worn thin or torn. An old rocking chair, with a red cushion, pulled up beside a wood-burning stove set in what must have been the original fireplace. To the left of the door, a dining table covered by an old, stained cloth was cluttered with all manner of bric-a-brac. A fishing rod and flies, boxes, and torn-open cartons of some kind of scientific supplies. There was a pair of large, padded white gloves, an SLR camera fitted into a bracket with a clamp on one end, a scattering of inch-long red plastic tubes with flip-over lids.

Through an open door that led into the

lean-to, she saw dirty dishes piled around an old Belfast sink. A gas cooker caked in grease. She heard the hum of a refrigerator. The air was thick with the odor of stale cooking and woodsmoke.

"Can I help you?"

The voice startled her, and she wheeled around to find herself faced by a tall figure wearing a white circular hat. Netting that hung from its wide brim obscured the face, like an alien from the same horror movie as the door with the sound effect. She let out a small, involuntary scream.

A hand shot up to whip away the hat and reveal the grinning, bearded face of the young man whose photographs she had seen on the Billy Carr Facebook page. His hair was longer. The beard, too. And it tangled around a tanned face that was more handsome in life than captured on a screen. He wore a grubby white T-shirt and jeans tucked into mud-caked boots. He said, "That's the trouble with this country practice of leaving your doors open. Sometimes folk wander in uninvited."

Karen recaptured a little of her composure. "I'm sorry. As you say, the door was open. I'm looking for Billy Carr."

He looked at her appraisingly. "Oh, are you? And I suppose you'll be the Karen who told my maw that I knew her from the Geddes." He chucked his hat on to the table and swung a pack from his back to set down on the floor at his feet. "She was pretty pissed off at you stealing my postcard and running off without so much as a thank you or goodbye. Good thing my email address was in her mailer, or she'd never have been able to get in touch with me." His smile had long gone. "So you want to tell me what the fuck your game is?"

Karen took a half-step back. "I've come a long way to see you, Billy."

The grin returned, although there was no humor in it that Karen could see. "All the way from Glasgow, no doubt. I'm flattered. There's not many lassies would travel that far just to see me. Must be my irresistible charm, eh?" The grin vanished again. "Or maybe not. What are you after, Karen?" And he put a heavily sarcastic emphasis on her name.

She was determined not to be intimidated and stuck out a defiant jaw. "I was hoping you could tell me whether or not my father is still alive."

It was as if a light had been switched out behind his face. Darkness fell across it like a shadow, and his black eyes widened. "Jesus Christ! Karen Fleming?"

■ ■ ■ ■

Karen sat at the space Billy had cleared for them on the table and smoked nervously as she waited for him to come back out from the kitchen. He had already broken the seal on a bottle of Australian shiraz and poured them each a glass of the dark purple wine. She didn't much like the taste of it, and left it untouched after the first sip.

Now he arrived with a wooden chopping board laden with chunks of cheese and glistening, freshly washed grapes, and half a French loaf, which he cut into pieces on the table and dropped into a basket with a hand engrained by grime and punctuated by the odd bee sting.

"Not really hungry," Karen said.

Billy sat down opposite her and shrugged. "Suit yourself." He cut some slices of cheese to lay along a piece of bread, which he wolfed down hungrily, washing it over with a mouthful of wine. As he picked a couple of grapes from the bunch, he said, "You know as well as I do that your father's dead."

"I know as well as you do that he's not."

He eyed her suspiciously. "And just how exactly would you know that?"

"He left me a letter, which I wasn't supposed to get for another year."

Billy paused, with a grape at his lips. "What, and he told you in this letter that he was still alive?"

"As good as."

"Fuck!" He popped the grape past his waiting lips and bit down on it to release its sweet juices into his mouth. "Why would he do that?"

"Because he figured that, by the time I read it, he wouldn't have to pretend any longer that he had committed suicide."

Billy gazed at her thoughtfully while he took another mouthful of bread and cheese. "Aye, well, since he didn't mean you to get it for another year, maybe he still wants people to go on thinking that. Does it not occur to you that by blowing his secret you could maybe be putting his life at risk?"

She drew on her cigarette and blew smoke into the thick, fetid air of the cottage. "Funny. You're the second person to suggest that in the last couple of days."

He frowned. "Oh, yeah? Who else?"

"Richard Deloit."

Billy's eyes opened wide. "Deloit spoke to you?"

"Well, no. I spoke to him, and he as good as told me to fuck off."

He breathed consternation through his

nose. "So why are you pursuing this?"

"Maybe if you'd ever lost your father, only to find out that he was still alive, you wouldn't have to ask."

He took a large gulp of wine. "Aye, well, I know what it's like to lose a father, right enough. It's tough. Especially when you're still a kid. Different for a girl, maybe, but for someone like me, suddenly it brings responsibilities."

"Your mother."

He nodded. "I'd fucking do anything for her, you know? She and my old man both. Sacrificed almost everything to send me to a good school. I mean, there's not many kids from Balornock get to go to Hutcheson's Grammar, do they? A working-class boy among all the toffs. School fees, university. I owe them everything. And my dad goes and dies just when she needs him most. So it's down to me now. Payback. Not that I resent it. I love that woman."

And Karen wondered how it must feel to love your mother. "So what are you doing here?" she said.

He placed his glass carefully on the table and thought about it. Then he stood up. "Come with me," he said. "I'll show you."

He lifted his beekeeper's hat and walked out from the gloom of the cottage into the dusky pink twilight of the clearing. Karen stubbed out her cigarette and followed. He led her then along a well-worn path that wound its way through the trees. A startled fawn bounded away into the darkness of the woods, crashing through the undergrowth and sending birds screeching and cawing into the high branches.

After just a few minutes they emerged into a natural clearing where trees had been brought down by rockfall from the hill above, and eighteen beehives stood secured to wooden pallets set among the rocks and the tangling remains of fallen tree trunks.

They cast shadows there in the dying light, among the trees, like sentinels standing guard over the future of mankind. A few bees were still making their return to the hives at the end of a long day of foraging for pollen. Billy went to the nearest of them and removed the lid and the crown board, setting them carefully on the ground beside it. He turned to see that Karen had not moved from her place on the clearing's edge.

"Come and see," he said. "They'll not sting you unless they think you present a threat." He grinned. "Though they like to crawl into tight, dark spaces, like nostrils and ears. That's why the hat." And he put it on, letting the netting drape itself over his shoulders, before reaching in to slide out one of eleven frames containing honeycomb and crawling with bees.

Karen approached cautiously, nervous of the bees that buzzed around the hive, and the netted figure of Billy Carr as he held up the frame. They were crawling all over his hands, but he didn't seem troubled by them.

"Look," he said. "Aren't they beautiful? A perfect matriarchal society, behavior elaborately preordained for perpetuation of the species. The honey and the beeswax and the propolis are just side products that we have learned to harvest. If there is some kind of intelligent design to this world, Karen, then bees are the key to the survival of Man. Even if it was only a random process of evolution, we can't do without them."

Karen nodded. "I know."

"What do you know?"

"I know that they pollinate two-thirds or more of the fruit and vegetables and nuts, and other crops that feed us. I know that without them tens of millions of people or more would probably starve to death."

He grinned. "Your father's daughter, I see."

"Actually, it was Chris Connor that told me about bees." Billy glowered. "Connor?

What the fuck's he been saying?"

"That you and my dad did an experiment proving that neonic pesticides are screwing with bees' brains."

"Fucking idiot! He should have known better than to go opening his mouth like that." Billy slid the frame back into place and started replacing the crown board and lid.

"That *fucking idiot* was my godfather. And he won't be opening his mouth again, because he's dead."

Billy turned, removing his hat, and she saw that his face had gone deathly pale. "Dead? How?"

"A car accident. Apparently. The day after he met me and told me all about you and my dad, and your experiment." She paused and cast her gaze over the eighteen silent sentinels. "You're repeating the experiment, aren't you?"

He sighed and seemed resigned to the fact that there was little point in trying to hide the truth from her anymore. He nodded. "Here and at two other sites. Chosen because of their purity. Areas uncontaminated by pesticides or herbicides. So that, when we introduce neonics to the diet of the bees, we know with certainty no other cause can be attributed to the effects. We even monitor the bees for disease and mites, though that's not really a problem, since we had the original colonies checked and declared disease-free before we brought them on site."

"So nine of these would be control hives?"

He raised his eyebrows in surprise. "Oh, you know about that, do you?"

"Chris explained." She nodded toward the hives. "I'm assuming that you let the bees in half of the hives forage for pollen naturally, and feed the other half with . . . what? Imidacloprid?"

Billy grinned now. "You must have been paying attention, girl. You'd make a good student." He paused. "We actually let both groups forage naturally, and at certain times feed both groups sugar syrup. The difference is that we introduce tiny quantities of imidacloprid into the sugar syrup of the non-control group. The kind of quantities they would expect to encounter in the pollen and nectar of any environment where crops have been treated by neonic pesticides. About 2.5 parts per billion, which is already proven not to kill bees."

"But it destroys their learning and memory."

He nodded grimly. "It does."

"How do you know that, Billy?"

"Because we monitor their performance."

"How? How's that possible?"

He shrugged. "Lots of ways. We measure the colony once a week by weighing the hives. But only at night, when they've all returned. We mark the queen to keep an eye on her and make sure she's not been replaced. We photograph all the frames, after shaking off the bees, to estimate areas of honey stores, and pollen, sealed brood, larvae, eggs. We place cameras above the entrance to the hives to collect data on activity levels. Mainly the number of bees returning with pollen. We can measure the amount of pollen gathered by using pollen traps. And we can use that same pollen, when foraging is good and they're not interested in the sugar syrup, to contaminate it with imidacloprid then give back to them the following day. We even screen foraging bees for gut parasites at the entrance to the hive using a handheld field microscope."

"So the effect of the pesticide is measurable?"

"Absolutely. And, Karen, it is seriously fucking with their ability to do their job." He grinned. "Which is . . . ?" He held open hands out toward her to prompt a response.

She tutted and raised her eyes skyward. "To feed the world."

He rang an imaginary bell. "Brrrrring! Well done, you've just won a microscope and a holiday for two in a tropical rainforest somewhere in South America."

She shook her head and smiled in spite of herself.

"What's amazing about bees, Karen, is their ability to associate color and smell with good food sources. You can actually teach them to remember and identify smells that will lead them to food. They are so good at it that the military are now using bees to sniff out explosives, like landmines, or IEDs. Feed them after exposing them to the smell of any explosive substance, and they will identify it with food. Release a bunch of bees where you suspect there are buried landmines, and they will immediately cluster around them, smelling the explosive. Without, of course, setting them off." His face clouded. "But the effect of the neonics is to destroy that ability. It damages their brain cells. The cells don't die, but they stop generating the energy that fuels their memory. So they don't remember the smell, or the color, or the way to the food or the way back. And, you know, bees communicate all this information to one another by these amazing dances they do in the hives. Where the good food is, what direction to go, how far. But, without memory, there is no accurate communication. And, without either, the colony will wither and die." He turned to wave his arm toward his hives. "And that's exactly what's been happening here."

He raised his head, and Karen followed his gaze up through the trees to where the first stars were appearing faintly as blue faded to black. He took her by the arm, and she was reminded momentarily of Richard Deloit and the way he had expelled her from the offices of OneWorld. "Come on, we should go back to the cottage before it gets dark and we get lost in the woohooooods." He waved his arms, ghostlike in the air, and laughed. "Actually, after eighteen months of this, I reckon I could make it back blindfolded."

Darkness fell suddenly, and evening became night even before they got back to the cottage. Strangely, it almost seemed lighter. The sky was clear and crusted with stars, and a nearly full moon rose up over the hills to cast its shimmering silver luminescence on the still, reflective surface of the loch.

Billy switched on a light when they entered the cottage, and the dismal yellow that washed over the room from the single naked bulb at its center made it seem even more miserable. It really was a mess, Karen saw now. The floor strewn with discarded food wrappers and cigarette ends, and dried mud from caked boots. Clothes lay over the backs of chairs, and socks and underwear hung drying from a rack near the stove. Karen looked around with disgust. The contrast with the pristine, sanitized middle-class existence that her mother had contrived for her in suburban Edinburgh could hardly have been more stark, or unpleasant.

Billy followed her eyes and looked embarrassed. He ran his hand back through his hair as if somehow trying to make himself more presentable. "If I'd known I was having a visitor, I'd have tidied up. Never seems much point when you're just on your own." He nodded toward a large flat-screen television in the corner. "TV's my only company. No signal up here, of course. I've got a satellite dish out back."

Karen could only imagine how depressing it would be. "And you've been here eighteen months?"

"Yep. Had a wee break during the winter months. Without that, I'd have gone stir-crazy a long time ago. Thank God it's just about over."

"Is it?"

"Pollen season's all but finished. We've got

two years of results from three separate sources. Identical experiments with eighteen hives, each in contaminant-free environments. Covers all the variables so that the statistician can draw incontrovertible conclusions."

"Statistician?"

"Yep. An independent fourth party, who takes all our figures and results and crunches the numbers. When his report on our experiment gets published, it's going to blow the agrochem industry out of the water, Karen."

"So you already know what the results are?"

"Well, we anticipated what they might be. But I haven't actually seen the final figures myself."

"Why not? If you're taking all these daily and weekly measurements, then you have all the figures yourself, surely?"

"Not the most important ones." He headed toward a door in the far corner of the room. "Come on, I'll show you."

Karen followed him into what must once have been a storeroom of some kind, built out from the back of the cottage under a sloping roof. The light he turned on here was much brighter than the one in the sitting room, throwing everything into sharp relief. In contrast to the chaos outside, there was a sense of order in the tiny secret lab that it revealed. Worktops set out with scientific equipment. Microscopes, micro-pipettes, tweezers and scissors. Electrical equipment, a laptop, a small freezer humming in the corner. Shelves laden with glass jars and Petri dishes and bottles. Everything was shiny clean, and, unlike the air in the sitting room, there was a smell in this little room of antiseptic, almost hospital-like.

"This is the nerve center, so to speak. Most of the rest of what we do is keeping and collecting numbers. Figures. Statistics. Here, under that microscope, we dissect contaminated bees toward the end of their pollen-collecting lives, which are only about three weeks long, by the way. We remove brain matter and send it in ice-packed flasks to a laboratory in Edinburgh." He laughed. "I'm sure the good folks in the Post Office down in Strathcarron must wonder what it is I've been sending away in these wee parcels every week. But, anyway, the lab in Edinburgh measures levels of the contaminant, and is then able to relate them to cell damage."

Karen looked at him. "But they don't send the results back to you?"

"No. They all go to the PI, along with all

my stats, and those from —" he grinned — "my coconspirator."

"PI?"

"Principal Investigator. He's the team leader. The third in our little triumvirate." Billy turned out the light and pulled the door shut behind them as they went back out to the sitting room. "All the data goes to him, and he's the one who feeds it to the statistician."

Karen shook her head. "I don't understand. Why wouldn't you all share in the data?"

"Because the PI trusts nobody but himself, Karen. Not even me, or Sam. And the PI's known Sam since his university days. But he's probably right to be so careful, because these bastards will go to any lengths to stop us publishing."

"Ergo?"

Billy nodded. "That's why all the secrecy. I'm sure they know what we're doing, just not exactly who's doing it or where." He sat down at the table and took out a tin filled with loose tobacco and a chunk of cannabis resin wrapped in silver paper. "See, nobody's done this kind of detailed research before, Karen, because the only people likely to fund it would be the industry themselves. And they just bury the results

391

that they don't like." His laugh lacked humor. "That's why, when your dad went to Ergo with the results of our accidental experiment, they buried *us*. Threatened to withdraw funding from the Geddes, got your dad sacked and my fellowship withdrawn." He turned to look at her. "I wasn't kidding when I said publication of our results would blow them out of the water. The European Union will be forced to extend its ban on neonicotinoids. The fucking British government, would you believe, has been trying to get that ban lifted, under pressure from the farmers' union. So they're going to have to change their tune pretty bloody fast. And then there's the Americans. They've been resisting all attempts at banning neonics. We are going to leave them with no choice."

"And the agrochem industry is not going to be very happy."

"Fucking right, they're not!" He held the flickering flame of his lighter under the little tinfoil package he had made containing the cannabis. "They don't care about the planet or the bees, Karen. They don't give a shit about people starving. All they care about is money. Profit. The bottom line. Like the tobacco industry's big five, they are just in total denial. And trust me, they will do anything, *anything,* to stop us from publishing."

He laid tobacco along a sheet of cigarette paper and crumbled the cooked resin into it, before rolling it up, licking the gummed edge and sticking it down. He put the deformed-looking cigarette to his lips and lit it, drawing deeply and holding the smoke in for some moments before blowing it out.

He held the spliff out to Karen. "Want a drag?"

She took it, and sucked hot smoke into her lungs. When she exhaled, she felt a sense of something like relief wash over her. She handed it back and looked very directly at Billy. "The PI. The Principal Investigator. That's my father, isn't it?"

Billy took another long pull, then slowly nodded as he blew smoke at the ceiling.

The moon was almost startling in its clarity. It had risen well above the hills now, shrinking in size as it rose above the Earth's atmosphere. But vivid in its illumination, sprinkling colorless light across the hills and the trees, reflecting in the waterfall at the far side of the loch and delineating the ripples it sent out toward Karen, who stood at the water's edge contemplating all the contradictions of her young life.

That her father was still alive was confirmed now beyond doubt. But elation in that discovery was tempered by the anger that still festered at what he had put her through these last two years.

Yellow light spilled out across the clearing as the door of the cottage opened, and Billy's shadow extended long across the dry, beaten earth. It grew even longer, then faded, as he moved toward her, until she saw his reflection in the water as he reached her shoulder. "A month ago," he said, "you couldn't have stood out here on a night like this. The midges would have eaten you alive." He chuckled. "Just one of the many joys of living here. Midges from June to September, cleggs in June and July, cold bloody weather in spring and autumn. We had snow here in May, and they're predicting an early frost next week." He looked at her. "Where are you staying tonight?"

She laughed. "Well, I was hoping that might be here. Not really anywhere else for me to go, is there?"

He shrugged. "You're welcome to stay if you want. But like I said, I wasn't exactly expecting visitors, so you'll have to take things as you find them. There's a bed in the back room. Never been slept in, so it might be a wee bit damp."

She looked at him, surprised. "Where do you sleep?"

"Sleeping bag on the couch. It's always been warmer in front of the stove."

She turned to gaze back out across the silvered surface of the loch. "Will you take me to my father?"

There was a long silence, during which she daren't even look at him. Then she heard him sigh. "Karen, I can't."

And a spike of anger shot through her. "Why not?"

"Because everything we're doing and have done has only been achieved through secrecy. Your father would kill me if I told you where he was. The whole point of the three of us living like this, no contact with friends or family, was so we'd drop below the radar. So Ergo wouldn't know how or where to find us."

She turned blazing eyes on him, and he very nearly flinched.

"Hey, don't look at me like that. None of this was my idea." He hesitated. Then, "Just how well do you know your dad, Karen?"

"Well enough." All her defiance apparent in the set of her jaw.

But Billy just shook his head. "I doubt it. You've never worked with him. You don't know him like I do." He gazed out over the loch. "He's brilliant, sure. No one's going to argue with that. But I've never known a more difficult man in my life. Obsessive. Relentless. Demanding. You wouldn't want him on your team, cos he'd never give you the ball. He'd have to be the gaffer, and you'd damn well do it his way or he'd deselect you in a nanosecond. And he's paranoid, Karen. *Paranoid.*"

"About what?"

"That Ergo might fuck him again."

"Well, he must have been pretty desperate to fake his own suicide."

Billy dragged his eyes away from the loch and turned them on Karen. "He didn't do that for himself."

"How do you mean?"

He paused only for a moment. "When your dad was forced out of the Geddes, he went around trying to raise finance to privately fund a repeat experiment. And that's when they told him."

Karen frowned. "Told him what?"

"That if he didn't drop it, they'd go after his family."

Her eyes opened wide in shock. "Who? Who told him that?"

Billy snorted and threw his hands loosely in the air. "Christ, Karen, who knows? These people never speak to you directly.

Threats are never specific. They're veiled. And, in a way, that almost makes them even more sinister. I don't know who threatened him, or how, but he was spooked. Man, was he scared. Not for himself. Cos, really, he's not the kind of guy who's going to back down from anything, or anyone. I bet he got a few doings at school for standing up to the class bully." He looked at Karen's upturned, wide-eyed face. "The only reason he faked his suicide was to protect you. If he was dead, you were safe. That's why he's spent the last two years living under an assumed identity in the back of beyond."

Karen felt like she was wearing lead boots. She could not have moved her feet from that spot if she had tried. Her whole body felt heavy, and stinging as if from an electric shock. And all she could remember were her final words to her dad. *I hate you, I hate you, I hate you.* She felt tears filling her eyes. Those were the words he must have taken with him as he faked his own death and embarked on a life of denial, sacrificing everything to protect her. If anything, her sense of guilt was even greater now than it had been when she learned that he had gone missing. "Please." Her voice felt very small and quiet. "You *have* to take me to him."

He turned and put his arms around her,

and she let him draw her to him, pushing her face into his chest and trying not to cry in front of this young man she had known for only a matter of hours. "Karen, I can't!"

She pushed away again, suddenly, misery morphing to anger. "Billy, you must. You've *got* to."

He shrugged helplessly. "Honestly, Karen. That's not even a decision I can make on my own."

"Well, who can make it, then?"

He sighed. "We could ask Sam, okay? That's as much initiative as I'm prepared to take on my own. And if he says no, then that's it. No argument."

"Who's Sam?" There was real aggression in her voice.

"Sam, your dad and me are the ones who've run this whole experiment. Sam Waltman. Your dad knew him from his time at University College, London. They studied cell biology together. One of the few people in the world he trusts. Our funder sponsored him on a two-year sabbatical to do the research."

"Well, what? Can you phone him? Email him?"

Billy laughed. "Karen, we don't communicate directly. Mobiles and emails are not secure. Not that I've even got a signal here. We'll have to go and see him."

"Now?"

Billy laughed again and shook his head. "No, Karen, not now. Tomorrow. We can go and see him tomorrow. He has his hives hidden away on the Waternish Peninsula on the Isle of Skye. It's just a couple of hours' drive from here."

Scattered moonlight somehow made its way down through thick foliage on the trees behind the cottage, to creep in around the edges of the frayed curtain Karen had dragged across the window. She wasn't sure why she had bothered. She had no intention of undressing, or getting into the bed, and in any case there was nobody out there to peek in at her even if she had.

She lay on top of a soft, damp-smelling quilt, and heard all the old springs of the bed creak beneath her. The room was small and square and cluttered, a dumping ground for anything and everything that had been displaced from the rest of the house, including beekeeping equipment and shelves of honey. The air was infused with the sweet smell of it, and the astringency of cedar wood and smoke. It was cold in here, too, and she understood why Billy preferred the couch in front of the stove. What kind of miserable, lonely existence must it have been, stuck out here on his own for a year and a half, cut off from friends and family, miles distant from the nearest human life? And she realized it could not have been so very different for her father, wherever it was he might be. Had it really all been worth it? To bring the results of some experiment about bees into the public domain? And no sooner had she asked the question in her mind, than she knew the answer.

This wasn't just some vague, scientific experiment he had sacrificed himself for. This was about the survival of one species, and the future of another. About naked greed versus the very existence of mankind. She got that. She understood what must have driven him, what still drove him. And, yet, there remained a part of her that resented it. Why had she, and her dad, and her family had to suffer? It made her mad at Ergo.

She heard the creak of the bedroom door, and a pencil-thin line of pale light fell across the room, zigzagging across the clutter. She sat bolt upright, heart hammering, and watched as the line of light widened and the door opened.

"Billy?" Her voice rang out in the dark, shrill, frightened.

"It's okay." His voice came reassuringly, and she saw his silhouette as he stepped into the room. "Just checking that everything's alright."

"Everything's fine."

But he didn't go away again. Standing hesitantly in the open doorway as if undecided about what to do or say. Then he started easing his way through the debris, toward the bed.

"I said everything's fine."

"I know, I know . . ." He sat down on the edge of the bed, and she moved away until her back was against the wall, and she felt the cold of it seeping through her clothing. "Just checking."

"You said that."

There was a long silence, in which all she could hear was her breathing and his. "You have no idea how lonely it's been here, Karen."

"Yes, I have. I can imagine it." Her voice sounded shrill.

"I'm mean, I'm just a young guy, you know? It's not normal to be cooped up on your own all this time. It's only natural."

"Billy, please go."

More silence. She felt him move in the dark, the squeak of the springs. But he was the merest shadow, and she couldn't tell if he was moving closer or about to get up. Until she felt his breath on her face, and his hands on her body, clumsy and clawing. His mouth trying to find hers.

She reacted violently, clenched fists flying blindly in the darkness, sometimes striking air, sometimes connecting with flesh and bone. But he was so much stronger than her, and it was only when she bit his lower lip hard that she felt, more than heard, his voice exploding in her face with pain. He recoiled immediately, slipping from the bed on to the floor, then clambering to his feet and staggering to the door. There, he flicked a light switch, and she blinked in the sudden harsh glare of the naked flickering bulb that hung from the ceiling.

He stood at the door, holding it open with one hand to steady himself, his other at his mouth. She could see blood oozing through his fingers, and she realized for the first time that he was wearing only boxer shorts. His skin was pale, apart from forearms, neck and face, which had been burned by the sun or weathered in the wind. He was wiry thin, but had well-developed pecs and the hint of a six-pack on his flat white belly. He took his hand from his mouth and looked at the blood on his fingers. It was smeared all around his mouth and beard, too. She had the iron taste of it in her own mouth, and she leaned forward on the bed to spit on the floor.

"You fucking little bitch!" he hissed at her, spraying blood into the blinding dazzle of electric light.

Karen was scared. By the attack, by his anger, by what she had done to him. But more than anything, scared that he wouldn't take her to see Sam tomorrow. "I'm sorry," she said. "You frightened me. I . . . I over-reacted."

"Fucking right you did." He put his hand to his mouth and brought it away with more blood. "Jesus, you damn near bit my lip off!"

She slipped off the bed, her heart still hammering, and crossed the room to pull his hand away from his mouth. "Let me see."

He submitted like a child, and stood acquiescent as she tipped his head down toward her and took a look at his lip. The blood was coming from the inside. She could see her own teethmarks on the outside, but they hadn't broken the skin, just bruised it.

"Do you have a first-aid kit?"

He nodded.

"Show me."

He took her through to the kitchen and

they found a green plastic box with a red cross on it, tucked away in a drawer. She opened it up to find a roll of cotton wool, a selection of plasters, a tube of antiseptic ointment and various silver-packaged pain-killers.

"Do you have salt?"

He opened a wall cupboard and pulled down a packet of salt, and she immediately took a clean glass to make a strong solution of salt and water.

"Here. Rinse your mouth with this. Don't swallow. Spit out in the sink and rinse again."

Once more, like a child, he did what he was told, and rinsed several times before she drew his head down and gently pulled out his lower lip to see inside. She held it open to slip in a wad of cotton wool, pushing it down between his lip and his front teeth. Then she rolled kitchen roll into a thick wodge and held it under the cold tap until it was soaking, then made him hold it hard against his outer lip. She took him by the arm and led him back through to the sitting room.

"Come and sit down. And hold the kitchen roll like that for five or ten minutes. The pressure should stop the bleeding. Mouths are great healers, and the salt solution should have disinfected it."

He sat meekly on the edge of the settee and looked up at her with now mournful eyes. Both his lust and his anger had dissipated. Perhaps, she thought, all he had really craved was the human contact.

"I'm sorry," she said again. "You really did scare me."

He nodded, but was afraid to speak in case he aggravated the bleeding. But the blood had stopped within a matter of minutes, and didn't restart when finally he removed the kitchen roll and cotton wool fifteen minutes later. His voice came muffled through lips that he didn't want to move. "Sorry I scared you." He met her eye. "Just wanted a cuddle."

It had seemed to Karen in the moment that he was after much more than that. But now she felt guilty, almost sorry for him. Gently, she encouraged him to lie down on the sofa. "You should get some sleep," she said. "The lip will be a bit swollen and bruised tomorrow. But you'll live to kiss again." She grinned, and he returned a pale smile. "I'd better get some sleep, too. See you in the morning."

She walked carefully across the room, as if afraid to break the spell of tranquility she had somehow managed to cast over his masculine aggression, and turned the light out before she slipped into the darkness of her bedroom, closing the door behind her and turning the key in the lock.

For a long time she stood with her back to the door, listening to the pulsing of blood in her head and allowing her breathing to subside slowly. Then she tiptoed through the shadows to lay herself carefully down on the bed, wincing with the creak of the springs, her body still rigid with tension.

It was going to be a long night, and she had no intention of sleeping.

CHAPTER TWENTY-SEVEN

In spite of best intentions, sleep had stolen her away sometime in the small hours, and she woke now with a start, sitting suddenly upright and hearing the sounds of someone moving around outside her door. She rubbed her eyes and blinked hard to clear them of sleep, and swiveled on the bed to put her feet on the floor.

All her fear and misgivings from the previous night returned. How was Billy going to be with her this morning? Would he still be prepared to take her to see Sam? If not, she had no idea what she was going to do. She was stuck here, miles from anywhere, with no transport, completely at the mercy of an unpredictable young man who might or might not have tried to rape her last night. Just how much resentment would he still be nursing after her violent rejection of his advances, and the biting of his lower lip?

Tense and stiff from a night braced on the

sagging mattress of her damp bed, she eased herself across the room to the door and turned the key very gingerly in the lock. She wasn't sure quite why, but she didn't want him to know that she had locked herself in. She opened the door abruptly and stepped out into the sitting room.

Her first reaction was surprise at seeing sunlight flooding in through windows and a wide open front door, where a startled hen cast a long shadow toward her before clucking away across the clearing. The sun was still low in the sky, and it reached right across the room to the far wall. Her second reaction was pleasure at the perfume of freshly brewed coffee and the sound of cooking that came from the kitchen. Something spitting and hissing in a frying pan, and good smells issuing from the open door. Bacon.

Billy turned as she appeared in the kitchen doorway. He was standing over the stove, breaking eggs into bacon fat. Cooked rashers sat on a plate next to the gas rings. He managed what seemed to Karen an almost cheery smile. "The big advantage of keeping hens is the freshest of eggs every morning. You want to grab a couple of plates?" He nodded toward one of the kitchen cupboards.

Karen retrieved plates and found cutlery, and he served up two eggs on each, along with half a dozen rashers of bacon. She carried them through to the table, and he followed her with the coffee pot and a couple of mugs. The milk and sugar were already out. She looked at him carefully as he sat down opposite. "How's the mouth?"

He shrugged. "A bit sore, but I'll live."

"I'm sorry." She repeated her apology of the previous night.

"Don't be. It's me that should apologize. I was out of order." He nodded toward her plate. "Tuck in. Who knows when we'll get to eat again."

She almost held her breath. "We're still going to see Sam, then?"

"Of course. The sooner we get on the road the better."

It was a stunning morning, cloudless and clear, the dark purple peaks of mountain ranges east and west rising up around them and reflecting on the still waters of Loch Carron as they headed south through Stromeferry and Plockton toward the Kyle of Lochalsh. Across the Sound of Raasay they saw the jagged outline of the Cuillins piercing the blue that framed the Isle of Skye, and the water of the Inner Hebrides lay flat and still in the windless silence.

They drove for a long while without a word passing between them, then out of the blue Billy said, "Amazing things, bees."

Karen looked at him. "Did you know much about them before you worked on this experiment?"

He shook his head. "Nothing. It was a steep learning curve. But, you know, totally fucking fascinating. The hive, the colony, it's completely run by women." He turned to grin at her, but winced in pain and raised a rueful hand to his mouth. "Shit," he muttered. Then, with both hands back on the wheel, "After all, it's a *queen* bee, not a king. And the women do everything. They clean the hive, they nurse the young, they guard the entrance, and when they're old enough they go out and do the foraging, bringing back the pollen and the nectar for storage." He chuckled. "That's why they're called the *workers*. The poor bitches only live for about a month, and never have any sex."

"That doesn't sound fair. What about the men?"

"Ah, well, the guys really have it cushy. Drones, they're called. They just hang around doing fuck all, eating and making a lot of noise."

Karen laughed. "Sounds like most guys I know. So what's the point of them?"

"Same as the male of any species. To get the females pregnant. Or, in the case of bees, one female. The queen. She goes on a weeklong fuckfest when she's still a pretty young thing. It's the only time she leaves the hive. Flies off looking for drones, who usually hang around high spots like church towers so they can see her coming. Imagine their excitement. Finally going to get their end away." He laughed. "Almost literally. Cos what they don't know is that they only get to do it once. Their tackle is barbed, you see, and gets stuck inside the queen, ripping away their insides as she flies off. She'll screw a dozen or more of these daft drones, and you'll often see her flying around with their remains dangling from her doodah."

Karen wrinkled her nose. "That sounds vile."

"Yeah, but what a way to go!" He glanced at her, eyes shining. "Don't you think?"

"I think I'd rather be the queen."

"Nah, I doubt if you would. She has a pretty tough life, as well. After a week of screwing around, she has enough sperm inside her to lay fertilized eggs for two or three years. And that's all she does. Goes back to the hive and lays eggs. And when she starts running out, the other women kill her and feed up one of their own with royal jelly to make a new queen."

"And the men?"

"Like I said, they just hang around the hive, feasting and spit-balling until the end of the season, when the women figure they have served their purpose and kick them out to die."

Karen blew air through her lips. "That's pretty brutal. Don't think I much fancy being a bee, of either sex."

He grinned. "You're never alone, though. There's anything up to sixty thousand bees in a hive. And all of them your relatives. Imagine writing the Christmas cards for that lot!"

Karen laughed out loud.

There was very little traffic on the Skye bridge as they swept down to cruise across the first stretch of it, before seeing it rise ahead of them in a perfect arch over the waters below. Mountains shimmered darkly against a distant blue sky as they looped down through Breakish and Broadford, turning north then and heading for Portree.

They had driven for perhaps another twenty minutes in silence before Karen glanced at Billy. "How can you afford a big four-wheel drive like this?" she said.

"Needed a big beast to get up and down to the cottage," he said. "Especially in the wet and the snow. Our sponsor covers the costs."

"Sponsor?"

"Well, we couldn't have done it without one, could we? I mean, financing the three of us for two years apiece, never mind the equipment we had to fork out for, and the lab tests in Edinburgh . . . It's all cost a bloody fortune." He glanced at her. "We get our funding from an environmental campaign organization."

She nodded. "OneWorld."

"Bet Deloit was not best pleased when you turned up threatening to blow the whole thing."

"I wasn't threatening to blow anything!" Karen said, indignant. "I was looking for my dad."

"Aye, who everyone thinks is dead, and who wants to stay dead till this is over."

She threw him a look.

"I mean, see it from their point of view, Karen. They've put out a small fortune on this. If Ergo cottoned on to what was happening, and where, it would be a total disaster. They could wreck the whole thing in any number of ways. Not least by exposing your dad as a liar and a fraud."

"I'm not going to blow anything," Karen said huffily. "No one even knows I'm here. All I want to do is see him."

"Well . . . we'll see what Sam says."

At Borve they turned off the main A87 on to the road for Dunvegan, winding through rolling, treeless green countryside, across the River Snizort, then heading west until they reached the turnoff for Waternish. The island was dazzling in the late September sun, still purple with heather, but mixed now with the golds and browns of autumn. The road north along the west side of the Waternish peninsula rapidly turned into single-track with passing places. But they only had to pull in a couple of times to let oncoming cars past.

After a while, they saw sunlight coruscating across the clear blue waters of Loch Bay, off to their left, passing the tiny communities of Waternish and Lusta and Stein. A single white-sailed yacht cut a straight line through the sea loch, leaving a spreading white wash in its wake. Billy slowed down, glanced several times beyond Karen to the waters below. "Perfect day to be out sailing," he said. "Wish it was me."

She looked at him, surprised. "You sail?"

He turned resentful eyes on her. "Why?

414

You think sailing's too middle class for a boy from Balornock? That's a bit elitist, isn't it?"

Karen was startled by his sudden umbrage. "No, I didn't mean it like that. I just didn't think you were the type, that's all. My dad was a great sailor."

"I know. He ran the sailing club at the Geddes. That's how I got into it. There were only about a dozen of us, but your dad got an instructor in from the Scottish RYA to coach us. Out on the firth almost every weekend. A really nice guy, Neal Maclean. Poor bugger died not long before your dad got kicked out. Heart attack. You'd never believe it, a guy that fit." And he fell into what felt to Karen like a sulky silence.

The road dipped down, midpeninsula, and they passed the homes that incomers had made in pristine whitewashed cottages nestling in anonymity behind shrubs and small trees splashed autumn red and yellow. Billy slowed down and took a tight right turn toward a place called Geary, or *Gearràidh* as it was signposted in the Gaelic, and the road climbed steeply uphill across virgin moor tinted mauve with heather in bloom. As they crested the hill, and passed a sign for schoolchildren crossing, a spectacular view across Uig Bay fell away below them toward the Trotternish Peninsula and the village of Uig itself. It was from there that the ferries left for Harris and South Uist, and the islands of the Outer Hebrides could be seen clearly, simmering darkly along the horizon. A little white schoolhouse sat on their left, and Karen marveled at the thought of going to a school with such a view. She would never have paid the least attention to any of her lessons.

Beyond the school they turned right, descending steeply then to pass through and leave behind them the small settlement of Gillen, houses hiding discreetly behind trees and tall shrubs. Less than half a mile later, Billy took a sharp, unexpected right turn on to what was little more than a dirt track, leading them up through a scattering of Scots pines into the shadow of hills rising steeply to the west. They bumped over ruts and potholes, and a crude wooden bridge across a tiny gushing stream, cresting a rise then and dropping suddenly into a small hidden valley where an old shepherd's cottage stood among a clutch of trees, glowing white in the sunlight that washed down from the peaks.

"Et voilà," Billy said, and pulled the Mitsubishi to a sudden stop on the grass in front of the cottage.

As she climbed down from the four-by-four, Karen saw how run-down the place was. A wooden fence around an overgrown garden was rotten and had collapsed in several places. The slate roof was almost green with moss, and the trees that crowded the flaking whitewashed walls cast their gloom all around it. A stream splashed and tumbled over the rocks behind the house, catching the sunlight and cascading down the hill beyond, before losing itself among the gorse and heather.

The rest of the valley was a shambles of rock spoil from the hills above, and thick tangling heather that grew abundantly in wet, black, peaty soil.

Billy stood scratching his head. "He's not at home."

Karen rounded the SUV, disappointment clouding this sunny morning. "How do you know?"

"His Land Rover's not here."

She followed him up an overgrown path to the front door and he pushed it open into a gloomy interior. It breathed dampness and old woodsmoke into their faces. A tiny square hall stood at the foot of narrow stairs that rose steeply to dormer rooms in the attic. On their left, old, overstuffed furniture gathered itself around a long-dead open fire in a small sitting room. On their right, a kitchen smelled of stale cooking, and on a scarred wooden table the remains of an abandoned meal had turned moldy.

Billy's voice was hushed and barely audible. "I don't like this."

He turned and almost ran out of the house. "What? What is it?" Karen called, then hurried after him as he started purposefully away through the heather and rocks, following what looked like a deer path. By the time she caught him up, they had reached the summit of a small rise and found themselves looking down into a sheltered hollow. Eighteen beehives lay smashed and scattered among the rocks.

Billy stopped abruptly. "Jesus," he whispered through breathless lips. And he ran on down into the hollow, moving among the remains of the hives, pulling out long-abandoned frames where honey and wax exposed to the weather had turned hard and black. Karen watched him with a growing sense of trepidation as she saw his panic mushroom. All the bees were gone, the hives destroyed by some hand determined to make them unserviceable. He looked up at her, and she saw how pale he had grown, his tan looking yellow now, like jaundice.

He strode up the hill, passing her without

a word and barely a glance. She turned and followed him back to the cottage, struggling to keep up. By the time she got to the front door he was on the landing at the top of the stairs. He vanished into the room on his left and she ran up after him. The door to the right stood ajar. Through it she saw an unmade bed, and smelled the sour odor of bodies and feet. Straight ahead, a door opened into a small, dirty toilet and shower room. The room to the left had clearly once been Sam's laboratory. Billy stood in the middle of it looking helplessly around him at the chaos of smashed equipment. The floor was littered with broken glass. Shelves had been pulled off the walls. A small freezer lay on its side with the door open. "His laptop's gone," he said.

He turned to push past Karen and run down the stairs. She heard him banging about the house, opening cupboards, pulling open drawers, and she walked slowly back down to the hall and out into the garden. On the surface, it was still a beautiful day. But somehow, now, it had turned ugly and she felt a chill in her bones. Something dreadful had happened here, and Sam was gone. And, along with him, the last chance of finding her father.

She swiveled around as she heard Billy

coming out behind her. He was out of breath, his face taut with tension. "Everything's been taken," he said. "Everything. All his records, his diary, his computer."

He gazed at her without seeing her for several long moments, lost in thought, then half-turned to look up at the cottage.

When he turned back he said, "Could you get my rucksack from the back of the Mits? It's got my iPhone in it. I want to take some pics of this."

"Sure." Karen felt glad to be useful, more than just a bystander. She walked briskly to the Mitsubishi and lifted the tailgate. The rucksack was right at the back of the boot space, and she leaned in to retrieve it. As she pulled it toward her, a sound behind her made her turn. In time to see a shadow cross the sun before light and pain exploded in her head. Darkness subsumed her before she even hit the ground.

It was still dark when consciousness returned, bringing with it a headache like none she had ever known. She screwed up her eyes tightly, hoping it would pass, but it didn't. It felt as if someone were hitting her repeatedly with a mallet. They say you can get used to anything, even pain, and after a few minutes, sensations beyond that pain began slowly to impinge on Karen's awareness.

She was curled up in a fetal position, hands bound behind her back, legs tied together at the ankles. Her mouth was full of something soft and wet. Something else was stretched taut across her lips, preventing her from opening them. She gagged, and fear of choking or drowning in her own vomit only just prevented her from being sick.

She realized there was daylight beyond the darkness, that there was something pulled over her head and tied at the neck. She could feel it against her face. Soft, caressing. And the air it contained was hot, rich in her own carbon dioxide. Almost suffocating.

For several minutes she struggled against whatever bound her wrists and ankles, but there was no give at all, and she quickly gave up, exhausted. Desperately, she tried to draw more air through nostrils that had begun to stream. She felt tears burning her eyes and cheeks, and was overcome by an abject sense of helplessness.

The sound, very close, of a car door opening suddenly brought with it a rush of fresh air, and momentary hope. Strong hands grabbed her arms and pulled her into a semiupright position, leaning back against something solid. Fingers at her neck loosened whatever it was that covered her head, and a hand tugged her hair as it grasped the cover to pull it away.

She had not thought it possible for the pain in her head to get worse, but the sudden exposure to bright sunlight seared her brain like a branding iron. She wanted to cry out, but her voice was muffled and choked by whatever was stuffed in her mouth. Tears coursed from her eyes and she blinked furiously, to see Billy standing beneath the open tailgate of the Mitsubishi, looking in at her. His face was devoid of expression, his eyes cold and dead, and he regarded her dispassionately, as if examining some inanimate object.

She tried hard to speak, to beg him to let her go, but heard only the pathetic muffled sounds that issued from her throat and nose. He paid her not the least attention, taking his iPhone from his pocket and examining it for some moments, tapping and swiping the screen, before holding it in front of him, in landscape mode, and taking several photographs of her. She heard its faux, electronic shutter-click five or six times before he switched it off and slipped it back in his pocket.

Without meeting her eye, he leaned in to retrieve her head cover and pulled it roughly over her head again, plunging her once more into suffocating darkness. She tried to struggle as he secured it at the neck, but it was pointless. He took her by the shoulders, half-turning her and tipping her over on to her side. The vehicle shook as he slammed the tailgate shut.

For some time, she struggled furiously, trying to kick out with her bound feet, but quickly running out of air and hope, and falling finally into a bottomless well of black despair.

The vehicle lurched as she heard him open the door and climb into the driver's seat. He pulled the door shut and started the motor, turning the SUV in three swift movements that threw her from one side of the boot to the other, then accelerating back down the track toward the road, bumping through potholes and over ruts, tossing her around in the back like some rag doll.

She fought hard not to throw up, and it was with some relief finally that she felt them turn on to the smooth tarmac of the road. Drawing breath through her panic was like trying to breathe through straws. She prayed she wouldn't pass out and vomit into her mouth, for if she did, she would be dead long before they got to wherever it was he was taking her.

CHAPTER TWENTY-EIGHT

There is sunlight streaming into the bedroom through the side window I left on the latch. I feel the heat of it on my legs as it falls across the bed, and I am sure that is what has wakened me.

I glance at the bedside clock and realize with a sense of shock that it is almost midday. I must have slept for well over twelve hours. No doubt I needed it, but if anything I feel worse. My head is thick, my nasal tubes stuffed up so that I have to breathe through my mouth. My eyes are gritty and clogged with sleep. My body is stiff and aching, and feels as if I have left it behind in the land of Nod, even though my brain has woken to the new day.

I swing my legs out of bed and stagger into the bathroom to lean against the wall and listen, eyes closed, to the stream of my urine as it splashes into the pan. Then plunge my face into the sink to splash it repeatedly with cold water, before rubbing it briskly dry with a fresh, soft towel.

I pull on jeans and a T-shirt and pad through to the kitchen to make coffee. Both kitchen and sitting room are flooded with the softest September light, and I look from the window at the incoming tide in all its shades of blue, reflecting sunshine in pools and eddies all across the bay. Bran is stretched out at the kitchen door and scrambles hopefully to his feet as I come through. I go into the boot room and open the front door to let him out. He goes haring away across the dunes and I return to the kitchen to sit at the table, sipping strong black coffee. I try to remember the idea that excited me sometime in those brain-fogged moments before sleep took me last night. It had seemed inspirational then. But now, as it comes back to me, it appears to have little merit. It had occurred to me that I hadn't checked the laptop in the shed.

I look at the other laptop sitting on the table in front of me, and wonder why I thought the computer in the shed might cast any more light on my situation than this one has done.

Still, I am a man who pays attention to detail. I know that now, and so I am aware that I must check the laptop out there, even if the rational part of my brain tells me I will be wasting my time.

In the boot room I slip bare feet into my wellington boots, and take my mug of coffee with me as I go out to the shed. The breeze is fresh and strong in my face as I step outside. I can smell the sea and the heather, and, somewhere on the edge of the wind, the faintest whiff of peat smoke. And I wonder who has lit a fire on a day like this.

The laptop takes some minutes to boot up, so I stand gazing around the shed as I wait for it. When my eyes alight, finally, on the beekeeper's mask, the gloves that I know make my hands too clumsy to wear, the tools, the smoker, I have a moment when I am so close to remembering everything, I feel that if only I reached out I could almost touch my forgotten past. I lift the beekeeper's hat and facenet down from its peg, feeling it soft in my hand, like memory itself. But frustratingly, it is all still just beyond recollection.

I realize that the laptop has finished loading its operating system and I turn to examine it, laying my mug to one side. Apart from the software that came by default with the OS, there is nothing on it at all. No applications, no files. Nothing.

How is it possible, I wonder, to work with a computer for a year and a half and leave no traces? Which is when I spot the black FireWire cable trailing away from the input sockets on the left side of the computer. It is about six inches long, a naked, shiny plug on the other end of it. And it dawns on me that I must have been using an external drive. Something loaded with software, where I stored all my files, leaving no trace of my activities on the computer itself.

But where is it?

I search the shed from top to bottom. Methodically, meticulously. It is not here. And I know it is not in the house. In a drawer, I find a cardboard box containing nearly a dozen USB thumb drives. One by one, I plug them into the laptop, but they contain no data, and never have, as far as I can see. Unused, virgin thumb drives, each with a capacity of 32 gigabytes.

In my frustration, I strike out and punch the wall, only to graze and bruise my knuckles and wave my hand in the air, cursing at the pain and my stupidity.

I grab my coffee and storm back to the cottage, aware, as I stride across the few yards between hut and house, of Mrs. Macdonald watching me from her window across the road. Bran has been waiting outside and runs into the house ahead of me. I slam the door shut, kick off my wellies and slump into my chair at the table again. I get absolutely no satisfaction from ticking off another thought from my list.

I hear my own voice reverberate around the kitchen before realizing that I have shouted at the facing wall, an unadulterated expression of pent-up anguish. My mug goes flying, and coffee spills across the keyboard of the laptop on the table. I swear, and leap up to grab a cloth from the sink and mop it up before it does any damage. Bran is barking his consternation at the ceiling, wondering what I am shouting at and why I haven't fed him.

The act of wiping the cloth across the keyboard wakens the laptop from its slumber, and its desktop throws gray light back in my face. I shout at Bran to shut up and am about to slam the lid shut when I notice for the first time, amongst all the software icons on the dock, a familiar white F on a blue background. I know immediately it is a Facebook application, and I wonder two things. Why did I not notice it before, and why would I have a Facebook app?

I find myself staring at it, a seed of excitement burgeoning somewhere deep inside me. Is it possible that I have a Facebook account? No matter how unlikely it seems, I feel a fresh flush of hope. I sit down to face the screen and, with trembling fingers, activate the application. Username and password are automatically entered from the computer's keychain memory, and the home page fills the screen. It is blank, apart from an open *Update Status* window, in which there is the silhouette of a white head against a pale gray background. The status is empty, too. On the blue menu bar along the top of the screen, there is a miniature postage stamp of the white head beside the name Michael.

I pause before clicking on it. Michael? Is that me? I steel myself for whatever might come next and click on the name. It brings up the personal page of Michael Fleming. Both profile and cover pic windows are blank. There is not a single entry on the page, no personal details, no education or work history. And only one friend.

Karen Fleming.

I am aware now that my mouth is quite dry, with my tongue in danger of sticking to the roof of it. I reach for my coffee mug but it is empty, and I am not about to get up and make another.

There is a profile pic of Karen. She looks midteens, with strangely short hair, shaved at the sides and dyed green on top. There are steel studs in her eyebrows and rings in her lower lip, a tiny sparkling diamond in her nose. She has ice-blue eyes like mine and is staring straight into the camera with a kind of challenging insolence. Nothing about her is familiar to me, except perhaps for the eyes, but maybe then only because they are the same color as mine. The cover photo on her personal page is of some heavy metal rock band with impossibly long hair and sneering faces. She has twenty-seven friends. Not many for a girl of her age. And her posts and shares are sparse and cryptic. Teenagers, I know, have a language that is all their own.

I click to drop down a menu and check my preferences. I have set everything to private, although since I have entered no personal information and made no posts, that hardly seems necessary.

Three icons along from the settings menu, there is a red dot next to a couple of square, overlapping speech bubbles. Someone has messaged Michael. I click on the icon to open a window that has a single message for Michael Fleming from Karen Fleming. It is dated just three days ago and reads, *Uncle Michael, I think dad might still be alive. Please get in touch.*

I sit back, stunned. So is that who I am? Michael Fleming? Karen's uncle? If that is the case, why am I not suddenly remembering everything? Why is recollection and all that detail of my life not flooding back into memory? My sense of disappointment is almost crippling.

After several long minutes just staring at the screen, I force myself to click on Karen's photos. There are a few dozen of them. I open up the first and then start scrolling through the others. Most of them are pictures of Karen with friends. Selfies. Stupid faces pulled for the camera. There are photographs of freshly acquired tattoos, and I am shocked by the extent to which this girl has vandalized her skin.

Then suddenly I am frozen in time and space, like an insect trapped in amber. A photograph posted of a much younger Karen. She is sitting on a wall beside a man, both of them smiling at the camera, his arm around her shoulder. Her post reads, *Happier days. Me and my dad when I was twelve.*

And the man is me.

It never seemed to occur to the police that I might have two keys for my car. I keep the spare in the glove compartment, and since the car is not locked I have no trouble retrieving it.

I take all the beekeeping equipment from the shed and throw it into the boot. Which is when I notice the large rucksack in the back. And I wonder now, as I pack everything into it — hat, gloves, smoker, kindling, hive tool — if this is how I carried all my stuff up the coffin road during my visits to the hives.

Bran jumps into the back seat, fed and happy, and stretches out as I start the car, reversing into the turning area, then accelerating hard over the cattle grid.

It takes me little more than ten minutes to get from the cottage to the parking area beyond the Seilebost causeway, turning off to where the tarmac ends and the mud track that is the old coffin road begins. The wind and the sun have mostly dried the mud, and the track is rutted and tricky underfoot, rainwater lying only in occasional pools, in holes and hollows.

Bran races ahead of me, pleased to be out and running free, stopping frequently to shove his nose at familiar smells, then galloping off in search of the next. It is hot in the afternoon sun, and only the wind cooling my sweat keeps me from overheating as I stride determinedly up the hill. I am not sure why, but I feel somehow as if the bees are the key. Not just to my memory, but to everything.

My name is Fleming. My daughter is Karen. Though nothing else has come back to me yet, memory seems only a breath away. Somewhere just beyond the most flimsy of membranes. I can almost see it, colors and shapes, blurred and refusing to come into focus. But somewhere in those hives, hidden among the rock spoil of ice-age explosions, I am convinced now that my memory is waiting for me.

It is what drives me on, refusing to stop for a breath, the rucksack weighing heavy on my back, legs aching from the relentless climb. Only once do I stop, to look back, and see dark storm clouds gathering along the distant horizon, incongruous in the sunshine that spills down here from the bluest of skies. But I know how fast the weather can change, and that it won't be long before equinoctial winds, whipping up their anger in the southwest, will blow in the storm.

The breeze is already freshening and gaining in strength, and I turn to push on toward the summit. The wind ridges the surface of the loch as we pass it, and I force myself up through the final 200 yards of grueling ascent, past ancient cairns, to the spot where I recognize the two stones that sit, unnaturally, one on top of the other.

The giant rocks away to our right, standing guard over my concealed hives, cut deep shadows into the incline. And the cracks and crevices in the face of the cliff above them are thrown into sharp relief by the sunlight.

Bran has already covered half of the distance between the rocks and the road as I set off across the peat bog in pursuit of him, black glaur sucking at my feet with every step. My legs are shaking from the effort by the time I reach the lip of the hollow and gaze down at what I know to be my hives gathered among the rocks below me.

I scramble down, swinging the rucksack from my back, and start lifting off lids and crown boards, stopping only to pull on my hat with its protective net and light my kindling, smothering it in the smoker with damp newsprint to produce clouds of white smoke that I puff into the hives to calm the bees.

Even though I have no recollection of it, I know I have done this many times. It comes to me as second nature.

There is a considerable traffic of bees, seduced to leave their hives by the good weather with its promise of pollen and nectar among the late-season heather.

All of the hives have sugar bags below the crown boards and I know, without even thinking, that the season is over and I have prepared them for winter. I know, too, that in the spring my bees will have flown down on to the machair, where they will have feasted upon the abundance of wild flowers there, and that it is during the summer lull, when the flowers have passed and before the heather is in bloom, that I will have fed them their first sugar syrup.

I can almost taste the sweetly perfumed heather honey that my bees produce, but then that moment of elation is followed by the shadow of depression descending suddenly upon me, like sunshine slipping behind a cloud. Something is wrong. The bees are dying. Not just here. Everywhere. I realize with shock, like a sudden slap on the face, how disastrous this is. Not just for me.

Bran's barking brings me back to the present, and I turn, startled, to see him dancing around the legs of a man standing at the top of the hollow. He is silhouetted against the sky and it is not until he climbs down among the hives that I realize it is the man with the binoculars from the caravan across the bay.

His hair, like lengths of frayed rope, blows out behind him in the wind. His face is deeply tanned and unshaven, and he examines me carefully with dark-ringed eyes. When he speaks, his voice seems familiar. "Local gossip has it that you've lost your memory, Tom." I return his gaze with an odd sense of apprehension. "Maybe it's about time that someone told you who you are."

But a moment of revelation causes me to shake my head, and I stare at him with new eyes. "No," I say. "No. There's no need, Alex."

CHAPTER TWENTY-NINE

Bran is running around the cottage like a daftie, chasing imaginary rabbits, or something else unseen. He seems infected by my excitement. Although, in truth, excitement does not do justice to how I feel. I am both elated and devastated. I know who I am, and I know what happened on Eilean Mòr. And I remember only too vividly what occurred that same night when the storm finally capsized my damaged boat. Although nothing of what followed, until I was washed up on Luskentyre beach. I know that I am extraordinarily fortunate to be alive.

But it is all, simply, too much. I cannot process everything at once. My brain is suffering from information overload and telling me, "Enough!" Like too much light, returning memory is blinding me. I can see the big picture in silhouette, but most of the detail is still burned out.

My name is Tom Fleming. I am a neuroscientist, and I used to work at the Geddes Institute of Environmental Sciences, until I was kicked out for conducting experiments that didn't please their sponsors, the giant Swiss agrochem company, Ergo. My wife is suing me for divorce. Or was. Now, presumably, she is treading water until I am declared legally dead after disappearing off my yacht in the Firth of Forth.

And Karen. I close my eyes. My little girl. I can see her now. That shining, happy face gazing up at me with unglazed affection. Love. Dependency. How I adored her. And still do. Despite the sulky, sullen teenager she became. I recall her final words to me before I faked my suicide. *I hate you, I hate you, I hate you.* And I wish I could just rewind time, and do it all again. This time differently.

I open my eyes and remember the message she left for my brother Michael, not realizing it was me who had friended her on Facebook. The only way I could maintain even the most tenuous of contacts without her knowing. Watching over her from an anonymous distance. *Uncle Michael, I think dad might still be alive. Please get in touch.* Somehow she knows I am not dead. I left that note with Chris, but he is not due to give it to her until she turns eighteen, when all of this is over.

But there are more pressing things. Sam is dead, and his killer is on the loose, almost certainly the same person who tried to stab me to death that night in the cottage. Impossible to express the relief I feel in knowing it was not me who murdered Sam. But equally impossible to shut out the guilt. Because I am responsible for his death as surely as if it were I who had killed him. In spite of the breach of security, I know that I must contact Deloit and tell him what has happened.

I sit at the kitchen table and draw the laptop toward me. My hands are shaking as I swipe the touch pad and waken it from sleep to open up the mailer.

To my surprise, there is an email waiting for me in the inbox. I frown and click to open it. In the moments that follow, I genuinely believe my heart has stopped. Before suddenly it kick-starts back to life and begins hammering against my ribs like someone with a sledgehammer trying to break out.

The email contains a single photograph. It is Karen. She is in the back of a vehicle of some kind, legs pulled up to her chest, and I can see bindings around her ankles. Her arms are behind her, and there is a broad slash of gray duct tape across her mouth. Tears have streaked black mascara down her cheeks, and her eyes are wide, staring at the camera, filled with fear. The message below it reads, *A fair exchange. Eilean Mòr, tonight.*

It is unsigned, but even before I look at the address of the sender, I know who it came from. And a chill of utter disabling despair forks through me.

"Hello? Anyone home?" Jon's voice startles me, and I look up as the door from the boot room opens to reveal Jon and Sally crammed into the small space among the waterproofs and wellingtons. Bran goes barking excitedly to greet them.

Sally looks at me, concerned, and I cannot imagine how I must look to prompt her question. "What's happened?"

But I turn my eyes toward her husband. "Jon, do you still have a boat at Rodel?"

He nods. "Only just. We were planning to take her south next week. Our time here is up."

But I barely absorb what he says, just the affirmative nod of his head. I stand up. "I need you to take me out to the Flannan Isles."

He is startled. "When?"

"Now."

CHAPTER THIRTY

DS George Gunn sat at his desk, leaning back in his chair and staring at the cursor blinking on a blank document on his computer screen. Progress on the case seemed to have ground to a standstill, and he had no idea what to write in his daily report to the CIO.

Circulating the photograph of the dead man in the media had produced nothing more than the usual crank calls, wasting a lot of man-hours in chasing them down. There was nothing back from the lab yet regarding the scrapings taken by the pathologist from beneath the victim's nails. Gunn was beginning to think they would have to ask the suspect's permission to circulate *his* photograph, in the hope that they could at least establish who *he* was.

He could feel the CIO's impatience reaching along the corridor to the open door of his office. Chisholm did not want to be here any longer than necessary, and would not be pleased to have Gunn's failure to close the case reflect on him. As it surely would, back in Inverness.

Gunn sighed and looked at the time. His shift would come to an end soon, when he would escape back to real life. His wife, he knew, would right now be poaching the salmon he had acquired for her yesterday, and in a few short hours Fin and Marsaili would arrive, finally, to have that long-awaited dinner with them. Gunn licked his lips. He could almost taste the rich firm flesh of the fish, and the subtly flavored garlic potatoes that his wife would serve with it. He sighed again, and swiveled in his chair as a shadow fell across the doorway. DC Smith stood, almost stooping to avoid the lintel, clutching a note in his hand.

"This might just be the one, sir."

Gunn cocked an eyebrow. "Tell me."

"Boat owner at Callanish. Says the man in our photo hired him to take him out to the Flannan Isles a week or so ago. And his vehicle's still parked where he left it. A Land Rover."

Gunn knew immediately that he would have to drive down to Callanish. And the chances were he wouldn't make it back in time for dinner.

■ ■ ■ ■

He saw the standing stones from a long way off, clustered together on the rise, with their commanding view over the coast of southwest Lewis. Fingers of gneiss pointed at a darkening sky, contours sculpted by weather and geology and time. There was something primordial about them. Older than Stonehenge, and raised by Man for who knew what purpose. Although they were cruciform in shape, they predated Christ by thousands of years, and Gunn had been fascinated by them from childhood. He remembered his father bringing him here for the first time. A day out, a family picnic, but something about the stones had spooked the young George, and nightmares had kept him awake most of that night, and for several more thereafter. He had never lost the sense of awe that they inspired in him.

These days, they were a tourist attraction more than anything else, and coaches rumbled daily to the visitor center along the single-track road that Gunn now took to the tiny jetty that nestled at the foot of the peninsula, well beyond the stones.

The machair was relatively flat here, dipping down to the seaweed-strewn rocks

444

along the loch side, and Loch Ròg An Ear itself was slate-gray and contoured by the rising wind. As it stretched west, out into the ocean, the waters of the loch were broken only by the low-lying islands of Chearstaidh and Ceabhaigh and the much larger mass of Great Bernera.

Iain Maciver was waiting for Gunn at the old stone jetty, standing at the end of it, leaning against the railing, smoking a cigarette and looking out across the water to a landscape dotted by sheep and the occasional croft. He looked round as Gunn drove up, and, because there was no place to turn here, Gunn realized he was going to have to reverse all the way back to the parking area at the top of the hill, where he had passed a beaten-up old Land Rover sitting back from the tarmac.

He got out and met Maciver halfway along the jetty. The two men shook hands. The fisherman had a leathery, weathered face very nearly the color of tar, and big-knuckled hands that crushed the one of Gunn's that he shook. There were a couple of small boats tied up along the right-hand side of the quay, and a narrow slipway on the left below a rusted old railing.

"Which boat's yours?" Gunn asked him, and Maciver nodded toward a garishly painted old hoor of a fishing boat anchored in the bay. "Bloody hell!" Gunn said. "You take that out to the Flannans?"

Maciver shrugged and grinned. "She's game for anything, that old girl."

Gunn looked at her, and couldn't imagine a trip he would less like to make. He took out the original photograph of the murdered man from Eilean Mòr and held it out.

Maciver looked at it and nodded. "Aye, that's him alright. Sam Waltman, he said his name was. Don't know why that stuck. Except I remember thinking Waltman, Walt Disney." He grinned to reveal a mouthful of bad teeth. "And Sam's not a name you hear much around here."

"How did he contact you?"

"He didn't. I got a call from a fella down in Harris. Neal something. Asked if I would take his friend out. A one-way trip. I wouldn't need to bring him back, he said, because he would be meeting him out there, and would give him a lift back himself." He took a long pull on his cigarette, then let the wind whip it away from his open mouth. "Dunno what happened, but he parked his Land Rover up the road yonder, and it's still there."

Maciver followed him slowly up the road on foot as Gunn reversed back to the parking area. He swung into it and got out, to feel the wind picking up as it whipped in off the water. The Land Rover was parked on the grass just beyond the square of tarmac. It was an old beast, an off-road warrior, scraped and dented by the years, wheels caked with mud. The windscreen was opaque except where it had been smeared by the wipers in two blurred arcs. Gunn tried the doors and tailgate. All locked. He shaded the driver's window from reflection and peered inside. It was littered with cigarette packs and chocolate wrappers. A well-thumbed road atlas of Scotland lay on the passenger seat next to what looked like the return half of a ferry ticket.

He walked around to the front of it and took a note of the registration number, then turned to Maciver. "I'm obliged to you, Mr. Maciver. We'll need to take a statement. Tomorrow'll be fine. If you can't come to Stornoway, I'll send someone to the house. Excuse me."

He turned away then and checked the signal on his mobile before calling the office, the phone pressed to one ear, a finger in the other.

"Hector, it's George. I'm pretty sure he's our man. Sam Waltman's his name. I've got the registration number of his Land Rover.

Let's run it through the DVLA and see who owns it." He reeled off the number from his notebook. "And we'll need a tow truck down here to get it back to Stornoway, and a mechanic to open her up for us."

The signal was breaking up and DC Smith's response was inaudible.

"Sorry, Hector, I'm on one bar here. Say again?"

After a couple of crackles, Smith's voice came through loud and clear. "We just got feedback from the Manchester police on the Harrisons, sir," he said. "I suppose it shouldn't be any surprise to us that the man's not in concrete at all." And Gunn kissed goodbye to even the remotest possibility of making it back in time for dinner.

On the single-track heading west toward Luskentyre beach, Gunn could see the storm gathering itself out at sea. Gone was the blue overhead, to be replaced by low gray skeins of cloud that cast their shadow over the bay. Two, maybe three miles offshore, the rain was already falling in intermittent patches of darker gray, curiously backlit in fleeting moments of dazzling sunlight that broke through the cloud bubbling along the horizon.

As he drove past the cemetery, he reflected

that its permanent residents must have seen many a storm come and go. The white Highland pony that habitually fed on the beach grasses that grew among the dunes would have seen a few, too. He was grazing near the fence below Dune Cottage, and Gunn noted with a grim sense of premonition that the suspect's car was gone. At the top of the hill, Sergeant Morrison from Tarbert was leaning against his car, which he had parked across the gate of the Harrisons' house. Gunn drew up in front of him and got out to shake his hand.

"Donnie."

"George."

"Well?"

"Nobody here. Car's gone."

Gunn nodded down the hill toward Dune Cottage. "And our man?"

"Not there either, and no sign of a vehicle."

"Shit." Gunn's involuntary curse, barely whispered, was lost in the wind. It was Gunn who had told the CIO that they had no reason to detain the suspect, but now they knew that it was Mr. No Memory who had arranged for Sam Waltman to be taken out to Eilean Mòr, where the two men had a rendezvous. A one-way trip was what he had ordered, as if he knew that Waltman

wouldn't be coming back. And now he was
gone. He looked up at the glass front of the
Harrison house wondering what, if any, connection the Harrisons had with this. In his
experience innocent people did not usually
lie. So why had Jon Harrison lied to him
about what he did for a living? "Let's talk
to Mrs. Macdonald," he said.

They walked down the road to her house,
and Mrs. Macdonald opened the door to a
cacophony of barking dogs. Her yappy little
dog growled and snapped at them from
behind the safety of her legs, while Bran
greeted Gunn like a long-lost friend, paws
up on his chest, almost knocking him over.

"Bran!" Her reprimand brought the Labrador back down to all fours, and she stood
glaring at the policemen. "I don't pretend
to know what's going on here, officers, but
I think we've all had just about enough of
it."

"I couldn't agree with you more, Mrs.
Macdonald," Gunn said. "I'm surprised to
see that you have —" he hesitated only
momentarily — "Mr. Maclean's dog."

She tutted and raised her eyes to the ceiling. "Well, I wouldn't normally take him,
but it's hardly the dog's fault that his
owner's a crook and a liar." Gunn wondered
what exactly it was she had heard about

him. "And they were off together, all three of them. In both cars."

"Mr. Maclean and the Harrisons?"

"That's right. It was Mrs. Harrison that came to the door with Bran. *He* wouldn't dare! Normally, she would take Bran. But since they were all going off together, she begged me to keep him. Just for a few hours, she said."

"And did she say where they were going?"

"Rodel, apparently. Looking for a boat." She glanced beyond the two policemen at the darkening sky blowing in across the bay. "But I can't imagine they'd be going out anywhere in that."

"How long ago did they leave?"

"About half an hour." She tipped her head toward the tall sergeant. "Mr. Morrison could only have missed them by ten minutes or so."

The light was fading fast as Gunn drove down into the shadow of St. Clement's Church and the shelter of the tiny harbor at Rodel. Sergeant Morrison, in his too small police car, drew in behind him and jackknifed himself out into the first spits of rain. He walked stiffly over to where the Detective Sergeant was standing on the quayside gazing helplessly out over the boats that rose and fell in the incoming swell, complaining and straining against the restraint of their ropes. There was nobody here, just a red SUV parked on the far quay.

"That looks like their cars over there," Morrison said, and Gunn swiveled his head to see two vehicles parked up on the grass below the Rodel Hotel. Lights from the hotel itself shone into the dusk, casting feeble shadows toward the harbor.

"Maybe they're in the hotel. Or someone there might have seen them." He turned to look at the cloud and rain blowing in through the Sound. "Nobody in their right mind would take a boat out in this." He started off toward the hotel, but Sergeant Morrison grabbed his arm.

"What was that, George?"

Gunn turned. "What was what?"

"Something banging."

"The wind, probably."

"No, there it is again."

And this time Gunn heard it too. It seemed to be coming from the nearest of the boats. The two men walked along the quay and stood listening intently. There were three sharp bangs from inside the white motor launch tied up below them. A blue canvas awning was stretched tightly over the driver's console, and the banging came from beneath it.

"Give me a hand," Gunn said, and the old sergeant grasped his hand to support him as he clambered down on to the rise and fall of the vessel. Morrison jumped down behind him, and together they began releasing the poppers that held the awning in place. When they peeled it back, they saw Coinneach Macrae lying curled up in the bottom of the boat, ankles and wrists bound by duct tape, a strip of it stuck across his mouth to stop him from calling out.

"Jesus Christ!" Morrison said, and he fished in his pocket for a Swiss Army knife, selecting a blade to open and cut through Macrae's bindings.

Gunn eased the duct tape away from the man's face, and saw the blood that had dried among his thinning hair from a gash in his head. "What the hell happened to you, man?" And he turned to Morrison. "Better radio for medical assistance."

Macrae took a moment to regain his composure, breathing deeply, straightening and stretching stiffened limbs. "The fucking wee bastard!" he said finally.

"Who?" Gunn heard the crackle of Morrison's radio behind him, and the sergeant's voice requesting an ambulance.

Macrae pulled himself up into the driver's

seat and fought for a breath. "Carr. That's his name. I remember it from his boat license. Hired a boat from me a week or so ago. Had all the right paperwork, so I'd no reason to doubt him." He fumbled in his pockets for cigarettes and lighter, and lit one with trembling hands. "Said he was going to spend a few days exploring the east coast. Do the Golden Road, but from the sea, going ashore to camp at night. Paid up front. But he was back the next day. Said the weather was too bad." He shrugged. "Didn't even ask for a refund."

"I take it he showed up again today, then?" Gunn said.

Macrae sucked on his cigarette, then curled a lip in anger as he blew out the smoke. "Aye, damn right he did. This afternoon, wanting to hire another boat. I told him there was a storm on the way, but he said he'd be safely berthed somewhere sheltered before it came. Wanted the same boat he had last time, with an inflatable tender for getting him ashore. But it's out on a hire, so I showed him another one." He howked phlegm up into his mouth and spat over the side into the water. "He's taking a look over it when I hear this thumping coming from inside his motor." He nodded toward the far quay. "That's it, over there.

The red Mitsubishi."

Gunn glanced up and saw the SUV he had spotted when they first arrived.

"So I go over to take a look. There's definitely something alive in the back of it, kicking and rocking the bloody thing. I'm peering through the smoked glass, and I see this . . . I don't know, kid, a girl or something. All tied up, a bag over her head, kicking shit out the tailgate. I'm turning to go and open it up, when, wham, that bugger goes and cracks me on the bloody head." He lifts a rueful hand to the gash in it. "Don't know what he hit me with, but he just about split my skull." Another drag on his cigarette. "Next thing I know, I'm lying in the dark, trussed up like a bloody chicken. Not even the first idea how long I'd been there. Started kicking the side of the boat like mad when I heard your voices."

Gunn held out a hand to him. "Come on, let's get you back on dry land. Can you stand up okay?"

"Aye." But still he staggered as he stood, and it took both policemen to help him up on to the quayside.

Gunn said, "I take it he took the boat?"

Macrae cast his eyes over the boats in the harbor. "Aye, it's gone alright."

"Any other boats missing?"

Macrae seemed surprised, glancing at Gunn, then passing his gaze over the harbor again. "Aye, there is," he said. "Harrison's boat's gone."

Gunn said, "You never mentioned that he had a boat here."

Macrae gave him a look. "You never asked, Mr. Gunn. And why would I even think to mention it? He's been berthing a boat at Rodel for about a year. Don't know why, though. He's hardly ever out in it." He thought about it for a moment. "I suppose I must still have been unconscious when it left. Never heard a thing."

"There's an ambulance on the way, George," Morrison said.

Gunn nodded and turned back to Macrae with the heaviest of hearts. He heard himself sigh before he said, "Is there anyone, sir, who could take us out to the Flannan Isles?"

"What, now?" Macrae seemed incredulous.

"Aye."

"You think that's where they've gone?"

"I'm pretty sure it is, sir. Both boats."

Macrae shook his head, then winced from the pain of it. "You'll not get anyone to take you out there on a night like this, Mr. Gunn. Yon folk might have reached the Flannans before the storm broke, but they'll not get back tonight, and the only way anyone else is going to get out there now is by helicopter."

Gunn couldn't help feeling something like relief.

CHAPTER THIRTY-ONE

No words have passed between us during the last hour as Jon's boat plows through mounting seas and the dying embers of the day. He has deferred to my superior seamanship and I am at the helm. But even I am afraid of the coming storm, for this is just the beginning of it. Only my fear for Karen is greater, and that is my single focus.

For some time now we have seen the beam of light fired out at regular intervals from the lighthouse on Eilean Mòr, piercing the gloom, reflecting on the underside of the dark, dangerous clouds that gather all around us. The Seven Hunters are shadows huddled along the horizon, intermittently obscured by the ocean swell.

Our silence is full of tension. I have given them the barest outline of the circumstance which has led me, and them, to make this journey that no sane person would undertake on such a night. They listened in grave silence, neither asking questions nor making comment. All color and animation left Sally's face, and I caught them once exchanging glances, a dark, troubled exchange conveying an unspoken understanding that I could not interpret.

But I have held my peace. I cannot afford to confront them with what I know before we reach the island. And they must realize that their success depends on my getting them and me there safely. They also know by now that I have my memory back, for I have told them. And so our silence preserves the pretense. But in my head a voice is screaming, and had I the means I would strike them both down, and hit them. And keep hitting. And hitting. Until I had extinguished all sound and movement and life.

We are upon the Flannans almost before I realize it, the sea breaking luminous and white all around the ragged contours of the rocks. The sound of the sea breaking over them from the southwest and the cry of the wind is very nearly deafening.

I have no choice but to turn on the spotlights mounted on our crossbar to light the way ahead. I know it means that Billy will see us coming, but without them we would founder on the rocks.

From the merest shadows fifteen minutes

ago, the Seven Hunters have risen above us now, as if they have somehow pushed up out of the sea, crowding around us, overlapping, dangerously obscure as I try to navigate between them. There is the merest lull in the force of the storm as we slip into the lee of Eilean Tighe, and I keep a wary eye on Gealtaire Beag, away to our starboard side. But then the sea gathers momentum and anger again as it rushes through the gap between the two Làmhs, and I try to hold a course for the southeast side of Eilean Mòr and the more sheltered of the two landing sites.

Finally, our lights pick out the shell-crusted steps cut so steeply into the side of the cliff, and the sea breaking ferociously around them as they vanish into the depths below. We see Billy's boat, anchored in the bay, rising and falling dangerously on the swell. And his inflatable, dragged up the steps and on to the broken concrete quay, where he has secured it to the great rusted ring that is sunk into the rock. I get as close as I dare to his boat, then drop anchor. A glance at my companions reveals fear in their faces. They know as well as I do that this is the most dangerous moment. The transfer from boat to tender, and the attempt to reach and jump out on to the steps.

I cut the motor and clamber into the back of our boat to swing the inflatable out on its jib and lower it carefully into black waters that seem alive with rage and a determination to suck us under. As the tender comes up on the rise, I jump in and feel it fall away beneath me again as the sea drops, and I fall backward into the bottom of it, grateful for the ropes around its smoothly inflated sides to grip and steady me as the boat rises again and water breaks over me, icy cold in the darkness.

Sally is next and, as she swings herself into the tender, I grab her arm to steady her. In that moment, I remember all the times we have made love. The feel of her skin beneath my hands and against mine. Her lips. Her breath in my face. Our eyes meet, but neither of us can hold the look, each for different reasons. And then Jon is there beside us, and the two of them sit, clinging to the ropes, as I pull the starter cord and the outboard comes to life, a roar we can barely hear above the sea and the wind. I cast off and, accelerating away from our boat, turn into the swell and steer us toward the cliffs.

As we approach the steps, I swing the inflatable around at the last moment to bring us alongside, nursing the engine and the throttle to try to keep us there and prevent the sea from throwing us against them. It is not an easy thing to do, for the sea is trying its hardest to smash us all to pieces as our tender lifts ten feet or more, riding the incoming waves. I accelerate hard against its drag until we drop again, suddenly. I hear Sally scream, but we are still in one piece. Jon turns his eyes toward mine and they are black with fear. I throw him the rope and shout at the top of my voice, "Next time we go up, jump, then hold us steady."

But he misses the moment. I see him brace for the leap, but he doesn't make it, fear breeding inertia.

"Now!" I scream at him as the sea tosses us high again. And this time he jumps. For a moment I lose sight of him and think he has gone into the water. But as the sea recedes and we drop once more, I see him standing on the steps, ashen, the rope in his hands. Sally looks at me, panicked at the thought that she is next. I nod, and she knows she has no choice.

In the event, she makes the jump easily, grabbing Jon's outstretched arm to set herself, and they both pull hard on the rope. This is the worst moment for me. I know I must cut the motor before jumping, and trust that the Harrisons will keep tension on the rope. If not, I will be gone, and there will be no one to protect my little girl from these people.

I see the next wave driving in and brace myself, feeling the tender lift on the crest of it. I stall the engine before leaping into space. I seem to fall through darkness for an eternity before my feet strike solid concrete and I feel Sally's steadying hand. It takes me only a moment to get my bearings, and then all three of us are dragging the inflatable on to the steps, and pulling it up above the reach of the water, to the old concrete landing stage. I can feel salt spray stinging my eyes and the cold of this September sea seeping into my bones.

We secure it to the same ring that Billy has used to secure his, and I stand for a moment, looking out at the incoming ocean caught in the sweep of light from above. The wind is almost strong enough to knock me off my feet, and I know that with the rising tide this will all soon be under water, and the chances are that neither inflatable will survive.

Without a word, I turn and start to run up the steps. The old rusted iron handrail is deformed beyond use, ravaged by countless storms, and for the briefest of moments I find myself in the company of the lighthouse men who lost their lives here. They had trodden these same steps many times, and perhaps their ghosts still do. But Jon and Sally are not ghosts. They are flesh and blood and a threat to me and mine, and they are right behind me.

At the elbow of the dog-leg, I stop to catch my breath. The wind is even stronger up here, the beam from the lighthouse sweeping through the night above us, twice every thirty seconds, reaching twenty miles and more out to sea. I see Sally's face and Jon's, caught ghostly white in its reflection. None of us knows what the next few minutes will hold, and all of us, I suspect, are afraid of them.

I push on up the steps, two at a time, feeling how every muscle in my legs aches and how the breath rips itself from my lungs with every step. From the landing platform, we follow the concrete path and the rusted lines left by the old tram tracks, until we reach what they once jokingly called Clapham Junction, where the tracks from the east and west landings converge to ascend that final stretch to the lighthouse itself.

There I stop again and look up at the shadow of the lighthouse standing stark against a stormy sky almost entirely devoid now of light. It flickers and fades like some phantom in the reflected light of its revolving beam. The wind hits us here like a physical blow, and it is not possible even to speak. The outside light at the entrance to the building is switched on, drawing us like moths to our fate.

The rain drives in horizontally as we run the last few yards to the comparative shelter of the outer wall of the complex, and I feel relief in escaping the relentless wrath of the storm. I crouch down in the lee of the wall, among the wet grass and the rubble, and the Harrisons do the same, three faces turned toward each other in the colorless light of the lamp above our heads. The time for pretending is over.

I say, "All I want is my daughter. Safe."

"So do we," Sally says, and the look I turn on her forces her to avert her eyes.

Jon is still gasping for breath. He says, "All we want is the data. That's all we ever wanted."

"What makes you think it's here?"

"Because it's not at the cottage. Do you think we haven't been through that bloody house a hundred times? Every time you went up the coffin road to your bees. All those nights that Sally kept you safe in your bed, asleep after sex." I glance at her but still she won't meet my gaze. "And Billy says you were manic about it, refusing to share with him or Sam. That you were the only one with all the data. Paranoid. And just crazy enough not to keep copies in case they fell into the wrong hands." He looks at me with cold, hard eyes. "We had your computer hacked." He shook his head. "Both of them. Nothing. No data on the hard drive. And you weren't uploading to the cloud. So you had to have some kind of hard copy. It's here somewhere, isn't it? All those trips backward and forward to the islands. That was all about keeping your data safe."

I nod.

"And you knew all about us, didn't you? You knew we were watching you?"

"Yes."

"Until you lost your bloody memory." He glares at me. "At first I didn't believe it, but Sally was convinced it was real. And then we were afraid that we wouldn't get our hands on it, because you didn't know where it was. And who knew when you might remember? If ever." He turns and looks toward the door of the lighthouse. "You've hidden it in there?"

I nod again. "It's all on a hard drive." And in the look I give him, I try to convey all the contempt that I feel. "You know what you're doing, don't you? All the time and money and effort that's gone into this. Proof positive that the poison these agrochem companies are pouring on our crops is destroying the bees. And all that that means for the future of our own species. This planet. And you don't care, because someone's paying you a lot of money."

"A helluva lot of money."

"You fucking idiot! Maybe one day, if you ever have children, you'll understand how you're selling their future down the river."

He is unmoved. He says, with a strangely quiet authority, "We'll go in there, get your data, and take Billy away with us."

But I shake my head. "Billy's not going to just walk away, Jon. I saw him kill Sam that night. And he'd have killed me, too, if I hadn't got away from him." I shake my head with the recollection of it. "I knew I was going to have to blow the whole project. Go to the police as soon as I got ashore. And I would have, if I hadn't struck rocks trying to clear the islands in the dark. Holed the bloody boat, and knew I was never going to make it back. Don't know how many hours I bailed her out after the engine got submerged. I don't even remember her going down in the end. Just the thought that I was going to die out there."

Sally's voice cut in for the first time. Frail and uncertain. "But you didn't."

I turn withering eyes on her. "No. Which is why Billy came looking for me at the cottage two nights later to try and finish the job."

Jon's voice forces me to tear my eyes away from Sally. "Billy was way off script, Tom. Freelancing. The stupid little idiot must have thought he could hijack the research data himself and hold Ergo to ransom. All he was supposed to do was keep me and Sally informed, and we'd have snatched the results from you ourselves when the time came. No need for anyone to get hurt."

"Except me." I turn my head toward Sally again. "And I don't mean physically. It must take quite an act of will to fake sex with someone so convincingly."

This time she forces herself to hold my eye. "It wasn't all an act, Neal." And speaking the name she has always used for me strikes us both, as if we have been slapped in the face. She quickly corrects herself. "Tom."

"Enough." Jon stands up, rising beyond the protection of the wall, and takes a step back as the full force of the wind hits him. He reaches behind him and draws a pistol from some hidden holster. His smile is dry and goes no further than his lips. "Don't worry, Tom. I have a license for it. And no intention of using it. But who knows how unstable our friend Billy Carr might be? He might require a little persuasion. And we might need a little protection."

The grilles protecting the outer door have been prised open, and the lock on the door itself smashed. Jon opens out one half of it and slips into the yellow light that illuminates the kitchen and the corridor that leads off to the sitting room. Sally and I follow, and I pull the door shut behind us.

The sound of the storm raging outside recedes immediately, and we are enveloped by a strange hush. Like stepping through some portal that takes us to another time in another world. I become aware that all three of us are soaked to the skin and trembling with the cold.

There is no sign of life. No sound. Yet I know that Billy must have seen us coming, and that he is waiting for us somewhere in here. I only hope to God that he has Karen with him, and that she is still alive.

"Billy!" Jon's voice thunders in the silence of the building.

"We're in the tower." Billy's shout echoes down the spiral stairs from the light room above.

"Don't be an idiot, son. Leave the girl up there and come on down. Tom's going to give us the hard drive and we'll be out of here."

But I know that they won't. No one is leaving the island tonight. Not in this storm. And I wonder if Jon has any intention of letting Karen and me leave at all. Because hasn't it all just gone too far by now? Ergo may never have intended causing anyone physical harm, but Sam is dead. Murdered. Billy is a loose cannon, and I am a witness. As, now, is Karen.

In focusing on the short term, in trying to save my daughter, I have not thought any further ahead than that. I have not projected possibilities into the future, played out the game in my head to visualize where it will end. And now I do. And see it clearly. Jon cannot afford for any of us to leave here alive. Not Billy, not me, not Karen. Not now. And I wonder if Sally realizes it.

I glance at her pale, frightened face and find it hard to believe she is really capable of this.

Billy's voice reverberates in the stairwell again. "He saw me kill Sam."

"That's just your word against his. There's no physical evidence to link you to this place. No other witnesses. And anyway, the police already think Tom did it. No point in making things worse."

But Billy is not listening to Jon's reason. "If he doesn't want me to hurt Karen, he'd better come up. Right now." I can hear the hysteria creeping into his voice. His intelligence must surely be telling him that this cannot end any way but badly. But something else possesses him, something beyond intelligence, and he seems driven on a course to self-destruction. Which makes him unpredictable and dangerous.

I glance at Jon. In a low voice I tell him, "He's going to kill me."

Jon shakes his head in disagreement. "Not until he has his hands on the data."

I close my eyes in desperation. No one, it seems, is thinking clearly or rationally. Except me. But I don't know what else I can do. Billy has Karen and I have no choice but to do what he demands. With a final glance back at Sally, I start up the stairs, steadying myself with outstretched fingers on the curve of the walls.

From the stairwell, I enter through a yellow door into the circular wood-paneled room beneath the light room itself. The light is dazzling up here, as the slowly revolving beam thrown out by the lamp passes just above my head. I duck to avoid the underside of the lamp mechanism and climb the rungs of the ladder through the hatch in the grilled floor, pulling myself up and into the circle of glass whose prisms magnify the light and launch it out to sea. Briefly, irrationally, I wonder if it is reaching any ships out there in the dark, guiding them safely away from us.

Almost immediately, a revolution of the lamp blinds me, and I stagger back against the glass. It passes quickly, but leaves me nearly blind, and I blink to bring Billy and Karen into focus out of the flare of negative color that fills my eyes. He is wearing a baseball cap pulled low over his eyes to protect them. Karen's hands are bound behind her, and she has a pillow case over her head that concertinas on her shoulders. He has a hand spread across her forehead, pulling her head back, and a knife against the cloth where her throat must be. I feel a terrible empty ache inside me. I cannot imagine what I will do or how I will feel if any harm comes to her.

"Where have you hidden the data?"

I see the lamp coming and close my eyes this time until it has passed. "What makes you think there's not a copy?"

He just laughs. "Because you're too fucking paranoid, Professor Fleming." A mocking parody of how he addressed me at the Geddes. "If there's one copy, and you have it, there's not the slightest danger of anyone else getting their hands on it. Unless, of course, you give it to them."

I shut my eyes again, but even so, the light burns through my lids.

And still Billy wants to talk. "All the data that Sam and I collected so faithfully every week. Sent to you. Never shared. All the samples we sent to the lab, results returned only to you. So nobody else, *nobody,* could put it all together. Except you. And the statistician. Whoever he might be." A sneering little laugh. "Just one more thing you kept from us. Playing God. Forgetting that it was me — *me* — who discovered it all in the first place. Not you. *Me.* And who was going to get all the credit?" He waves a finger of admonition at me. "Not right, Professor Fleming. Not right at all."

I shut my eyes against the glare one more time, and feel someone at my side. I open my eyes, still in the blaze of light from the lamp, and even before I can shout, "No!" I hear the shot. Deafening in the confines of the light room. I see Billy step back, the glass behind him red with his blood, the light fired from the lamp off into the night turning momentarily pink.

473

I am knocked roughly aside as Jon steps over Billy's body, which has slumped into a sitting position against the wall, head tilted forward, eyes closed. He whips away the cover from Karen's head and I see her blinking frantically in the sudden, blinding blaze of light. Her mouth is taped over and, as her pupils contract, I see her terror.

I want to throw myself at Jon, but he holds her upper arm and pushes his gun against her temple.

"This was never going to work." He has, it seems, lost all patience. "I want the data. Now!" His voice reverberates around the light room almost as loudly as his gunshot of moments earlier.

I nod. "It's downstairs."

I am strangely calm as I kneel on the floor with the screwdriver that I have recovered from its hiding place in the kitchen. Above me, set into the wall, are the coat hooks where the men who tended this lighthouse once hung their waterproofs. Their boots would have stood where I now kneel. One of them, in contravention of all the rules, had left his coat hanging here on the night that Ducat, Marshall and McArthur disappeared in a storm just like this one.

One by one, I remove the screws that hold

the wood paneling in place below the hooks, and start lifting away the panels. Jon stands over me with his gun, Sally just a few paces behind us in the corridor, holding Karen firmly by the shoulders.

Jon says, "How the hell did you ever get keys for this place?"

I chuckle, though there is really nothing to laugh about. It is the irony, I suppose. "The first summer I was here, I landed one day to find that the Lighthouse Board had sent in decorators to paint the place. Everything was opened up. The guys were okay with me taking a look around and we got chatting. The forecast was good, and they expected to be here for a few days. So I spun them the story about writing a book and said I would probably be back tomorrow. And I was. Only this time with a pack of Blu-tack. When they were having their lunch, I took the keys from the inner and outer doors and made impressions. Dead simple. Had keys cut, and access to the place whenever I wanted thereafter."

The final panel falls away in my hands, and I reach in to retrieve a black plastic bag. I hand it up to Jon, and he peels back the plastic to look inside. As I stand up, I lift one of the wooden panels. I know that this is the one chance I will get, while he is distracted, and I swing the panel at his head as hard as I can.

The force with which it hits him sends a judder back up my arms to my shoulders, and I actually hear it snap. He falls to his knees, dropping the hard drive, and his gun skids away across the floor.

Sally is so startled, she barely has time to move before I punch her hard in the face. I feel teeth breaking beneath the force of my knuckles, behind lips I once kissed with tenderness and lust. Blood bubbles at her mouth.

I grab Karen by the arm and hustle her fast down the corridor, kicking open the door and dragging her out into the night. The storm hits us with a force that assails all the senses. The wind is deafening, driving stinging rain horizontally into our faces. The cold wraps icy fingers around us, instantly numbing.

Beyond the protection of the walls, it is worse, and I find it nearly impossible to keep my feet as I pull my daughter off into the dark. Only the relentless turning of the lamp in the light room above us provides any illumination.

We turn right, and I know that almost immediately the island drops away into a chasm that must be two or three hundred feet deep. I can hear the ocean rushing into it. Snarling, snapping at the rocks below and sending an amplified roar almost straight up into the air.

I guide Karen away from it, half-dragging her, until we reach a small cluster of rocks and I push her flat into the ground behind them. I tear away the tape that binds her wrists, then roll her on to her back to peel away the strip of it over her mouth. She gasps, almost choking, and I feel her body next to mine, racked by sobs, as she throws her arms around me and holds me as if she might never let go. Her lips press to my cheeks, and I feel the explosion of her breath on my face as she cries, "Daddy!" One simple word that very nearly breaks my heart.

"Baby. Baby, it's okay. We're going to be okay." I squeeze her so hard, I'm afraid I might break her.

We are, both of us, soaked through, the sodden ground beneath us stealing away the last of our body warmth. The rain is as relentless as the wind, and it feels as if it is flaying the skin from our faces.

I untangle myself from Karen and lift my head up over the rocks to look back toward the lighthouse. It is almost spectral in the strange reflected light of the beam that sweeps across the island and off out into the night. And I am just in time to see Jon and Sally run out from the protection of the outer wall. He has a torch, but its light is all but snuffed out by the blackness of the night and the ferocity of the storm. He turns it in an arc around them, searching, I imagine, for some sign of us. But he must know it is pointless. He grabs Sally's hand and they run down the concrete path, in the tracks of trams long gone, and are swallowed by the dark. I am aware, then, of Karen's face close to mine, watching, too.

"You can't just let them go," she says.

"Why not?"

"Because they've got the data."

I turn, and for the first time in a long time find myself able to smile. "And I've got you. And that's all that matters." I gaze off into the dark. "Anyway, there's no way they will get off the island in this."

Karen looks at me very directly, and I see myself so clearly in her blue eyes. "You can bet they'll try, though."

I struggle to my feet. "You wait here."

But she grabs my hand and pulls herself up. "I'm not letting go of you again. Ever."

I nod. And I don't want to let go of her either. "Come on, then."

We run, crouching into the wind, across

the grass, and join the concrete path again just above Clapham Junction. We turn to our left, water flowing in spate across the concrete beneath our feet, and make our way down to the concrete platform, where the crane would have dropped its loads in days gone by. From there, a short flight of steps leads down to the concrete block where the crane itself was mounted, and we find ourselves looking on to the steps far below. I pull Karen to her knees, and we lie on the concrete, offering less resistance to the wind, easing ourselves closer to the edge of the platform, so that we are looking over it into the maelstrom beneath us.

The sea is like some wild animal, possessed, and thrashing itself in a fury against the rocks. Out in the bay it is just possible to see the two anchored boats being tossed around in waves that break across them in bursts of almost luminescent spume, threatening to engulf them completely. And I know that those anchors will not hold for long.

Two hundred feet below us, Jon and Sally try to reach the inflatables. But the sea has beaten them to it. Both tenders, still tethered to the ring, are being thrown about and smashed against the rocks. The Harrisons retreat ten or fifteen feet back up the steps, and I hear a roar so human that it sends a chill through my very soul.

"Jesus!" I hear Karen say. "Look!"

I lift my head and see a huge wall of black water thundering between the islands to our right, gaining in strength and momentum. I have heard stories from old sailors of freak waves that carry all before them, but I have never seen one like this. It must be a hundred feet high or more.

The Harrisons hear and see it too, and I watch them turn and run in panic back up the steps. But they are too late. The luminous white that has been brimming on the brink of the wave finally spills over as it crashes into the island, completely engulfing the figures below us. I feel the force of the spray lash my face.

I blink to expel the water from my eyes, and when I can see again, the wave is receding with an enormous sigh, retreating into the bay in a whirlpool of green and black and white. And Jon and Sally, and both of the inflatables, are gone. Like the three lighthouse keepers on the west landing more than a hundred years before them.

Almost immediately I hear the sound of a motor rising above the storm and see a searching beam of light that sweeps across the island. Karen and I roll on to our backs and look up to see the coastguard helicopter as it swings dangerously in the wind, dropping on to the helipad just below the lighthouse and touching down with a bump on the concrete.

CHAPTER THIRTY-TWO

They say that after a storm the sun always shines. Not necessarily true in the Hebrides, but it is this morning.

I have spent most of the night here in this interview room in Stornoway, giving my statement. They took Karen to hospital for a medical examination. She has a nasty head-wound where that bastard hit her, and they were concerned that she might be concussed, or have a fracture to her skull, so I have barely seen her since everything that passed on the island.

Neither have I slept, and as the morning sun floods this room with its light and warmth, I can feel my eyes grow heavy and begin to close. Only to be startled wide again by the door opening. Detective Sergeant Gunn comes in carrying a fat folder that he places on the table before sitting down to cast curious eyes over me. He sighs.

"Hard as it is for me to believe, Professor,

everything you have told me seems to check out." He pauses, and there is something like a smile playing about his lips. "To be honest with you, sir, I've never heard anything quite like it in all my years in the police."

I am too tired even to think about it. Everything in my life these last two years has been hard to believe. He opens up his folder and scans the first few pages.

"The Harrisons were brother and sister. They ran a private detective agency in Manchester. Whoever was employing them —"

"Ergo," I tell him.

He demurs. "That may be, sir, but I doubt we'll ever prove it. Whoever it was paid more than a million pounds into their business account in several installments over the past year. Obviously, they felt it was more than enough to justify putting the rest of their business on hold for twelve months to come up here and keep an eye on you."

I shake my head, still a sense of mourning in me for the woman I may even have thought once that I loved. "Hardly worth dying for, though."

"No, sir. No amount of money would be worth that." He turns his attention back to his folder. "Billy Carr is still in the ICU at the Western Isles Hospital, but the doctors seem confident that he'll recover alright."

He looks at me. "I apologize, Professor, for giving you such a hard time over the murder of Mr. Waltman. But you must appreciate how it looked to us."

"I do, Mr. Gunn. For a time, I even believed myself that I had killed him."

"Well, we finally got a report back from the lab. They have recovered DNA from the scrapings taken from beneath Mr. Waltman's fingernails."

And all I can see is the two men locked together, falling to the ground, rolling over and over, punching and grabbing each other like schoolboys fighting in the playground. Until they broke apart and Billy laid his hand on that rock and struck poor Sam on the head, dropping him to his knees. Then hitting him again. Three, four times, in a bloody, fatal frenzy.

"We've taken a swab from Mr. Carr. I imagine there will be a match." He looks to me for confirmation, and I nod, grim still from the memory. Then he sits back in his chair, folds his arms across his ample stomach and shakes his head. "I think, sir, you might also find yourself in a bit of hot water for faking your own death."

From somewhere, I find enough amusement in his words almost to laugh. "The least of my problems, Mr. Gunn. Though I didn't actually fake anything. You can read what you want into my suicide note." And I make inverted commas in the air with my fingers around "suicide." "But it doesn't say anywhere that I was going to kill myself. People drew their own conclusions when they found my empty boat out in the firth."

I run a hand back through the salty tangle of my black curls. "What's the word on Karen?"

Gunn closes his folder. "She's fine, sir. No fracture. No sign of concussion. A very lucky girl. One of the constables has just gone to fetch her from the hospital. He'll give you both a lift back down to Harris."

My sense of relief is enormous, and I feel now that an end to this nightmare that my life has been since my sacking from the Geddes is just in sight. "My car must still be at Rodel."

"Sergeant Morrison went to get it this morning. It's waiting for you at the cottage."

"I'm allowed to drive it now, then, am I?"

"Provided you have a valid license, sir."

I smile. "I can assure you, Mr. Gunn, I do."

I see her in the street outside, for the first time in daylight. She is so pale it is almost painful. In the photographs I saw of her, she had rings and studs in her face. Not now, though. Just the holes they have left, and I wonder if they will ever close up.

She seems so tiny. Frail. And yet, a million miles from the little girl in the blue dress and straw hat. The photograph that sat on my desk for all those years. The features are the same, though the hair is different, and I realize what has changed. She has grown from child to adult. And in the process lost her innocence. Not lost it, perhaps. Had it taken from her. By me. What damage have I done to my own wee girl by trying to save the world?

We stand there on the pavement in Church Street, with the sun slanting down between tall buildings and the sound of gulls rising with the breeze from the harbor at the foot of the road. People pass us without a second glance. A father and daughter. Nothing remarkable about that. Not even when we hug, and hold each other with silent tears on our cheeks. Because I was dead, and am alive again. We were lost, and now we are found.

When, finally, we part, and I blink away my tears to see her more clearly, my eyes light on the tattoos that deface her arms and neck. Blue and black outlines, blocks of color. Weird and wonderful designs. I say,

"When did you get these?"

She closes her eyes and sighs. Then opens them again and says, "Dad . . ."

"What?"

"Don't start!"

The light at Luskentyre is stunning. The wind is brisk but soft. The land has soaked up everything thrown at it last night by the storm. It has, it seems, an endless capacity to do so. The sky presents itself in torn strips of blue interspersed by teased-out cotton wool, and the sun reflects in countless shades of turquoise across an outgoing tide that leaves silver sands shining.

Karen is seeing it for the first time. "Jees, Dad! Is this really where you spent the last two years?"

I nod, and see our driver smiling.

"And you expect me to have sympathy for you?"

We are barely through the door of Dune Cottage when a frozen-faced Mrs. Macdonald arrives with Bran. "Overnight is hardly a few hours," she says coldly and marches back across the road without another word.

Karen raises an eyebrow in query. "Long story," I say, then turn to ruffle Bran's ears as he leaps about my legs. "Karen, meet Bran. Bran, meet Karen. I have a feeling you two are going to get on like a house on fire."

Karen crouches and Bran turns to her, sniffing excitedly. Maybe he can tell from her scent that she is a part of me, and that she deserves his love as much as, if not more than I do. She spreads her hands on his head and he licks her face, and when she puts her arms around him, he leans in to her, making funny little noises, looking up at me with big soulful eyes as if seeking my approval.

When she stands up, she says, "I phoned Mum."

"How was she?"

"I think, incandescent would probably describe her best. Of course, she was pleased to hear I was safe. But the bit she liked most was when I told her you were definitely still alive."

I grin. "That must have been disappointing for her." But Karen doesn't smile, and I see only pain in the face she turns up toward mine.

"You have no idea what you put me through."

I put my arms around her and pull her to me. "I think I do." And I make her look at me. "And I'm so, so sorry. I would never have done it this way if I'd had a choice."

She nods. "I know. Billy told me. They threatened me."

"You were my one weak spot. My Achilles heel. And they knew it."

"In spite of how horrible I was to you?"

My smile is rueful. "We are all teenagers once, Karen. Your mum and I had already burned ourselves out. But leaving you behind was the hardest thing I ever had to do in my life." I turn toward the laptop on the kitchen table. "That Facebook page of your Uncle Michael's . . . That was me. So I could watch you, even from here. See you growing up. From your posts and your photos. It was just about the only thing that kept me sane."

She nods. "I think I figured that out by now."

A shadow falls across her face, just as if the sun had slipped behind a cloud. "And I fucked it all up for you."

I am shocked to hear her swear. But more disturbed by what she says. "How?"

"All that data. Lost. Because of me. Two years of research. You'll never be able to set that up again, will you? You could never finance a repeat of it all."

I take her into my arms again and rest my chin on the top of her head, closing my eyes. "I don't have to."

She draws back and looks at me. "Why not?"

"Karen, I may be all the things that Billy accused me of. Manic, selfish, paranoid." I pause. "But I'm not stupid." I take her hand. "Come on, there's someone I want you to meet."

Chapter Thirty-Three

This is the first time I have driven out across the machair to where the old caravan is roped down and pegged into the sandy soil. I could never risk being seen here, or having any contact with the man known as Buford.

My car is not well suited to this track with its ruts and potholes, and it lurches from side to side, creaking, and banging as the underside of it hits bump after bump.

The breeze is stiffening again as we step out into it, but the clouds gathering to the west are light and blow in shreds across the sky, sending shadows careening ahead of them over the sand. I breathe deeply and know I am going to miss this place.

I guide Karen around the giant satellite dish and a generator whose motor is barely audible, and we hear the radio mast vibrating and singing in the wind. At the front of the caravan, a Land Rover sits proud on the machair, a stone's throw from the beach.

The caravan door opens, and the man with the binoculars and the straggling hair grins out at us. He steps down on to the machair and we embrace. A long, heartfelt embrace. He grins at me and shakes his head. "Man, I really thought I was never going to see you again."

I turn to my daughter. "Karen, this is Alex. He's my statistician. Being an obsessive twitcher, and a man who likes his own company, he jumped at the chance of a six-month sabbatical from St. Andrew's University, funded by OneWorld, to come up here and crunch the numbers on our research." She shakes his hand. "And be glad he did, because he saved my life."

Alex scratches his head ruefully. "Aye, and very nearly got myself killed in the process." He steps back into the caravan. "Come in."

It is the first time I have been in here, and I am immediately struck by the smell of stale cigarettes and cooking and body odor. Alex might well be a genius with figures, but I fear his personal hygiene leaves much to be desired.

One half of the caravan is a shambles of clothes that lie in crumpled heaps, a tiny sink piled high with dirty plates and tin cups, a table littered with books and papers and an ashtray overflowing with the remains of roll-ups and who knows what else. Three blackened pots crowd together on a two-ring cooker.

The other end is like some high-tech IT lab. There are several computer screens on a table that groans with black and silver boxes that spew cable in all directions. There are three keyboards and umpteen mice. Beneath the table, I see at least two large processing units.

"Contrary to appearances," I tell Karen, "Alex is not an avid watcher of satellite TV. The dish provides him with a high-speed internet link, and the little generator out back supplies him with power. He also has secure radio comms with OneWorld, so he is in constant touch with our funders."

"Wow." Karen gazes at the computer equipment that Alex has assembled. "You'd never know there was all this stuff in here from the outside."

"That was the idea," Alex says. "Everyone thinks I'm a traveler, or a New Age hippy. The kids are scared of me and stay away. The adults want me gone, but the authorities can't move me, so here I am."

I clear away some laundry and sit down. "I was afraid from early on that the whole research project might be compromised.

Billy was right, I didn't trust anyone. And when the Harrisons turned up, it just seemed a little too pat. So I asked One-World to check them out. And guess what. They weren't at all who they said they were. Which meant that someone on the inside had sold out to Ergo."

"Billy," Karen said.

I nod. "Deloit had someone run the rule over him. Turned out he had an awful lot more money sloshing around than they were paying him. So security became paramount. I stopped sharing with both Sam and Billy. We funneled all the results through me, and from me to Alex. Nobody but me and Deloit knew about Alex. I worked on an external hard drive that I hid out on Eilean Mòr when there was anything of any value on it. I copied my data on to thumb drives that I left for Alex in waterproof bags under a couple of stones up on the coffin road, near where I have my hives."

Alex said, "So all the research data was coming to me, and I was doing the statistical analysis as it came in. I have everything on my hard drives."

I smile. "And just to be extra safe, we backed everything up on the internet." I turn to Karen. "Remember that web space I got you about three years ago? You were going to try your hand at website development." I pause. "And never did."

She looks guilty. "Like all those things I was going to do and never did. It's what Gilly was doing. I guess I just wanted to keep up. But I was never really that interested."

"Just as well," I tell her. "That's the space we used to store our backup. On private pages. Somewhere no one would ever think of looking."

"So what happened out on the island between Billy and Sam?"

I exchange a dark look with Alex. "That was a bad idea," I say. "And I only have myself to blame. I thought, if we could draw Billy out in the open, confront him with the fact that we knew he'd sold out . . . I thought I could talk him round. Get him on our side again, then maybe we could find out what Ergo and the Harrisons were planning." I shake my head in raw regret. "I confided in Sam and we hatched a plan to snare Billy. Stupid! Sam deliberately let it slip to him that he and I were meeting up to exchange final data, and the statistician's analysis."

"At the lighthouse?"

"Yes. A lie, of course. I arranged for someone to take Sam out to the island. I was going to meet him there, and we would see who, if anyone, turned up. Billy is who we expected, and Billy it was. But I got held up by the bad weather, and by the time I got there, Billy had beaten me to it and he and Sam were knocking lumps out of each other. I don't know what happened between them, or what was said, but when I tried to intervene I got knocked to the ground. And the next thing, Billy's grabbed a rock and he's smashing it into Sam's head. Again and again. Totally out of control. And when he looks at me, covered in Sam's blood, I see only madness in his eyes and I know he's going to try and kill me, too. Nothing I could do for Sam, so I ran. Back down to the boat, and off into the night. Only to hit a damn rock in the dark and hole my boat below the waterline." I am trembling from the recollection of it. "I suppose I must have been trying to make it back here, and by the time she finally went down I couldn't have been that far offshore. But the first thing I know is I'm lying out there on the beach and I can't remember a thing. Not who I am, nor what I'm doing here, nor anything that happened on the island." I shake my head. "Which damn near blew the whole project."

Karen has been listening in rapt silence.

And now she looks from me to Alex and back again. "So how did Alex save your life?"

"Billy showed up at the cottage two nights later. Tried to kill me. Finish off what he failed to do on the island."

Alex says, "It was a golden rule. Your dad and I would never have any personal contact. Never. But I saw him that day, washed up on the shore. And the next day, when he took Sally up to the hives, I knew that something must be badly wrong. I was going to go and see him at the cottage that night, but she was there. So I waited a day, and went back the next night. Which is when I saw Billy sneaking into the house, well after midnight."

"A good job you broke that golden rule," I tell him. "If you hadn't, I'd be dead."

Karen's eyes are wide with wonder, and consternation. "And it's all been worth it, Dad, has it? Three lives, and everything you've all been through?"

I sigh deeply. "It's hard to measure the worth of anything against the loss of even a single life, Karen. Sam was a great friend. It breaks my heart that he died the way he did. I can't speak for him, but if I had died achieving what we've achieved, then I would have felt that I had given my life for something worthwhile. Call me naive, but I have to believe that what we've done here will make a difference." An extra-strong gust of wind rocks the caravan, and we hear it whistling around every window. "As for the Harrisons, they brought what happened on themselves. I find it hard to sympathize." Though my heart still aches for Sally, and I wonder what, after all, she really felt about me.

Karen nods gravely. "So it's been a success?"

I nod. "We stopped collecting data a few weeks ago. Alex completed his statistical analysis and I have written my paper on it. We have proved, scientifically, beyond any doubt, that neonicotinoid-based pesticides are destroying bee colonies by robbing them of their memory. Ergo and the rest will deny it till they're blue in the face. Governments will try to ignore it, but they'll be forced to act by public opinion. All that remains for us to do is publish." I turn to Alex. "It's all set?"

He nods and crosses to his computer screens. He pulls up several documents. "Press release. PDFs of the stats and all the data. Your paper." He stands back. "All you have to do is hit the *return* key, and it's out there. Everywhere across the web. There won't be a single hiding place left for Ergo, or any of the rest of them." He looks at me. "And your story, when you start giving interviews to the media, is going to go global."

I stand up and take Karen by the hand, leading her to the computer. "You do it."

She looks up at me. "What do you mean?"

"You hit the *return* key. Tell the world. Save the bees. No one deserves that more than you."

I see tears well in her eyes as the enormity of it all dawns on her. "This is only the beginning," she says. "Isn't it?"

I nod. "It is."

She turns to gaze at the screen for a moment, then looks down at the keyboard and hits *return.*

ACKNOWLEDGMENTS

I would like to offer my grateful thanks to those who gave so generously of their time and expertise during my researches for *Coffin Road*. In particular, I'd like to express my gratitude to Dr. Christopher N. Connolly, an associate of the Center for Environmental Change and Human Resilience (CECHR), University of Dundee, Scotland, on whose research the science in my story is based; Joe Cummins, Professor Emeritus of Genetics at the University of Western Ontario, Canada, whose presentation to the European Union on links between neonicotinoids and the collapse of bee colonies predated the current controversy by several years; Gavin Jones, beekeeper, Isle of Harris, and Iain Smith, beekeeper, Isle of Lewis, Scotland, for their advice on Hebridean beekeeping; Dr. Steven Campman, Medical Examiner, San Diego, USA, for his advice on pathology; George Murray, for his insights into Hebridean policing; Murray Macleod of Seatrek, Uig, Isle of Lewis, for his expertise in accessing the Flannan Isles by boat; Lorna Hunter of the Northern Lighthouse Board, for photographs and information provided on the lighthouse at Eilean Mòr in the Flannan Isles; and Judy Greenway, acting trustee for the Wilfrid Gibson literary estate, for her kind permission to quote lines from Wilfrid Wilson Gibson's poem "Flannan Isle," about the unresolved disappearance in 1900 of the three lighthouse keepers on the Flannan Isles.

LP 30 $\frac{99}{}$